About the Contributors

MARGARET WEIS lives in a converted barn in Wisconsin with daughter Elizabeth Baldwin; two collies, Laddie and Robbie; and two cats, Nickolai Mouse-slayer and Motley Tatters. Weis presently is working with Tracy Hickman on the fifth book in the Death Gate Cycle, and will be starting book number four in her own galactic fantasy series, Star of the Guardians.

TRACY HICKMAN lived in Wisconsin before moving to Arizona with his wife and four children. He and Margaret Weis wrote the Chronicles and Legends trilogies and edited the first Tales trilogy. Hickman also cowrote the best-selling Darksword Trilogy and Rose of the Prophet series for Bantam Spectra and is in the throes of writing the Death Gate Cycle.

MARK ANTHONY pursues a career in science as a graduate student in biological anthropology at Duke University. He cowrote the DRAGONLANCE® novel *Kindred Spirits* and is writing a FORGOTTEN REALMS® novel, *Crypt of the Shadowking*.

TONYA R. CARTER earned a journalism degree from the University of North Carolina at Chapel Hill, where she met her husband, Greg Cook, and her collaborator, Paul B. Thompson. In addition to having written several DRAGONLANCE novels and the TSR® novel *Red Sands* with Thompson, she has penned science fiction, fantasy, and horror short stories and is working on a fantasy novel. She lives in Ithaca, New York.

TODD FAHNESTOCK is a dreamer whose lucky streak alone exceeds his love for fantasy. He has settled (for the moment) in Colorado Springs, Colorado, where he lives with friends in "The Inferno."

RICHARD A. KNAAK makes his home in Bartlett, Illinois. A University of Illinois graduate with a degree in rhetoric, he has been a full-time author for four years. He is the author of *The Legend of H̶̶̶̶ and K̶̶ the Minotaur. He is writing *Dragon Tome, ̶̶̶̶̶̶̶̶̶̶̶̶y series, published by W̶̶̶

ROGER E. MOORE has been the editor of DRAGON® Magazine since 1986 and is the author of the SPELLJAMMER® novel *The Maelstrom's Eye*. Besides writing, his interests include his son, John, cooking, aikido, and wishing he didn't need to sleep. He thanks Deborah Wiegand for her part in inspiring his story.

DOUGLAS NILES has been an amateur student of history since before his teenage years, so the bookish historian Foryth Teal grew naturally from his interests. He is the author of *The Kinslayer Wars* and coauthor of *Flint, the King*, both in the DRAGONLANCE® world.

NICK O'DONOHOE has written short stories for both the Tales and Tales II series, as well as the science-fiction murder mystery *Too, Too Solid Flesh*. He never thought his experience of removing beer kegs from a jackknifed semi would be useful—until now.

DAN PARKINSON lives in Lake Jackson, Texas. He is a prolific writer whose work ranges across many genres. He is the author of the TSR® novel *Starsong* and *The Gates of Thorbardin*.

PAUL B. THOMPSON grew up in rural North Carolina. His works include articles on military history, science history, and the occult, as well as the novel *Sundipper*. With Tonya R. Carter, he wrote *Red Sands, Darkness and Light, Riverwind, the Plainsman*, and two volumes in the Elven Nations Trilogy. He recently forsook his longtime bachelorhood at the age of thirty-four.

MICHAEL WILLIAMS is best known for his poetry in the DRAGONLANCE series and for his four novels, two of which (*Weasel's Luck* and *Galen Beknighted*) are also set in the world of Krynn. His most recent book, *The Oath and the Measure*, tells of Sturm Brightblade's early adventures. Williams lives in Louisville, Kentucky, with his wife, Teri, and three long-haired dachshunds.

TERI WILLIAMS is a native Floridian, potter, and writing instructor at the University of Louisville. She was chosen by the National Endowment for the Humanities to attend a summer seminar on medieval culture, specializing in the works of Chaucer. She gratefully acknowledges that the ideas and people she encountered there, especially professor Russel Peck, continue to influence her work.

THE CATACLYSM

With an introduction by
Margaret Weis and Tracy Hickman

Cover art by Larry Elmore

Interior art by Karl Waller

DRAGONLANCE® TALES

THE
CATACLYSM

First Printing: July 1992
Printed in the United States of America
Library of Congress Catalog Card Number: 91-66500

9 8 7 6 5

ISBN: 1-56076-430-9

TSR, Inc.   TSR Ltd.
201 Sheridan Springs Rd.   120 Church End, Cherry Hinton
Lake Geneva, WI 53147   Cambridge CB1 3LB
U.S.A.   United Kingdom

TABLE OF CONTENTS

INTRODUCTION

The world was forged upon three pillars: good, evil, neutrality. In order to progress, a balance between the three must be maintained. But there came a time in Krynn when the balance tilted. Believing himself to be the equal to the gods in knowledge and in wisdom, the Kingpriest of Istar sought the gods in arrogance and pride and demanded that they do his bidding.

Having viewed with sorrow the tilting of the scales of balance, resulting in hatred, prejudice, race divided against race, the gods determined to restore the balance of the world. They cast a fiery mountain upon Ansalon, then withdrew their power, hoping those intelligent races who dwelt upon Krynn would once again find their faith—in the gods, in themselves, and in each other.

This catastrophe became known as the Cataclysm.

Michael Williams tells a tale of vengeance in his epic poem, "The Word and the Silence." He and his wife, Teri, continue the tale and turn it into a mystery, as the accused murderer's son seeks to end the curse on his family in "Mark of the Flame, Mark of the Word."

Matya, a very cunning trader, stumbles onto the bargain of her life—literally—in Mark Anthony's "The Bargain Driver."

In Todd Fahnestock's story, "Seekers," a young orphan boy embarks on a perilous journey to ask the gods a question.

For most people, the Cataclysm meant sorrow, death, ruination. For the entrepreneurs in Nick O'Donohoe's story, "No Gods, No Heroes," the Cataclysm means opportunity.

Richard A. Knaak tells the tale of Rennard, known to readers of *The Legend of Huma*. Now a ghost, doomed to torment in the Abyss, Rennard finds himself transported back to Ansalon during the Cataclysm. Is it an accident, or has he been brought back for a reason?

Dan Parkinson continues the adventures of the Bulp clan of gully dwarves. Led by their valiant leader, Gorge III, the Bulps leave Istar in search of the Promised Place. What they find instead is certainly not what they expected, in "Ogre

Unaware."

Roger E. Moore reveals why Astinus never hires kender to be scribes, in his story, "The Cobbler's Son."

A ship bound for Istar may be making its final voyage, in Paul B. Thompson and Tonya R. Carter's story, "The Voyage of the *Sunchaser*."

Doug Niles continues the adventures of his scribe, Foryth Teal, as that intrepid historian sets out to investigate a priest's claim that he can perform miracles, in "The High Priest of Halcyon."

In "True Knight," we continue the story of the cleric of Mishakal, Brother Michael, and Nikol, daughter of a Solamnic Knight. The two survive the Cataclysm, but now they want answers. Their search leads them to an encounter with the knight who, so rumor has it, could have prevented the Cataclysm.

Margaret Weis and Tracy Hickman

The Word and the Silence

Michael Williams

I

ON *Solamnia's castles*
ravens alight,
dark and unnumbered
like a year of deaths,
and dreamt on the battlements,
fixed and holy,
are the signs of the Order
Kingfisher and Rose—
Kingfisher and Rose
and a sword that is bleeding forever
over the covering mountains,
the shires perpetually damaged,
and the blade itself
is an unhealed wound,
convergence of blood and memory,
its dark rain masking
the arrangement of stars,
and below it the ravens gather.

Below it forever
the woman is telling the story,
telling it softly
as the past collapses
into a breathing light,

---

and I am repeating her story
then and now in a willful dusk
at the turn of the year
in the flickering halls of the keep.
The story ascends and spirals,
descends on itself
and circles through time
through effacing event
and continuing vengeance
down to the time
I am telling her telling you this.

But bent by the fire
like a doubling memory,
the woman recounts and dwells
in a dead man's story,
harsh in the ears
of his fledgling son,
who nods, and listens again, and descends
to a dodging country
of tears and remembrance,
where the memories of others
fashion his bent recollections,
assemble his father
from mirrors and smoke
and history's hearsay
twines and repeats,
and the wavering country,
Solamnia, muses and listens.

Out on the plains, Orestes,
the woman is saying, *out among fires*
which the bard's voice ignited
in rumor and calumny,
there they are burning your father,
his name and our blood
forever from Caergoth
to harboring Kalaman
and out in the dying
bays of the North:

all for a word, my son,
a word masked as history
shielding a nest of adders.
With words are we poisoned,
Orestes, my son, she repeats
in the fragmenting darkness,
the firelight fixed
on her hair, on the ivory
glove of her hand
and the tilted goblet.

And always Orestes listened
and practiced his harp
for the journey approaching,
and the world contracted,
fierce and impermeable,
caged in the wheeling words
of his mother, caged
in a custom of deaths.

II

Three things are lost
        in the long night of words:
history's edge
        the heart's long appeasement
the eye of the prophet.
        But the story born
of impossible fragments
        is this: that Lord Pyrrhus Alecto
light of the coast
        arm of Caergoth
father to dreaming
        and to vengeful Orestes
fell to the peasants
        in the time of the Rending
fell in the vanguard
        of his glittering armies
and over his lapsing eye

 wheeled constellations
the scale of Hiddukel
 riding west to the garrisoned city.
It is there that the edge
 of history ends:
the rest is a song
 that followed on song
the story involved
 in its own devising
tied in devolving circles until
 truth was a word
in the bardic night
 and the husk of event
was a dim mathematics
 lost in the matrix of stars.

 III

But this is the story
 as Arion told it,
 Arion Corvus, Branchala's bard
the singer of mysteries
 light on the wing
 string of the harp.
Unhoused by the Rending,
 traveling west, his map
 a memory of hearth and castle,
unhoused, he sounded forever
 the hymns of comet
 and fire perpetual
sounded the Time of the Rending,
 betrayals and uprisings
 spanning the breadth of the harper's hand,
and history rode
 on the harp incanting
 the implausible music of breath.
His was the song I remember,
 his song and my mother's retelling.
 O sing the ravens

perpetually wronged
    to the ears of my children,
        O sing to them, Arion Stormcrow:

Down in the arm of Caergoth he rode:
    Pyrrhus Alecto, the knight of the night of betrayals
firebrand of burning that clouded the Straits of Hylo,
    the oil and ash on the water, ignited country.
Forever and ever the villages burn in his passage,
    and the grain of the peasantry, life of the ragged armies
that harried him back to the keep of the castle
    where Pyrrhus the Firebringer canceled the world
beneath the denial of battlements,
    where he died amid stone with his covering armies.
For seventeen years the country of Caergoth
    has burned and burned with his effacing hand,
a barren of shires and hamlets,
    and Firebringer history hangs on the path of his name.

IV

Look around you, my son
for the fire in Arion's singing:
For where in this country,
in forgotten Caergoth,
where does a single village burn?
Where does a peasant suffer
and starve by the fire of your father?
Somewhere to the east
before a white arras,
gilded with laurel
and gold adulation,
the bard sings a lie
in a listening house,
and Caergoth burns
in the world's imagining,
while the bard holds something
back from his singing,
something resembling the truth.

But let not the breath
of the fire touch your father,
Orestes, my son,
my arm in the dwindling world,
my own truth
my prophecy,
soothed the effacing mother,
and darkly and silently
Orestes listened, the deadly harp
poised in his hand circuitous.
And the word turned to deed
and the song to a journey by night,
and the listening years
to a cloak and a borrowed name,
as the boy matured
in his mother's word,
and the harp strings droned
in the facing wind
as he rode out alone, seeking Arion.

V

High on the battlements
of Vingaard Keep
as the wind plunged over
the snow-covered walls,
Orestes perched
in a dark cloak huddled,
the window below him
gabled in light,
and he muttered and listened,
his honored impatience
grown loud at the song
of the bard by the fire.

Melodiously, Arion sang
of the world's beginning,
the shape of us all
retrieved by the hands

of the gods from chaos,
the oceans inscribing
the dream of the plains,
the sun and the moons
appointing the country
with light and the passage
of summer to winter,
the bright land's corners
lovely with trees,
the leaves quick with life
    with nations of kestrel
    with immaculate navies of doves,
    with the first plainsong
       of the summer sparrow
and the song from the bard
sustaining it all,
breathing the phase
of the moon's awakening,
singing the births
and the deaths of the heroes,
all of it rising
to the ears of Orestes.
And rising beyond him
it peopled the winter stars
with a light that hovered
and stilled above him,
as nightly in song
the old constellations
resumed their imagined shapes,
breathing the fire
of the first creation
over the years to the time
that the song descends
in a rain of light
today on your shoulder
with a frail incandescence
of music and memory
and the last fading green
of a garden that never
and always invented itself.

For the bard's song
is a distant belief,
a belief in the shape of distance.

All the while as the singing
arose from the hearth and the hall,
alone in the suffering wind, Orestes
crouched and listened
slowly, reluctantly
beginning to sing,
his dreams of murder quiet
in the rapture of harp strings.

VI

Hieronymo he called himself,
Hieronymo when down from the battlements
he came, supplanted and nameless
entering the hall
in the wake of the wind and darkness.
Arion dreamt by the fire,
and his words were a low, shaping melody:
the tongue of the flame
inclined in the hall of his breath
and the heart of the burning
was a map in the eye of Orestes,
who crouched by the hearth
and offered his harp
to his father's slanderer,
smiling and smiling
his villainous rubric,
Teach me your singing, Arion, he said,
adopting the voice and the eye
of imagined Hieronymo
deep in disguises,
and none in the court
knew Alecto's son—
Teach me your singing, memorable bard,
the light in the heart of winter,

singer of origins, framer of history,
drive my dead thoughts over the winter plains
like withered leaves to quicken a new birth!

Old Arion smiled
    at the boy's supplication
    at the fracture of coals,
    at the bright hearth's flutter
    at the nothing that swirled
    at the heart of the fire:
for something had passed
in his distant imagining,
dark as a wing
on the snow-settled battlements,
a step on a grave
he could only imagine
there in the warmth of the keep
where the thoughts were of song
and of music and memory,
where something still darker
was enjoining the bard
to take on the lad
who knelt in the firelight.
Some things, he said,
the poet brings forth.
Others the poet holds back:
for words and the silence
between them commingle,
defining each other
in spaces of holiness.
Softly the old hand
rose and descended,
the harp-handling fingers
at rest on the brow
of the bold and mysterious boy.

The apprenticeship was sealed
in Orestes's bravado,
the name of *Hieronymo*
fixed to the terms of indenture,

all in the luck of an hour,
and depth of a season,
but somewhere within it
a darker invention
that sprawled in the depths
of the heart and the dwindling earth.

VII

So masked in intention,
in a sacred name
for a year and a day
Orestes surrendered
his anger to music and wind,
apprenticeship honed
on the laddered wires
of a harp that the gods whispered over,
of a wandering in lore
and the cloudy geographies
tied to the fractured past,
and he dwelt by the poet
and traveled to Dargaard
  to the heart of Solanthus,
  to imperiled Thelgaard,
  to nameless castles of memory
   where the knights abided
   in yearning for something
   that moved in the channels of history,
   redeeming the damaged blood of the rose,
while the story that Arion sang,
his back to the dream
and incredulous fire,
discovered the years
and the fading arm of the sword.

Seven songs of instruction
arose from the fire and the dreaming:
  the spiral of Quen
   love's first geometry

the wing of Habbakuk
        brooding above the world
the circle of Solin
        rash and recurrent heart
the arc of Jolith
        dividing intention from deed
the white fire of Paladine
        perfected song of the dragon
the prayer of Matheri
        merciful grammar of thought
and the last one the high one
        light of Branchala
that measures all song
        in the shape of words

Alone in the margin
of darkness, Orestes
surrendered and listened
singing reluctantly, joyfully,
as the gods and the planets
and the cycle of years
devolved in a long dream of murder
and the cleansing of harp strings.

VIII

A year and a day the seasons encircled,
according to fable and ancient decrees of enchantment,
        as the gnats' choir of autumn surrendered to ice
and the turn of the year approached like a death
        and the listening castles mislaid under snow.
Orestes's apprenticeship led to a circle of fire,
        where the harp he had mastered and the seven songs
and the fourteen modes of incalculable magic
        circled him back to the night and the keep
and the wintry eyes of the bard singing memory
        into flesh, into stone, into dreaming and wind,
and *Arion*, he said, and *Arion, tell me of time*
        of the Rending of Krynn and betrayals.

The bard took the harp in the foreseen night:
    for his memory darkened the edge of the past
when knowing devises the shape of creation,
    and the Rending changed as he spoke of its birth
in the spiral of prophecy, the brush of its wing
    on the glittering domes and spires of Istar
the swelling of moons and the stars' convergence
    and voices and thunderings and lightnings and
        earthquakes
and Arion told us that night by the hearth
    that hail and fire in a downpour of blood
tumbled to earth, igniting the trees and the grass,
    and the mountains were burning, and the sea became
        blood
and above and below us the heavens were scattered,
    and locusts and scorpions wandered the face of the
        planet,
as Arion told us, and Orestes leaned closer
    and *Arion*, he said, and *Arion, teach me of
        time*
of the famine and plague and Pyrrhus Alecto.
    Arion stroked the harp and began, his white hair
cascading across the gold arm of the harp
    as though he were falling through song into sleep
and the winter stilled at the touch of the string,
    and he sang the last verses as hidden Orestes
reclined and remembered and listened:
    Down in the arm of Caergoth he rode:
Pyrrhus Alecto, the knight of the night of betrayals
    *firebrand of burning that clouded the Straits of
        Hylo,*
the oil and ash on the water, ignited country.
    Forever and ever the villages burn in his passage,
and the grain of the peasantry, life of the ragged armies
    that harried him back to the keep of the castle
where Pyrrhus the Firebringer canceled the world
    beneath the denial of battlements,
where he died amid stone with his covering armies.
    For seventeen years the country of Caergoth
has burned and burned with his effacing hand,

a barren of shires and hamlets,
and Firebringer *history hangs on the path of his name.*
　　Orestes listened, as honor and song,
as blood and adoption warred in the cell of his thoughts,
　　his father redeemed by poison, by blade
by the song of the harp string rendered a garrotte,
　　closing the eloquent throat of Arion
silencing song, reclaiming his father,
　　and transforming Caergoth from desert to garden:
yet the hand of Orestes stilled in the arc of reprisal,
　　and into the night he warred and remembered,
and as I tell you this, memory wars with him still.

IX

　　The mourning began when the doves circled Vingaard:
the poison had passed through the veins like imagined fires:
　　and alone in his quarters, the poet's apprentice
abided the funerals, settled accounts, awaited
　　the search of the Order through ravaged Solamnia
for rivals and villains, for the trails of assassins,
　　and late on the fifth night after the burning,
when the ashes had settled on Arion's pyre,
　　only then did Hieronymo bring forth the harp
(though some there were curious, who late in the night
　　had heard, or had thought they heard, the apprentice
weeping and playing the sonorous mode of the Rending),
　　and late on the fifth night after the burning
Hieronymo sang for the host at the Vingaard Keep
　　and the Rending changed as he spoke of its birth
in the spiral of prophecy, the brush of its wing
　　on the glittering domes and spires of Istar
the swelling of moons and the stars' convergence
　　and voices and thunderings and lightnings and
　　　　earthquakes
as Hieronymo told them that night by the hearth
　　that hail and fire in a downpour of blood
tumbled to earth, igniting the trees and the grass,
　　and the mountains were burning, and the sea became

blood
and above and below us the heavens were scattered,
and locusts and scorpions wandered the face of the
planet,
as Hieronymo told us, and then he leaned closer
and *Now*, he said, *now, I shall teach you
of time*
of the famine and plague and Pyrrhus Alecto.

*Down in the arm of Caergoth he rode:
Pyrrhus Alecto, the knight on the night of betrayals.
When a firebrand of burning had clouded the Straits of
Hylo.
Like oil on water, he soothed the ignited country.
Forever and ever the villages learn his passage
in the grain of the peasantry, life of the ragged armies.
They carried him back to the keep of the castle
where Pyrrhus the Lightbringer canceled the world
beneath the denial of battlements,
where he died amid stone with his hovering armies.
For seventeen years the country of Caergoth
has turned and turned in his embracing hand,
a garden of shires and hamlets,
and Lightbringer history hangs on the path of his name.*

X

His duty dispatched
and the old bard murdered,
Orestes returned
toward rescued Caergoth,
skirting the foothills,
and long were his thoughts
as he passed over Southlund,
the Garnet Mountains
red like a memory
of blood in the distance:
There is no law,
Orestes murmured,

his hand on the harp strings,
        no rule unwritten
that your father's slanderer
        cannot instruct you,
that the man you murder
        your heart cannot honor,
even as your hand
        concocts the poison.
The landscape ahead
        was diminished and natural,
no thing unforeseen
        sprang from the heavens,
the waters were channeled
        and empty of miracles.
So this is history,
        Orestes considered,
so this is history
        now I can understand
as the road lay before him
        uninherited, heirless
cut off from its making
        and silenced by blood.

At the borders of Southlund
        the smoke was rising,
the Arm of Caergoth
        harbored incessant fire:
Orestes rode swiftly
        through billows of prophecy,
the stride of his horse
        confirming the dead words of Arion.

The cavalry plundering
        the burgeoning fields,
leveling villages,
        approaching invulnerable Caergoth,
heeded little the ride
        of a boy in their column
cloaked in the night
        and in helpless mourning.

_____

A bard, some said,
>   or a bard's apprentice
returned to his homeland
>   burning and desolate.
The captain of cavalry
>   turned to the weeping boy
and addressed him as soldier
>   as fellow and brother:
Sooner or later, sing you this,
>   *bard or bard's apprentice.*
For the voice of the harper
>   *the musician, the piper*
shall no longer be heard
>   *in the Arm of Caergoth,*
long kept from the fire
>   *by the song of a poet*
who said she was burning already:
>   *for a fresh fabled country*
is the nest of invasions,
>   *the quarry of cavalry,*
ripe for the sword and the fire.
>   Orestes rode forth
and the captain continued,
>   turning his pale horse
as a star tumbled down
>   from the fixed dream of heaven:
For the bard's song, they tell me,
>   *is a distant belief*
in the shape of distance.
>   *For Caergoth was burning*
when she said in her heart,
>   *'I am queen, not a widow*
and sorrow is far from me,
>   *elusive as thought*
or the changes of memory.'
>   *Sooner or later, sing you this.*
And he vanished in histories
>   of rumor and smoke,
and sooner or later,
>   a bard will sing this,

in beleaguered castles
             abandoned to night
and the cough of the raven.
             Sooner or later,
someone will sing
             of Orestes the bard,
for some things the poet
             brings forth and fashions,
and others the poet holds back:
             for words and the silence
between them commingle,
             defining each other
in spaces of holiness.
             and through them the story
ascends and spirals,
             descends on itself
and circles through time
             through effacing event
and continuing vengeance
             down to the time
I am telling and telling you this.

Mark of the Flame, Mark of the Word

Michael and Teri Williams

It began when I was fourteen, the burning, in the winter that the fires resurged on the peninsula.

I awoke with a whirling outcry, my face awash in fire, the blankets scattering from the bed. The dogs raced from the cottage, stumbling, howling in outrage. Mother was beside me in an instant, wrapped in her own blanket, her pale hair disheveled, her eyes terror stricken.

The burning spread down my neck and back, the pain brilliant and scoring, and I clutched at her hand, her shoulders, and shrieked again. Mother winced and fumbled silently, her thick fingers pressing hard, too hard, against my scarred lips.

And then we were racing through the forest night.

The freezing rain lanced like needles against the hissing scars on my neck and face. *Quiet, my darling, my dove, lest they hear you in the village,* her hands flashed.

We moved over slick and glittering snow, through juniper and *aeterna*, and my breath misted and crystalized on the heaped furs, and the dogs in the traces grumbled and yapped.

Then it was light, and I lay in a dry, vaulted cavern on a hard pallet.

Above me the druidess L'Indasha Yman rustled, draped in dried leaves and holly bobs like a pageant of late autumn. She was young for medicine, young even for divining, and I was struck by her dark eyes and auburn hair because I was fourteen years old and just becoming struck by such things.

She gave me the *beatha* to help with the pain, and it tasted of smoke and barley. The burning rushed from my scars to my throat, and then to the emptiness of my stomach.

"They've matured, the lad's scars," she said to my mother. "Ripened." Expectantly, she turned to me, her dark eyes riveting, awaiting our questions.

Mother's hands flickered and flashed.

"Mother wants to know . . . how long . . ." I interpreted, my voice dry and rasping.

"Always," said the druidess, brushing away the question. "And you?" she asked. "Trugon. What would you ask of me this time?"

She should have known it. Several seasons ago, the scars had appeared overnight without cause, without warning. For a year they had thickened slowly, hard as the stone walls of our cottage, spreading until my entire body was covered with a network of calluses. I could no longer even tell my age. I was becoming more and more a monstrosity, and no one could say why.

"Why. I would know why, my lady." It was always my question. I had lost hope of her answering it.

Mother's gestures grew larger, wilder, and I would not look at her. But when L'Indasha spoke again, my heart rose and I listened fiercely.

"It's your father's doing," the lady said, a bunch of red berries bright as blood against the corona of her hair.

"I have heard that much," I said, wincing as Mother jostled me frantically. The pain drove into my shoulders, and still I turned my eyes from her gestures. "I want all the rest, Lady Yman. How it was his doing, and why."

The leaves crackled as the druidess stood and drifted to the mouth of the cave. There was a bucket sitting there, no doubt to catch rainwater, for it was half filled and glazed with a thin shell of ice. With the palm of her hand, the druidess broke the ice, lifted the container, and brought it back to me, her long fingers ruddy and dripping with frigid rain. She breathed and murmured over it for a moment.

I sat up, the heat flaring down my arms.

"Look into the cracked mirror, Trugon," she whispered,

kneeling beside me.

I brushed Mother's desperate, restraining hand from my shoulder, and stared into the swirl of broken light.

There was a dead man. He was small. His shadow swayed back and forth in a room of wood and stone, dappling the floor below him with dark, then light, then dark. His fine clothing fluttered and his hood lifted slightly. I saw his face . . . his arms . . .

"The scars. Lady, they are like mine. Who is he?"

"Orestes," she replied, stirring the water. "Pyrrhus Orestes. Your father, hanged with a harp string."

"And . . . *who*?" I asked, my sudden urge for vengeance stabbing as hot as the *beatha*, as the burning.

"By his own hand, Dove," L'Indasha said. "When he thought he could neither redeem nor . . . continue the line."

Redeem nor continue. It was quite confusing and I was muddled from the potion and the hour.

L'Indasha's face reflected off the fractured ice in the bucket: it was older, wounded, a map of lost lands. "You weren't told. But Orestes got his desire and now the scars have ripened."

Mother clutched my shoulder. The pain relented a bit.

"Continue what? Lady, 'tis a riddle."

A riddle the druidess answered, there in the vaulted cave, as the weather outside turned colder still and colder, on a night like those on which the fisherman claim you could walk on ice from Caergoth across the waters to Eastport.

She told me that my father, Orestes, had ridden desperately westward as the peninsula burned at the hands of the invaders. He rode with freebooters—with Nerakans and the goblins from Throt, and they were rough customers, but he passed through Caergoth unharmed. None of them knew he was the son of Pyrrhus Alecto—"the Firebringer," as the songs called my grandfather.

"Why did he . . . why *didn't* he . . ." I began to ask. I was only fourteen.

The druidess understood and lifted her hand. "He was just one, and young. And there is a harder reason. Orestes, *not your grandfather*, had brought the fires to the peninsula. You see, he murdered his master. Your grandmother had fostered his apprenticeship with Arion of Coastlund. She taught him from childhood that he must recover his father's honor at any cost. Your grandfather's honor. So he killed Arion, that he should sing no longer of your grandfather's shame."

Mother's grip tightened on my shoulder. I shrugged her away yet again. Again the scars on my neck and face bit and nettled.

"Go on."

"Then the goblins came, when they heard the new song Orestes sang. . . ."

When Orestes saw what his words had wrought, he ran. It was at the last village seawards—Endaf, where the coast tumbles into the Cape of Caergoth—that Orestes could abide no more of the plunder and burning. Caergoth was in flames behind him, and Ebrill, where the bandits first camped, then Llun and Mercher, vanished forever in the goblin's torchlight.

He was just one man, and he was young, but even so, surely it shamed him as much as it angered him.

At Endaf he stopped and turned into the fray. He dismounted, broke through the goblins, and joined in a frantic attempt to rescue a woman from a burning inn. Orestes was sent to the rooftop, or he asked to go. The beams gave way with him, and the goblins watched and laughed as Orestes fell into the attic, which fell around him in turn, crashing down and up again in a rapture of fire.

But he lived. He was fire-marked, hated of men, and they would know him by his scars henceforth. The burns had bitten deep and his face was forever changed into a stiffened mask of grief. A fugitive and a vagabond he was upon Krynn, and wherever he traveled, they turned him away. To Kaolin he went, and to Garnet, as far north as Thelgaard Keep and south to the coast of Abanasinia. In all places, his scars and his story arrived before him—the tale of a bard who, with a single verse of a song, had set his country to blaze and ruin.

He took to bride a woman from Mercher, orphaned by the invasion and struck mute by goblin atrocity as they passed through with their flames and long knives. Orestes spirited her away to the woods of Lemish, where in seclusion they lived a dozen years in narrow hope.

A dozen years, the druidess said, in which the child they awaited never came.

That part I knew. Mother had told me when I was very little, the soft arc of her hand assuring me how much they had waited and planned and imagined.

That part I knew. And Mother had shared his death with none but me. But I had never heard just how he had died.

"In despair," the Lady Yman told me, the cavern lapsing into shadow as her brown, leafy robes blocked out the firelight, the reflection on the ice. "Despair that his country was burning still, and that no children of his would extinguish the fires. He did not know about you. Your mother had come to me, and she knew, was returning to your cottage to tell him, joyous through the wide woods.

"She found what you've seen. Orestes could wait no longer. Your mother brought me his note to read to her: *I have killed Arion, and the burning will never stop,* it said. *The land is cursed. I am cursed. My line is cursed. I die.*"

L'Indasha reached for me as I reeled, as the room blurred through my hot tears.

"Trugon? Trugon!"

Redeem nor continue. I understood now, about his anger and guilt and the terrible, wicked thing he had done. The *beatha* raced through me, and the torchlight surged and quickened.

"Why did you finally tell me?" I asked.

"To save your life," the lady replied. She passed her hand above the broken water, and I saw a future where fires arose without cause and burned unnaturally hot, and my scars were afire, too, devouring my skin, my face, erasing all reason and memory until the pain vanished and my life as well.

"This . . . this is what will be, Lady?"

"Perhaps." She crouched beside me, her touch cool on my neck, its relief coursing into my face, my limbs. "Perhaps. But the future is changeable, as is the past."

"The past?" The pain was gone now, gone entirely.

"Oh, yes, the past is changeable, Trugon," L'Indasha

claimed, passing from firelight to shadow, "for the past is lies, and lies can always change." She was nearing the end of the answer and the beginning of another riddle.

"But concern yourself now with the present," she warned, and waved her hand above the troubled water.

I saw four men wading through an ice-baffled forest, on snowshoes, their footing unsteady, armed with sword and crossbow.

"Bandits," L'Indasha pronounced, "bound to the service of Finn of the Dark Hand."

I shivered. "The bandit king in Endaf."

The druidess nodded. "They are looking for Pyrrhus Orestes. Remember that only your mother and you know he is dead. They seek him because of the renewed fires on the peninsula. They are bent on taking your father to the beast, for the legend now goes, and truly, I suppose, that no man can kill a bard without dire consequence, without a curse falling to him and to his children."

She looked at me with a sad, ironic smile.

"So the bandits are certain Orestes must die to stop the fires."

Mother helped me to my feet.

"I . . . I don't understand," I said. "It's over. He's killed himself and brought down a curse on me."

L'Indasha waved her hand for silence. "It wasn't the killing that cursed you. It was the words—what he said before he died. Now you must go from here—anywhere, the farther, the better. But not to Finn's Ear, the bandit king's stronghold on the Caergoth shore."

"Why should I leave?" I asked. "They are after my father, not me. I *still* don't understand."

"Your scars," she replied, emphatically, impatiently. "The whole world will mistake you for your father, because of the scars."

"I'll tell them who I really am!" I protested, but the druidess only smiled.

"They won't believe you," she said. "They will see only what they expect. Hurry now. *Find* the truth about Orestes. The finding will save your life and make the past . . . unchangeable."

I thanked her for her healing and her oracle, and she gave me one last gift—her knowledge.

"Although now you may regret your blood," she said, "remember that you are the son of a bard. There is power in all words, and in yours especially."

It was just more puzzlement.

We climbed, Mother and I, into the sled, moving quickly over thick ice on our way back to the cottage. Mother slept, and I guided the dogs and looked into the cloudless skies, where Solinari and Lunitari tilted across the heavens. Between them somewhere rode the black abscess of Nuitari, though I could not see it.

The black moon was like the past: an absence waiting to be filled. And looking on the skies, the four big dogs grumbling and snorting as they drew us within sight of the cottage, I began to understand my scars and my inheritance.

* * * * *

Frantically, as I gathered my clothing in the cottage, Mother told me more: that my grandfather, Pyrrhus Alecto was no villain. He had kept the Solamnic Oath, had fallen in the Seventh Rebellion of Caergoth, in the two hundred and fiftieth year since the Cataclysm. She showed me the oldest poem, the one that Arion had taken and transformed. The old parchment was eloquent. I read it aloud:

"Lord Pyrrhus Alecto
    light of the coast
arm of Caergoth
    father to dreaming
fell to the peasants
    in the time of the Rending
fell in the vanguard
    of his glittering armies
and over his lapsing eye
    wheeled constellations
the scale of Hiddukel
    riding west to the garrisoned city.

"And that was all?" I asked. "All of this trouble over a poem?" I hated poetry.

I gave voice to her answer as she held forth rapidly, as the words slipped from her fingers into my breath and voice. "No, Trugon, not over that, over the other one."

She did not know the words of the other poem. She had not even seen or heard it. It was the poem of trouble, she insisted, crouching nervously by the door of our cottage. It was the poem that Father . . .

"Changed?"

She nodded, moving toward Father's old strongbox.

"Then Father lied as well as betrayed?"

Mother shook her head, brushed her hair back. She opened the strongbox.

I knew what was inside. Three books, a penny whistle, a damaged harp. I had never asked to see them. I hated poetry.

Mother held up one of the books.

It was the story of the times since the Rending, since the world had opened under Istar. The work of the bard Arion, it was, but more. It was his words and the words of others before him: remote names like Gwion and Henricus and Naso, out of the time when Solamnia was in confusion.

The book was battered, its leather spine scratched and cracked. As Mother held it out to me, it opened by nature to a page near its end, as though use and care had trained it to fall at the same spot, to the same lines.

She gestured that the lines were in Father's hand. Indeed, the whole book was in Father's hand, for neither Arion nor any of the bards before him had written down their songs and tales, preferring to pass them on to a listening apprentice, storing their songs in the long dreaming vaults of their memories. But Father thought he was heirless and alone, and had written them all—every poem and song and lay, from the edicts to the first shaking of the city, down through the dark years unto this time. A dozen lines or so of one verse he had worried over, scratched out, revised, and replaced, only to go back to the first version, to his first choice of wording.

I mouthed the lines, then read them aloud:

> *"Down in the arm of Caergoth he rode:*
> *Pyrrhus Alecto, the knight on the night of betrayals.*
> > *When a firebrand of burning had clouded the*
> > > *Straits of Hylo.*
> *Like oil on water, he soothed the ignited country.*
> > *Forever and ever the villages learn his passage*
> *in the grain of the peasantry, life of the ragged armies.*
> > *They carried him back to the keep of the castle*
> *where Pyrrhus the Lightbringer canceled the world*
> > *beneath the denial of battlements,*
> *where he died amid stone with his hovering armies.*
> > *For seventeen years the country of Caergoth*
> *has turned and turned in his embracing hand,*
> > *a garden of shires and hamlets,*
> *and* Lightbringer *history hangs on the path of his name."*

It was as though Father had never been satisfied. Something had drawn him to these lines again and again, as if changing them would . . .

Would straighten the past, make it true.

" 'Tis here, Mother," I announced, so softly that at first she did not hear, though she was staring directly at me as I read.

She cupped her ear, leaned forward.

" 'Tis in the poem. Or, rather, *not* in the poem."

Mother frowned. I knew she saw Orestes in me now—poetic and full of contradictions.

I tried to be more clear about it.

"These lines Father wrote and rewrote and worked over are . . . are the lie. Don't you see, Mother? The druidess said that *the past is lies, and lies can always change.* These are—" I thumbed through the book, looking early and late "—these are the only lines he has fretted over.

"It's as though . . . he was trying to . . ." I looked at Mother. ". . . change the lies back to the truth."

I did not know whether that was so or not. I stepped quietly to the strongbox and took out my father's harp, one thick string missing, and held it for a long moment. It fit my hand exactly and when I put it down, I could not shake away its memory from my grasp. When I looked at Mother again, her eyes had changed. We both knew what I would say next.

"Yes, I *must* go, but not because they seek me. I will go because I have to find the lost song," I announced. "Father's words are still hiding something."

One of the dogs rumbled and rose from the shadows, stretching and sniffing lazily in the dwindling firelight. Then his ears perked and he gave a low, angry growl.

Mother scrambled to her feet and to the door, a confusion of soundless sobs and flickering hands.

"I know. They're coming," I said. "I must hurry. Finding the truth is saving my life. The druidess said so."

I stroked the ears of Mateo, the largest of the dogs, who looked up at me solemnly, his thick shoulders pressing against my legs until I staggered a little at the weight. I had no thought of how small I was—how things far greater would press against me when I stepped across the threshold into the early winter morning.

Mother moved slowly aside as I passed into the pale sunlight, her fingers brushing softly, mutely against my hair. I gave her a smile and a long hug, and she assured me of her own safety. In the sled lay an old hide bag, big enough for the harp and the book, a loaf of bread, and a wedge of cheese. I tossed everything in and moved off, as quickly and silently as I could.

One of the dogs barked as I lost the cottage behind a cluster of blue *aeterna* branches, and the high wind shivered faintly at their icicles like the vanished notes of a song. Above the hillside nearest my home, four long shadows fell across the trackless snow.

*   *   *   *   *

There were other adventures that led me back to the peninsula—a wide arc of years and travels across the continent, Finn's men at first only hours behind me, then less constant, less menacing the farther south I traveled. I sent the dogs back to Mother soon and traveled alone, sometimes working for a while at jobs where nobody knew me or thought they knew me, where nobody cared that I never removed my hood.

It was a year, six seasons perhaps, before I realized exactly what it was about the song I was searching for.

It has long been practice that when a bard travels and sings, his songs are attended, remembered, and copied by those in the regions nearby. If a song is a new one, it carries to still farther regions by word of mouth, from bard to bard, from orator to folksinger to storyteller to bard again.

It is a tangled process, and the words change sometimes in the telling, no matter how we try to rightly remember. The old lines from Arion's song I heard in Solamnia as

> *the prayer of Matheri*
> *merciful grammar of thought*

I had heard in the small town of Solace as

> *the prayers of Matheri*
> *mercy, grandmother of thought*

and the southern lines made me laugh, distorted like gossip in their passage across the straits.

For I had the book with me, and within it the truth unchangeable. As I traveled, I knew I would come to a place when I would hear those scratched and worried lines of my father's—the lines about Pyrrhus Alecto, about Lightbringer and history and glory—but I would hear them in a different version.

And I would know at last what Pyrrhus Orestes had altered.

* * * * *

Across the Straits of Schallsea I once stowed away on a ferry. The enraged ferryman discovered me under a pile of badger hides, and he threatened to throw me overboard for evading his fee. He relented when he pushed back my hood and saw the scars from the burning.

"Firebringer," he snarled. "Only my fear of Branchala, of the curse upon bard-slayers, stays my hand from your murder." I cherished his greeting. It was the first of many such conversations.

Over the grain fields of Abanasinia I wandered, in a journey from summer to summer and threat to threat. Three times I heard "Song of the Rending"—once from a minstrel in Solace, again in the city of Haven from a seedy, unraveled bard who had forgotten entire passages about the collapse of Istar, whereby his singing lost its sense, and finally from a blind juggler wandering the depths of the plains, whose version was wild and comical, a better story by far than Arion's.

The minstrel and the juggler repeated Father's altered lines word for word. But the juggler recited them with a curious look, as though he was remembering words contrary to those he was speaking. Although I asked him and asked him again about it, he would tell me nothing. Faced with his silence, I began to believe I had imagined his discomfort, that it was only my hope and dreaming that had expected to find the missing lines.

And so, back across the straits I sailed, in the summer of my sixteenth year, and again the ferryman called me Firebringer, cursing me and spitting at me as he took my money.

On Solamnic shores once more, I started for home, but discovered that no village would shelter me on the journey. "Firebringer," they called me, and "Orestes the Torch," meeting me on the outskirts of the hamlets with torches of their own, with stones and rakes and long peninsular knives.

Some even pursued me, shouting that the fires would die with the one who brought them. Like the ferryman, like Finn, they thought I was my father.

*　*　*　*　*

To the north lay the great Solamnic castles—Vingaard and Dargaard, Brightblade and Thelgaard and DiCaela. Each would take me in of a night for the sake of my grandfather. These families would nurse me on occasion, for my scars burned with growing intensity as the seasons turned and the fires to the west raged and the years passed by me. Sometimes the knights let me stay for a week, perhaps two, but the peasants would clamor, would talk of traitors and firebrands, and I would be asked to leave, would be escorted from Solamnic holdings by a handful of armed cavalry.

The knights would apologize there at the borders, and tell me that their hearts were heavy for me . . . that the welfare of the order and the people took precedence . . . that, had there been another way, they would have been glad to . . .

In all those high places, I asked after Arion's song. Solamnia was, after all, the bard's sanctuary, the harp's haven. All of the schooled poets had retreated to these courts, and all knew the works of Arion of Coastlund.

I showed around the scratched and amended passage near the poem's end. All the bards remembered it, and remembered no other version. As I sat alone in the vaulted hall of Vingaard Keep, my thickened hands strumming Father's harp in the vast and echoing silence, it almost seemed to me that the walls shuddered with my clumsy music, the one string still and always missing.

*   *   *   *   *

In my seventeenth year, the peninsula had burned clear up to Finn's own holdings.

Out of the stronghold of his lair in the seaside caverns at Endaf, from which his horsemen could harry the trade routes north from Abanasinia and his notorious ships, the *Nuitari* and the *Viper*, could find safe harbor, Finn terrorized the cape and covered the shore with the husks of schooners and brigantines, off course in the smoke from the mainland.

It was rumored by some that an ancient evil had returned, in those brief years before the War of the Lance. Finn was one of those who harbored them, the populace whispered. For in the depths of his seaside cavern lay an intricate web of still larger caverns, tunnel devolving on tunnel, the darkness slick and echoing. This was the legendary Finn's Ear, where it was supposed that all sounds muttered in shelter of stone eventually and eternally circled and spoke. At the heart of Finn's labyrinth was said to lay a monster, his black scales glittering with cold malice and devouring acid.

They said that the beast and the bandit had struck an uneasy truce: Finn soothed the monster with the music of well paid but exhausted bards, and, lulled by continual song, the great creature received in turn the company of the bandit king's uncooperative prisoners. And as to the fate of those poor wretches, even the rumormongers were silent.

In the rough border country between Lemish and Southlund, cooling myself in the high foothills of the Garnet Mountains, I pondered the looming necessity of actually going to Finn's Ear, where the bards were singing and the caverns echoing. It was the only place I had not searched for the song.

Hooded as always to hide my livid scars, I crossed that border and stalked through the burning peninsula, keeping the towers of Caergoth to the north as I traveled toward the little villages in the west. My route took me within Finn's own sight, had he cared to leave his rocky throne and look west from the beetling cliffs.

For days I wandered through hot country and distant rising smoke. I would stand outside the village pubs, hooded and shrouded like a highwayman or a self-important mage, and through open windows I heard the nervous talk, the despair of farmer and villager alike.

Spontaneous fires arose in the dry grain fields, leaving the countryside a wasteland of ash and cinder. In droves the farmers were leaving, no longer able to fight the flames. All this disaster, they claimed, had enraged Finn to the point where, in the search for remedy, he had offered an extravagant bounty to any bard or enchanter who could extinguish the fires with song or incantation.

Hard words about a curse drifted through one of the windows. I heard the name of my father. It lightened my steps somehow, as I passed through the deserted village of Ebrill in the early morning, then over the ruins of Llun and Mercher, moving ever westward, believing now that my quest would at last be done. Endaf was the last place Finn would look for a far-flung quarry, and my father's name rode on the smoky air.

It was midmorning when I reached Endaf. I wandered the village for a while, weaving a path amid the deserted cottages and charred huts and lean-tos, all looking like a grim memory of a village. And it was odd walking there, passing the old flame-gutted ruins of the inn and knowing that somewhere in its vanished upper story my father had received the scars I had mysteriously inherited.

I turned abruptly from the ashes. I was eighteen and impatient, and had come very far for the truth. The old acrid smell of Endaf faded as I walked from the ruins on a rocky and shell-strewn path, and as I trudged west I caught the sharp smell of salt air and heard the faint cries of gulls and cormorants.

* * * * *

About a mile from the center of the village, Finn's Ear burrowed into a sheer limestone cliff overlooking the Cape of Caergoth. Black gulls perched at its edge, the gray rock white with their guano, loud with their wailing cries.

Steps had been chopped in the steep rock face, whether by the bandits or by a more ancient hand it was hard to tell, given the constant assault of storm and birds. I took my place in the middle of a rag-tag group of beggars, farmers, bards and would-be bandits, each awaiting an audience with King Finn of the Dark Hand.

As I waited, the bards talked around and over me in their language of rumor. The gold thread at the hems of cape and cloak was tattered, frayed; each wooden harp was chipped and warped, each bronze one dented and tarnished.

No famous poets these, no Quivalen Sath or Arion of Coastlund. They were courtiers with trained voices and a studied adequacy for the strings. Now, in single file on the rocky steps, each encouraged the other, thereby encouraging himself.

Being praise-singer to a bandit king was a thankless and shabby job, they said.

Well, generally.

But Finn, they said, was different. Of course.

It was hard to keep from laughing. In the rationale of such men, a bandit, a goblin, even a monster was *different* when coin and a warm hearth were offered.

Finn, they claimed, had joined resolutely in the search to lift a curse brought upon Caergoth and the surrounding peninsula years ago by the fire-bringing Solamnics, Pyrrhus Alecto and his son Pyrrhus Orestes. His search had entered its fourth year, his seers and shamans telling him that the curse would last "as long as Alecto's descendants lived," his hirelings telling him always that they had just missed catching Orestes. Desperate, Finn hoped that a transforming hymn would lift the curse with its beauty and magic.

The bards needled one another cynically, each asking when they would write that certain song, make their fortunes among the bandits. They all laughed the knowing laughter of bards, then fell silent.

I leaned against the cold rock face, awaiting uncertain audience. Pelicans and gulls wheeled over the breaking tide, diving into the ardent waters as the sun settled over the eastern spur of Ergoth, dark across the cape.

Carelessly, I touched the strings of the harp, felt in my pockets for the poet's pen and ink. I had traveled hundreds of miles to this stairwell, this audience. The pain of my scars rose suddenly to a new and staggering level.

The song of the bards around me was skillful and glittering and skeptical . . . and empty of the lines I sought. I would have to brave the echoing caverns below Finn's lair.

The druidess had told me that I could find the truth. *And the finding would save my life and make the past unchangeable.* The song had to be here, or there was no song. And could the final pain of the monster's acid be any worse than this perpetual burning?

"You'll have it, Father," I muttered into the dark of my hood. *"Redeemed and continued.* The past will be unchangeable. Whatever you have, it will be the truth. And whatever I have, it will be better."

* * * * *

Finn of the Dark Hand sat in a huge chair hewn from the cavern wall. He looked hewn from stone himself, a sleepless giant or a weathered monument set as a sign of warding along the rocky peninsular coast. His right hand was gloved in black, the reason known only to himself.

Around him milled his company of bandits, rough and scarred like burned villages. They bared their knives as they watched the singers, smiling wickedly one to another, as though keeping a dreadful secret unto a fast-approaching hour.

I hovered at the mouth of the cave, listening for an hour to the technically brilliant and lifeless songs of the bards. They claimed to play the music for its own sake, for the sake of the glory of song, but they all knew otherwise, for always music serves some master.

Even Finn knew they were liars. Finn, who had held neither harp nor flute, whose poetry was ambush and plunder. He leaned into the eroded throne, dismissing the pearly singer from Kalaman, the pale lad from Palanthas and the merchant turned poet from Dargaard. Each gathered a heel of bread for his song and turned, grumbling, eastward toward Solamnic cities and the possibility of castles and shelter.

It was night. Bats rustled in the upper regions of the cavern, and I remembered an old time, a winter time, a cavern and a dry rustling sound. Two last supplicants stood between me and the bandit: a beggar whose leg had been damaged in a field accident, and another bard.

While the beggar begged and was given a loaf, and while the bard sang and received a crust, I waited in the shadow of the cave.

None of them had the song. None of them. Neither bard nor minstrel nor poet nor troubadour. Their songs rang thinly in the cave, echoing back to them and to us, throwing the music into a doubling confusion.

I had come this far, and for me there was still more to discover, more than thin music and mendicant rhymes. When summoned, I stepped to the light, and when the dulled eyes of the bandit king rested upon me, I threw back my hood.

* * * * *

"Firebringer," he rasped, and "Orestes the Torch."

As all the bandits hastened to be the one to slay me, to end the line and the curse before the approving eye of their leader, Finn raised his hand and stayed theirs.

"No," he rumbled. "The blood of the line of Pyrrhus should not stain the floors of this cavern. For remember the curse. Remember the harm it might visit."

One shaman, seated by the stone foot of the throne, nodded in agreement, beads rattling as he fondled his bone necklace.

I followed the bandit guards into the throat of the cave, to a confusing depth where all light had vanished except the glow of candles wedged in rocks and later only the torch that guided us. In a great rotunda hundreds of feet below the surface they left me, the last of the guards covering their tracks, candle by extinguished candle, and their footsteps echoed over each other until the cavern resounded of a passing, vanished army.

I sat in a darkness most absolute. After only a moment, I heard a voice.

The language was quiet, insinuating, weaving with the fabric of my thoughts until I could no longer tell, especially in this darkness, what words lay outside me and what within.

Oh, to a wandering eye . . . it began, a fragment of song in the darkness.

I scrambled to my feet and lurched toward, I hoped, the passageway. Bones clattered beneath my feet, rattled against rotting wood and rusted strings, striking a hollow music. Spinning blindly in the dark, I realized I had left father's harp behind, and knew at once that I could not find my way back to it.

A second voice caught me standing stupidly in the same place, huddled in my cloak, expecting the fangs, the monster's fatal poisons. At the new sound, I jumped, flinging my pitiful knife away into the darkness, where it clattered much too loudly against the rock wall.

"Est Sularis oth Mithas . . ."

And then, behind me, or what I thought was behind me, another.

Build ye the westernmost wall in three parts . . .

And, beyond that, another voice, and yet another, until I spun about dizzily, buffeted by voices, by echoes, by wandering sound from centuries before. For not only did the voices of Southlund and Coastlund mingle in the darkness with a chorus of High Solamnic, but the ancient ritual language seemed to change as I heard it, traveling from voice to voice, each time its pronouncements varying slightly until I realized that the last voices I had heard were another language entirely and that I had followed a passage of familiar words, familiar sounds, back to a voice that was entirely alien, speaking a tongue as remote as the Age of Might, as the distant and unattainable constellations.

I would know why, said a young man's tortured voice.

You can find the truth, another voice said—softer, more familiar.

And the finding will make the past . . . unchangeable.

I followed the familiar voice of the druidess L'Indasha Yman, my shoulder brushing against stone and a cool liquid draft of air rushing into my face, telling me I had found a passage . . . to somewhere else.

The voices were ahead of me now, ahead and behind, contained, I suppose, by the narrow corridor. Some shouted at me, some whispered, some vexed me with accents curious and thoughts fragmentary. . . .

. . . se the for Dryhtnes naman deathes tholde . . .

. . . here on the plains, where the wind erases thought . . .

. . . our medsiyn is a ston that is no ston, and a thyng in kende and not diverse thynges, of whom all metalles beth made . . .

. . . Your one true love's a sailing ship . . .

. . . Down in the arm of Caergoth he rode . . .

I stopped. In the last of the voices, somewhere behind me in the corridor, the old words had sounded. I forgot them all—the druidess, the erasing wind of the plains, the medicine and bawdy songs—and turned about.

In the midst of a long recounting of herb lore I discovered that voice again . . . the bard's intonation masking the accents of Coastlund. I followed the northern vowels, the rhythmic sound of the verse. . . .

And I was in another chamber, for the echo swirled around me and over me, and I felt cold air from all quarters, and a warmth at a great distance to my left. The voice continued, louder and unbroken by noise and distraction, and it finished and repeated itself as an echo resounds upon echo.

I held my breath, fumbled for pen and ink, then remembering the monster, sniffed the air for acid and heat.

It was indeed Arion's "Song of the Rending," echoing over the years unto this cavern and unto my listening.

So I waited. Through the old narrations of the sins of the Kingpriest, through the poet's account of the numerous decrees of perfection and the Edict of Thought Control. I waited as the song recounted the glittering domes and spires of Istar, the swelling of moons and the stars' convergence, and voices and thunderings and lightnings and earthquakes. I listened as hail and fire tumbled to earth in a downpour of blood, igniting the trees and the grass, and the mountains were burning, and the sea became blood, and above and below us the heavens were scattered, and locusts and scorpions wandered the face of the planet. . . .

I waited as the voice echoed down the generations, from one century to the next to the third since the Cataclysm, awaiting those lines, not letting myself hope that they would be different from the ones in the leather book in my pack, so that when the lines came, they were like light itself.

Down in the arm of Caergoth he rode:
Pyrrhus Alecto, the knight of the night of betrayals
firebrand of burning that clouded the Straits of Hylo,
the oil and ash on the water, ignited country.
Forever and ever the villages burn in his passage,
and the grain of the peasantry, life of the ragged
armies
that harried him back to the keep of the castle
where Pyrrhus the Firebringer canceled the world
beneath the denial of battlements,
where he died amid stone with his covering armies.

*For seventeen years the country of Caergoth
          has burned and burned with his effacing hand,
a barren of shires and hamlets,
          and* Firebringer *history hangs on the path of his
               name.*

I sat on the cold stone floor and laughed and cried quietly, exultantly. I waited there an hour, perhaps two, as the
"Song of the Rending" ended and began again. I wondered
briefly if this were the echo of Arion himself, if I was hearing not only the words but the voice of the bard my father
had killed a generation back.

I decided it did not matter. All that mattered was the
truth of the words and the truth of the telling. Arion's song
had marked my grandfather as a traitor, but it had preserved the land, for what bandit or goblin would care to
invade a fire-blasted country? Orestes's song had rescued
Alecto's name, at the price of flame and ruin and his own
life. So when Arion's song returned again, I was ready to
hear it, to commit it to memory, to wander these caves until
I recovered the light, the fresh air, the vellum or hide on
which to write the lines that would save my father's line, my
line.

It did return, and I remembered each word, with a memory half trained in the listening, half inherited from a father
with bardic gifts. For the first time in a long while, perhaps
the first time ever, I was thankful for who he was, and I
praised the gifts Orestes had passed on to me.

And then, with a whisper that drowned out all other
voices, at once the beast spoke. It was a dragon!

*So he has sent another from up in the light . . . O most
welcome . . . the struggle is over is over . . . rest there
rest . . . no continuing . . . no . . . no . . .*

Oh. And it seemed not at all strange now to fall to the
monster without struggle or issue, to rid myself of the shifting past and the curse of these scars and their burning, and
to rid all above me of the land's torture . . .

So I stood there, ridiculously clutching pen and ink, and
though it was already darker than I could imagine darkness
to be, I closed my eyes, and the alien heat engulfed me, and

with it the evil smell of rust and offal and old blood. The jaws closed quickly around me as I heard a man's voice, saying, *I have killed Arion, and the burning will never stop. The land is cursed. I am cursed. My line is cursed. I die.*

And then, like a last sudden gift, a woman's whisper: *There is power in all words, and in yours especially.*

* * * * *

It was the hot fetor that awakened me. I gasped and coughed and closed my eyes immediately to the fierce and caustic fumes.

I was sitting upright in very confined quarters.

Slowly I tested my surroundings, my eyes clasped tightly against the foul biting mist. I stretched my arms, and to each side I felt slippery leather walls.

It came to me slowly what had happened.

I sat in the dragon's stomach, like a hapless sailor at the end of an ancient tale.

I cried out in panic and kicked against the pulsing walls, flailing frantically, but it seemed that the great beast had settled and fallen asleep, assured by long experience that the dark corrosives of his stomach would do the rest.

I felt my scars hiss and bubble. The tissue was old and thick as hide, and it would take hours for the acid to eat through. There was a fair amount of air, though it was foul and painful to breathe. What was left to me was the waiting.

For a while, for the space, perhaps, of a dozen heartbeats, the absurdity of my quest rushed over me like a harsh, seething wave. Four years of wandering across two continents, hiding away in castles and marshes, under the abutments of bridges and in filthy, narrowing alleys, enduring searing pain in silence . . .

Only to come ignobly to the filthiest, narrowest end of all, and with me the line of Pyrrhus Alecto, dissolved and digested miles beneath our beloved peninsula. I had gone down to the depths of the mountains, and the earth with her bars was about me forever.

I cried out again, certain no one would hear me.

Then it seemed almost foolishly simple. For after the weeping, the vain recollection of my hundred adventures, I recalled the last thing I had heard:

"There is power in all words, and in yours especially."

My first purpose, many seasons past and a hundred miles away, when I left my mother and home, had been to discover and make known the truth about Orestes and Grandfather.

I had discovered. Now I must make it known. I would salvage the truth in the last dissolving hour. And though I assumed the words would never see light or catch a willing eye, I brought forth quill and inkhorn, and said aloud, canceling my father's words as he had canceled Arion's, "The fires are extinguished. The land is free. I am alive."

Dipping the quill, I began to write blindly on the quivering stomach walls of the dragon.

Down in the arm of Caergoth he rode . . .

* * * * *

Some men are saved by water, some by fire. I have heard stories of happy rock slides releasing trapped miners, of a ship and its crew passing safely through hurricanes because the helmsman nestled the boat in the eye of the storm, in sheer good fortune.

I am the rare one to be saved by nausea.

Credit it to the ink, perhaps, or the incessant, swift scratching on the walls of the dragon's stomach. Whatever it was, the fishermen skirting the coast of Endaf, the good folk of Ergoth who drew me sputtering from the water, said that they had never seen the likes of it on sea *or* land.

They said that the caverns of Finn of the Dark Hand had exploded, the rubble toppling down the cliff face and pouring into the circling waters of the cape, that they thought for certain it was an earthquake or some dwarven enchanter gone mad in the depths of the rock until they saw the black wings surge from the central cavern, bunched and muscled and webbed like the wings of a bat. And they told me how a huge creature pivoted gracefully, high above the coastal waters, plunged for the sea, and inelegantly disgorged above the Cape of Caergoth.

It seemed a clear, sweet grace to me, lying on the deck of their boat as they poured hot mulled wine down me and wrapped me in blankets, their little boat turning west toward the Ergoth shore and the safety of Eastport, a haven in that ravaged and forbidding land.

The fishermen's attentions seemed strange, though—as if, in some odd, indescribable way, I was one of their fellows. It was not until we reached the port itself and I looked into a barrel of still water that I noticed my scars had vanished.

But the memory of the burning returns, dull and heavy in my hands, especially at night, here in this lighthouse room overlooking the bay of Eastport. Across the water I can see the coast of my homeland, the ruins of the bandit stronghold at Endaf. Finn, they tell me, dissolved with two dozen of his retainers when the dragon thundered through their chambers, shrieking and flailing and dripping the fatal acid that is the principal weapon of his kind.

And the creature may as well have dissolved himself. He has not been seen since that day on the Caergoth coast. But the same fishermen who rescued me claim that, only the other night, a dark shadow passed across the face of the red moon. Looking up, they saw nothing but Lunitari and a cloudless sky.

They saw an omen in this, and now carry talismans on board, but sailors always were a superstitious lot, fashioning monsters out of clouds and the wind on the waters.

At night I sit by the window, by lamplight, and watch the constellations switch and wink and vanish in this uncertain time, and I set before me a fresh page of vellum, the lines of each day stored in my memory. For a moment I dwell on the edges of remembrance, recalling my mother, L'Indasha Yman, the reluctant knights, and the fortunate fishermen. But, foremost, I recall my father, come down to me in an inheritance of verse and conflicting stories. It is for him, and for Grandfather before him, and for all those who have vanished and been wronged by the lies of the past, that I dip the quill into the inkwell, and the pain in my hand subsides as I begin to write . . .

*On Solamnia's castles
ravens alight,
dark and unnumbered
like a year of deaths,
and dreamt on the battlements,
fixed and holy,
are the signs of the order
Kingfisher and Rose—*

The Bargain Driver

Mark Anthony

I'll give you the two bronze knives, the string of elven beads, and the silver drinking horn, but that is my final offer."

"Are you mad, Matya?" the grizzled old trader said in exasperation. He gestured to the bolt of fine cloth that lay between them on the counter, in the center of the trading post's one dingy, cluttered room. "Why, this was woven for a noble lord in the city of Palanthas itself. It's worth twice what you're offering me. Nay, thrice!"

Matya watched the trader calculatingly with her bright brown eyes. She could always tell when she was about to best Belek in the driving of a bargain, for his nose invariably would begin to twitch.

"If the cloth is so fine, why did the noble lord for whom it was made not buy it?" Matya asked pointedly.

Belek mumbled some excuse, but Matya waved it away with a ring-covered hand. "You may take my offer or leave it, Belek. You'll not get so much as a bent nail more."

The trader sighed, a look of dismay on his haggard face. "You're determined to drive me out of business, aren't you, Matya?" His bulbous nose gave a violent twitch.

Matya smiled inwardly, though she did not let the trader see her satisfaction. "It's simply business, Belek, that's all."

The trader grunted. "Aye, so it is. But I'll warn you, Matya. One day you'll drive a bargain too cleverly for your own good. There are some bargains that aren't worth taking, no matter how profitable they seem."

Matya laughed at that. "You always were a sore loser, Be-lek." She pushed the goods she had offered across the counter. Belek sighed—his nose twitching furiously—and pushed the bolt of cloth toward her. Matya spat on her palm. Belek did likewise, and the two shook hands. The bargain had been struck.

Matya bade Belek farewell and loaded the bolt of cloth into her wagon outside the ramshackle trading post. The wagon was a colorful, if somewhat road-worn, affair—a wooden box on wheels, painted in countless bright but peel-ing hues. Hitched in front was a single dun-colored donkey with patient eyes and extraordinarily long ears.

Matya's wagon was filled nearly to overflowing with all manner of wares, both mundane and curious: pots and pans, cloaks and boots, arrows and axes, flints, knives, and even a sword or two, plus countless other objects she had bought, haggled for, or—most of the time—scavenged. Traveling from town to town, trading and striking bar-gains, was how Matya made her living. And it was not a bad one at that.

Like the wagon, Matya herself was a bit worn with the years. Her long hair, coiled in a thick braid atop her head, had been flaxen, but now was ash gray. Countless days of sun and wind had tanned and toughened her ruddy cheeks. Fine wrinkles touched the corners of her eyes and mouth, more from smiling than frowning, and so were attractive. And, like the wagon, Matya was clad in a motley collection of clothes representing all colors of the rainbow, from her ocean-blue skirt to her sunflower-yellow shirt and forest-green vest speckled with tiny red flowers. Her willowy, fig-ure had plumped out, but there was still an air of beauty about her, of the simplest and most comforting kind—when her nut-brown eyes weren't flashing fire, that is.

"Let's be on our way, Rabbit," Matya told the donkey as she climbed onto the wagon's wooden bench. "If we hurry, we can reach Garnet by nightfall. There's a merchant there who's an even worse haggler than Belek." The donkey gave a snort that sounded uncannily like laughter.

Matya tied a bright red kerchief over her graying hair and

grasped the wagon's reins in her strong, thick fingers. She whistled sharply, and Rabbit started off at a trot down the dusty highway, pulling the gaudily colored wagon behind.

* * * * *

It was midafternoon when she saw the ravens circling lazily against the azure sky not far in the distance. Matya knew well what the dark birds portended: Death ahead.

"Keep those ears up, Rabbit," she told the donkey as the wagon jounced down the heavily rutted road. "There's danger on the road these days."

Matya watched warily as the serene, rolling hills slipped by. Autumn had touched the land with its frosty hand, coloring the plains of southern Solamnia in a hundred shades of russet and gold. The honey-colored sunlight was warm and drowsy, but Matya resisted the temptation to doze, as she might have done otherwise. The land was beautiful, but beauty could conceal danger. She remained wide awake and alert.

The wagon crested a low rise. Below her, the road split, and it was here the ravens circled. The highway continued on to the north, and a second road led east, toward the dim purple range of mountains marching on the horizon. Scattered about the dusty crossroads were several queer, twisted objects. A raven dived down and pecked at one of the objects before flapping again into the air, and only then did Matya realize what the strange things were: corpses, lying still in the dirt of the road.

She counted five of them as Rabbit—eyeing the dead nervously—pulled the wagon to the crossroads. Matya climbed down and knelt to examine one of the bodies, an older man's, dressed in neat but threadbare attire. A crudely made arrow with black fletching protruded from its throat.

"Goblins," Matya said in disgust. She had heard rumors that the verminous creatures were creeping down from the high places of the mountains of late to waylay travelers. By her guess, these had been pilgrims, making for Caergoth, to the south, to visit the temples of the new gods there.

"They found their gods sooner than they thought," Matya muttered. She spoke a brief prayer to speed the dead on their journey, then began rummaging about the bodies, seeing if any of them carried something that might be worth trading. After all, the dead had no use for objects of value. Matya, on the other hand, did.

After several minutes, however, she gave up in disgust. Like most pilgrims, these owned little more than the clothes on their backs. She would not have scorned even these, but they were threadbare and stained with blood. All she had got for her trouble was a single copper coin, and a bent one at that.

"There's nothing for us here," Matya told Rabbit as she climbed back into the wagon. "Let's be on our way. Men riding out from Garnet will find these folk soon enough and lay them to rest—hopefully dead with the goblins."

Rabbit let out a low bray and started into a trot, anxious to be away from the crossroads and the smell of blood. Matya guided the donkey down the east road, but after a hundred paces or so she pulled hard on the reins, bringing the wagon again to a halt.

"Now what on the face of Krynn is that?" Matya asked herself. Something glinted brightly among the nettles and witchgrass to the side of the road. She started to ignore it, flick the reins, and continue on—the hour was growing late—but curiosity got the better of her. She slid from the wagon's bench, pushed through the weeds, and headed toward the glimmer she had seen. The nettles scratched at her ankles, but in a moment Matya forgot the sting.

"Why, 'tis a knight!" she gasped aloud, staring at the man who lay, unmoving, in the weeds at her feet.

The man was clad in armor of beaten steel, but his visage was more that of a shiftless vagabond than a noble knight. His eyes were deeply set, his features thin and careworn, and the mouse-brown moustache that drooped over his mouth was coarse and scraggly.

Whether he was, in truth, a knight or a looter in stolen armor, it didn't much matter now, Matya thought. His hair was matted with blood, and his skin was ashen with the pallor of death. She said the familiar words to appease the spirit of the dead, then knelt beside the corpse.

The steel armor alone would be worth a fortune, but it was terribly heavy, and Matya was not entirely certain she would be able to remove it. However, the knight wore a leather purse at his belt, and that boded well for Matya's fortunes. Deftly, she undid the strings, peered inside, and gasped in wonder.

A woman's face gazed out of the purse at her. The tiny face was so lifelike that, for a moment, Matya almost fancied it was real—a small, perfect maiden hidden within the pouch.

"Why, it's a doll," she realized after a heartbeat had passed.

The doll was exquisitely made, fashioned of delicate bone-white porcelain. The young maiden's eyes were two glowing sapphires, and her cheeks and lips were touched with a blush of pink. It was a treasure fit for a lord's house, and Matya's eyes glimmered like gems themselves as she reached to lift it from the purse.

A hand gripped her arm, halting her. Matya froze, biting her lip to stifle a scream. It was the dead man. His fingers, sticky with dried blood, dug into the flesh of her arm, and he gazed at her with pale, fey eyes.

The knight was very much alive.

* * * * *

"Tambor . . ." the knight whispered. He lay slumped against the wheel of Matya's wagon, his eyes shut. "She sings . . . Tambor . . ." His mumbling faded, and he drifted deeper into a feverish sleep.

Matya sat near the small fire, sipping a cup of rose hip tea and watching the knight carefully. Twilight had descended on the grove of aspen trees where she had made camp, transforming all the colors of the world to muted shades of gray.

Tambor, Matya thought. There's that word again. She had heard it several times in the knight's fevered rambling, but she did not know what it meant, or even whether it was the name of a place or a person. Whatever it was, it was important to him. As important as that doll, she thought. Even now, in his sleep, the knight clutched tightly at the purse that held the small porcelain figurine. It had to be valuable indeed.

While Matya was not one to go out of her way to help others when it was unclear what—if any—reward she might gain from it, neither was she without a heart. The knight would have died had she left him there by the road, and she would not have wanted that weighing on her conscience to the end of her days. Besides, she suspected there was a good chance the knight would die regardless of her aid, in which case the doll would be hers, free and clear. Either way, it was worth her while to help.

Getting the knight into her wagon had been no simple task. Fortunately, Matya was a strong woman, and the knight had roused himself enough to stumble most of the way with her help. She had hoped to make Garnet by nightfall, but she had tarried too long at the crossroads. Shadows were lengthening, and the town still lay many leagues ahead. Knowing night was not far off, fearful of Rabbit stumbling into a hole or missing the trail in the dark, she had made camp in the grove of aspen by the road.

She had tended to the knight's wounds as best she could. The cut on his scalp was shallow, but he had lost a good deal of blood from it. More troubling had been the wound in the knight's leg. She had found the broken shaft of an arrow embedded in the flesh behind his knee. Goblin arrows were wickedly barbed, Matya knew, and there was only one way for her to remove the arrow tip. Steeling her will, she had pushed the broken shaft completely through the flesh of his leg. Mercifully, the knight had not awakened. Blood flowed freely from the wound, which she had deftly bound with a clean cloth. The bleeding soon stopped.

The night deepened, and the stars came out, one by one, like tiny jewels in the sky above. Matya sat by the fire to eat a supper of dried fruit, nuts, and bread, regarding the knight's sleeping form thoughtfully through the back of the wagon.

If he still lived when she reached Garnet the next day, she would leave him at one of the monasteries dedicated to the new gods—if the brethren would accept a Solamnic Knight into their sanctuary, she amended. There were many who frowned upon the Knights of Solamnia these days. Matya had heard tales that told how, long ago, the knights had been men of greatness and honor, who had protected all Solamnia against creatures like goblins. Matya, however, was not certain she believed such tales.

Most Solamnic Knights she had ever heard of were little more than fools who expected others to be impressed simply because they wore ridiculous suits of rusting armor. Some folk even said it was the knights themselves who brought about the Cataclysm, the fiery destruction that had rained down upon the face of Krynn more than half a century ago, bringing an end to the Age of Might.

"Not that I think the Cataclysm was really such a terrible thing," Matya said to herself. "I daresay I wouldn't make as good a living as I do if these self-important knights still patrolled the highways. And while times may be hard, it only means that people will spend more dearly for the sort of things I can bring them in my wagon. If anything, the Cataclysm has been good for business, and that's all that matters to me."

With a start, Matya realized that the knight had heard her talking, was watching her. His eyes were pale, almost colorless.

"To whom do I owe my life?" he asked her.

Matya stared at him in surprise. Despite his unlikely looks, the knight's voice was resonant, deep and almost musical, like the sound of a hunting horn.

"My name is Matya," she said briskly, recovering her wits. "And as for what you owe me, we can discuss that later."

The knight inclined his head politely. "I am Trevarre, of the House of Navarre," he said in his noble voice. "For your assistance, I thank you, but if it is a reward you seek, I fear we must discuss it now, not later." He gripped the wagon's side and tried to pull himself up, heedless of his injuries.

"What are you doing?" Matya cried.

"Leaving," Trevarre said. A crooked smile touched his lips, and determination shone in his deep-set eyes. "You have been more than kind, Matya, but I have traveled day and night to reach the end of my journey. I cannot stop, not yet."

"Why, you knights are greater fools than the tales say," Matya said angrily, hands on her hips. "You'll only kill yourself."

"So be it," Trevarre said, shrugging as if this prospect did not disturb him. He grimaced, breathing hard, as he slid from the wagon and balanced on his good leg. "I must go on." He took a step onto his injured leg. His face went white with pain. He groaned and slumped to the ground.

Matya clucked her tongue, helped him sit back up against the wagon wheel. "I don't think you're going anywhere, except to a monastery in Garnet—or the grave, if you try that again." She poured a cup of water from a goatskin and handed it to him. The knight nodded in thanks and drank it down.

"You do not understand, Matya," Trevarre said, an intent look on his weathered face. "I must journey to Tambor. I have received a plea for help. I cannot refuse it."

Matya scowled. "Why ever not?"

Trevarre sighed, stroking his scraggly moustache. "I do not know if I can make you understand this, but I will try. I am a Knight of the Sword, Matya." He rested his hand against his steel breastplate, decorated with the symbol of the sword. "This means I cannot live my life as other men do. Instead, I must live by another, higher standard—by the Oath and the Measure. It is written in the Measure that there is honor in aiding those who cry out in need. And, by the Oath, I swore that my honor is my life. I will fulfill my quest, Matya." A faint light glimmered in his pale eyes. "Or die trying."

"And what reward will you get for performing this 'honorable' task?" Matya asked with a scowl.

"My honor is reward enough."

Matya sniffed. "This 'Oath and Measure' hardly sounds practical. It's rather difficult to eat one's honor when one gets hungry." She paused a moment. Her real interest was in the doll, but she couldn't think of how to ask about it without rousing the knight's suspicion. Maybe, if she could keep him talking about himself, he'd tell her what she wanted to know. "And how is it you came to hear this plea for help, Knight? How do you know it's not simply a trick to lure you into a den of robbers?"

"I know." The crooked smile touched Trevarre's lips once again. "By this, I know." He slipped the porcelain doll from the leather pouch.

Matya was thrilled. She had not thought to get another glimpse so easily. Seeing it closely now, Matya realized the doll was even more beautiful than she had thought. She clasped her hands behind her back so she would not be tempted to reach out and touch its smooth surface.

"Passing fair, would you not say?" Trevarre said softly. Matya could only nod. "It is a most remarkable thing. I came upon it some days ago, by the banks of a stream that flows from the mountains. It lay in a small boat woven of rushes, caught in a snag by the shore." He slipped the figurine back into its pouch. "By it, I learned of a maiden who lives in a village called Tambor. She is in dire need. The code of the Measure is most clear on this. I must go to her."

Matya raised an eyebrow. It was a peculiar tale. She guessed Trevarre had stolen the doll and simply was making up the story. After all, he looked more like a thief than a knight, despite his armor. If so, stolen goods were fair game. Ask any trader.

"How is it you learned of this maiden?" she asked, hoping to trip him in his lie. "Was there a message in the boat?"

"No," the knight replied, "not as you mean, at least. You see, the doll is magical. Each night, when Solinari rises, the doll speaks with the maiden's voice. That is how I heard her call for help."

Matya laughed aloud, slapping her knee. "A wondrous tale indeed, Trevarre, but I believe you have taken up the wrong vocation. You should be a storyteller, not a knight."

Trevarre's expression became grave, serious. "You must know, Matya, that on his life a Knight of Solamnia cannot speak falsehood. I can understand why you do not trust in magic. We knights do not think much of sorcerous powers either. But wait until Solinari is on the rise. Perhaps you will change your mind."

Matya studied the knight attentively. His was not exactly a trustworthy face, despite his pretty voice. Still, there was something about the intentness of his pale eyes.

"Perhaps I won't," she said.

* * * * *

It was nearly midnight. The knight had slipped into a doze, less fitfully this time, and Matya rummaged through a wooden box in the back of her wagon. The light of a single candle illuminated scrolls and parchments. Finally, she found what she was searching for—a bundle of yellowed sheets of vellum.

Matya untied the bundle's silken ribbon and unrolled the sheets, spreading them out on the lid of the box. They were maps, rendered in fading ink. A kender had given them to Matya some years ago in exchange for a silver knife. It had proved to be one of the few unprofitable trades Matya had ever made. She soon had learned that the maps contained many mistakes. They showed land where there were seas, mountains where there were deserts, and populous cities in which no one lived. She should have known better than to trust a kender. They were little tricksters, all of them. Still, poor as the maps were, they were the only maps she had, and she was curious about something.

She shuffled through the maps until she found one that had *Solamnia* written on the top. The mountains were missing, and the map showed Caergoth to be an inland city, while Matya knew very well that it stood on the coast. Some features had been added to the map in a bold, scrawling hand, and Matya suspected these were the kender's own additions. Among other things, the kender's scrawls showed the highways leading to Garnet and Caergoth, and the crossroads as well.

"Now where is it?" Matya muttered, running a finger over the yellowed, cracking vellum. "It has to be here." Then she found what she sought. Written in small, faded letters was the word *Tambor*. By the markings on the map, the village of Tambor was no more than ten miles north and east of the crossroads. "But that would put it in the foothills of the mountains, though this map shows southern Solamnia to be nothing but plains," she added in disgust.

The kender had written something beside the spot marked *Tambor*. She had to squint to make out the scrawling words. They read, *Deestroyd in Kataklism*. Matya mumbled an oath under her breath.

If this was true, then the village the knight sought had been destroyed more than fifty years ago. So much for his plea for help! A liar, as she'd suspected. She didn't know why that hurt her.

Trevarre called out. Matya hastily put away the maps. She found the knight still sitting by the wagon wheel. The porcelain doll stood on the ground before him.

"It is almost time," he said, nodding toward the west. A pearly glow had touched the distant horizon. Solinari, the largest of Krynn's three moons, soon would rise.

Matya sat on a fallen log near the knight, eyes on the doll. While she did not believe Trevarre's story, she was curious to see what he would do when the doll failed to speak.

"Wait," Trevarre said softly. "Just wait."

Matya sighed, resting her chin on a hand, and waited. This was rapidly growing tedious. Finally, a thin, silvery sliver of Solinari lifted above the far-off horizon.

The doll began to sing.

Matya stared at the porcelain statuette in shock. The maiden's lips moved. A sweet, wordless song drifted upon the night air. There was no doubt but that the song came from the doll.

Matya shot a look at Trevarre. The knight's pale eyes were triumphant. The song continued, a sad melody that tugged at Matya's heart. Finally the sweet music ended, and the doll spoke.

"Please, come to me, whoever finds me," it said, its voice cool and lilting but filled with sorrow as well. "I beg you. Come to the village of Tambor. I need help desperately. Please."

Solinari lifted full above the horizon, and the doll fell silent. Matya's eyes glimmered as she stared at it calculatingly.

"An enchanted doll!" she said to herself. "Why, it is

worth a king's ransom."

"Do you believe my tale now?" Trevarre asked, a slight smile beneath his mousy moustache.

Matya nodded. "I believe you." She was glad to believe in him, too, but she didn't tell him that.

"I have something to ask of you," the knight said. "It appears my legs are set on betraying me. I cannot journey to Tambor on foot, but your wagon could carry me. Take me there, Matya. Take me to Tambor, please."

"And what would I gain for my trouble?" Matya asked coolly.

Trevarre reached inside the collar of his woolen cloak and undid the clasp. He held it out to her. "Will this do?" The clasp was fashioned of finely wrought silver, inlaid with pearl and lapis lazuli. Matya appraised it with a practiced eye. The jewel obviously was quite valuable. By any measure, the trade would be a good one, but it was not enough.

"Give me the doll as well," Matya said crisply, "then I will take you to Tambor."

Trevarre gazed at her for a long moment, but Matya did not so much as blink. Finally he laughed. "You drive a hard bargain, I see. It appears I have little choice but to accept. Very well, I will give you the doll—but only after we reach Tambor."

"Agreed," Matya said, her eyes flashing. She took the jeweled clasp from his outstretched hand and spirited it away to a pocket in her dress. "I will keep this as assurance." She knew that Trevarre likely would be distressed when he found Tambor in ruins and his quest proved a folly. However, if he was a man of honor, he would keep his word. The doll would be Matya's. "I'll take you to Tambor, Knight."

She spat in her hand and held it out. Trevarre looked at her in puzzlement for a moment, then nodded solemnly and did the same. They shook hands firmly. The bargain had been struck.

* * * * *

Matya and the knight set out with the dawn, traveling east down the road to Garnet. The mountains loomed high before them, like great gray giants. Their summits were already dusted with a coating of snow, bespeaking the winter that soon would blanket the rest of Solamnia.

Matya studied the kender's map as Rabbit plodded on, pulling the wagon along the jouncing road. The map was terribly faded and crumbled a bit each time she touched it, but Matya could make out the line of a faint road leading south from the place marked Tambor. If the kender had drawn in the highway to Garnet at all accurately, they ought to reach the road to Tambor sometime around midmorning.

" 'Two giants point the way,' " Trevarre said. Matya looked questioningly at the knight, who was propped up on the bench beside her. "That was the sign the doll spoke of that would guide me to the village," he explained. "I imagine it means two mountains, or some such thing."

"You were going to try to find the village with directions like that?" Matya asked.

Trevarre only shrugged.

"Humph!" Matya snorted. "If this maiden of yours was going to all this trouble to get rescued, she might have given you clearer instructions."

Before Trevarre could reply, one of the wheels hit a deep rut, and he winced as the wagon lurched roughly. He was in better shape today than he'd been the night before, but his face was still pale, and the roughness of the wagon's ride obviously was causing him pain. He did not complain, however.

Midmorning passed and noon approached, and still Matya saw no sign of a road leading north from the highway. Finally she pulled on the reins, and Rabbit came to a halt. "It's time for a rest," she said.

She fastened a feedbag over Rabbit's muzzle, then found food for herself and Trevarre. A jumble of massive, oddly shaped granite boulders, warmed by the sun, lay next to the road. The two sat on these as they ate a meal of cheese, bread, and dried fruit. When they had finished, Matya checked Trevarre's bandages. "Your hands are gentle, though your tongue is sharp," said the knight, smiling at her. Matya blushed, but ignored him and nodded in satisfaction. The knight's wounds had closed, and none of them showed signs of festering.

"We had best be on our way," she said, eyeing the sun, which now shone directly overhead. She helped Trevarre stand, offered him her shoulder to lean on. He smelled of oiled steel and leather, not an unpleasant scent, she thought, as the two started making their way back to the wagon. Suddenly Matya froze.

"What is it?" Trevarre asked, looking quickly about in alarm. "Goblins?"

"No," Matya whispered. "No, it's a face."

She pointed to the boulder Trevarre had been sitting on. They had not noticed it earlier, because the shadows had obscured it, but with the sun directly overhead, Matya now saw it as plain as day. The boulder was carved in the face of a man.

The carving was weathered and cracked—it must have been ancient—but Matya still could make out the proud, kingly features, the aquiline nose, and deep, moss-filled eyes. Looking around, she saw that other overgrown boulders were parts of a man—one shaped like a hand, another like a shoulder, still another like a boot.

"It is a statue," Trevarre said in amazement, "a gigantic statue. It must have fallen over years ago, by the looks of it, probably in the Cataclysm."

"Wait, there are two of them," Matya said, pointing to another broken boulder, which was carved in the form of a regal-looking woman.

"The two giants," Trevarre said. "It seems the maiden's directions were not so inadequate after all."

* * * * *

The road beyond the ruined statues was all but hidden by a tangle of willows and brambles. Matya doubted that anyone had come this way in a long time. The way was passable but overgrown and rutted. Trevarre winced each time the wagon's wheel hit a bump, but he said nothing.

"He has courage, if not sense," Matya told herself. She glanced at him, and for a brief moment her hard expression softened. She found herself wondering just how old Trevarre was. He was not a young man, she suspected, despite his foolhardiness.

The narrow road wound across the rolling foothills, over grassy knolls and through groves of aspen and fir. In places the trail was so faint Matya could hardly see it, and several times it ended abruptly, only to be found continuing a hundred paces to the left or right. It was almost as if the land itself had shifted beneath the road, breaking it into pieces.

As the hills slipped away to either side, Matya began to feel a growing sense of unease. The land around them was strangely silent. There are no birds here, she realized with a start, here where the meadows should have been filled with birds.

It was late in the afternoon, and the amber sunlight had grown heavy and dull, when the wagon crested a low ridge. Below lay a small, grassy dell, and in its center stood—

"Tambor," Trevarre said triumphantly.

Matya shook her head in astonishment. She had expected to see a pile of ruins in the dell, the burned-out husks of a few cottages perhaps, and some crumbling stone walls. Instead she saw a prosperous village. More than a score of well-tended cottages lined a main street, busy with people, horses, chickens, and dogs. Smoke rose from a low stone building—probably a smithy—and a mill's waterwheel turned slowly in a small stream.

"You have kept your end of the bargain, Matya," Trevarre said solemnly. "Now it is my turn." He handed her the leather pouch that contained the doll. Matya gripped the purse with numb hands.

The kender had been wrong, she told herself, that was all. Tambor had *not* been destroyed in the Cataclysm. Matya didn't know why she was surprised. Still, there was something about this that did not seem entirely right.

"What is such a prosperous village doing at the end of such an overgrown road?" she asked herself, but she had no answer. Not that it mattered. She had the doll now. That was all she cared about.

59

"I can walk the rest of the way," Trevarre said, starting to climb down from the wagon, but Matya stayed him with a hand on his arm.

"I know it's hard, but try not to be a fool, Knight. I'll take you into the village. I'll need to stay here anyway. It's growing late. I'll set out again in the morning."

Matya guided the wagon to the banks of the stream. A small stone bridge arched over the clear, flowing water. A young woman stood on the far side of the stream. She was clad in a gown of flowing white, and her hair was as dark as jet. She was beautiful, as beautiful as the porcelain doll.

"My knight, you have come to me!" the woman cried out. Her voice was the doll's sweet voice. Matya thought this odd, disconcerting, but it didn't bother Trevarre. His pale eyes shining, he slipped from the wagon and limped across the stone bridge, ignoring the pain of his injury. He knelt before the young woman and kissed her fine-boned hand.

Matya scowled. He never kissed my hand, she thought sourly.

"I am Ciri," said the sweet voice. "Welcome, Sir Knight. My deliverance is at hand."

*   *   *   *   *

Ciri led Trevarre and Matya around the edge of the village. "Quickly," she said softly. "The fewer the folk who see us, the better."

Matya wondered why, but it wasn't *her* place to ask. Trevarre tried to walk faster, but it was clear his wounded leg was causing him great pain. Ciri laid a fine hand on his elbow, and the grimace eased from the knight's face. He walked more easily with her hand on his arm. Matya noticed that Trevarre seemed to have taken more than a passing interest in Ciri's lovely face. "I'll warrant he's more interested in her looks than his honor," she muttered, suddenly annoyed for no particular reason.

As they walked, Matya looked at the village in the ruddy light of the setting sun. Nothing appeared out of order, but something was not right. You're tired, Matya, that's all, she told herself. Tomorrow you'll ride into Garnet and leave this knight and his foolishness behind. That thought should have made her feel better, but it didn't.

Ciri led them to a small, thatch-roofed cottage standing slightly apart from the others. She looked about to make certain no one was watching, then opened the door, gesturing for Trevarre and Matya to enter.

The cottage was warm and neatly kept. A fire burned on the fieldstone hearth, and the wooden floor had been scrubbed clean. Ciri bade them sit down. She filled a wooden cup with crimson wine for each of them. Matya raised the cup of wine, then set it down without drinking it. It had a funny smell to it. Trevarre, however, drank deeply, thanking the woman for her hospitality—all politeness, as his Measure called for, Matya supposed with a frown.

"And now, my lady, you must tell me why you have called to me," Trevarre said.

Ciri smiled at him, a sweet, sorrowful smile.

"And I hope your reason is a good one," Matya noted, crossing her arms. "It was no mean feat getting this knight here, I'll tell you."

Ciri turned her gaze toward Matya for a moment, and suddenly her smile was neither sweet nor sorrowful.

"For that, I do thank you, my good woman," Ciri said.

Matya could not mistake the coldness in Ciri's otherwise lovely voice. It was clear that Matya's presence had not been expected; neither was it wanted.

Ciri's gaze turned soft again as she regarded the knight. Matya scowled, but she said nothing. If the young woman feared competition for the knight's attention, then she was as much a fool as Trevarre. There was little room in a bargain driver's life for love. Such fancies dulled the sharp edge Matya depended on for her livelihood. Besides, there was nothing about the knight she liked, even if his pale eyes were strangely attractive and his voice *did* remind her of a trumpet's call.

The gloom of twilight descended outside the cottage's window. Ciri began her tale. "I fear the fate that lies before me is dark, my knight. A terrible wizard—my uncle—means to force me to marry him, against all propriety and my own wishes. He is a mage of great power, feared by all the folk of Tambor, and even beyond. He is away now, gathering components for his magecraft, but when he returns, he will compel me to wed. You have arrived none too soon, my knight."

"Well, why don't you simply run away?" Matya asked.

Ciri gave her another chill look. "I fear it is not so simple. You see, my uncle dabbles in the *black* arts, heedless of the peril to his soul. He has cast an enchantment upon me. I am unable to leave the village. The banks of the stream are as far as I may tread. Should I take but one step beyond, I would perish."

"But what of your father?" Trevarre asked. "Will he not protect you from your barbarous uncle?"

Ciri shook her head sadly. "My father and mother both died many years ago. There is no one here to protect me. That was why I wove the boat of rushes and sent the doll down the waters of the stream, hoping someone might find it and hear my plea."

"How does the doll speak with your voice?" Matya asked, not caring if she aroused more of Ciri's displeasure.

"It was but the echo of my voice," Ciri explained, her eyes on the knight. "The doll is a magical thing. My father brought it all the way from Palanthas for me when I was a child. If you speak to it, or sing it a song, it will echo your words back to you with the rising moon, exactly as you spoke them."

Matya's eyes glittered brightly. This was better and better. The doll would be almost beyond price. *Almost*, that is. Matya always had a price.

"And how can I break this grievous enchantment?" Trevarre asked earnestly. He was good at this knightly business, Matya had to admit, despite his sorry looks. Ciri stood and walked to the window, gazed through it sadly a moment, then turned to the knight.

"There, in the center of the village, stands a shrine. In that shrine is an altar carved of marble. The altar is the focus of all my uncle's dark powers. I know, for I have seen him work his wicked spells there. From it, he draws his strength. But the magic of the doll has the power to counter it. If one who is strong of heart sets the doll upon the altar of his own free will, the enchantment will be broken."

"And what will happen to the doll?" Matya asked suspiciously.

"Its magic will be dissipated," Ciri answered. "It will become an ordinary doll and nothing more."

She walked to Trevarre then, and he rose to meet her. She laid a hand gently upon his breastplate. Matya could see the pulse beating rapidly in the man's throat. It was clear Trevarre was not immune to Ciri's bewitching beauty. Another weakness of knights, Matya thought acidly. Not that she cared one way or the other, she reminded herself.

"Will you do this task for me, my knight?" Ciri pleaded. "I cannot break the enchantment with my own hand, and there is none in the village brave enough to defy my uncle. Will you help me?"

Trevarre sighed and glanced at Matya. "I would, with all my heart, that I could do this thing, my lady, but I fear I cannot. You see, I have given Matya the doll in payment for bringing me to this place. On my honor, I cannot ask her for it back."

Ciri's face twitched. She shot Matya a look so filled with malice that Matya shivered. Then, aware of the knight's eyes on her, Ciri's sweet, sorrowful look had returned to her lovely face. She bowed her head.

"Then I am doomed, my knight."

"No," he said, with a fierce smile. "No, I cannot think that. I am no sorcerer, but I expect there is another—albeit cruder—way to free you." His hand moved to the hilt of the sword at his hip. "I will stand before your uncle when he returns, and I will demand a duel. The enchantment will be broken when your uncle lies dead at my feet. Won't that solve your problem, my lady?"

Ciri sighed. "My knight, you are indeed brave," she murmured. "So very brave."

Matya noticed, however, that Ciri did not answer Trevarre's question.

* * * * *

Matya awoke in the gray light before dawn. Ciri had provided her a bed. Trevarre slept soundly on a bed of furs before the cottage's hearth. Matya looked around the cottage, but Ciri was nowhere to be seen.

Just as well, Matya thought. This way she would not have to bid the strange young woman good-bye.

Matya knelt beside the sleeping knight before she left. His careworn face was peaceful in slumber, his brow untroubled.

"I hope you find your honor truly reward enough, Knight," she whispered softly. She hesitated a moment, then reached out a hand, as if to smooth his mouse-brown hair over the bandage on his head. He stirred, and she pulled her hand back. Quietly, Matya slipped from the cottage.

"Trevarre has what he wants," she reminded herself, "and so do I."

The ruddy orb of the sun crested the dim purple mountains to the east as Matya made her way through the village. A few folk already were up at this hour, but they paid her no heed as they went about their business. Once again, Matya had the feeling there was something peculiar about this village, but she could not quite fathom what it was. She hurried on toward her wagon and the restless Rabbit.

Then it struck her.

"The shadows are all wrong!" she said aloud.

Her own shadow stretched long before her in the low morning sunlight, but hers was the only shadow that looked like it was supposed to look. The shadow cast by a two-story cottage to her left was short and lumpy—much shorter than she would have expected for a building so high. She looked all around the village and saw more examples of the same. Nowhere did the outline of a shadow match that of the object that cast it. Even more disturbing were the villagers themselves. None of them cast shadows at all!

Her sense of unease growing, Matya gathered up her skirts and hurried onto the stone bridge. She suddenly wanted to be away from this troubling place. She was nearly across the bridge when something—she was unsure exactly what—compelled her to cast one last glance over her shoulder. Abruptly she froze, clapping a hand over her mouth to stifle a cry.

The village had changed.

Well-tended cottages were nothing more than broken, burned stone foundations. The smithy was a pile of rubble, and there was no trace of the mill except for the rotted remains of the waterwheel, slumped by the bank of the stream, looking like the twisted web of some enormous spider. There were no people, no horses, no dogs, no chickens. The dell was bare. The dark ground was hard and cracked, as if it had been baked in a furnace.

Matya's heart lurched. She ran a few, hesitant steps back across the bridge, toward the village, and she gasped again. Tambor looked as it had before, the villagers going about their business. Blue smoke rose from a score of stone chimneys.

Perhaps I imagined it, she thought, but she knew that wasn't true. Slowly, she turned her back to the village once more and walked across the bridge. She looked out of the corner of her eye and again saw the jumbled ruins and blackened earth behind her. Slowly, she began to understand.

Tambor *had* been destroyed in the Cataclysm. The people, the bustling village, were images of what had been long ago. It was all illusion. Except the illusion was imperfect, Matya realized. It appeared only when she traveled *toward* the village, not *away* from it. But how did the illusion come to exist in the first place?

Resolutely, Matya walked back across the bridge. She found that, if she concentrated, the illusion of the bustling village would waver and grow transparent before her eyes, and she could see the blackened ruins beneath. She walked to the center of the village, toward the single standing stone of pitted black basalt. This was the shrine of which Ciri had spoken. At the base of the standing stone was an altar, but it was not hewn of marble, as Ciri had claimed. The altar was built of human skulls, cemented together with mud. They grinned at Matya, staring at her with their dark, hollow eyes.

"Did you really think I would allow you to leave with the

doll?" Ciri spoke behind her in a voice cool and sweet.

Startled, Matya turned around. She half expected to see that Ciri had changed like the rest of the village. The woman was as lovely as ever, but there was a hard, deadly light in her sapphire-blue eyes.

Ciri gazed at Matya, then understanding flickered across her face. "Ah, you see the village for what it is, don't you?"

Matya nodded silently, unable to speak.

Ciri shrugged. "It is just as well. It makes things easier. I'm glad you know, in fact."

"What do you want from me?" Matya asked.

"To strike a bargain with you, Matya. Isn't that what you like to do above all things?"

Matya's eyes narrowed, but she said nothing.

"You have something I want very much," Ciri said softly.

"The doll," Matya said, eyeing the woman.

"You see, Matya, despite the illusions I have used to mask the appearance of the village, much of what I told you last night was the truth. An enchantment does prevent me from leaving the village, and only the doll can break it."

"How is it you came to be here in the first place?" Matya asked.

"I have always been here," Ciri said in her crystalline voice. "I am old, Matya, far older than you. You see me now as I was the day the Cataclysm struck the face of Krynn, more than half a century ago."

Matya stared at her in shock and disbelief, but Ciri did not pause.

"By my magic, I saw the coming of the Cataclysm. I prepared an enchantment to protect myself from it." A distant look touched her cold eyes, and her smile grew as sharp and cruel as a knife. "Oh, the others begged at my door for me to protect them as well. The same wretches who had mocked my magic before wanted me to save them, but I turned my back on them. I wove my magic about myself, and I watched all of them perish in agony as the rain of fire began." Ciri's face was exultant, her fine hands clenched into fists.

Matya watched her with calculating eyes. "Something went wrong, didn't it?"

"Yes," Ciri hissed angrily. "Yes, something went wrong!" She paused, recovered her composure. "I could not have foreseen it. The power of the Cataclysm twisted my magic. The enchantment protected me, as I commanded, but it also cursed me to remain here alone in this ruined town, not aging, not changing, and never able to leave."

Matya shuddered. Despite herself, she could not help but pity this evil woman.

"I want to be free of this place—I *will* be free of this place," Ciri said, "and for that I need the doll."

Matya was no longer afraid. Magic was Ciri's element, but bargaining was Matya's own. "And what would you give me in exchange for the doll?" she asked. "It is worth a lot to me."

"I made that one, and once I am free I will have the power to make more," Ciri replied. "I will fashion you a dozen such dolls, Matya. No one in Ansalon will be wealthier than you. All you have to do is give the doll to Trevarre. *He* wants more than anything to rescue me, to preserve his precious *honor*." She said this last word with a sneer. "He will place the doll upon the altar, and I will be free. And so will you. I swear it, by Nuitari."

"And what will happen to Trevarre?" Matya asked, as if she didn't much care.

Ciri shrugged. "What does it matter? You and I will have what we want."

"I'm curious, that's all," Matya said, shrugging.

"You'll find out anyway, I suppose," Ciri replied. "He will take my place in the enchantment. He will be imprisoned within Tambor even as I am now. He will not suffer, however. I will see to it that *his* soul is destroyed. The empty husk of his body will dwell here until the end of all days." Ciri arched her eyebrow. "Are you satisfied?"

Matya nodded, her expression unchanging. "I'll need to think this bargain over."

"Very well," Ciri said, annoyed, "but be swift about it. I grow tired of waiting. Oh, and if you are thinking of warning the knight, go ahead. He won't believe you." The enchantress turned and stalked away, vanishing among the ruins of the village.

* * * * *

Matya retrieved the leather pouch with the doll from its hiding place in her wagon and tied it to her belt. She sat for a time on the wagon's bench, alone with her thoughts, then finally made her way back to Ciri's cottage. Like all the others, this building was in ruins. The roof was gone, and two of the walls had fallen into a jumble of broken stone.

Trevarre had risen and was in the process of adjusting the straps of his ornate armor. He looked up in surprise.

"Matya. I did not hear you open the door."

Matya bit her tongue to keep from telling him there *was* no door.

"Have you seen Ciri this morning?" he asked. He ran a hand through his lank brown hair.

"I saw her out in the village," Matya said, afraid to say more.

"Is something wrong, Matya?" Trevarre asked her, frowning.

Matya's hand crept to the leather purse. She could have everything she had ever wanted, if she just gave Trevarre the doll. He would take it. She knew he would. As unlikely as Trevarre looked on the outside, the heart that beat in his chest was a knight's, true and pure. He would break the enchantment, and Ciri would be free. She had sworn her oath by Nuitari—a vow no sorcerer could break. Matya would be rich beyond her dreams. It would be the greatest bargain Matya had ever struck.

Her hand reached into the pouch, brushing the smooth porcelain. "I wanted to tell you . . ." She swallowed and started over. "I just wanted to tell you, Trevarre . . ."

"Go on," he said in his resonant voice, his pale eyes regarding her seriously.

Matya saw kindness in his gaze, and, for one brief moment, she almost imagined she saw something more— admiration, affection.

Matya sighed. She could not do it. How could she live with herself, knowing it was she who had silenced Trevarre's noble voice forever? She could strike a bargain for anything—anything but another's life. Belek had been right. There were some bargains that weren't worth making.

"There *is* something wrong," Matya blurted. "Something terribly wrong." She told Trevarre of her conversation with Ciri. "You see, we must leave—now!"

The knight shook his head.

"She is evil!" Matya protested.

"I cannot believe it, Matya."

"What?" she said in shock. Although Ciri had warned her, Matya still was shocked. She had given up the greatest bargain of her life, and now he claimed that he didn't believe her? "But what reason would I have to lie to you, Trevarre? Has her loveliness made a slave of you already?" Her voice was bitter.

He held up a hand. "I did not say that I do not believe you, Matya. I said that I *can*not. I cannot believe evil of another without proof." He sighed and paced about the ruined cottage, which to his eyes still looked warm and hospitable. "How can I explain it to you, Matya? It has to do with the Measure I swore to uphold. Ciri sent out a plea for help, and I have answered it. Yes, she is lovely, but that is hardly the reason I cannot heed your warnings, Matya. She has shown me nothing but courtesy. To leave without aiding her would be a grave dishonor. And you know—"

"Yes, I know," Matya said harshly. " 'Your honor is your life.' But what if she tried to harm you?"

"That would be different. Then I would know she is evil. But she has not. Nothing has changed. I will help her break the enchantment that keeps her here in this village if it is at all in my power to do so."

Trevarre fastened his sword belt about his waist and walked to the door of the ruined cottage. Before he stepped outside, he laid a gentle hand upon Matya's arm. "I doubt that it matters to you," he said hesitantly in his clear voice, "but, to my eyes, you are every bit as lovely."

Before Matya could so much as open her mouth in surprise, Trevarre was gone.

Matya stood in silence for a long moment, then muttered angrily under her breath, "The Solamnic Knights aren't fools. They're idiots!" She stamped out of the open doorway after Trevarre.

Ciri was waiting for her.

"Do you have an answer for me, Matya?" Ciri asked in her lilting voice.

Trevarre stood before the enchantress, the wind blowing his cloak out behind him. He would not raise a hand against her, Matya knew. What happened next was going to have to be up to her.

"The answer is no, Ciri," Matya said calmly. "I won't accept your bargain."

Ciri's eyes flashed, and the wind caught her dark hair, flinging it wildly about her head. Anger touched her lovely face. Trevarre, startled, fell back before her fury.

"That is a foolish decision, Matya," Ciri said, all pretext of sweetness gone from her voice. "I will find another who will break the enchantment for me. I'll have the doll back! You both will die!"

The enchantress spread her arms wide, and the wind whipped about. Dry dust stung Matya's face. Trevarre looked around, shock on his face. The illusion had vanished. The evil-looking ruins were laid bare and undisguised.

Ciri spoke several strange, guttural words. Instantly the swirling wind was filled with dead tree limbs and dry, brown leaves. As Matya watched, the broken branches and leaves began to clump together, growing denser, taking shape.

"Trevarre, look out!" Matya cried out in terror.

The dead, brittle branches and clumps of rotting leaves had taken the shape of a man. The tree creature was huge, towering over the knight. It reached out a bark-covered arm that ended in splintery claws. Its gigantic maw displayed row upon row of jagged, thorny teeth.

Trevarre drew his sword, barely in time to block the creature's swing. Branches and splinters flew in all directions, but the knight stumbled beneath the blow. His face blanched with pain; his wounded leg buckled beneath him. He was too weak to fight such a monster, Matya realized. One more blow and he would fall. Ciri watched the battle with a look of cruel pleasure on her face. The tree monster roared again, drawing back its arm for another bone-crushing blow.

Matya drew the doll from the leather pouch and stared at it. She hesitated for a moment, but the sight of Trevarre— standing before the monster, his face grim and unafraid— steeled her resolve. Regretfully, she bade her dreams of wealth farewell . . . and hurled the doll at the altar.

Too late Ciri saw Matya's intent. The enchantress shrieked in rage and reached out to catch the doll. Her fingers closed on thin air.

The figurine struck the altar and shattered into a thousand pale shards—dirty, broken bones. The wind died as suddenly as it had started. The tree monster shuddered and collapsed into a pile of inanimate wood and leaves. Trevarre stumbled backward, leaning on his sword to keep from falling. His face was ashen, his breathing hard.

"What have you done?" Ciri shrieked, her sapphire-blue eyes wide with astonishment and horror.

"I've given you what you wanted," Matya cried. "You're free now, Ciri. Just let Trevarre go. That's all I ask."

Ciri shook her head, but her lips moved wordlessly now. She took a few steps toward Matya, each one slower than the last. Her movements had become strangely halting, as if she were walking through water, not air. The enchantress reached out a hand, but whether the gesture was one of fury or supplication, Matya did not know. Suddenly, Ciri shuddered and stood motionless. For a moment, the figure of the enchantress stood there among the ruins, as pale and perfect as a porcelain doll. Her eyes glimmered like clear, soulless gems.

Then, even as Matya watched, a fine crack traced its way across the smooth surface of Ciri's lovely face. More cracks spread from it, snaking their way across Ciri's cheeks, her throat, her arms. As if she had been fashioned of porcelain herself, Ciri crumbled into a mound of countless fragments, a heap of yellowed bones—all that was left of the enchantress.

*　*　*　*　*

The doves were singing their evening song when the gaudily painted wagon bounced past the fallen remains of the gigantic statues and turned eastward down the road, heading toward the town of Garnet. Matya and Trevarre had traveled in silence most of the way from the ruined village of Tambor. The knight, still recovering from his wounds, had slept the better part of the day. Matya was content to occupy herself with her thoughts.

"You gave up your dreams to help me, didn't you, Matya?" Trevarre asked.

Matya turned her head to see that the knight was awake, stroking his mousy brown moustache thoughtfully. "And what reward do you have to show for it?"

"Why, I have this," Matya said, gesturing to the jeweled clasp she had pinned to her collar. "Besides, I can always find new dreams. And I am certainly not ready to give up bargaining. I'll make my fortune yet, you'll see."

Trevarre laughed, a sound like music. "I have no doubt of that."

They were silent for a time, but then Matya spoke softly. "You would do the same again, wouldn't you, if you heard a call for help?"

Trevarre shrugged. "The Measure is not something I can follow only when it suits me. It is my life, Matya, for good or ill. It is what I am."

Matya nodded, as if this confirmed something for her. "The tales are right then. The Knights of Solamnia *are* little better than fools." She smiled mischievously. "But there's one more bargain that must be struck."

"Which is?" Trevarre asked, raising an eyebrow.

"What are you going to give me in return for taking you to Garnet?" Matya asked slyly.

"I'll give you five gold pieces," Trevarre said flatly.

"I'll not take less than fifty!" Matya replied, indignant.

"Fifty? Why, that's highway robbery," Trevarre growled.

"All right," Matya said briskly. "I'm in a kindly mood, so I'll make it twenty, but not one copper less."

Trevarre stroked his moustache thoughtfully. "Very well. I will accept your offer, Matya, but on one condition."

"Which is?" Matya asked, skeptical.

A smile touched Trevarre's lips. "You must allow me this." He took Matya's hand, brought it to his lips, and kissed it.

The bargain had been struck.

Seekers

Todd Fahnestock

Gylar Radilan, of Lader's Knoll, set his mother's hand back onto her chest, over the rumpled blanket. It was done then. Gylar wasn't sure whether to be relieved or to crumple into the corner and cry. Finally, though, it was done. Stepping back, he fell into the chair he'd put by her bed, the chair he'd sat upon all night while holding her hand.

His head bowed for a moment as he thought about the past few days. The Silent Death had swept through the entire village, killing everyone. It had been impossible to detect its coming. There were no early symptoms. One minute, people were laughing and playing—like Lutha, the girl he had known—and the next, they were in bed, complaining weakly of the icy cold they felt, but burning to the touch. Their skin darkened to a ghastly purple as they coughed up thicker and thicker phlegm, and in a few hours their bodies locked up as with rigor mortis.

Poor Lutha. Gylar swallowed and sniffed back tears. She'd been the first one, the one who had brought about the downfall of the village. Gylar could remember going with her into the new marsh, the marsh that hadn't been there before the world shook. People had told their children repeatedly not to go in. They said it had all sorts of evils in it, but that had never stopped Lutha. She'd never listened to her parents much, and once she got something into her head, there was no balking her. She'd had to know about their tree, his and her tree.

Now she was dead. Now everyone was dead. Everyone, of course, except Gylar. For some reason, he hadn't been affected, or at least not yet. His parents had seemed to be immune as well, until the day they collapsed in their beds, shivering.

Gylar rose and crossed the room. He looked out the window to the new day that was shining its light across the hazy horizon and sifting down over the trees skirting the new marsh. He clenched his teeth as a tear finally fell from his eye. If it hadn't been for the marsh, none of this would have happened! Lutha never would have brought the evil back with her, and everyone would be okay. But, no, the gods had thrown the fiery mountain. They'd cracked the earth, and the warm water had come up from below, and with it whatever had killed the town.

Gylar banged his small hand on the windowsill. Why did they do it? The villagers all had been good people. Paladine had been their patron; Gylar's mother had been meticulously devoted to her god, teaching Gylar to be the same. She had loved Paladine, more than anyone in the village. Even after the Cataclysm, when everyone else turned from the gods in scorn and hatred, Gylar's mother continued her evening prayers with increasing earnestness. What did she, of all people, do to deserve such punishment? What did any of them do to deserve it? Was everyone on Krynn going to die, then? Was that it?

Gylar was young, but he wasn't stupid. He'd heard his parents talking about all the other awful things now happening to people who'd survived the tremors and floods. Didn't the gods care about mortals anymore?

Caught up in a slam of emotions, Gylar turned and ran from the house. He ran to the edge of the new bog and yelled up at the sky in his rage.

"Why? If you hate us so much, why'd you even make us in the first place?"

Gylar collapsed to his knees with a sob. Why? It was the only thing he could really think of to ask. It all hinged on that. Why the Cataclysm? How could humans have been evil enough to deserve this? How could anyone?

For a long moment he just slumped there, as though some unseen chain were dragging at his neck, joining the one already pulling at his heart. Gylar sniffled a little and ran his forearm quickly across his nose.

Stumbling to his feet, he looked at the sky again. Clouds were rolling in to obscure the sun, threatening a storm. Gylar sighed. Although he had nowhere else to go, he didn't want to stay in this place of death. His eyes swept over Mount Phineous. The towering mountain still looked overpoweringly out of place, like a sentinel sent by the gods to watch over the low, hilly country. The top fourth of it was swept by clouds. Another result of the Cataclysm, the mountain seemed a counterpart of the new swamp. Brutal and imposing, powerful, the towering rock was the opposite of the silent, sneaky swamp of death.

His fatigue overcame his sadness and revulsion, at least for the moment. Slowly, he made his way back to the house, back to the dead house. Stopping in the doorway, Gylar turned around to look at the land that was growing cold with winter. It was likely going to snow today.

He turned and slammed the door shut behind him. It didn't matter. Nothing much mattered anymore. His limbs dragged at him heavily. Sleep, he thought, that's all. Sleep, then, when I wake up—if I wake up—I'll figure out what to do.

So, for the first time in three days, Gylar slept.

* * * * *

Eyes focused on his prey, Marakion stilled his breathing, though a haze of white drifted slowly from his mouth. The scruffy man before him leaned heavily against the tree, huffing frosty air as he tried to recover from the run. Although exhausted, the man never once turned his fearful eyes from Marakion.

"A merry chase, my friend," Marakion said in a voice that was anything but merry. "Tell me what I wish to know. This will end."

The man stared in disbelief. Marakion was barely winded. The man gulped another breath and answered frantically, "I told you! I never heard of no 'Knight-killer Marauders!' "

Marakion hovered over the thief, his eyes black and impenetrable, his lip twitching, barely holding his rage in check. The bare blade of his sword glimmered dully. "Knightsbane Marauders," he rumbled in a low voice. The scruffy man quivered under the smoldering anger. "You are a brigand, just like them. You must know of them. Tell me where they are."

"I told you!" The thief cringed against the tree. "I don't know!"

In brutal silence, Marakion let loose his pent up rage. One instant his sword, Glint, was at his side, and the next, the flat of it smashed into the man's neck. The thief was so surprised by the attack that he barely had time to blink. The strike sent him reeling. Two more clubbing strokes dropped him to the frosty earth, unconscious.

"Then you live," Marakion said, breathing a bit harder. Leaning down, he searched the body thoroughly for the insignia that gave his life burning purpose.

There was none to be found.

Furiously disappointed, he left the useless thug where he lay and headed for the road.

The town that had been his destination before the small band of ruffians had attacked him lay ahead. He had searched all of the towns and outlying areas east of here, only to come up empty-handed, forever empty-handed. But this desolate area showed promise. Marakion was sure the marauders were here. They had to be. During the last few days, he'd come across numerous wretches like the one he'd just felled. None of them belonged to the Knightsbane, but their presence might be a sign that he was getting close to their hideout.

It wasn't long before sparse trees gave way to a huge, rolling meadow. On its edge stood a squat, dirty little town. Marakion didn't even look twice at the ramshackle buildings, the muddy, unkempt road, the muck-choked stream. The sight of people living in such squalor was not unusual to him, not unusual at all. In fact, this place was better than some he'd seen.

The few people he saw as he followed the road to town gave him quick, furtive glances from beneath ragged, threadbare cowls. Marakion ignored them, made his way to the first tavern he could spot.

He didn't even read the name as he entered. It didn't matter to him where he was, and the names only depressed him—new names, cynically indicative of the time, such as "The Cataclysm's Hope," or old names, which the owners hadn't bothered to change. Those were even worse, sporting a cheerful concept of a world gone forever, their signs dangling crookedly from broken chains or loose nails.

Marakion opened the door; it sagged on its hinges once freed of the doorjamb. He pushed it shut, blocking out the inner voice that continued to remind him how worthless life was if everything was like this.

Marakion turned and surveyed the room, walked forward to the bar that lined the far wall.

The innkeeper had smiled as Marakion had entered, but now blanched nervously at sight of the hunter's stony face, the dark, deliberate gaze.

"Uh, what can I do for you, stranger?"

"What do you have to eat this day, innkeep?"

"Fairly thick stew tonight. Mutton, if you've the wealth."

"Bread?"

"Sure, stranger, fairly fresh, if you've the wealth."

Marakion did not return the man's feeble attempts to be friendly. "A chunk of fresh bread and the stew." He tossed a few coins on the bar. "I'll be at that table over there."

The innkeeper scooped the coins off the counter in one movement. "I'm Griffort. You need anything, I'm the man to talk to. I don't suppose you'll be staying for the night. Got a couple of rooms open—"

"One room," Marakion interrupted, "for the night." He left a stark pause in the air and waited.

"Uh, um, another of those coins'll do it," the unnerved innkeeper stuttered.

Marakion paid the man and made his way to the table he'd indicated. As he sat down, he touched his money pouch. Not much left. A filthy inn, rotten food, a room likely crawling with rats, and costing him as much as a night in Palanthas—that was the type of world he was living in now.

The type of world he lived in now . . .

Marakion put his fingers to his face and massaged his eyes gently. He couldn't make the memories go away. Even if he blocked the images, the essence of them still came to him. He couldn't seem to shut that out. It infected his every thought, his every action.

He relaxed, and his muscles began to unknot from the day's exercise. He could feel the pull of exhaustion on him. His fingers continued to massage closed eyelids, and the inn slowly drifted from his attention.

Where is she, Marakion? A familiar voice asked the question again inside his head.

"I don't know. Nearby somewhere. I don't know," he muttered.

That's not good enough, Marakion. Where is she? Where?

"I'm looking, trying to find her!"

Not good enough, Marakion. There can be no excuses. They'll kill her, you know. Every day you fail to find them is another day they could kill her, or use her.

"I know. I'll find them. If I have to rip apart this entire continent. I will."

You'd better.

The accusing voice drifted away, to be replaced by the vision that haunted his nights when he slept and his waking hours whenever he lost the concentration that kept it at bay.

* * * * *

Fire. Fire and smoke. The flames licked the top of the tower windows. The smoke spiraled up from every part of the castle, blackening the sky. Despair wrenched at Marakion's heart. He had returned home in time to see it fall to the hands of a pillaging group of brigands.

His horse slipped on the cobblestones that led into the castle. He yanked brutally on the reins, pulling the galloping animal to a stop. The horse almost stumbled to its knees. Marakion leapt from its back and raced into the castle gardens. They were trampled, destroyed, burned.

"Marissa!" he shouted above the crackling flames and tearing, rending sounds of destruction that came from within the castle proper. "Tagor! Bess!" He was across the garden in a heartbeat and ran through the entryway. The great double doors lay broken and scattered on the floor. The huge foyer was destroyed, a shambles, a mockery of its original grandeur. One scruffy-bearded ruffian stood guard at the entrance.

The marauder charged. He had determination and purpose in his eyes; Marakion had murder. Rage fueled Marakion's sword arm, fear for his family infusing his body with uncanny speed. He smashed the invader's sword aside and delivered a vicious return stroke at the head.

The marauder ducked under the powerful attack and slipped a cut at Marakion's midriff. Marakion parried, stepped inside the invader's guard, and ran him through.

The invader fell and gasped as his life seeped away. Marakion put his foot on the man's chest and kicked violently, freeing his blade. The dying man's screams ended by the time Marakion reached the top of the left-hand stairs.

"Marissa!"

Marakion raced to his younger sister's room, the first room on the second level. She was not there, but, as with the foyer, her room was cast into disarray—books thrown on the floor, the bed a smoldering pile of burned sheets, straw, and wood. Next to the burning mass lay a piece of cloth. He recognized it, grabbed it: a scrap of her dress, the lavender dress she always wore for his homecoming. A spattering of blood tainted the remnant.

"Marissa!" he yelled in impotent rage. His sixteen-year-old sister, his best friend, so bright, so alive . . . Marakion uttered a strangled cry, clutched the cloth in his fist. . . .

* * * * *

"Sir?"

Sir . . . ?

"Sir, are you asleep?"

Marakion started awake as the hand touched him. He was disoriented, thought he was still there, still back at his burned and devastated home. His hand reacted to the touch with the quickness of a snake. Snatching the thin wrist, he held it tightly. There was a gasp of pain. Marakion stared hard, trying to focus his eyes.

Marissa?

The eyes of the woman were wide, and she was frozen where she stood.

Marakion's harsh stare did not relent, but his grip lost some of its steel. No, not Marissa, a barmaid, just a barmaid.

"What?" he asked shortly, releasing the woman's wrist. Her hair was a dirty red, and as unkempt as the plain, rumpled brown dress she wore.

She appraised him coolly with shrewish eyes. "Griffort wants to know if you want pepper in your stew."

"Fine," Marakion said, "that's fine."

"I'll tell him," she said curtly, and left.

Marakion slowly withdrew something from his tunic. Unfolding it, he laid the piece of lavender cloth out in front of him. It was worn, faded; dark brown spots stained it.

Closing his eyes, Marakion pressed the cloth against his cheek.

"Marissa. . . ."

*　*　*　*　*

The following morning dawned cold and unpleasant. It was snowing. As Marakion shouldered his pack and tied on his cloak, he stared out the window in his room and thought that today would be the day he found the marauders. Today would be the day he found where the scum holed up.

Griffort was wiping down the bar, looked up to see him.

"Morning, sir," he said. "Breakfast for you today? I might be able to scrape together some eggs, if you've the wealth for 'em."

"No. I'm leaving."

Griffort nodded. "Which way you headed?"

"West."

Griffort's face darkened, and he motioned Marakion closer. The innkeeper spoke in a low voice, "You want a copper's worth of free advice?"

Marakion nodded for him to continue.

"Don't go west, at least not straight west. Skirt Mount Phineous if you can. Evil things going on up there."

Marakion was interested. "How so?"

"Lader's Knoll." The innkeeper shook his head. "We used to have an arrangement with a farmer up there in Lader's Knoll. 'Taters don't grow down here, as well as other stuff Bartus likes for his cooking, so we'd swap bread and the like for vegetables and such—but I can see you're not into long stories, so I'll cut it short. One day, the farmer stopped bringing his wagon down. I sent one of the town boys to Lader's Knoll to see what had happened. The kid never came back. Something bad's going on up there, stranger—" Griffort stopped at the sight of Marakion's smile.

"Perfect," Marakion said. "Does the name 'Knightsbane Marauders' mean anything to you? Have you heard of them?"

The disconcerted innkeeper shook his head slowly. "No."

Marakion stared at him hard, then turned and left the inn. Behind him he heard the innkeeper's comment to the barmaid: "Must'a got his noggin cracked somewhere. World's full of crazies nowadays."

* * * * *

Gylar awoke the next morning in a better mood. He'd slept all the previous day and all night. His confusion and fear were replaced by purpose. He wanted to know why the gods killed everyone, why they allowed people like his mother, and like Lutha, to die needlessly. Well, he would ask them.

The question turned over again and again in his head as he buried his mother next to the rest of his family. The snow fell lightly on him and the ground at which he worked. It was almost as though the skies knew Gylar didn't want to look at the village anymore.

When his mother was resting with his little brother and father, Gylar went back inside the house.

He closed the door on the storm outside, went to his father's room, and pulled down the pack he'd kept on the wall, the pack Gylar had seen his father use countless times when they'd gone hunting together. A brief wash of memories splashed over Gylar. He sniffled and ran a sleeve across his nose.

Turning his thoughts to more immediate tasks, Gylar took the pack into the kitchen. He collected some food suited to traveling, a good kitchen knife, a spoon, and a small pot. Gylar looked about for anything else he might need. A bedroll, he thought. He went to his room, stripped the woolen blanket off the bed, and rolled it up, tied it onto his father's already laden pack.

He put on a thick cloak and pulled the pack to the door. The snowfall had sheathed the ground in white. Mount Phineous was hidden in the distance, but its presence still loomed in Gylar's mind. What better place to contact the gods than from the top of their latest creation?

He adjusted his cloak more snugly, threw the heavy pack over his shoulder. It unsteadied him for a moment, but he regained his balance and thrust an arm through the remaining strap, securing the burden. He turned and looked one last time at what once had been his home. Gylar said nothing, bowed his head, and began walking toward the great mountain.

*   *   *   *   *

Marakion watched as the young boy, bundled to the teeth, left Lader's Knoll.

"Off on a journey, are we?" he said quietly from the shadow of a wall. "And just where are you going, little looter?"

Marakion had been in the small village for about half an hour, and he hadn't seen a living being. His disappointment was acute. He'd assumed that Lader's Knoll was the marauders' camp. It was perfect, a desolate place; all those within traveling distance were scared to visit.

But instead of seedy shacks full of murderers and cut-throats, he'd found fresh graves or, sometimes, a few bodies, sleeping the slumber of the dead. The gaunt faces were a faint purple, and dried blood covered their lips.

Another false trail. His frustration was painful almost beyond bearing. He wandered the town in search of some sign, any sign that this had been the hideout of the marauders, but it appeared that the only curse to take up residence in this town was a plague.

"There's your evil, Griffort," he'd muttered.

He'd been about to start off from the devastated village when he'd seen a door to one of the houses open. He slid from view behind one of the nearby buildings.

With a quick-beating heart and silenced breathing, Marakion watched the boy leave the village. "Well, well. Looting the dead, eh? Where are your cohorts, Marauder? Or did they just send you to scout the area?"

Marakion exulted in his discovery. The boy was headed toward Mount Phineous! Marakion berated himself for not thinking of it before. What better place for a band of brigands than a Cataclysm-spawned, uninhabited mountain?

Marakion detached himself from the shadow of the house and followed. He was not about to reveal himself to his guide, at least not until the sanctuary was found.

"I'm coming, Marissa," he whispered as he fell into a loping stride behind his prey.

* * * * *

Occasionally during the trek up the mountain, the boy turned to look at the sky, or at how far he'd separated himself from the village. The ever alert Marakion moved skillfully into a nearby copse of trees, ducked behind an outcropping of rock or shrubbery. It wasn't difficult for Marakion to remain hidden from the youngster's view. The cloud cover made the terrain gloomy, and the falling snow decreased visibility dramatically.

It was afternoon when the boy first stopped. After extracting a few things from his pack, he dumped it on the ground, sat on it, and began eating.

Marakion watched from just over a small hillock, built up by a tremendous snowdrift, then settled down to a meal of his own, consisting of some strips of dried rabbit.

The snow stopped falling sometime before noon, and the afternoon opened up clear and bright, making Marakion's stalking much more difficult, but not impossible. He smiled. It wouldn't be long now.

While tearing at the rough meat with his teeth, Marakion studied the youngling with interest. The boy was not very large; Marakion guessed him at about eleven or twelve years old. He looked innocent enough, sitting there, chomping on his lunch, not much like a sneak-thief. But, no, he was one of them—a messenger, maybe, or a pick-pocket. He had to be.

Marakion's teeth fought the dried meat for another bite. He gauged the size of the mountain. It was not the biggest he'd seen, but impressive in its own right.

Marakion turned his attention back to the boy. He wasn't going anywhere for the moment. Obviously he'd settled down for a long rest. Marakion set his excellent hearing to guard and hunkered down comfortably.

Relaxing, he slipped into a light drowse, waiting for the boy to make the next move. He was startled back to wakefulness. His ears caught a crunching sound from up the mountain. Rolling to his feet, he peered over the drift.

The boy had heard the sound, too. He scrambled upright. The bramble-breaking noise grew louder. Marakion tensed his body, relaxed his mind, letting it disappear, allowing the energy to flow. This was it. This must be some rendezvous point. The entire band, maybe! He was ready.

But the boy did not run into the trees to welcome a gang of murderers. He did not call a greeting to comrades. Instead, he let out a fearful yell and, stumbling over himself, began running down the hill. Marakion stared curiously into the trees to see what was following.

A huge ogre burst from the foliage. Sallow and crusty-skinned, the ogre charged forward with long, quick strides. Wet brambles and a few straggling pine needles showered off the creature as it ran, sending snow flying in a blinding flurry.

Marakion cursed as he watched the ogre closing on the boy. The damned ogre was ruining everything! Scaring off Marakion's guide, the ogre might kill the boy before Marakion could question him!

* * * * *

Gylar's heart beat against his rib cage like a woodpecker. The snow impeded every step of his short legs, while the ogre's strides cleared the terrain as though it were midsummer ground. It was just a matter of time. Gylar gulped for air as he struggled onward. His mind had gone numb, and all he could think of was escape. He'd heard stories about what ogres did to children. . . .

Just at the height of his despair, when the ogre loomed over him, casting a nightlike shadow that engulfed Gylar, the strap of his pack slipped off his shoulder.

If Gylar had been thinking straight, he'd have abandoned his pack and kept going, but he reflexively hung onto it as it scraped the snow. Too late, he realized his error. The momentum of his flight sent him sprawling, then tumbling down the hill. He careened into a snowbank in a fluff of white.

The massive arm of the ogre plunged into the snow, groped around, then plucked out a struggling Gylar. The ogre's craggy mouth split like a crack in a tree's bark, revealing a fairly complete row of sharp teeth as dingy yellow as the ogre's mottled skin.

* * * * *

Twenty feet away, Marakion leaned against a tree, listening. A shimmer ran the length of Glint.

The ogre chuckled at the boy as it began to walk home. "Glad came," the ogre said, with a thick, grating accent. "Hungry, me. We eat, I and you." The ogre chuckled again, sounded like someone scraping rough rocks together. "Take home you to me. Dinner, we have—"

"Not today." Marakion said clearly in the frosty air as the

two walked past the tree he stood behind. The ogre took one look at Marakion and dropped the boy into the snow with a snarl.

But Marakion was on the ogre before it could even raise its arms in defense. Marakion kicked out, struck the ogre in the knee, swung the flat end of Glint into the side of the ogre's head.

The creature went down in a tumble of arms and snow. Marakion stood ready as the ogre surged onto its feet. It was calm, imposing.

"Leave, friend. The boy is under my protection. If you have any wits at all, you'll seek food elsewhere. Surely catching a deer could not be as much trouble as this little one will cost you."

The ogre growled, flexing its muscles under its rough yellow skin, but it did not take a step forward. It was accustomed to fearful enemies, not one facing it with confidence. The ogre showed its teeth viciously. "Hungry. Food mine. You leave."

"Not on your life." Marakion smiled, his stance immobile. It felt good to fight, for whatever reason. The despair, the frustration, the hopelessness—all disappeared when Marakion went into combat. "You leave, or we fight. If you insist, I must say I'm really in the mood for the battle. Is it worth it?"

The ogre stood swaying back and forth, wondering, perhaps, what it was that made this human brave enough to challenge it. It showed its teeth again. "Hungry!" it growled, clenching and unclenching its clawed fists anxiously.

Marakion's eyes narrowed. "Times are hard for all of us, friend. Everyone's got—"

Marakion didn't have time to finish his sentence. The ogre—a madness in its eyes, claws extended—charged the knight.

Having thought he was actually having some effect with his words, Marakion was surprised by the sudden onslaught. Quick reflexes moved him to the side of the hulking swing that cracked a tree trunk behind him.

Marakion slid under the ogre's arm and dodged behind

the yellow giant. His sword flashed out, slashing once, twice on the ogre's back. Blood welled from cuts, a muted crack sounded. Broken bone, Marakion realized. The ogre roared in pain, struck out with its huge fist. Yellow-fleshed arm bone and steel whacked together harshly, and the ogre howled again.

Another huge yellow hand came down. Marakion didn't have enough leverage to sidestep. The jagged claws raked his left side. He grabbed hold of the forearm and slammed Glint's pommel into the ogre's left eye. A follow-up strike cracked into the side of the bark-skinned head. The ogre reeled backward, stunned. Marakion hit it again and again.

Snow exploded outward as the huge body fell heavily to the ground. Jumping forward, Marakion hovered over the ogre like a dark angel, clenching Glint tightly in his fist. His breathing was hard and quick. He stared down at the ogre, waiting for it to rise again, waiting for it to attack.

The ogre didn't rise, though the eyes fluttered open. Marakion raised his finely honed arm, preparing to end the creature's life, then he paused. The rough yellow hide was pulled tight over the protrusion of the creature's ribs; the bloody, bruised face was gaunt. The ogre's muscles were thin, hunger-wasted.

Marakion lowered Glint. The ogre struggled sluggishly to get up, only to fail and plunge back into the snow. It raised its arms a bit in a feeble attempt to ward off another blow—one that never descended.

This wasn't a monster, Marakion thought, just another creature devastated by the Cataclysm, whose life had been turned upside down, ruined, like his own. The ogre was just trying to survive. Marakion wondered what lengths he would go to if he were starving. Definitely he wouldn't be above eating ogre flesh.

Marakion noticed the young boy watching his deliberation.

"Go on," the man said harshly to the ogre. "I gave you one chance. This is your second. You won't get a third."

The emaciated ogre finally made it to its feet. Its unswollen eye gave one final, hungry look at Gylar, then it turned and limped slowly into the woods from which it had come, blood drops dotting its tracks.

Marakion's brow furrowed. Sheathing Glint, he turned to face the boy.

"What's your name?" Marakion asked harshly.

The boy looked dazed, still recovering from shock and fright. "Uh, Gylar, sir. I . . . Thanks," he tacked on lamely.

"You shouldn't be out here alone. Ogres might not be the worst you'll find. I hear there's a dangerous band of brigands in these hills."

Marakion watched for some reaction. Gylar's face gave no telltale signs of anything but relief.

"I—I'm on a quest, and . . . Who are you?" Gylar couldn't contain his curiosity any longer. "What are you doing up on the mountain here? My village is the only one for miles."

Marakion noted the honest innocence in the boy's face, and he cursed again, silently.

"I do a bit of traveling. Just passing through, really." He paused and looked at Gylar closely once more. He began to doubt again. The boy might be a cunning liar.

"Tell you what, kid. Looks like we both need to rest a little." He touched his raked side gingerly. "What do you say to putting your quest on hold and setting up camp? I saw a cave, over there a ways. . . . When we get a good fire going, you can tell me all about it."

Gylar smiled and nodded.

*　*　*　*　*

"I went with Lutha. I knew she wasn't supposed to go in there. Mom had told me about the evil in the new marsh, and Lutha's parents had told the same thing to her. But Lutha wasn't afraid. You see, there was something we'd put in an old tree before the marsh came, before the Cataclysm and Mount Phineous. A couple of necklaces we made out of leather and wooden disks." Gylar's mouth became a straight line, and his brow furrowed.

The warm fire popped and crackled, illuminating Marakion's intent face and the makeshift bandages that he was wrapping slowly around his middle.

Gylar sighed and continued, "She was always doing stuff like that. Anyway, the marsh wasn't really scary, just wet and mucky. The only thing that happened was that Lutha fell down in the water once.

"But Mom was real mad when I got back. She knew where we'd been. I guess the smell of the marsh and my wet boots gave us away. Anyway, I snuck out of the house later, when Mom was down at the stream washing and Dad was chopping wood. I went to see Lutha.

"I didn't knock at the door, because her parents were probably just as mad at her as mine were at me. Instead, I went around back and looked in the bedroom window. Lutha was in there and she was shivering real bad. And her face was real red. That was the first time I saw the sickness on somebody. Lutha was the first. . . ."

Gylar tossed a twig into the fire. "I didn't see Lutha again." He wiped his nose. "The day after that, it was the talk of the village. Lutha had died of a strange sickness. Then her parents died. No one knew how to stop the sickness. Everybody went into their houses and didn't come out, but it didn't matter. I'm not sure who died after that, because Dad closed us up in our house, too. When Rahf died, my little brother, Mom said it didn't matter anymore that we stayed in the house."

Gylar sighed again. "It was awful. Hardly anyone was alive in the village when we came out. We went from door to door, looking for people. Everyone was in their beds, shaking with the fever or already dead. I wanted to leave. Since we hadn't caught it yet, I told Mom we should run away from it. She shook her head and didn't answer me. We helped those who had it. We took care of them, but it didn't matter, just like staying in the house didn't matter anymore. They were going to die, but Mom said we could help them. I know now she didn't mean help them live, but help them to die better. I guess . . .

"Then Dad died." Gylar's voice was subdued. He shook his head; his cheeks were wet. "He went just like everyone else, shivering but so hot. I didn't want . . ."

His eyes focused again on Marakion. "He was one of the last ones to go, then it was my mother. When she died, I felt so alone, so alone and numb. I could touch something, like the blanket, or—or her hand, and I wouldn't really feel it. I had to go. I had to get out."

Gylar looked intently at Marakion. "Why did the gods do it, sir? I just don't understand. Why did they have to kill so many people? It doesn't make sense. We didn't do anything! We just lived. We worshiped Paladine. But Krynn was still cracked, and then the new marsh rose and Lutha caught the sickness and now everyone . . . everyone I ever knew is dead." He bowed his head.

Then his mouth set defiantly and his brows came together in anger. "And so I'm going to ask them. I want them to answer just one question. Why? Why did they do it to everyone? What did we do wrong?"

Marakion smiled. "Supposing the gods even respond, they might drop another mountain on you."

"I don't care," Gylar said petulantly, gathering his blanket around him and resting his head on his pack. "I don't care if they do. If they do, they don't care about us and it won't matter. But . . . but I will ask." He yawned. "I will ask *him* . . . Paladine."

Gylar fell asleep. Marakion gazed at the young face. The flame's light played off the round, boyish features that would not fade for several years yet. Marakion sighed aloud this time. Watching the boy tell his story, the knight had realized Gylar was indeed no marauder's lackey. He actually was what he claimed: a simple country boy in search of divine answers.

Gylar's story made Marakion think of all the things he'd lost because of the Cataclysm. If the gods had not dropped the fiery mountain, his home would not have been attacked.

"You're right, Gylar," he said to the sleeping boy. "Paladine should be confronted, asked . . ." Marakion's iron doors creaked open. "So much like Tagor," he said to himself. "A victim, like Tagor. I wonder what will happen to you?"

Flames and smoke danced in the fire inside his head. Very much like Tagor. *What will happen to you?*

---

* * * * *

Screams. Clanging steel. The sounds of battle. The cry of his younger brother.

"I'm coming, Tagor!" Marakion shouted from Marissa's destroyed bedroom.

The yell had sounded from down the hall. Marakion propelled himself toward it. The library! Tagor was trapped in the library.

Marakion slammed through the door with the force of a battering ram. He knocked one of the invaders to the floor. His sword took out another.

Five more waited. Tagor stood on top of a table in the corner, fighting off the men who were harassing him. The teasing grins they wore turned to scowls when Marakion entered.

"The knight! Keep him there!" a thick-bearded man yelled. "I'll finish this young one off."

Marakion shoved his fallen foe away and slammed into the next, trying desperately to come to the aid of his younger brother, but his new opponent was a skilled swordsman, not a brawler. Marakion slashed insanely at the man's guard, trying at the same time to see Tagor.

Perched on the studying table, wielding their father's sword, Tagor delivered a wicked slash to the bearded man, opening up his forehead. He was holding his own momentarily, but that wouldn't last long. Although Tagor was a fine swordsman for fifteen, he was no match for the brigands' strength, or their numbers.

Marakion let out a roar. "Bastards! Leave him alone! Fight me!"

Tagor twisted sideways, screamed. A sword slashed through his leg. He stumbled to the edge of the table and lost his footing, crashed to the floor below.

Marakion bashed through the swordsman's guard, sent the man's hand spinning from his wrist in a trail of blood.

Marakion ran forward. There were three left. Two charged him and kept him from his brother. The third . . . The third was clubbing . . . clubbing a body on the floor.

"Tagor!"

* * * * *

Marakion started, beat the vision down into the recesses of his memory. Breathing hard, he closed his eyes. Think of *now*, only of *now*. Forget Tagor. Forget all of it.

He sat still for long moments, trying to forget, holding his breath with gritted teeth, but the pent up air hissed out slowly in a shudder. Marakion crumpled and sobbed. "Tagor . . ."

* * * * *

Marakion beat his way through those three marauders, killed them all. He knelt at Tagor's side.

"They came . . . from the north. . . . They took Marissa. They called themselves the Knightsbane, Marakion. . . . The Knights—Knightsbane. Why, Marakion? . . . Why?"

It was his last word, then he died.

* * * * *

Marakion's cheeks were wet with tears. He turned and gazed down at another brave youth.

Yes, why?

"I hope you get your answer, kid. I really do. There's quite a few questions I'd like to ask Paladine myself." Marakion turned his face heavenward and focused on the constellation of the platinum dragon, high above. "At least a few."

* * * * *

Marakion came out of a reverie that had slipped into a doze. The fire was dwindling. Blinking his eyes, he picked up a couple of sticks and tossed them on, poking at the embers to stir the flames up again. After he'd tended the fire and stoked it for the night, he turned to adjust his bedding for sleep when he heard Gylar give a low moan. Marakion hurried to the young boy's side.

Gylar shuddered a little, his eyes moving under shut lids,

as he huddled deeper into his blanket. He shivered again, turned over, pulled the covers closer about him. Marakion pulled his cloak off and draped it over the boy.

Beneath the double cover, Gylar still quaked. Marakion moved his hand to the boy's forehead.

It was as hot as fire to the touch.

Marakion closed his eyes. "What will happen to you?" He repeated his thought of earlier in the evening. "Yeah, that's what, same as everyone else. It doesn't matter what you've already suffered. It's not enough yet, is it? It's never enough."

Marakion lay awake, staring silently at the cave's ceiling, for a long, long time. He could not sleep with the anger that burned through him as hotly as the fever now burned through Gylar's body. The brutal injustice galled him.

"I'm going to take you to the top, kid. It's not going to end like this, not without a fight. No, not without an answer. By my dead brother, I swear you'll get to ask your question."

He turned over and tried to go to sleep, but it wasn't until morning that exhaustion closed those eyes that were very tired of looking at the world.

*　　*　　*　　*　　*

The morning broke, warm and sunny. A few clouds drifted through the sky, but gave no threat of any type of storm. Snow gathered on tree limbs, slipped heavily from leaves, as the warmth of the day melted it. Pine needles shrugged off sheets of snow and rustled as they adjusted to their newfound freedom from winter's blanket.

Marakion stood at the cave's entrance. Nature was adapting to the freak warmth of the winter's day. The snow on the ground was glazed with a sheen of wet sparkles. Everything was adapting—everything except Gylar.

The sickness moved fast once the fever started. Gylar had slept late into the morning without knowing it, and Marakion had not come to a decision about waking him yet. As he stood there, though, he could hear the boy coming to.

He scuffed a groove into the wet snow. Casting a scathing glance heavenward, he turned and made his way back into the small cave.

Marakion stopped a half-dozen paces from the boy. Gylar knew what was happening to him. Maybe he'd realized it in the middle of the night—the fear was on his face—but the fear was held at bay by determination.

Gylar looked up. The boy tried to manage a smile, but failed. Tears stood in his eyes. Marakion wanted to say something, some word of comfort, but he knew if he tried to talk, it would come out choked.

"I have it, Marakion."

I know, Marakion spoke in a voice with no sound. Clearing his throat, he said again, "I know."

"I'm going to die." The boy's eyes were wide. They blinked once, twice.

Marakion nodded and lowered his gaze, his boots again scuffing a trench in the dirt floor. "Yeah," he said.

A different kind of fear entered Gylar's voice. "Marakion, you have to leave me, now. You have to go." His teeth chattered. Closing his mouth, he tried again. "You might have it already, but . . . but maybe not. You have to go."

Marakion knelt beside Gylar. The man smiled. "You want to try to make me, kid?"

Gylar was puzzled. "No . . ." His brows furrowed in confusion. "Make you? No, but, Marakion, if you don't leave—"

"I'm staying."

"But, sir, I told you what happened to—"

Marakion shrugged. "Do you want to make it to the top of this mountain?"

"Yes."

"Then I'm staying."

Gylar started to protest, but Marakion cut him off with a motion of his hand. "You've got heart, I'll give you that, but you aren't going to make the summit without me." He smiled expansively. "Even if you try."

Gylar nodded, warmed by the smile. Marakion suddenly reached out, held the small boy close.

"I'm afraid, Marakion," Gylar whispered, his shaking hands clinging tenaciously.

"I know." The man patted the small back. "I know."

"But it's all right." Gylar sniffed and let go. Running a sleeve across his nose, he smiled with effort and looked up at Marakion. "I just want to make it to the top, before . . . well, before . . ." He gulped. "I just want to make it there, that's all."

"Yeah." Marakion took a deep breath. "You will, I promise." Standing, he extended his hand. "Let's go, kid."

Gylar grabbed it, and they began again.

The cave they'd spent the night in was near a natural groove—almost like a trail—worn in the side of the mountain. Once the groove ended, the terrain became exceedingly precarious. More than once, Gylar slipped, and only Marakion's quick reflexes and strength saved the boy.

About three hours after midday, Gylar stumbled and had a hard time getting to his feet again.

"I'm sorry, Marakion," he said, shivering as he tried to stand up once more. "It's—It's just so cold. I can't seem to make my legs work right."

Marakion helped him to his feet. "You sure you want to keep going, kid?"

"Yes. I—I have to." Shakily, Gylar moved forward again.

By evening, Marakion had to carry him.

* * * * *

A few hours after nightfall, Marakion gently set the boy down in the snow at the summit of Mount Phineous. Lunitari was a thin crimson slash in the sky. Solinari was full and bright; it bathed them in a sparkling wash. The untouched snow looked like flawless, molten silver that had been poured over the top of the mountain and had hardened there. The only thing that marred the icy, detached beauty was a straggling trail gouged up the mountainside, a trail that led to the two solitary figures who had reached their destination.

The stars shone brightly from all around. Marakion's cloak, wrapped around the boy, furled and straightened softly in the breeze. His heavy breathing plumed out white in front of his face.

"Here . . ." Gylar said in a whisper. He nodded, with a smile. "Yes, this is perfect, so perfect."

Marakion swallowed hard and knelt next to Gylar. He spread a blanket and moved the boy onto it, then covered him with his own bedroll, trying to make him as warm as possible.

"Let me be alone now, Marakion." Gylar whispered, "I want to call Paladine. It's time for me to call him."

Marakion nodded, slowly rose from his kneeling position, and walked a distance away. He scuffed the snow with his boot, wondering again about this whole thing.

For an hour, Marakion walked about in the cold. He turned to watch Gylar from time to time. He could see the boy's mouth move, hear him talking to the skies.

Another hour passed, this time in silence. Nothing answered Gylar's feeble summons. Marakion tromped about, fuming. He knew he shouldn't have expected an answer, but suddenly he was furious that none was coming.

After a time, Marakion realized the boy was beckoning weakly to him. The man was instantly at the boy's side.

Gylar's flesh was almost completely wasted away. The effect of the fever over such a short time was astounding. But there was a smile on the boy's face. "Marakion . . ." He could barely speak.

Marakion leaned forward. "Yes, Gylar."

Gylar shook his head. "Paladine's not coming. He's not even going to—" The boy was cut off by a coughing fit. "He's not even going to drop a mountain on me, Marakion."

Gylar set a shaky hand on Marakion's forearm. "Remember the ogre, Marakion? I was s-so scared. It was going to eat me. You remember?"

Marakion nodded.

"You let it go, Marakion," Gylar whispered. "You said for it to choose something else, a deer or something. You said it had made the wrong choice. It didn't believe you, and you beat it up, but you let it go. You forgave it, Marakion. You forgave it for being itself. It didn't realize what it was doing."

Marakion swallowed a lump in this throat. Gylar closed his eyes. His hand still gripped the warrior's arm.

"Maybe Paladine didn't either, Marakion. Maybe he still doesn't. B—But that's okay. I forgive him. It's okay. I forgive them all. . . ."

Gylar's grip went slack on Marakion's arm. Marakion grappled for the hand and caught hold as it started to slip off. Squeezing his eyes shut, he bowed his head.

"Damn!" was all he said.

* * * * *

Hours later, Marakion stood next to a grave he'd had to fight the cold earth and snow to dig. His hands were blistered; Glint was caked in dirt.

Marakion did not speak a eulogy. Everything had already been said. Who would he speak words of comfort to, anyway? The only ones able to hear on this distant, isolated mountaintop were the gods, and they hadn't listened. This boy, alone, beneath the frosted, snow-swept ground, could pardon a god for his mistake, though that one mistake had destroyed everything Gylar had held dear.

Marakion adjusted the clasp at the neck of his cloak and pulled the edges together. He took a last look at the sky from the summit of Mount Phineous.

"Somebody learned something from your show of godly power. *He* forgives you."

Marakion slowly began his descent down the mountain, continuing on his own hopeless quest.

"Revel in it, Paladine, because, by the Abyss, I don't."

No Gods, No Heroes

Nick O'Donohoe

The road was blocked just over the crest of the hill. The ambush was nicely planned. Graym, leading the horses, hadn't seen the warriors until his group was headed downhill, and there was no room to turn the cart around on the narrow, wheel-rutted path that served as a road.

Graym looked at their scarred faces, their battered, mismatched, scavenged armor, and their swords. He smiled at them. "You lot are good thinkers, I can tell. You can't protect yourselves too well these days." He gestured at the cart and its cargo. "Would you like a drink of ale?"

The armored man looked them over carefully. Graym said, "I'll do the honors, sir. That skinny, gawking teenager—that's Jarek. The man behind him, in manacles and a chain, is our prisoner, name of Darll. Behind him—those two fierce-looking ones, are Fenris and Fanris, the Wolf brothers. Myself, I'm Graym. I'm the leader—being the oldest and"—he patted his middle-aged belly, chuckling—"the heaviest." He bowed as much as his belly woud let him.

The lead man nodded. "It's them."

His companions stepped forward, spreading out. The right wing man, flanking Graym, swung his sword.

Darll pulled his hands apart and caught the sword on his chain. Sparks flew, but the chain held. Clasping his hands back together, he swung the looped chain like a club. It thunked into an armored helmet, and the wearer dropped straight to the ground soundlessly.

Jarek raised his fist, gave a battle cry. The Wolf brothers, with their own battle cry—which sounded suspiciously like yelps of panic—dived under the ale cart, both trying unsuccessfully to wedge themselves behind the same wheel.

The cart tipped, toppling the heavy barrels. The horses broke their harnesses and charged through the fight. A cascade of barrels thundered into the midst of the fray. One attacker lay still, moaning.

That left four. Darll kicked one still-rolling barrel, sent it smashing into two of the attackers, then leapt at a third, who was groping for his dropped sword. Darll kicked the sword away, lifted one of the barrel hoops over the man's head. The attacker raised his arms to defend himself, neatly catching them in the hoop. Darll slammed him in the face with his fist.

Jarek yelled, "Yaaa!" and threw a rock at the leader. The rock struck the man, knocked him into Darll's reach.

Darll whipped his chain around the man's throat, throttling him. Hearing a noise behind him, Darll let the man drop and spun around.

Two of the others were crawling to their knees. Darll kicked one and faced the other, prepared to fight.

A hoarse voice cried, "No!"

The leader was gasping and massaging his throat. "Leave them. Let Skorm Bonelover get them," he told his men.

The attackers limped away, carrying their two unconscious comrades.

It was suddenly very quiet. The Wolf brothers, still under the cart, were staring at Darll in awe. Jarek—a second rock cradled in his hand—was gazing at the fighter with open-mouthed admiration. Graym took a step toward Darll, glanced at the fleeing attackers, and stepped away again.

"Six men," Graym said. "Six trained men-at-arms, beaten by a man in chains."

"It'll make one helluva song," Darll said acidly. "I suppose I'm still your prisoner?"

After a moment's thought, Graym nodded. "Right, then. Let's reload the barrels."

Graym and Jarek tipped the cart back upright and propped a barrel behind the rear wheel. The first barrel was easy to load. Too easy. Graym handled it by himself. He stared at it in surprise, then worked to load the second.

The third barrel was on, then suddenly and inexplicably it was rolling off.

The Wolf brothers, working on top, grabbed frantically and missed. The barrel slid down the tilted cart. Darll fell back. Jarek, standing in the barrel's path, stared up at it with his mouth open.

For a fat middle-aged man, Graym could move quickly. He slammed into Jarek, and both went sprawling. The barrel crashed onto a rock and bounced off, spraying foam sideways before it came to rest, punctured end up.

Graym, unfortunately, came to rest on top of Jarek.

Darll, manacles clanging, pulled Graym to his feet. "You all right?"

"Fine, sir, fine." Graym felt his ribs and arms for breakage.

"Pity," Darll grunted. "What about you, boy?" He bent down and helped Jarek up. "If you only hurt your head, we're in luck."

Jarek wheezed and gasped.

"He'll be fine," Graym said, slapping Jarek's shoulder. Jarek collapsed again, and Graym helped him up again. "Probably do us both good. Exercise new muscles."

"Try thinking. That should exercise a new muscle for you." Darll looked down at their feet. Foam was seeping quickly into the ground. The smell of ale was overpowering.

Graym followed his glance. "Only another loss," he said cheerfully. "Crisis of transport, sir. Part of business." He and Jarek limped over to the broken barrel.

Jarek, still wheezing, managed to say, "I'm sorry, Graym. You said 'Stop pushing when I say now,' and that was when you said 'now,' so then I thought you meant 'now.' "

"Don't you feel bad at all, boy." Graym looked at the damp rock and the damp soil below it. "This'll drive the price up when we reach Krinneor. Supply and demand."

He added, struck by it, "Makes the other kegs worth more."

He finished, convinced, "Best thing that could happen,

really."

Graym shook Jarek's limp hand. "Thank you for upping profits. A bold move—not one I'd have made—but worth it in the long run."

Jarek smiled proudly. Darll snorted.

The Wolf brothers looked down from the perch on top of the cart. "Want us to roll another off?" Fenris asked eagerly.

"Say when," Fanris added.

Graym shook his head. "Let's take inventory first."

The Wolf brothers slid cautiously off the wagon. They looked (and claimed) to be several years older than Jarek, but no one would ever know their real age until one of them washed, which was hardly likely. From their narrow beetle-browed eyes to their black boots, they looked wickedly dangerous.

A songbird whistled, and the two jumped and crouched low behind the wagon wheel.

"Don't crawl underneath," Graym pleaded. "That's how you tipped it the last time. It's all right now. The bad men are gone. And they weren't that bad, once we got their weapons away from them."

"*We? We?*" Darll demanded.

"I helped," Jarek said proudly. "I threw a rock at one. You did most of it," he added honestly. "But you should have. You're supposed to be a great mercenary."

"I'm *supposed* to be your prisoner," Darll said bitingly.

Graym put a hand on Darll's shoulder. "Don't take it so hard, sir. You're the Bailey of Sarem's prisoner. We're just transporting you to Krinneor." He patted Darll. "Think of us as company."

"I think of you," Darll said bitterly, "the way I'd think of the underside of an owlbear's—"

"I'm going to be a mercenary like you someday," Jarek broke in.

Fenris came out from behind the wagon wheel. He looked worried. "Did you hear what that man said just before running off?"

"You mean the part about 'Let Skorm Bonelover take them'?" Fanris finished nervously. "I heard it. What does it mean? Who's Skorm Bonelover?"

Graym was checking the fallen barrel. "An idle threat. Poor man, I don't think he was happy." He examined the sprung staves.

"You may be a cooper," Darll said, "but you can't mend that."

Graym felt along the keg sides, skilled hands finding the sprung barrel stave. "Not on the road," he said reluctantly. "And it's over half full still."

The Wolf brothers edged forward hopefully. "Be a shame to let it go to waste, Fan."

"Right again, Fen."

Jarek, rubbing his head, looked meaningfully at the bung-puller stored inside the cart.

"Half a keg of Skull-Splitter Premium. Well . . ." Graym sighed loudly, then smiled. "Not a bad place to camp."

* * * * *

They waited until nightfall to light the fire, so no one would see the smoke. They hung a shield of blankets around the fire to hide the light. Both were Darll's idea. Graym saw no need for such precautions, but was willing to humor him.

The sunset was blood red, like every one had been since the Cataclysm.

Graym sipped at the bowl of Skull-Splitter and said, to no one in particular, "Life is attitude—good or bad." He waved an arm at the desolate landscape. "What do you see?"

Darll grunted. "What else? Disaster. Broken trees, clogged streams, fallen buildings, and a godsforsaken broken road rougher than a troll's—"

"That's your problem, sir." Graym thumped Darll's back. "You see disaster. I see opportunity. Look here." He traced a map in the dirt. "See this road?"

He looked up and realized that Darll—ale rolling in his mouth, eyes shut to savor the flavor—wasn't seeing anything. "Excuse me, sir, but do you see the road?"

"The road from Goodlund to Krinneor," Jarek breathed reverently.

"Right. And do you know what's ahead?"

Darll opened his eyes. "Nothing. The end of the world."

Graym downed an entire bowl of Skull-Splitter, wiped his lips on his sleeve, and smiled genially. "Maybe it is, sir, but I say"—he waved the empty dipper for emphasis—"if I'm going to see the end of the world, I should see it with a positive attitude." He gazed up at the sky. "I mean, look at the world now. No gods, no heroes." He sighed loudly and happily. "It makes a man feel fresh."

"We were heroes this afternoon," Jarek objected, "me and Darll. We whipped those bastards."

"Now, now," Graym said admonishingly. "You hardly knew them, Jarek. Don't speak ill of people just because they tried to kill you."

Darll agreed. "Other than being the usual low, sorry sort of lowlifes you find in these parts, they weren't bad at all. They were bounty hunters." He eyed Graym suspiciously.

"Seems an unfriendly way to make a living," Graym said. He scratched his head, belched, and settled back. "Inventory," he announced.

The others suddenly looked nervous. "Will we have to sign for things?" Jarek asked. "I hate that."

Graym shook his head. "Nah, nah. This is just counting, and remembering"—he took another sip of ale—"and history. We started with nine barrels. Remember the loading? We pushed them on from all sides, and they shifted when we started rolling."

Fenris nudged his brother. "And one rolled away and smashed on Dog Street."

Fanris kicked him. "I couldn't hold it. It was hard to see, it being dark and all."

Darll's eyes opened. "You loaded in the dark? For the love of Paladine, why?"

Jarek said reasonably, "We didn't want to be seen."

Darll laughed, a short bark. "No wonder the horses ran off. They didn't even know you, did they? You stole them! *And* the cart, I'll wager."

"Jem and Renny, poor flighty nags. They never liked us," Graym said sadly. "Well, that's one barrel. Eight left."

"There was the barrel on the bridge," Jarek offered, "outside of town."

"We'd picked up Darll, and he was putting up a fight—"

"That's right, blame me." Darll glared at them all. "I only wanted to leap off at the bridge."

"And hit us," Fenris said.

"And kill us," Fanris added, hurt.

"And hit and kill you," Darll agreed. "I did fairly well, for being hung over."

"You might have drowned, sir," Graym said. "That wouldn't do when you're in our charge, would it?"

"He hit me," Jarek said, rubbing his head.

"And me," Fen said.

"And me," Fan added.

Darll settled back. "Stop whining. I didn't kill you." His scowl, fierce under his salt-and-pepper beard, seemed to add an unspoken "yet."

After a short silence, Graym continued. "One of the barrels dropped into Mirk River, leaving seven. After that, we didn't lose a one—not in the Black Rain, not in the Dry Lands, not in the swamps. We can be proud of that."

Jarek squared his shoulders. The Wolf brothers grinned, exposing teeth best left hidden.

Graym went on. "And today we beat back a better-trained force—"

"Any force would be better trained," Darll muttered.

"That's harsh, sir. We won through strategy—"

"Luck."

"Or luck, but not," Graym said sadly, "without casualties. We smashed two barrels, a major loss." He stared, brooding, into the fire.

Jarek counted on his fingers twice, then said proudly. "I know! I know! That leaves six barrels—"

"Yes. Five full barrels," Graym said. He walked unsteadily to the wagon. "And one other." He thumped it three times, pausing to let it echo. "One . . . empty . . . barrel."

The others ducked their heads, avoided his eyes. "It leaked," Darll said, shrugging.

Graym rocked the barrel back and forth and ran his hands around it. "Bone dry. No water marks, no foam flecks."

"Ghosts." Jarek looked solemn.

Graym snorted. "Ever seen a drunk ghost?"

Since none of them had seen a ghost of any sort, drunk or sober, they all shook their heads reluctantly.

"Might have been magic," Fenris said.

"True enough," Fanris said quickly.

Graym wiped the mud off the barrel end to expose a second, cleverly hidden bunghole. He felt in the corner of the wagon and pulled out a second tap. "And which one of you," he said firmly, "was the mage?"

He folded his arms. "Now, I know it's been a long, hard, dusty trip. A man gets thirsty. And you've all known me as long as you've worn dry pants. I'm not a hard man."

"You're a soft man," Darll said, but wouldn't look him in the eye.

"I'm a forgiving man."

"Hah! If you were, you'd let me go, but no—"

"It's a matter of principle, sir," Graym said firmly.

"And the money," Jarek reminded him.

"And the money, of course."

"Tenpiece," Darll said bitterly. "Took me straight from the Bailey of Sarem with a promise and a bag of tenpiece."

"Plus twenty when we get to Krinneor," Fen said.

"When we hand you up," Fan said.

"Thirtypiece." Darll shook his head. "The best fighter in Goodlund, second or third best in Istar, carted off to prison for thirtypiece."

"But enough prologuizing." Graym was swaying on his feet. "I can't stand a fella who prologuizes all the time. Let's say I'm forgiving and let it go at that. And, now, I'm going to ask who's been sneaking ale while I wasn't looking. I expect an honest answer. Who was it?"

Jarek raised one hand.

The Wolf brothers each raised a hand.

Graym looked at them in silence.

Darll raised a hand, his chains pulling the other after it.

After a long pause, Graym sighed. "Good to have it out in the open at last. Better to be honest with each other, I say."

" 'True thieves best rob false owners,' " Darll muttered.

"I've always thought that a fine saying, sir," Graym said. "Witty, yet simple. But I don't see it applying here."

Darll shook his head.

"Still and all," Graym continued, "we've done well. Three months on the road, and we've four barrels left." He shook a finger at the others. "No sneaking drinks from here. We'll need it all at the end of the road in Krinneor."

Jarek said eagerly, "Tell us about Krinneor, Graym."

"What? Again?"

"Please!"

Jarek wasn't alone. Fen and Fan begged to hear the story, and even Darll settled, resignedly, to listen.

Graym picked up a bowl and took a deep swig of Skull-Splitter. "I've told you this night after night, day after day—in the Black Rains, when the dust clouds came through, and in the afterquakes, and when we'd spent a long day dragging this wagon over flood-boils, potholes, and heaved-up rock on the road. And now you say you're not tired of it." He looked at them fondly. "I'm not either.

"Back in Sarem, I was nobody. Every town needs a cooper, but they don't care about him. They buy his barrels and leave. And I'd watch them, and I'd know they were off—to fill the barrels, travel up roads, and sell their stock."

Jarek leaned forward. "The city, tell us about the city!"

"I'm coming to that." Graym loved this part. "Every time a stranger came down the road, I'd ask him where he'd been. And he'd talk about Tarsis by the sea, or the temples of Xak Tsaroth, and one even showed me a machine from Mount Nevermind, where the gnomes live. The machine didn't work, of course, but it was a lovely little thing, all gears and sprockets and wires.

"But one and all, dusty from the road and tired from travel, told me about Krinneor, and the more I heard, the more I wanted to see it." Graym's eyes shone. "Golden towers! Marble doors! And excellent drains." He looked at them all earnestly. "I hear that's very important for a city."

They nodded. Graym went on. "After the Clay-chasm—"

"Cataclysm," Darll snapped.

"Cataclysm, thank you, sir. I keep forgetting. After that

night, when the ground shook and the western sky was all fire, people were frightened. They quit buying barrels, saying that trade was too risky. That's when I realized that no one was coming down the road from Krinneor, and no one was going there."

He tapped the bowl of Skull-Splitter, which he had emptied again. "And that's when I realized there was no more good Sarem ale going from Sarem to Krinneor. The poor beggars there would be as dry as a sand pit in no time.

"So I made these." He thumped the broken barrel, refilled the bowl from it. "Extra thick staves, double-caulked, double-banded. Bungs four fingers deep. Heads of the last vallenwoods in stock this far west. Harder than any man has seen. I spent everything I had making them, then borrowed from you all to finish them. And when the bailey heard we were going, he asked me to take you, sir, to the Bailey of Krinneor for safekeeping." He nodded respectfully to Darll.

"For prison, you fat fool," Darll said. "I can't believe I let a man like that capture me, especially after I beat the town soldiery. A scrawny, bald-headed, weak-armed man with no more strength in him than in a dead dwarf's left—"

"You wouldn't have if you hadn't been drunk," Jarek pointed out. He looked at Darll admiringly. "Single-handed, and you beat them all. If you hadn't been drunk—"

Graym interrupted. "And I hope it serves to remind you, sir, that ale is not only a blessing, but can also be a curse, and not to be taken lightly." He downed the bowl of Skull-Splitter. "Back to my story. I took you, sir, and the tenpiece from the bailey—"

"Then we got the ale," Jarek said.

"And the horses," Fen and Fan said together.

"Without paying for them," Darll finished.

"And I gathered victuals and water and spare clothes and knapsacks, and off we set"—Graym pointed to the east— "down the long, dangerous road! Facing hardship! Facing hunger and thirst . . ." He broke off. "Not as much thirst as I thought, apparently, but some thirst. Facing the unknown! Facing a ruined world! And for what?" He looked around at the watching faces. "I ask you, for what?"

Jarek blinked. "For Krinneor."

"True enough. For the golden spires, the marble towers, the excellent drains, and the fortunes that made them. Think of it!" Graym waved an arm unsteadily. "A city with all the gold you can dream of, and nothing to drink. And us with a cart full." He glanced to one side. "A cart *half* full of the best ale left in the world!"

"Our fortunes are made. We can ask what we want for it, and they'll pay twice what we ask. One barrel of Sarem ale will be worth the world to them, and five barrels leaves us one apiece."

Darll looked up, startled. "You're counting me?"

"You did your share on the road, sir," Graym said. "Each of us gets profits from one barrel of ale. And, if we're all clever—" he looked at Jarek and amended hastily, "—or at least if we stick together, we get exclusive Sarem trade rights to Krinneor. We'll have all the food we want, and houses."

"And a sword?" Jarek asked eagerly. "I've always wanted a sword. My mother wouldn't let me have anything sharp."

Graym smiled at him. "And a sword. And maybe a quick parole for friend Darll, and a tavern for me to run—"

"And a woman for me," Fenris said firmly.

"And me," Fanris echoed.

Graym scratched his head, looked dubious.

"Right," Darll said. "I'm sure that somewhere in Krinneor there's a pair of dirty, nearsighted women with no self-respect left."

The Wolf brothers brightened considerably.

*　*　*　*　*

By late night, the blanket screens were down and they'd piled wood on to make a man-high flame. The Wolf brothers were singing a duet about a bald woman who'd broken the heart of a barber, and Darll was weeping.

"You 'member," he said, his arm around Graym, "'member when the bounty hunters attacked, and I saved us?"

"You did well, sir," said Graym.

Darll snuffled. "I was going to run off, but then I remembered you had the keys to the manacles."

Graym patted his pocket. "Still do, sir."

Darll, tears running down both cheeks, wiped his nose. "You know that when you free me, I'm going to kill you."

Graym patted Darll's shoulder. "Anybody would, sir."

Darll nodded, wept, belched, tried to say something more, and fell asleep sitting up.

Graym lay down, rolled over on his back, and stared at the stars. They were faint in the dusty air, but to Graym they shone a little clearer every night. "I used to be afraid of them," he said comfortably to himself. "They used to be gods. Now they're just stars."

* * * * *

When the sun came up the next morning, it rose with what Graym heard as an ear-splitting crack.

He opened one eye as little as possible, then struggled to his feet. "Isn't life an amazing thing?" he said shakily to himself. "If you'd told me yesterday that every hair on my head could hurt, I wouldn't have believed you."

Fenris stared out at the dusty field nearby and quavered, "What's that terrible noise?"

Graym looked where Fenris was pointing and found the source. "Butterflies."

Fenris nodded—a mistake. His eyes rolled back in his head and he fell over with a thud. Fanris, beside him, whimpered at the sound of the impact.

Graym, moving as silently as possible, crept over to Darll, shook him by the shoulder. Darll's manacles rattled.

Darll flinched and opened two remarkably red eyes. "If I live," he murmured fuzzily, "I'm going to kill you."

Graym sighed and rubbed his own head. "I thought you already had, sir."

* * * * *

By midmorning, they were back on the road and near the first rank of western hills. Graym, pulling the cart along with Darll, was almost glad they had lost so many barrels.

The wagon lurched to a stop at every rock in the road . . . and there were many rocks.

At least the companions were feeling better. Skull-Splitter's effect, though true to its name, wore off quickly. Jarek was humming to himself, trying to remember the Wolf brothers' song of the night before. Darll, after swearing at him in strained tones for some time, was now correcting him on the melody and humming along.

Fenris, perched on the cart, yelled, "Trouble ahead!"

Fanris gazed, quivered. "Are they dangerous?"

Darll grated his teeth. "Kender! I hate the nasty little things. Kill 'em all. Keep 'em away. They'll rob you blind and giggle the whole time."

Graym looked up from watching the rutted road. Before he knew what was happening, he was surrounded by kender: eager, energetic, and pawing through their belongings. The kender had a sizable bundle of their own, pulled on a travois, but the bundle changed shape ominously.

"Ho! Ha!" Darll swung two-handed at them, trying to make good on his threat to kill them all. They skipped and ducked, ignoring the length of chain that whistled murderously over their heads.

"Here now, little fellers," Graym said, holding his pack above his head. "Stay down! Good morning!" He smiled at them and skipped back and forth to keep his pack out of reach, and he seemed like a giant kender himself.

One of the kender, taller than the others and dressed in a brown robe with the hood clipped off, smiled back. "Good morning. Where are we?"

"You're in Goodlund, halfway to Sarem if you started from just west of Kendermore." Graym snatched a forked stick from the hands of the tall kender—who didn't seem to mind—and hung his pack from it, lifted it over his head.

"Where are you going?"

"Oh, around." The tall kender took a forked stick from one of the others, who didn't seem to mind either. "East, mostly." He spun the stick, making a loud whistle. "Do you know, the gods told me that the world's greatest disaster would happen in a land to the west? Only it didn't."

"What are you talking about?" Graym looked openly astonished. "The Catcollision?"

"Cataclysm!" Darll snarled.

"Cataclysm, thank you, sir. I keep forgetting." Graym turned back to the kender. "All that happened in the east, you know."

"I know," the kender said, and sighed. "The gods lied to me. They did it to save our lives—we were going west to see the fun—but still, a lie's a lie." He fingered the torn collar of his cleric's robe. "So we don't believe in the gods anymore."

"Good enough," Graym said, brightening. "Smashed the world, didn't they? We're well rid of that lot."

"But they did save our lives," Fenris pointed out.

"From horrible deaths," Fanris added, "like being smashed."

"Or squished, Fan."

The tall kender shrugged. "You miss a lot, worrying about things like that. Say, what's that smell?" His nose wrinkled.

"Dirt, mostly," Jarek said.

The Wolf brothers scowled. "It's a perfectly natural smell," Graym said. "Strong, but natural." He smiled down at the kender. "My name's Graym."

The kender smiled back. "Tarli Half-kender. Half man, half kender."

Graym looked startled, then shrugged. "Well, I'm liberal-minded."

He offered his hand, taking care to keep his pack and pockets out of reach. But at a shout from Jarek, Graym whipped his head around.

"Here now! Off the cart. Mind the barrels." His knapsack fell from the stick.

Tarli caught the pack nimbly, flipped it over once in his deft fingers, and passed it to Graym, who was surprised that a kender would return anything. "Thank you," he said to Tarli, but his mind was on the kender falling and climbing all over the cart. The barrels, three times their size, wobbled dangerously. "Don't they know they could be killed?"

Tarli looked puzzled. "I don't think it would make much difference. Like I said, you can't worry about things like that, like Skorm Bonelover, coming from the east."

"Who?" The name sounded vaguely familiar to Graym's still-fuddled mind.

"Skorm," Tarli said helpfully, "the Fearmaker, the Crusher of Joy."

"Oh, *that* Skorm. You know him, do you?"

"Only by reputation. Everyone's talking about him." Tarli looked to the east. "Well, we'd better keep going if we want to meet up with him." He put two fingers into his mouth and whistled.

The crowd of kender scrambled off the cart and scampered down the road again, pulling the travois behind them. To Graym's watchful eyes, their pockets seemed fuller, and their bundle of supplies seemed larger, but there was nothing he could do about it.

"Cunning little things." Graym watched the kender running happily away. "Good attitudes, the lot of them. You can't keep them down."

"I'll try," Darll grated, "if you'll let me go." He held out his manacled hands.

"Ah!" Graym reached into his pack. "Can't do that, sir, but I could give your arms a rest while we're dragging the cart. You promise not to run off, sir?

He vaguely remembered Darll's saying something last night that should make Graym nervous, but dragging the cart was hard work, and Darll deserved a reward.

Darll looked sly. "Word of honor." He braced his feet for a quick start and smiled at Graym.

The Wolf brothers ducked under the cart. Even Jarek looked suspicious.

"Right, then." Graym fumbled in the pack, then reached into his left pocket . . .

Then checked his right breeches pocket, his hood, and his jacket . . .

Then stared at the departing kender. He looked back at Darll's impatient face. "Life," he said thoughtfully, "can be funny, sir . . ."

When Darll understood, he shook both fists at the kender and swore until he was panting like a runner.

* * * * *

Darll and Graym started off again. They grabbed the crosspiece of the wagon tongue, braced their feet in the dirt, and pulled. The wagon rolled forward quickly. Graym dropped the crosspiece.

"That was too easy. Jarek?"

Jarek hopped into the cart and counted loudly. "One, two, three, four—"

After a pause, Graym said, "And?"

"That's all," Jarek said.

Graym stared, disbelieving, at the distant dust cloud of the departing kender. "They walked off with a *barrel*?"

"Cunning little things," Fenris said.

"Industrious, too," Fanris said.

Jarek finished the inventory. Finally he hopped down and announced, "They got the barrel of Throat's Ease lager, our spare clothes—"

Graym laughed. "Picture one of those little fellows trying to wear my canvas breeches!"

"And most of the food."

Graym fell silent.

"So we make it to Krinneor in one night or go hungry," Darll said.

"We can do it," Graym said confidently. Landmarks weren't hard to read, but he had often discussed the road—wistfully—with merchants buying barrels and casks. "There's this hill, and one little town, and a valley, then, and a downhill run from there to Krinneor."

"And prison for me, and a forced march to get there," Darll said gruffly. "I'd be running away free, and you'd be—" He looked at Graym sharply. "I'd be gone if it weren't for those nasty, little, pointy-eared thieves."

Graym said gruffly, "You ought not to criticize others, sir. Not to drag up the past, but you've done worse."

Darll glared at him. "That wasn't a fair trial. The bailey wanted blood, and he got it."

"Of course, he wanted blood. You hurt his dignity. You had only a sword, and you half-killed ten soldiers armed with spears, maces, and swords."

Darll objected. "When I half-kill ten men, I leave only five left alive. I beat them badly, but that wasn't the charge against me, anyway, unless you count resisting arrest."

"True enough, sir," Graym said agreeably. "You scarpered the town treasury and then nicked a hay wagon."

"Nice way to put it. A real sophisticate, you are."

"Assault, theft, intoxication, breaking and entering, reckless endangerment, incitement to stampede, vandalism, arson." He paused. "That's the lot, isn't it, sir?"

"Still and all," Darll said stubbornly, "it *was* a first offense."

"First offense?" Graym gaped. "From you, sir?"

"Well, for this sort of crime."

Graym shook his head. "You tell your side of it well, sir, but I have a contract."

"It's the money, then."

"No, sir." Graym shook his head violently. "I gave a promise. Even if I persuaded the others to agree to forfeit the twentypiece we have coming, I'd still be unable—outstanding warrant and all—to go back to Sarem and return the ten—" He felt in his pocket. . . .

He sighed, didn't bother feeling in his other pockets.

Darll, watching his face, smiled. "Cunning little things."

"Thrifty, too," Graym muttered.

* * * * *

By midday, they had reached the top of the first large hill—low and rocky, with a fault crack running across it. Jarek, scouting ahead for the easiest route for the cart on the broken road, returned, announcing, "People coming."

Fen said fearfully, "What if they're robbers?"

Fan added, "Or maybe they're the bounty hunters."

The Wolf brothers edged toward the back of the cart.

Graym grabbed their shirts, pulled them back. He then wiped his hands on his own shirt. "Wait till we've seen them, at least."

He edged to the top of the hill and peered over the top.

A group of humans was walking toward them—townsfolk, seemingly, coming from the small knot of cottages standing on the road.

Graym retreated below the crest of the hill, reported what he'd seen. "We can't run, and there's no place to hide. Best we go forward and be friendly. Folks like that."

Jarek looked dubious. "They might rob us."

"Not of much."

"Or we might rob them. Are they rich?"

"I didn't grow up with 'em," Graym retorted. "How should I know?"

Jarek dug in the dirt with his boot. "Well, if they are, and we robbed them, then we'd be better off, right?"

Graym considered. "Now that's an idea. We rob from the rich. And then . . ."

"And then what?" Jarek asked.

"Can't rob from the poor," Fenris said.

"No future in it," Fanris agreed.

Jarek objected, "There's more poor people than rich people. Easier to find."

"Ah, but they don't have as much, do they?"

"Now that's telling him what, Fen."

"Thank you, Fan."

Darll said firmly, "You're not robbing these people."

Graym wasn't too keen on robbing, but he thought Darll was being a bit bossy, for a prisoner, even if he was a mercenary. "And why not, sir?"

Darll shook his head wearily. "Because they have us surrounded."

While they had been talking, the townspeople had encircled the hill and closed ranks. They approached silently. There were thirty or forty of them, dressed in ragged, ill-fitting clothes. Several wore robes.

Graym looked around at the circle of men and women. "Good to see so many of you here to greet us." He waved an arm. "I'd offer a drink, but we're running short."

A robed and hooded figure came forward. The robe was too long, clearly borrowed, and had been dyed a neutral color. "I am Rhael," said the person. "I am the elder."

The voice was strong and clear, strangely high. Graym said dubiously, "Are you sure? You sound kinda young for an elder."

"Quite sure." The woman pulled back her hood and shook her hair free of it.

Darll snorted. "Who are you all?"

"I am Rhael. These are my people. We come from the village of Graveside."

Darll asked, "A law-abiding village?"

She nodded.

"Good." He raised his manacled hands. "Arrest these fools and free me."

"Arrest them? Why?"

"Because they're crooks."

"What have they done?"

"What haven't they? Theft, resisting arrest, drunk and disorderly plenty of times, drunk but not disorderly at least once, sober and disorderly a few times—"

Rhael seemed impressed. "What are they like as fighters?"

"Terrible," Darll said truthfully. "Awful to watch. You can't imagine."

"Brutal?"

"That man—" Darll pointed to Graym—"drove off a band of bounty hunters, with only me in chains to help him."

"That one . . ." He pointed to Jarek. "He nearly killed a man with one blow." More or less true, counting a thrown rock as a blow.

"And those two . . . ?"

Darll glanced at the Wolf brothers, who waited eagerly to hear what he could say about them.

"Well, just look at them," Darll said.

The folk of Graveside looked them up and down. The Wolf brothers did look dangerous, both as criminals and as a health risk.

Darll held out his arms, waiting for his release.

Rhael walked straight up to Graym. "Would you be willing to lead an army?"

Darll choked. Graym's mouth sagged open.

"We need brave men like you," Rhael said. "We're facing a scourge."

One of the elders quavered, "A terrible scourge!"

"I didn't think it would be a nice scourge," Darll muttered.

"His name," Rhael lowered her voice, "is Skorm Bone-lover."

"Not his given name, I take it, Miss?" Graym said.

"He is also called the Sorrow of Huma, the Dark Lady's Liege Man, the Teeth of Death, the Grave of Hope—"

"I've always wanted a nickname," Fen said wistfully.

"We've had some," Fan reminded him.

"Not ones we've always wanted, Fan."

"True enough, Fen." He sighed.

Darll said, suddenly interested, "Don't you people have any fighters, or a bailey or something?"

They all looked sorrowful. "Gone, gone," one said.

"Killed?" Graym said sympathetically.

Rhael shook her head. "The Protector came to me one morning and warned me about the coming of Skorm. A stranger had come in the night and told him, said that he had already fled before Skorm's army. The Protector said the only sensible thing to do was flee, leaving all our things behind, so that Skorm would stay and plunder instead of pursuing us."

Graym frowned. "This Protector wasn't much of an optimist."

"He was terrified," Rhael said. "He said that Skorm would drink the blood of one victim, only to spit it in the face of another. He said Skorm once bit through the arm of a warrior and stood chewing on it in front of him. He said—"

"Never mind," Graym said hastily. His stomach had been wobbly all day. "Where is this scourge?" He looked around fearfully. "Not with you, I take it."

"He and his troops are camped in the bone yard—"

"Picturesque," Graym murmured, approving.

"In the Valley of Death, beyond Graveside. There are more than a hundred of them now. Every dawn," Rhael said with a voice like death, "we see more warriors standing by Skorm's tents. Every day his troops increase."

Graym turned to his companions. "And you all told me no one was hiring. It was nothing but a necessary market downturn, and you call it a Catechism."

"Cataclysm," Darll hissed.

"Right you are, sir." Graym turned to Rhael. "And, now, young elder . . . I can't get used to that, by the way. Why are you an elder, Miss?"

"Elders aren't chosen because they are old," a man next to her, quite old himself, explained. "We are chosen because each of us represents one of the elder virtues."

"And what," Graym asked, feeling his ears turning red, "is Miss Rhael's virtue?"

"Elder Rhael embodies fearlessness."

"No wonder she's so young," Darll said dryly. "Fearlessness never reaches old age. What about you?" He pointed with both chained hands at the elder who had spoken. "Who are you?"

The old man stepped back from Darll. "I am Werlow," he said. "I embody caution."

"Good for you," said Darll. "And what did you do about Skorm?"

"I convinced the rest of the people to evacuate," Werlow said. "We elders have stayed, to pray for the coming of heroes."

"We're here," Jarek said happily. "We're heroes, aren't we?" He looked to Graym for support.

Graym cleared his throat. "I don't like to boast. We're desperate men . . . and bold warriors, but we've left our robbing ways behind us. We have trade goods"—he didn't want to say 'ale,' though the barrels made it obvious—"that we're taking all the way to Krinneor, where our fortunes will be made and our lives will be good, in the richest city in the world." His voice went husky. "The golden towers, the marble doors, the excellent drains."

The elders exchanged glances. They were silent.

Finally Rhael said, "The road to Krinneor winds around the Valley of Tombs. There is no way there, except through Skorm's army."

The Wolf brothers made most unwarlike whimpering sounds. Darll edged over and kicked them each, hard.

Graym frowned. "Don't they ever move out of the cemetery, Miss? Parade, or bivouac, or do any of those nice martial things that make armies so popular with politicians?"

Rhael shook her head. "They have no need to," she said

sadly. "They just grow strong and plan to attack us."

"How much, to fight them?" Darll asked suddenly.

The elders looked at each other.

"Nothing," a reed-slender old woman said. "We heard of your fight with the bounty hunters. That is why we sought you. If you refuse to fight, we'll inform every hunter we can find, and you'll be taken or killed."

"That seems harsh, Ma'am," Graym said. "Fight or die? For nothing?"

"And what elder virtue are you?" Darll asked.

The old woman smiled thinly. "Thrift."

Graym made up his mind, turned, and addressed his companions. "These pick-me-up armies are all bluff. Farm boys and fishermen, not one real soldier in twenty."

Jarek was counting on his fingers. "How many real soldiers does that make against each of us?"

"One," Fenris said flatly.

"Maybe even two," Fanris added.

Graym waved his hand. "What's that to us? Nothing at all. They're just trainees. We're road-tested. Months of hardship, baking sun, blinding rain—"

"Great ale—" Jarek said, caught up in the enthusiasm.

Graym interrupted hurriedly. "And there you are. We'll frighten off this lot in no time and be back on the road." He raised a fist and shouted, "To Krinneor!"

"To Krinneor!" Jarek shouted. Darll said nothing. The Wolf brothers looked worried.

The elders had tears in their eyes. Graym was pleased to think he had moved them. He held out his hands. "As long as we're fighting the good fight for you, so to speak, can you lend us your swords?"

The elders stared at him.

"We didn't bring any," he added.

"It's not as if we needed them," Jarek said.

The elders were suitably impressed.

"The Protector fled with most of our good weapons. We still have a few." Rhael lifted a rag-wrapped bundle and gave it to Graym. "This is Galeanor, the Axe of the Just."

"Just what?" Jarek asked.

Graym took the axe, eyed it dubiously. "Just kidding."

Darll muttered in his ear. "Perfect. The fat man fights and dies with the Axe of the Just Kidding."

Rhael handed the others dented weapons, the few the Protector had left behind. Darll examined his sword with distaste. Jarek looked at his with delight. The Wolf brothers picked up two badly corroded maces, after touching them gingerly to be sure they weren't dangerous. They stood there, then, staring at one another.

"Don't you think you'd better take up positions opposite the enemy?" Rhael suggested.

"You're absolutely right, Miss," Graym said firmly. "Move out." With only a small twinge of guilt, he added, "And we'll take the cart with us—for supplies . . . and . . . strategy."

They traipsed down the hill, walked through Graveside. It was, Graym noted, a pleasant enough place, not much bigger than Sarem. There were cart tracks in front of the homes and manure piles in the tilled fields. It obviously was a farm-to-market town for a larger city. "Krinneor isn't far now," Graym said to the others. "We're closer to the city itself. I know it. Now, if we can just shake this lot . . ."

Graym glanced behind him. Werlow began organizing the elders for a safe retreat down the road. Rhael had gone into one of the cottages.

Graym smiled; they continued on.

At the crest of the hill, Darll raised his hand in silent warning. The others obediently stopped the cart.

"Keep low!" he ordered. They dropped to the ground and peered into the valley below.

Tombstones and open graves, white tents and a great many ropes stippled the valley and spread up the opposite hill. A hundred helmeted, armored warriors stood in line, ready for inspection. Graym looked shocked.

"These scum robbed the graves," said Darll. "And they're wearing the corpses!"

"Odd taste in armor, made out of bones. What for, d'you think, sir?" Graym asked.

"Wolves love bones," Darll said bitterly. "Sheep shy away from them. No use in shying, though. The wolves always win." He smiled grimly. "I know. I'm a wolf."

He pointed downhill cautiously. "The two in front with the swords are drillmasters, showing close-quarter thrusts. The ones checking the lines are lower-rank officers."

A man dashed up to a soldier, who was twisting this way and that, cuffed him, and yelled in his face. The shouting carried all the way to the hilltop.

"That," Darll said dryly, "would be the sergeant."

"Which one is Skorm?" Graym whispered.

"My guess would be the big guy, wearing the sawed-off skull."

They watched as Skorm paced calmly and evenly, inspecting the troops. The warlord, stepping over a skeleton, kicked the skull. It shattered on a tombstone.

Graym peered down at him. "Now there's a man who knows the value of appearances."

"Don't you ever say anything bad about anybody?"

Graym shrugged. "There's more than enough of that around, sir, if you want it."

"What if we split them down the middle?" a voice said.

They rolled and turned around, Graym snatching the axe from his belt. Rhael, a battered spear with a mended haft in her hands, was standing behind them. She was dressed in leather armor that probably had been trimmed from a butcher's apron.

"I've always heard that was how to deal with a larger force," she said.

"Young Elder Rhael," said Graym, "why don't you go back to town and keep bad folk from climbing the hill to surround us?"

Rhael looked at Graym admiringly. "You have the mind of a warrior." She stood stiffly. "I won't let you down. I promise."

They watched her run back over the hill crest. "I wish I could move like that," Graym said, envious.

"Wouldn't look good on you," Darll muttered.

Graym rubbed his rotund middle. "True enough, sir."

"Now," Darll said, "what's your battle plan?"

"Battle plan, sir?"

"You left Rhael to guard our rear—and an ugly rear at that. What's your plan of attack?"

Graym shuddered. "Attack? Don't even think it, sir. My plan is to run around Skorm and go on to Krinneor. Why do you think we brought the cart?"

The Wolf brothers looked vastly relieved. Darll stared at him, then began to laugh. "I like your style, fat man."

Graym hefted the axe. "Right. The chains, sir."

Darll was suspicious. "You're setting me free?"

"On good behavior." Graym glanced sideways down the hill at the soldiers. "I can't send you running past that lot in chains. They'd hear the rattle for sure."

Darll dropped to one knee and laid the chain on a boulder, turning his head away and shutting his eyes tightly.

Graym swung the broadaxe overhead, brought it down. Sparks shot in all directions. The Axe of the Just Kidding sliced through the chain and gouged the rock. Shards flew, grazing Darll.

He raised his right hand to wipe his cheek. His left hand automatically followed, a chain's length behind, then dropped. He looked with wonder at his hands, then looked longingly at the horizon ahead of them, beyond the army. "Right. Ready to run for it?"

He pulled a thong from his pocket, wrapped it around the sleeve of his right arm. Then he bent, tightened his boots, and stood straight.

Graym stared. With only a few tucks and touches, Darll had gone from prisoner to razor-sharp man of war. Graym stared down the hill, where an army was blocking their way. "Just think, sir," he said, "earlier today, the world was sweet, and I wanted it to last forever. Isn't life amazing?"

"While you've got it," Darll said. He poked at Jarek, who was playing mumblety-peg with his sword. "Tighten everything, boy. You want free limbs. Loosen for marches, tighten for fights or retreats."

Jarek tightened his belt hurriedly. Groaning with the effort, Graym bent and tucked his breeches down into his boot tops. He stood puffing and stared down the hill.

Jarek said eagerly, "Are we going to fight now?"

Graym shook his head. "That, my boy, would be the worst disaster since the Cattle-Kissing."

"Cataclysm!" Darll said automatically. "I think we can

run around the end of the valley there and be safely on our way to Krinneor before they know what happened."

"We'll be the first traders through Skorm's blockade," said Graym suddenly. "They'll call us heroes and pay triple the value on every glass of ale."

He raised the Axe of the Just Kidding. "To Krinneor!"

Skorm turned around, looked in their general direction.

The Wolf brothers shrieked and dived for the cart.

"No!" Graym shouted.

It was too late. In the struggle to fit underneath the cart, Fanris's foot dislodged the chuck block. The cart started rolling downhill.

"The ale!" Graym ran forward. Darll followed, swearing. Jarek whooped and charged alongside him. The Wolf brothers, terrified at being left alone, jumped up and ran after them.

Cart and barrels hurtled down the hill, bouncing over rocks, heading straight for Skorm and his officers.

The officers took one look and ran.

Astonishingly, none of the rank-and-file warriors budged. "Training's training," Darll panted, "but that's not possible."

The lead barrel, now thundering down faster than a man could run, bounced off a dirt pile and into the first row of warriors, who didn't even look up.

The second barrel hit the second row. The third barrel tangled the ropes that had strung the soldiers together. The bodies fell apart.

Darll gripped Graym's shoulder. "They're fake! Nothing but armor on sticks and bones!"

He ran toward the "officers," apparently the only living men on the field. Skorm shouted a command in a harsh voice.

Two of the men sidled around Darll, keeping out of range of his sword. One of them raised a throwing mace and swung it with a deadly whir.

Graym, desperate, flung the axe end-over-end. It thunked handle-first into the mace-swinger, knocked him senseless.

Darll leapt over the fallen man, stepping on his back.

"Officer material," he grunted, and wrapped his dangling manacle chain around the other man's sword and pulled. The sword flew out of the man's hand.

Darll shouted back to Jarek. "Pick up his sword!"

Jarek picked it up, dropping his own sword. Graym punched an opponent in the stomach and doubled him over, sent him stumbling into two men behind him.

The men staggered back and raised their swords, jumping at the Wolf brothers, who were closest.

Fanris and Fenris looked at the armored, bone-covered sword-carrying men. Panic-stricken, the brothers both shrieked, "We surrender!" and tossed their maces in the air.

The maces hit each man squarely in the head. Fenris and Fanris looked at each other in relief and turned to run away.

The remaining men, daunted by five berserkers crazed enough to charge an entire army, fled.

Skorm turned his skull face toward Graym. The grave-robber charged, aiming a vicious two-handed sword straight for Graym's heart.

Darll yelled, "The axe!" picked it up, and threw it.

Graym caught the axe by the thong, just as it struck Skorm's sword and shattered the blade. Graym grabbed the axe handle clumsily, and smacked Skorm on the head.

Skorm Bonelover, the Sorrow of Huma, the Dark Lady's Liege Man, the legendary Eater of Enemies, dropped to the ground with a whimper.

The fat cooper, axe in hand, stood panting over him. Rhael ran down the hill, spear in hand.

"We won!" she cried exultantly.

Halting, she looked down at Skorm's shattered sword and frowned. "That looks familiar," she said. "That's the Protector's Sword of Office!"

Graym bent and pulled the skull off Skorm's face. He was conscious again and looked pinched and scared, but fairly ordinary beyond that.

"Protector!" Rhael gasped.

Darll kicked the Protector's sword hilt away from him and stood watching over him.

Rhael was staring admiringly at an embarrassed Graym. "I heard the noise. I saw the whole thing. You charged an army by yourselves!"

Darll opened his mouth to explain, but Jarek trod on his foot. "We toppled our barrels on them. Then Graym was the first one down. Not even Darll could outrun him."

Rhael sighed. "What a wonderful idea. But your trade goods—your ale—you sacrificed them for us?"

"One barrel made it," Jarek told her. "It rolled off to one side and didn't hit anybody." He shook his head. "But I bet all those other soldiers are drinking it now."

"There are no other soldiers, rock-brain!" Darll growled. "This Protector and his friends built them out of corpses, tugged on ropes to make them move, pretended to train them. They wanted to scare everyone out of town, then loot it, and it nearly worked."

Jarek scratched his head. "Why didn't the town set up a bunch of fake soldiers to fight back?" he asked.

Darll looked at Graym, at Jarek, and at the Wolf brothers, who, seeing the fight was over, had returned. Darll grinned.

"They did set up fake soldiers. Sort of."

Graym cleared his throat. "Well, we'd best get on the road." He handed the Axe of Just Kidding back to Rhael. "Business calls, Miss. Glad we could help, and all."

She brushed his cheek with her finger. "You knew," she said wonderingly. "Even before you attacked, you knew Skorm was a fraud."

Graym looked uncomfortable. "Well, I had an idea. Couldn't be sure, of course."

Darll rolled his eyes.

Graym, feeling awkward, said simply, "Nice meeting you, Miss." He turned and walked through the graves and the shattered mock soldiers.

They collected the cart and the single surviving barrel. Graym tried, briefly, to find the barrel taps and the rest of their belongings, then said, "Give it up." They dragged the cart through the scattered armor, framework, and bones of the open graves.

The cart rolled freely. Jarek looked at the single barrel in it and said happily, "The price of ale must be way up now."

"Best thing that could happen, really," Graym said, but he

sounded troubled. He and the Wolf brothers drew the cart alone. Darll and Jarek walked alongside as they moved up the last hill before Krinneor. Darll was trying to learn the second verse of "The Bald Maid and the Barber."

Fenris, beside Graym, said, "I hate to turn him in."

Graym nodded. "He's not a bad lot. Wanted to kill us or jail us, but face it. Who wouldn't?"

Fanris, on his other side, said, "Can't we just let him go?"

Graym stared at the road. "He's expected. We were paid half in advance. We can't just two-step into Krinneor—"

"Do we need to go there so bad?" Fenris asked softly.

Graym looked back at the cart, bouncing easily with one barrel of ale and no supplies. "It's all we've got left."

They walked in silence, watching Darll try to teach Jarek to juggle. The mercenary, even while mocking Jarek's efforts, had a hand affectionately on the man's shoulder.

The road cut through a pass and angled to the left.

Jarek sniffed the air. "I smell something funny."

"That's the sea, boy," said Graym.

But Darll looked troubled. "I didn't know there was an arm of the sea here."

"A port city," Graym explained. "Not just rich, but a trade center. We're nearly here. Beyond this curve, we'll see the road on the shore, probably a lovely seaside view, all the way to Krinneor—"

They rounded the corner.

The hill plunged down to a sandy beach strewn with rocks. The road ended, half-covered with sand, sloping down into the water and disappearing. Ahead was water, all the way to the horizon,. a new sea, still gray with the silt and mud of the land collapsing and the waters rushing in.

A half mile out from shore, a group of battered golden spires stuck upright, barely a man's height above the waves. Gulls were nesting on them.

The men rolled the cart to the beach and stood.

"The golden towers," Fenris said.

"The marble doors," Fanris said.

"And excellent drains," said Darll.

Graym, staring at the spires in shock, murmured, "I hear that's very important for a city."

The others laughed for quite a while. Graym sat on a rock by the shore, staring.

Jarek moved down the beach, picking up stones to skip. The Wolf brothers, once they were over their fear of gulls, took off their boots and went wading. Darll walked up to Graym. "Where to from here?"

"Nowhere." Graym stared, unseeing, over the open water. "No horses, no food, no money. No Krinneor." He blinked his eyes rapidly. "All gone."

Darll was shocked. "There's a world out there. You can start over."

Behind them, a voice said, "You can stay here."

Rhael came forward, holding some sort of medallion and twisting it in her fingers. Her determination was gone; she looked unsure of herself.

Graym stared at her a moment. "You knew the truth about Krinneor, didn't you?"

"We all knew. No one wanted to tell you before you helped us."

"I don't suppose you did, Miss," Graym said heavily. "And after?"

"Afterward, Elder Werlow was afraid of you. You're fierce warriors."

Darll had the grace not to laugh.

"So you let us go. Good joke." Graym sighed.

She twisted the medallion chain almost into a knot. "I argued with them and said I'd follow you and apologize, and—and give you this."

She held up the medallion, realized how twisted it was. "Sorry." She untwisted the chain nimbly, then dropped it over Graym's neck. "There."

The medallion was a small shield with a single piece of black opal in the shape of an axe. Graym looked down at it. "It was brave, your coming here when you were embarrassed. Thank you, Miss. I'll keep this."

"Until he gets hungry," Darll said bluntly, "then he'll sell it. He'll have to."

Rhael ignored the mercenary. "Why not stay in Graveside?" she asked. She touched the medallion. "To fill the office that goes with this."

"Office?" Graym said blankly, opening his eyes.

"Of Protector," Rhael said. On impulse, she kissed his cheek. "Please take it. Your men, too. You'll have food and lodging, and we know we can trust you."

Graym stared bemusedly at her. "Me, a law officer?" He turned to Darll. "Would I be any good, sir?"

"Unless you rob them, you can't do worse than the last one they had." He looked at the dangling chain. "I suppose you'll put me in jail there?"

Graym sighed. "Can't do it, now that I'm their Protector. Wouldn't be right, would it, sir? I mean, you're their war hero and all."

He frowned, concentrating, then smiled and slapped Darll on the back. "You can go, sir. It's all right. You're pardoned."

Darll's jaw fell and he goggled at Graym. "You're pardoning me?"

"First offense, like you said, sir. You've matured since then. Probably be an upstanding citizen of Graveside." He puckered his brow, thinking, and suddenly brightened. "You could stay and be my military advisor."

"You lead? Me advise?" It was too much. Darll shook his head and walked away, swearing, laughing, and muttering.

"What's he upset about?" Jarek asked. "He fought all right."

"You all fought wonderfully," Rhael said firmly. "You're our heroes." She kissed Graym again, then walked swiftly back through the pass toward Graveside.

"Heroes?" the Wolf brothers said at once, and laughed.

Graym said gruffly, "There've been worse."

Darll looked back up the road toward Graveside, at the retreating Rhael. "Lucky for them they found us, in fact."

Graym grinned at the others. "Best thing that could have happened, really."

Suddenly he was back at the cart, tugging on one of the shafts. Darll joined him. "Right, then. Let's get back." Graym pointed at the remaining barrel of ale. "Skull-Splitter all around, when we get there, on the house."

It was a surprisingly fast trip.

Into Shadow, Into Light

Richard A. Knaak

The knight stalked across the hellish landscape, sword in hand. The fog failed to conceal the desolation around him. Gnarled trees and churned dirt were sights all too familiar after so long. His world, his cursed world, was always much the same: dry, crackling soil, no sun, no shadows, no refuge, no life, just endless devastation . . . and somewhere in the fog, those who ever hunted him.

The fever burned, but, as always, he forced himself to withstand the pain. Sweat poured down his face, trickling into his armor. The plague that coursed through him never rested. Oddly, it had been a part of him so long that he probably would have felt lost without it.

The rusted armor creaked as the knight stumbled up a small hill. Beneath the rust on his breastplate there could still be seen a ravaged insignia marking him as a knight of the Solamnic orders. He rarely looked down at the fading mark, for it was a mockery of his life, a reminder of why he had been condemned to this existence.

The price of being a traitor had been heavier than he had ever thought possible.

As he started down the other side of the ravaged hill, the knight caught sight of something odd, something out of place in this wasteland. It seemed to glitter, despite the lack of sunlight, and to the weary knight it was worth more than a mountain of gold. A stream of clear, cool water flowed no more than a few yards from where he stood.

He smiled—a rare smile of hope. The knight staggered forward, moving as fast as he could manage, ignoring pain, fatigue, fear. How long since his last drink of water? The memory escaped him.

Kneeling before the stream, he closed his eyes. "My Lord Paladine, I beseech you! Hear this simple prayer! Let me partake this once! A single sip of water, that is all I ask!"

The knight leaned forward, reached out toward the stream . . . and fell back in horror as he stared into its reflective surface.

"Paladine preserve me," he muttered. Slowly leaning forward again, he stared at his image in the stream.

Pale as a corpse, his face was gaunt, almost skull-like. Lank, wispy hair—what could be seen beneath his helm—was plastered to his head. His eyes were colorless; had they always been that way? A faint, sardonic smile briefly touched his countenance. "I look like a ghost. How appropriate now," he said to his reflection.

The water continued to flow past, and he recalled the purpose for which he had paused. Again he stretched forth his gauntleted hand. The water might rust the metal, but the parched knight did not care. All that existed was the hope that this once—just this once—he might be allowed a sip.

His fingertips reached the surface of the tiny river, passed through it without even touching.

He cursed, cursed the gods who had doomed him to this wretched life. In frustration, he thrust his hand as deep into the water as he could. The stream flowed on. He didn't create so much as a ripple.

Growing more desperate, the knight thrust his other hand into the water. He tried to cup some of the liquid, but each time his hands came free of the stream, they held nothing. This land might have been a desert for all he could drink.

His head lowered. The sound of mocking laughter came to him, but he did not know if it was real or his imagination. He had never known.

"How long must I pay?" the knight demanded of his unseen tormentor. "What must I do to earn a sip of water?"

He pounded his fist against the ground, but even that much comfort was denied him. His hand could not touch the soil. There was always a small distance between the world and him. The ground, like everything else, refused to accept his touch, refused him peace.

"I am dead!" he roared at no one. "Let me rest!"

Dead. He was nothing more than a ghost now, a ghost sentenced to pay in death for the darksome deeds he had performed in life. Now and forever, the Abyss was his home, his reward for living that life.

How long since his death? He had no idea. Time meant nothing here. But he thought the Dragon War must be long over. What was happening now in the world of his birth, Krynn? Had centuries passed since his spirit had been exiled to this phantom plain where no one existed but himself and those who sought vengeance? Or had it been only days?

The clink of armor warned him that he was no longer alone. His pursuers had found him again. The knight reached for his sword, but it was flight that was on his mind. Combat was a last, desperate effort; it was predestined that he would lose any battle.

Then the whispers began.

Rennard . . . We come!

His name. After so long, he often forgot. They were always there to remind him, however. They could never forget the name of the one responsible.

Rennard!

Betrayer . . .

Oathbreaker . . .

Rennard may not have remembered his name, but now the other memories were too terrible to forget.

His pursuers could not be far behind. Despite his danger, the cursed knight could not help but take one last desperate glance at the cool, sparkling stream.

"One sip," he prayed, reaching his hand a last time toward the water. "Is that so much to ask?"

And then . . . it was as if the world, *all* worlds, shrieked in agony, began to shake.

Rennard found himself cast out into an invisible maelstrom, caught up in some new, inventive torment of the gods.

The whispers died. He wondered if his pursuers, too, had been caught up by this chaos. Rennard stood. The desolate realm that was his home, his prison, began to fade before his eyes. He caught a glimpse of shadowy forms, swords, and bitter eyes, then they dwindled away to nothing. He heard a sound—one so out of place that he could not believe he heard it.

> "The Honor of Huma survives
> The Glory of Huma survives
> Dragons, hear!
> Solamnic breath is taken
> Life; hear!
> My sword is broken of Dragons"

It was a human voice singing. And he heard a name . . . Huma? How could such a thing be? What did it mean? The melody drew the knight. Without thinking, Rennard moved toward it, followed it. . . .

He found himself standing in a fogbound, desolate land.

Something is different, Rennard thought. This is not the Abyss!

The song faded away, but Rennard barely noticed. He stared at his surroundings. Some sort of terrible upheaval had wrecked this land. Trees—leviathans—lay broken on the ground. What once had been a well-traveled road was cracked and half buried under rubble. Thick clouds filled the heavens. A mortal might have thought this some variation of the infernal Abyss, but Rennard knew better. The living forest, struggling to survive, a bird fluttering overhead, the sounds that assailed him—all spoke of *life*.

He fell to his knees.

"Krynn!" Rennard whispered. "How have I come here? Is this truly the real world?"

A part of him was afraid it was a dream, that any second he would find himself once more fleeing his ever-present enemies. "Is this Krynn? Or have I merely entered some new phase of my punishment?" he asked bitterly.

A low laugh—or was it the wind?—teased him. The spectral knight twisted around, searching for the source. "Morgion, dark Lord of Decay and Disease, master of my grief, do I still entertain you?" he cried out.

No answer came.

Was that a tall, bronze tower he saw in the distance, a tower perched upon the edge of a precipice? A tower dedicated to Morgion, used by those who served him? The knight stared, but all he saw was a lone tree leaning precariously over the edge of a newly formed cliff. It was not the sanctum of the malevolent deity.

Bewildered, confused, he stared at his surroundings and made a bitter discovery. The muddy ground in which he knelt was soft. Despite the weight of his bulky armor, Rennard had not sunk so much as a finger's width into Krynn's blessed soil. He made not the slightest impression.

The knight rose to his feet. He cursed the gods who had brought him to this new fate. He was free of his prison, but not free of his damnation. Ansalon—if this was Ansalon—offered him nothing more than the demonic plain from which he had been cast out. Rennard raised his fist to the shrouded sky and wished that there had never been gods.

Dread, familiar sounds—the pounding of hooves, the clash of armor—jolted him. His pursuers had followed him!

The knight turned at the sound, the sight strengthening his fear.

A knight in war-scarred armor, riding a black horse, came at him. The steed—spittle flying as it strained to keep its mad pace—covered the distance between itself and Rennard in great strides. The horse's master, riding low, urged the animal on in harsh, unintelligible cries.

The horse charged straight at Rennard, but it was not a demonic phantom. It was a flesh-and-blood horse, a flesh-and-blood man—a man whose armor marked him as a Knight of Solamnia.

To see a living being, even one wearing the armor of those Rennard had betrayed, was so overwhelming that the ghost could not readily accept the vision. Rennard stretched a tentative hand toward the oncoming knight. The ghost longed to touch a living, breathing person.

The horse shied, nearly throwing its rider. The other

knight cursed and turned the animal back on the path, the path upon which Rennard stood. The horse stared fearfully at the wraith, then galloped forward.

It took Rennard several seconds to realize the truth. The horse, unable to swerve, had run *through* him. The ghost stared after the knight and his dark steed, riding madly down the broken road.

Rennard had to follow. Here was the first living being he had seen since his death, and a knight! Although he had betrayed the knighthood, Rennard felt a kinship for the warrior. Besides, here might be a chance to discover why the ghost had come to be once more on the face of Ansalon.

"I must catch him . . . But it's too late. I'll never be able to keep pace with the swift animal." As he started forward, the world seemed to ripple.

The ghost found himself standing in a new location, several yards *ahead* of the rider.

The other knight rode past. Rennard followed. Once more, the world rippled. Once again, Rennard had journeyed to a location ahead of the mortal.

Suddenly, the rider brought his horse to a halt, forcing his mount to veer off the path.

Rennard joined the mortal.

A body—that of an elderly man, a peasant by his clothes—lay in the brush, no more than a day dead.

The knight couldn't force his steed nearer. Rennard gradually realized that he was at fault. The animal could sense the ghost, though its master could not. Rennard stepped back a few paces, out of sight. The skittish horse grew calm.

The rider dismounted and approached the body. Rennard was amused to note that the knight drew a sword, just in case the wretched figure rose from the dead. A moment later, Rennard realized that perhaps the knight was not so foolish. Rennard was proof that anything was possible.

The knight pushed back his helm, bent down to study the remains, and carefully noted the direction the old man had been traveling. Rennard took time to study the knight. He was young, though still old enough to bear the symbol of the Order of the Rose on his breastplate.

Rennard sneered. Arrogant and self-serving, that was the

Order of the Rose. Most of the high lords of the Solamnic brotherhood came from the ranks of the Rose.

Rennard had murdered one of them, and here was the epitome of the handsome and heroic warrior that peopled the stories of bards and the dreams of maidens: perfect, honed features; dark, brooding eyes and firm jaw; black hair that curled from under his helm; a well-groomed moustache in the style still traditional among the Knights of Solamnia.

The ghost touched his own marred features. Here was everything that Rennard had never been. He'd rather look at the corpse, and the young knight was studying the corpse, too, with more than casual interest.

Although the hapless peasant evidently had suffered from many things, disease had killed him. Rennard, who knew of such things, could see the signs.

"Aaah, good folk of Ansalon," Rennard muttered as he looked at the corpse, "the gods treat you so well!"

The young knight had lost interest in the corpse and was now gazing down the road.

The peasant had not been alone. The tracks of more than a dozen people and one or two animals spoke of a long, arduous journey by a group of people in great haste. Rennard saw an endless trek, much like a journey he once had made. One by one, the members of the party had collapsed and been left behind, like this, left behind by those too terrified to stop to bury their dead.

The young knight began to talk, and at first Rennard wondered if another ghost haunted this region, for there was no one to respond.

"A day, Lucien, not much more. They're on foot. I'll surely catch up tomorrow. Then I will avenge you!" The young knight kicked the body with the heel of his boot, kicked it again and again until he wearied of the sport. Then, face twisted in bitterness and rage, the knight turned away.

Vengeance? Not—if Rennard recalled correctly—an act approved of by the knighthood.

Virtuous on the outside, foul within. Rennard had been a traitor and murderer—that was true—but others in the knighthood carried their share of dark secrets as well. Eyeing the mortal with growing distaste, he muttered, "And what are *your* secrets, great Knight of the Thorny Rose?"

His living counterpart stiffened, then looked in the ghost's direction, a trace of puzzlement on the young knight's features. His exhaustion was evident. Rennard saw rings under the eyes; the eyes themselves had the sunken look of a man who had driven himself for days. After a few moments—moments in which Rennard would have held his breath (provided he still breathed)—the young fighter rubbed his eyes, turned away, and resumed his inspection of the corpse and the trail.

The young knight took a few steps, following the direction of the dead man's footprints. Each step was less certain than the last. He was almost too tired to go on. Perhaps realizing this himself, the young knight returned to his mount and used the tired beast as support.

"Tomorrow, Lucien. I'll find them tomorrow." He clenched his fist. "They'll pay, the murderous carrion! They'll pay a hundredfold for your life. As my name is Erik Dornay, so I swear over and over it shall be!"

With some effort, Dornay mounted. He didn't give the corpse a second look, but for a brief instant his eyes returned to the general area where the ghost stood, watching. Frowning, Erik finally urged his horse along the trail. The animal needed no encouragement; it set off at a brisk pace, fueled by its obvious desire to get as far from Rennard as possible.

The horse's desperate efforts were useless. This young knight interested Rennard too much to let him go. The mortal might know where Rennard was, why he was here. And the ghost was anxious to know the reasons behind the vengeance that drove the young Solamnian to turn against the Oath and Measure.

Rennard had one other reason, one that he did not like to admit to himself. Night was fast approaching and night—in his mind—brought the hunters. But would they close the circle with a living person nearby?

Perhaps not.

Better the company of a Knight of the Rose than yet another confrontation with the bitter souls who owed their damnation to Rennard.

Rennard gripped the hilt of his sword and vanished after the diminishing figure of Erik Dornay.

* * * * *

Shortly after nightfall, Dornay ended his ride and made camp in a small copse of tangled trees. The halt was not by choice, if Rennard was any reader of expressions, but made out of necessity. The horse's breathing was ragged; it was doubtful that the unfortunate animal would have lasted much longer without rest. Dornay himself nearly collapsed as he dismounted, but the young knight took care of his horse, fed and tethered the animal. He built a small campfire, over which he set a piece of meat to cooking.

The aroma of the cooking meat drifted over to Rennard. The smell brought a terrible hunger for food. Without thinking, he stepped toward the fire. The horse, sensing him, neighed loudly and pulled on its reins.

Erik, just removing his helm, looked swiftly around. Rennard paid no attention to the knight. The ghost bent down by the fire and stared at the meat. He nearly forgot the agony of the plague that eternally tormented him.

"Paladine, Kiri-Jolith, Morgion, Takhisis . . . Gilean . . ." Rennard chanted in rapid succession. "If there be one who still watches over me, let me eat! Let me taste it . . ."

The meat sizzled. The ghostly knight reached out.

His fingers went through it, just as they had passed through the water earlier.

"Not again!" Frustrated, Rennard swung his hand at the makeshift spit.

Dornay's meal, spit and all, collapsed into the fire.

Rennard stared at his hand. Erik leapt forward and tried to rescue his meal. Cursing, the young knight dusted off his food and reset it to cooking.

"Did I do that?" wondered the ghost. He reached out again, but, to his dismay, his fingers could not touch it. He could only watch as Dornay removed the hot flesh a minute or two later and began to eat. Rennard envied every bite.

"This is madness!" Rennard cursed. "Better the ravages of plague or the thrust of a thousand swords than to suffer this hunger!" He stepped back, intent on departing but strangely reluctant to leave.

Dornay lifted a flask of cool water to his mouth.

Rennard rushed from the encampment. He had traded the endless running for this? Which was worse, he wondered, the fear or the desire?

Searing pain made him stumble—the ever-present torture of the plague. Rennard gritted his teeth and struggled to remain standing. Fever consumed his already dead flesh. Chills shook a body that did not exist.

Then a melody drifted to him, a melody that seemed to ease the plague's torment. Rennard slowly recovered, and as he did, his attention focused on the song.

> "Dragon-Huma
> temper me now
> Dragon-Huma
> Grant me grace and love
> When the heart of the Knighthood
> wavers in doubt
> Grant me this, Warrior Lord"

"Huma . . ." he whispered. It was the same song that had carried him through the chaos and into the plane of the living. The singer was Erik Dornay.

Walking toward the camp, the ghost listened to the words.

Heroes existed only in tales, not reality. They were the products of the ignorant, who had no other hope. The knighthood itself was proof, as far as Rennard was concerned. No heroes there. More darkness than light.

Yet even Rennard could not deny Huma's courage, his honor, his compassion . . . for one who had betrayed him.

Step by step, Rennard moved closer to the fire. Erik Dornay sang quietly, with a tenderness and awe that seemed out of place after his callous treatment of the corpse, his sworn oath of vengeance.

Rennard stared at the young knight. Dornay had thrust

his sword into the ground. He knelt before it, still singing. Rennard realized that it was the young knight's way of easing his mind, preparing for the evening rituals that were an integral part of a knight's training.

> "Honor is Huma
> Glory is Huma
> Solamnic Knight Huma survives
> Glorified Huma survives
> Life: hear!"

Huma. Erik began to pray, spoke of him as Huma of the Lance, spoke about a lance that had won the Dragon War and swept the Dark Queen from the heavens.

Seeing Erik in the dim light of the campfire, Rennard could almost imagine his former comrade kneeling there. Huma and Erik Dornay were similar in appearance, even without the hypnotic influence of the song.

"So, Huma, young squire—my kinsman—you have become a hero. A hero." The irony was not lost on the ghost. He had betrayed the knighthood, betrayed Huma—one of the few Rennard had ever thought worthy of the ideals of the Oath and the Measure. "And it was I who helped train you, not knowing you would cause my downfall."

Was this the reason he was here? the cursed knight wondered. A reason involving the mortal before him? Or was it mere coincidence?

The singing and prayers had ceased. Dornay was on his feet now, and the sword, which had stood like a monument, was in his hands—a deadly weapon in the grip of one well-versed in its use.

"Who's there? Who spoke? Enough of this! I've heard you before! Show yourself!"

Rennard, alarmed, looked to see if his pursuers had come while he had been lost in reverie. For a moment, the shadows of night became the hunters, but the ghost soon saw that there was no one, living or dead, other than Dornay and himself.

"You hear me, then, Knight of the Prickly Rose?" Rennard asked, not expecting an answer.

"I hear you too well, cur! Come out of hiding! Reveal yourself to me or I will let my blade find you!"

Dornay shifted to face the location where the ghost stood.

Rennard stared, amazed.

"You would not like me, mortal," the ghost replied, testing. "And your blade would be sorely disappointed."

"Where are you?" Exhausted as he was, Dornay was calm, alert. "I hear where you must be, but I see nothing there!"

Rennard walked slowly toward his young counterpart. "There is something here, Knight of the Rose, but nothing you can touch, not even the smallest bone remains. The physical shell I once wore was burned shortly after I killed myself, so very long ago."

"Killed yourself?" Erik's eyes rounded. "So you claim to be a ghost? You lie! More likely a spellcaster in hiding! Yes, that's who you must be!"

Rennard shook his head. "I am no mage, Erik Dornay. Do you recall the body you found not too far from here? The old man? I was watching you then. You thought you heard something . . . even saw something, didn't you?"

Dornay's countenance was nearly as pale as that of his unholy companion. The young knight backed slowly away, the sword stretched out before him. Rennard could guess some of what the knight must be thinking. Exhaustion could do things to the mind, especially one filled with grief and a burning desire for vengeance. Dornay probably debated which was more terrible—the thought that he had gone insane or the prospect that he faced a spirit from beyond.

"A trick," he muttered.

"I am real, Erik Dornay, as real as the armor you wear, but as insubstantial as your faith in the oaths you took when you donned the mantle of a knight." Rennard laughed.

Erik put a hand to his breastplate and touched the rose symbol. "Why do you haunt me, specter? Why reveal yourself to me now? Leave me! Go back to your rest!"

"Rest?" The word struck Rennard as sharply as a well-honed sword. "I cannot rest! I am not allowed to rest!" He stalked forward until he was almost face-to-face with the other knight, who continued to stare wildly around. "Gladly would I call an end to this accursed existence of mine! Gladly would I earn my *rest!*"

Erik stepped back again, aware that whatever haunted him lurked just ahead, but not at all certain what could be done about the situation.

Rennard found relief in venting his centuries-old anger on someone. "Would that I could reveal myself to you, Knight of the Rotting Rose, so that you could see the fate I've been condemned to!"

And there and then, Erik Dornay, staring in mute horror, nearly dropped his sword and fled, for the ghost, without knowing it, had done just that.

"A knight! . . . You are a knight. . . ." Dornay stared at the ghost's ruined face—the pale, drawn skin, the boils, and the scarlet patches.

"Plague!" Erik's sword arm extended as straight as possible. "Keep back!"

Rennard moved closer.

"Where is your brotherly concern?" he mocked. "I am in need. The plague still thrives within me, gnaws at me even after death. Surely, it is for you to aid a comrade!" He opened his arms, as if to embrace Dornay.

"May the gods forgive me!" Erik leapt forward and thrust his sword between Rennard's helm and breastplate.

The young knight's aim was true, so much so that the ghost expected to feel the death blow. Then, to Rennard's bitter amusement and Erik's disbelief, the blade passed through without obstruction.

The young Solamnian dropped his sword and stared at his hand, as if *it* were somehow to blame for the impossible sight he had just witnessed.

"Had it been my choice," Rennard said, "the blade would have sheared my head from my body, once and for all ending this accursed existence!"

"Paladine save me!" Erik cried.

"Paladine cannot save you. He did not save *me,*" the ghost knight hissed. "That was for another, darker lord to do. Morgion it was, who finally heard my plea, but he demanded a heavy price."

"Who—" The young knight pulled himself together. "Who are you, wraith? Why does your tragic existence haunt me now, in my grief?"

"You should know. It was *you* who called me. You—with your song."

"The . . . song?" Erik eyed the phantom, more perplexed than he was anxious. He frowned. "I am no foul necromancer, like the followers of Chemosh!"

"Nonetheless, it was your song." Rennard circled Dornay, his eyes never leaving the mortal. "The one you sang about . . . Huma."

"Huma? Huma of the Lance?"

"Just Huma to me, a knight who believed and, because he believed, fought as few others could. I knew him well, you see, even aided in his training. That was before . . ."

Erik's eyes were wary and thoughtful. One did not rise to the Order of the Rose without being able to adapt to the unknown, even if that included the undead.

Rennard guessed what he was thinking. "If you have a way, Mortal, to rid yourself of me, by all means try. I would welcome rest after so long. I am tired of running, of fighting in futility." Here, at last, Rennard could not hide his own despair. "Tired of the pain."

"Your name, Ethereal One. You still have not said."

The flickering flames of the tiny campfire caught the ghost's attention. He reached down and passed his hand through the fire. "You see? Nothing, not even now." He straightened. "My name? You probably would not know it. I daresay it was stricken from the rolls when the truth of my betrayal was known. I had, after all, murdered one grand master and attempted to kill his successor. Although many servants of the Dark Queen fell by my sword, I betrayed the plans of the knighthood whenever possible and caused the deaths of many men by my actions, all in the name of Morgion, dread Lord of Disease and Decay."

Dornay gasped. "I know *you*! I know the tales that they whisper, even now!" His handsome face twisted. "Rennard the Oathbreaker!"

Bowing, mocking, the ghost replied, "I thought myself forgotten. Yes, I have the dishonor of being him."

Erik snatched his sword from the ground, held it before him. His eyes were narrow slits, his breathing rapid. He began muttering under his breath.

Rennard recognized the litany and was amused. "Exorcising demons? You are not so well-versed for one of your rank. I doubt I will be so easily dismissed, even if you should happen upon the proper chant."

"Why does the ghost of a traitor and murderer visit me? Do the gods think you will stop me in my chosen course? Lucien's death demands justice! He was murdered needlessly, and I will see that his killers pay! Now begone!"

Rennard turned his horrific face toward the mortal. "I would very much like to be gone, Erik Dornay, but not to where I have been since my death. Peace is what I ask . . . peace and a sip of water." He stared into the flame, recalling the past. "I want nothing to do with you, but something has drawn me here. This is not the first time I have heard the song you sang tonight, a song about him. Huma never would have believed it. He would have shaken his head—"

"Do not speak his name!" Erik pointed the useless sword at the ghost as if he still intended somehow to run Rennard through. "He was everything that you were not, traitor! He was everything that I wanted to be!"

Wanted to be? thought the ghost. "And so you no longer desire to be like him?"

The young knight stiffened, then lowered his sword. "I cannot, not now, not after I kill them." His gaze strayed to the woods beyond. "So much has changed since the Cataclysm. At first they begged for our help. Then, with a swiftness unmatched even by the wind, the rumors began! Some of the rumors were not without foundation, but to blame the knighthood as a whole is unthinkable! If we were spared the brunt of the disaster, surely it meant that we were Paladine's chosen! We should have been their guides on the path of recovery. Instead, the scum we tried to protect turned on us. 'Look!' they cried. 'Ansalon shakes and quivers, people die, and the knights are untouched!' "

The young Solamnian laughed harshly. "Some even

claimed we had conspired with the gods, for it was Ergoth, our ancient tyrant, and Istar, our magnificent rival, who suffered most. Lucien tried to reason with them—the ignorant offal. And they dragged him down from his horse and murdered him!"

None of this made much sense to Rennard. "And was the knighthood responsible for this . . . this Cataclysm?"

Erik glowered. "How can you ask that? You were a knight!"

"Yes," said Rennard dryly, "I was a knight."

"I swear that we were not!" Dornay's voice shook. "It could never be!"

"I see."

After a pause, Erik asked, "Did you really know him?"

"Very well." Rennard stood silently, his mind a whirlpool of memories. He stared at the mortal before him and saw Huma. The similarities were more than skin deep.

Am I supposed to turn him along the proper path? Rennard asked whoever had sent him. *I was a puppet in life. Am I to be one in death? Better he make his own destiny, whatever the consequences! At least the choice will be his!*

Rennard saw, to his surprise, that the young Knight of the Rose was staring at him, not in fear and loathing, but in desperate need. "Huma . . . What would he have done? Would he have understood? Lucien was my friend, more than friend . . . he was dearer than any brother. Please, specter, tell me, what would Huma—?"

"Huma would have done what Huma would have done," Rennard interjected quickly. Thinking of Huma stirred memories and emotions that the ghost refused to acknowledge. "Just as you will do what you will do."

"That is no answer!" Dornay said angrily. "Would he have understood my need for vengeance? Tell me!"

I will not do this! Rennard told those who'd sent him. *Dornay's path must be his own! What course his life takes will be his choice, not that of some interfering deity!*

The ghost thought he heard whispers then, but perhaps they were only his own thoughts, speaking back to him: *Would you condemn anyone, even your worst enemy, to a fate such as yours?*

A fate such as mine? Erik's thirst for vengeance could hardly be as great a crime as those I committed. But, Rennard could not help wondering, once he's done murder, he might sink lower still. One day, he might find himself trapped in a futile flight from those he killed and who, because of him, would never be able to rest either.

The "Song of Huma" ran through his mind.

"Huma," Rennard whispered. The man who was now legend never abandoned me, he even looked up to me. Huma—the man, not the legend—had been there in the end, trying to save me from myself. Rather than face him, I took the coward's way out. I slit my own throat.

Rennard turned his eyes briefly to the murky heavens. "I will do this for you, Huma . . . of the Lance. I will do it for you, not the gods. Never them."

Pale eyes narrowing, the ghost answered the young knight's question. "He would have understood *very* well what you were doing, Erik Dornay. You have my oath on that. Unlike you, however, Huma would have understood the meaning and the consequences as well. And, therefore, he would never have considered your dark course." Rennard shifted so as to allow the fire to illuminate his features. "Huma would have known that such a course can lead one only to a fate . . . like mine. Each life I took follows me, punishes me." Rennard shivered, the flickering shadows caused by the fire too lifelike at that moment. "The number still horrifies me, when they begin to gather."

"But they killed Lucien! They don't deserve to live! I have to . . . to . . ." Backing away, Dornay stumbled over to his horse. He untied the animal and wearily mounted, ignoring the fact that his helm still lay on the ground.

"You may deny me, mortal. You may even deny Huma, whom you claim to admire. Can you, though, deny yourself?"

Erik Dornay did not respond. He turned his horse and urged the animal on with a harsh kick to the ribs.

Rennard materialized in front of him. "Huma—the squire I trained, the knight I fought beside and against, the legend that led you to the Solamnic orders—watches us. He had a way of affecting others, Erik Dornay, even me. For that reason and that reason alone, I will not let this end. I will haunt you day and night if I have to."

The Knight of the Rose kicked his protesting charger again, forcing the horse to ride through Rennard.

The ghost disappeared, made himself reappear in front of the startled animal. The horse tried to turn away, but Erik once more forced the terrified beast to keep to the chosen route. Snorting in frustration and anxiety, the mount again raced through the apparition and galloped down the path.

Rennard followed. He'd wait until the horse could go no farther, which couldn't be very long. What would Erik do when he realized it was impossible to escape the ghost? Rennard did not know. The young knight was wavering in his desire for revenge, but it was at such an emotional junction that the greatest danger lay. Erik might go through with his dark plan merely to prove to himself he was not a man of weak resolve, that he kept his promises to his friends. The ghost was all too aware of what people had done for lesser reasons.

Dornay's flight took them into thickening woods. A number of the trees had been uprooted, but most had more or less survived intact. The forest should have meant nothing to the ghost. Yet, for some reason that made no sense to him, he was reminded of Morgion. Rennard grew more cautious, even drawing his sword, just in case.

Ahead of him now, the Knight of the Rose suddenly reined to a halt. The flatter land gave way again to hills.

There was a campfire in the distance.

The refugees? Those he pursued? Dornay evidently thought so, for he moved with more stealth now.

Rennard debated with himself. He stared at the not-so-distant flame and decided it would be wise to take a closer look. Erik would not reach the camp for several minutes, whereas the ghost could flit in and out in less time than it took to draw a breath.

It proved easy to pick out a spot near, but not too near, the encampment. As a precaution, Rennard was careful to hide behind a gnarled oak, on the off-chance that he was visible to all, not merely Erik.

In the dim light of Solinari, the ghost saw the terrible

mob that had murdered the knight Lucien.

These wretched people looked little more alive than Rennard. They hardly seemed like a dangerous lot: sick old men, desperate young men, worn down women, crying children. With not enough to eat or wear, they were lost, with no knowledge of surviving off the land.

They will not survive their journey. If Erik doesn't kill them, they will wander around in circles until they all fall from disease and exposure and starvation.

Without raising a finger, the knight could sentence them all to death. With Erik's help, the group could survive.

Rennard returned to Erik, materialized next to him. The young knight had found another corpse.

In the light of the moon, the dead man's visage was nearly as horrible as that of the ghost. Rennard shivered, though not from fear. There was no doubting that the peasant—a man younger and much more burly than the previous corpse—had not died easily. He had struggled until the end.

"Do not touch him!" Rennard commanded.

Erik looked up, his surprise giving way quickly to nervous annoyance. "What are you doing here, phantom?"

"Saving you. This man died of plague."

Dornay quickly backed a respectable distance away. Rennard moved closer, noted the man's contorted features, the red splotches on his hands and face. A dusty film that sparkled a bit in the moonlight had already settled on the upturned visage. It had been a cruel death.

"Did you touch him?" Rennard demanded.

"No, thank Paladine, but I was almost ready to do so."

Rennard turned from the corpse, Morgion's legacy.

Legacy? Rennard turned back.

He thought of all disease as originating from the dark lord, but some had origins more human than godly. Rennard leaned close and studied the film on the unfortunate man's visage. Even in the dim moonlight, the dust shimmered with a metallic gleam.

"So some accursed things continue," Rennard muttered.

The victim had not died of plague. To the unknowing, it would seem so, but Rennard recognized the dust. The other symptoms, too, made sense, now that he knew the truth.

The legacy of Morgion had indeed killed this man, but it was human hands that had done the work—an evil powder, a poison, whose signs mimicked the plague. The ghost knew its uses all too well. The powder was a favorite tool of those who served the Master of the Bronze Tower. It was sacred to them, as if they held the very power of their god in their hands. The poison could be created by anyone with the knowledge. The Lord of Decay was not a trusting god, even with his followers. Only the most devout learned the secrets of his worship. Morgion's powers were reserved for those who guided the cult, the Nightmaster and his acolytes.

Any loyalty Rennard had ever owed to his dread master had died with his body. Morgion rewarded failure with death. Rennard had failed to kill the Solamnic warrior who had discovered that there was a traitor in their midst. Rennard had failed to kill Huma.

Rennard knew then the fate of the doomed peasants. They would die, a few at a time, in the name of the faceless god he once had called master.

"What do you see, specter?" Erik demanded.

"I see that your sword would be a kind fate to these folk, Erik Dornay. They are being culled and sacrificed in the name of Morgion."

The Knight of the Rose gripped the hilt of his sword tightly. "You are certain?"

"I think I know well enough. The poor wretches are easy prey for the cultists. Look at what lies here. They do not have the strength to bury their dead anymore."

The young knight was grim, pale. He sheathed his sword. Slowly, Erik returned to his horse.

"What will you do?" Rennard asked.

Dornay would not look at him. "I am leaving. I have no need to stay. You should be pleased. I won't kill them."

As the Knight of the Rose mounted, the wraith appeared before him. "You haven't spared the people. You merely have given their deaths into the hands of others."

"They are no more concern of mine." The young Solamnian mounted his steed, trying to depart. "I'm finished with the knighthood, Oathbreaker. I have sung the 'Song of

Huma' for the last time."

He sounded resolved, but he was shaking. Rennard knew that a battle was going on inside the young knight, one that in some ways was as painful as the one Rennard himself constantly fought.

"Very well," the ghost knight told him. There was only one thing he could think of to do, and he prayed that both his memory and the spirit of Huma—who seemed to have a hand in this—would guide him. "I will stand aside."

Erik began slowly riding away. As he passed the wraith, however, Rennard began to sing.

> "Huma's death calls me!
> His death!
> Temper me with such death!
> Paladine, lord god of knights!
> Huma's life is all our lives!
> Dragon-Huma survives!"

Dornay halted. The cursed knight continued to sing, finding that the words—or words enough—were given to him. The melody would forever play in his mind.

Erik pulled tightly on the reins, turned the horse around, and gazed at the phantom. Rennard continued to sing softly, his own memories of Huma adding a vibrancy to the saga that made it come alive, for his memories were tinged with truth, not stretched by time and legend.

"You—" Dornay began.

A stone whistled through the darkness and struck the young knight soundly on the side of the head.

He grunted and fell from his mount. His charger hesitated, but when Rennard ceased singing and started toward the fallen knight, the terrified animal shied away.

Rennard stood over Erik, wondering what had happened, what a ghost could do to help. Even if he were able to touch the mortal, he might do more harm than good. He might infect Dornay with the plague he carried. Morgion would laugh at that.

When the shadows began to move, the ghost drew his sword, prepared to face his own enemies. Then he saw that these were not the ones who hunted him, but mortal men, well-versed in hiding from their victims.

"The armored one is down," said one.

Someone else spoke, but his words were too quiet for the ghost to hear. Then there came an answer.

"Crazy or not, he is a Knight of Solamnia! No, I have something different in mind for him. Perhaps *he* will please our lord."

Seven figures, more like ghosts than the ghost himself, gathered around the fallen knight. They did not see Rennard, who stood among them.

"Take him," said one whose voice was a harsh rasp. He turned to another, who was trying to catch the reins of the horse. "Forget the beast! If he causes trouble, a little dust will settle him!" The hooded figure rolled Dornay over, peering at his armor. "A Knight of the Order of the Rose! This must be a sign, that one of the servants of the Great Enemy should fall into our hands so easily! Our infernal Lord Morgion *must* find this sacrifice satisfactory."

"What of the others, Nightmaster?" The newcomers were covered from head to toe in enveloping cloaks and hoods. Only the Nightmaster's features were visible. He had a long, vulpine face, and his skin looked mottled.

"This one will die this eve. The rest are sheep and will be sacrificed as needed. The knight is of utmost importance. For him, we must plan a ceremonial death, a slow, debilitating death, with one of the slower, more intricate poisons."

"But, Nightmaster," pleaded another, "we've tried before and failed. Some are saying the gods have all abandoned Krynn—"

"Blasphemy!" The leader's shout silenced the questioner. Under the cleric's baleful gaze, the other cultists reached down and took hold of the knight.

"Bind and gag him . . . just in case."

The acolytes obeyed with cold efficiency.

Desperate, Rennard swung his sword at the closest, but his weapon passed through the man without harm. Rennard stared at his hand, thinking how useless it was despite the heavy gauntlet. *To all living things, I am less than the wind!*

A wave of agony sent him to his knees. His frustration had left him open to the curse. The plague was coursing through his body. He fought back the pain. Through blurred eyes, Rennard watched the cultists carry Dornay away.

"Paladine . . . great lord . . . you cannot want this! I do not want this and neither does Huma, your most loyal servant! Will you give another victim to the foul, faceless Master of the Bronze Tower?"

This plea, however, went ignored as far as he could tell. The cultist had spoken of a rumor of the gods leaving Krynn. Was that so? Was there no one, then, who could save the young Solamnian?

No one . . . except a ghost . . . ?

"It seems I am always too weak! To save my life, I gave myself to Morgion. Later, I killed myself, as Huma watched. Now, I must let Erik die."

Unbidden, the "Song of Huma" came to his mind. Try as he might, Rennard could not drive the melody away.

"Huma," the ghost whispered, "why must you, of all people, continue to have faith in me?"

He struggled to his feet and started to follow, each movement sheer torture. Every dead muscle, every long-decayed organ, every broken joint in his body burned with pain and fever. What he hoped to accomplish, the ghost did not know. Rennard knew only that he could not yet give in.

He could hear the acolytes whisper.

" . . . death of another knight . . ."

" . . . Morgion reigns . . ."

" . . . another soul to add to his collection . . ."

Rennard doubled his pain-filled efforts to keep pace with them. Fortunately, the servants of Morgion were hampered by Erik's armored body.

Too soon, the Nightmaster signaled his acolytes to stop.

"This will do." The leader pointed to a small, cleared patch of ground by a stream. Morgion's servants preferred privacy for their work. It would not do for some peasant to stumble on them. He might escape and warn the others.

The Nightmaster began chanting a litany that brought back to Rennard faint memories of stench-ridden ruins and dark practices for the glory of the despotic deity who was their lord. It would not be long before the sacrifice. The special death of a Knight of the Rose was a great gift to the dark god. Small wonder that the Nightmaster might think it sufficient to at last reunite the cultists with their master.

Rennard had willed himself to be visible to the young knight. Now the ghost sought to do the same with the cultists, hoping that his horrific appearance would send them fleeing. Exactly how he had accomplished the feat the first time, the ghost didn't know. Intense need, anger, bitterness . . .

At first, he thought he'd failed, for surely someone should have noticed him, then one of the acolytes raised his head. His eyes settled on where the ghost stood.

An indrawn hiss alerted the others. Hoods shifted as the servants of Morgion turned to see what had so startled their companion. The acolytes quickly retreated at the sight of an armed knight, but the Nightmaster held his ground.

"Have you come for your companion, Knight of Solamnia? Come and take him . . . or join him, perhaps. Morgion will be doubly pleased, yes." The cloaked figure held out his hands, presumably to show he had no weapon.

Rennard stepped forward, his eyes on the Nightmaster.

A cloud of dust shot forth from the hand of the cult leader. Rennard stopped. The assassins leaned forward in expectation, awaiting the horrible death that soon would come to the knight.

He did not need to look down to see that the poison had ended up settling on the ground beneath his feet. "I am beyond your deadly trick, mortal. The poison dust affects only those who still draw breath. I am long past that."

He stepped closer, enabling them, even in the dim light of Solinari, to see him clearly.

Not entirely certain whether what they saw was truly what they saw, two of the acolytes drew daggers. If the blades were as Rennard recalled, each was coated with one of the cult's concoctions.

The nearest thrust his dagger into the ghost's throat. The weapon found no substance.

The acolyte dropped his dagger, turned, and fled. Another joined him.

"Who are you, phantom?" the Nightmaster demanded.

"One who knows your ways, servant of Morgion. One who once went by the name Rennard."

His name meant nothing to the acolytes who dared to remain, but the Nightmaster reacted with glee. "Rennard—still called Oathbreaker by the knighthood! He has sent you to me as a sign! Our work has not been in vain. Our Lord Morgion has not abandoned us after all! The lies that the gods left Krynn have been disproved! All our sacrifices, all the lives we have sent to our lord, have at last won his notice again!" He eyed Dornay's still form with pleasure. "We must do something special for you, Sir Knight."

Rennard had visions of more and more sacrifices made in the name of Morgion . . . all deaths for which he would be accountable.

More shadows to haunt him.

"I do not come to you . . . but *for* you!" Acting instinctively, his anger deluding him into believing he was flesh and blood, Rennard leapt at the unsuspecting Nightmaster, grappling for the man's throat.

The ghost's hand touched cloth and flesh.

The discovery was so shocking that he almost lost his grip on the Nightmaster. The man's hood fell back as the ghost dragged his captive forward. His pale, ravaged face was almost as horrible as the ghost's, but Rennard was well used to such sights from when he had been one of them. Slowly and carefully, he spoke, his voice as chill as death. "There is no Morgion. The god of disease has indeed fled us." The ghost felt his pain ease. "There will be no more sacrifices."

The leader of the cultists shivered and, at first, the ghost thought that the chills were from fright. Then he saw the man sweat, saw the patches of inflamed skin that gave the scarlet plague its name.

Rennard had transmitted his accursed disease to the Nightmaster . . . and like a flame on dry kindling, it was spreading rapidly.

"Please!" the man begged. He knew what was happening. No one understands poison better than the poisoner. "Let me go, before it's too late!"

A grim satisfaction filled Rennard. "You wanted Morgion. Here is his legacy. You should be happy, Nightmaster."

He threw the infected cultist into the remaining acolytes, who were staring, frozen in fear. They fell together in a jumbled heap, the servants frantically trying to separate themselves from their stricken leader. It was too late for them, however. They were infected the moment the Nightmaster touched them, for such was the intensity of the malady the gods had granted to the traitorous knight after his death. For the only time he could recall, Rennard was grimly pleased at the rapid speed of the plague. He doubted any of them would live to see morning.

During the chaos, Erik Dornay woke from the blow that had laid him unconscious. He stared at the screaming acolytes, then his unholy companion.

"Rennard?" he asked, still dazed from the blow.

The Nightmaster rose and took a step toward Erik. The ghost shifted, standing in front of the assassin. The Nightmaster stumbled back. His remaining followers ran away. When the Nightmaster tried to join them, however, he found the spirit before him. Rennard drew his sword.

"I regret I cannot leave you to the fate you deserve. I can take no chances, mortal."

The ghost knight thrust his blade into the man's chest. The sword proved very solid.

"Why did you kill him?" Erik asked, struggling to free himself from his bonds. "His face . . . he looked as if he was dying already."

Rennard glanced down at the body. "The others will run back to their temple, beg Morgion to save them. He won't. He can't. When they die, the scarlet plague dies, for such is its way. This one, however, would serve his master to the end. Nightmasters are chosen from among the most fanatical of Morgion's followers. If I had let him go, he might have tried to spread the curse to those poor souls in the camp."

"You . . . you have my gratitude for saving me."

"Huma saved you, not I," Rennard remarked, thinking of the song. Sheathing his blade, he moved to Erik's side and tried to take one of the young knight's daggers in order to cut the ropes. His hand passed through it. Dornay managed to free himself.

Rising, Erik stared at the body of the cleric, then back in the direction of the refugee camp. "You were right. These fiends were trailing them."

"Yes, Morgion's toadies were sacrificing them one at a time in the hope of calling the Faceless One back. Come now, there is something I want to show you."

"What?"

"Your friend's murderers."

On foot, it took several minutes to reach the outskirts of the encampment. Someone evidently had heard the short, fierce struggle, for the party had gathered close around the fire. Four of the more fit were keeping watch. Women clutched whimpering children. Men held sticks of wood for weapons. All looked terrified.

"There they are," Rennard said. "What will you do?"

"They look . . ." Erik hesitated.

"Hopeless? Desperate? In the Dragon Wars, I saw many who looked that way."

Erik eyed him. "You're asking me to go to them, aid them? But the danger is past!"

"If the cultists do not get them, then bandits or starvation will. Look at them, Erik Dornay. They need your pity, not your hatred. Huma would have tried to help them. He would have understood that a moment of despair turned them into an inhuman mob. His duty would have been to restore their humanity."

The Knight of the Rose still hesitated. "If I go to them, they'll attack me. I'll be forced to kill them! I am not Huma! He was a—"

"Huma was a man." Rennard saw movement and glanced around. The shadows seemed to thicken, come to life.

"What's wrong?" Dornay began to move closer. Rennard kept him at bay with his sword.

"Come no closer. I have already risked you once. If I can spread my curse to those curs, then I can spread it to you."

Erik stepped back with great reluctance.

The shadows, Rennard saw, were taking shape and form.

"Now it is time for you to go, Erik Dornay."

"But what about you?"

Rennard heard no whispering yet, but he was certain the eyes of the hunters burned into him. The ghost readied his blade and moved farther from the encampment. "I must attend to matters of my own."

"Matters . . ." Erik looked into the shadows. "Paladine save us! What are they?"

"I told you that even ghosts may be haunted by ghosts, Erik Dornay. These are mine—the shadows of every knight who died by my hand or by my actions. They cannot rest, and so I cannot."

"What will they do?" the mortal whispered in awe.

"Pursue me, fight me, and kill me. Then, when their need for vengeance is sated, I will rise, and the entire tragedy will happen all over again."

"That's monstrous!"

"It is justice. Even I know that."

"What can I do?" Dornay began to reach for his sword.

"Help those people."

"I mean for you!"

The ghost laughed. "So I now have two champions—you and Huma! Both trying to save me from what I am!" Rennard shook his head. "There is one thing you can do for me, my . . . my friend. Go to those you sought to kill. Let me see that I have accomplished my task."

Dornay looked at the shadows of long-dead knights, gathering to attack, then at their intended victim. At last, he straightened and brought his sword up to his face in the knight's salute. "I will pray for you, Sir Rennard."

The shadows still had not moved. They, too, were waiting. "Once you depart, do not look back," Rennard said. "I would prefer it that way."

Erik nodded and turned away. The ghost watched, his own renewed pain and the nearing shadows forgotten. The young Solamnian moved through the woods and, without pause, entered the camp. The people were frightened, staring at him uncertainly. Those who held weapons waited for the knight to attack.

The Knight of the Rose planted his sword in the earth and

held up a hand in a sign of peace. He said something that Rennard could not hear, but which caused the refugees to lower their weapons.

One of them stepped forward. Erik held out his hand. The man grasped the knight's hand thankfully.

Rennard nodded, satisfied. He turned away from the mortals to face the shadows who waited for him, across a stream. Fog began to envelop him, and he knew that his brief journey to Krynn soon would be only a memory.

Had it all been coincidence? Or did the gods, who had left Krynn, still have ways of watching over those who interested them?

The hunters waited, even when the sounds of mortal beings faded away in the fog. Rennard tensed. Around him, the fog gathered thicker.

"Why do you wait?" he shouted. "Why now?"

They made no answer. Even their whispers were preferable to the silence, he realized.

The sound of sword striking shield came from behind him. Rennard turned and stepped into the stream.

Water splashed. His boot struck the surface and sank in.

Rennard stared at the water. He dropped his sword and fell to his knees. Fearfully, the ghostly knight reached down.

Small ripples spread out from his fingers. The tips of his fingers *touched* the stream. Rennard thrust his hands into the water. He cupped his hands together.

His own words came back to him. *What must I do to earn even a sip of water?*

Rennard brought the liquid to his parched lips and drank. For the first time since his death, the eternal fever that burned within him cooled.

Rennard lowered his hands into the stream again. Another sip. He needed another sip.

This time, however, all was as it had been. The stream flowed through his fingers as if they were not there . . . which they were not.

The shadows moved. He had been granted his drink of water. Now, it was time to return to the Abyss.

Krynn faded completely then. The stream disappeared

before his eyes. In its place lay the familiar plain of death.

Rennard grabbed his sword and began to back away from the oncoming knights. Oddly, he did not feel as afraid as before, even knowing that this flight, like so many others, would end with his downfall.

Another question came to his mind, one that he often had asked before without hope.

"I earned the sip of water. Will I earn my rest as well?"

The shadows closed in. Rennard thought he heard the distant strains of a song.

SONG OF HUMA

Tracy Hickman

Sularus Humah durvey	The Honor of Huma survives
Karamnes Humah durvey	The Glory of Huma survives
Draco!	Dragons, hear!
Solamnis na fai tarus	Solamnic breath is taken
Mithas!	Life; hear!
Est paxum kudak draco	My sword is broken of Dragons
Draco-Humah	Dragon-Huma
oparu sac	temper me now
Draco-Humah	Dragon-Huma
coni parl ai fam	Grant me grace and love
Saat mas Solamnis	When the heart of the Knighthood
vegri nough	wavers in doubt
Coni est Lor Tarikan	Grant me this, Warrior Lord
Sularus Humah	Honor is Huma
Karram Humah	Glory is Huma
Solamnis Humah durvey	Solamnic Knight Huma survives
Karamnes Humah durvey	Glorified Huma survives
Mithas!	Life; hear!
Humah dix karai!	Huma's death calls me!
Ex dix!	His death!
Oparu est dix!	Temper me with such death!
Solamnis Lor Alan Paladine!	Paladine, lord god of knights!
Humah mithas est mithasah!	Huma's life is all our lives!
Draco-Humah durvey!	Dragon-Huma survives!

Ogre Unaware

Dan Parkinson

Through most of a day—from when the sun was high overhead until now, when the sun was gone behind the dagger-spire peaks of the Khalkist Mountains and night birds heralded the first stars glimpsed above—through those hours and those miles he had trailed the puny ones, thinking they might lead him to others of their kind. Now they had stopped. Now they were settling in on the slope below him, stopping for the night, and his patience was at an end.

Crouching low, blending his huge silhouette with the brush of the darkening hillside, he heard their voices drifting up to him—thin, human voices as frail as the bodies from which they issued, as fragile as the bones within those bodies, which he could crush with a squeeze of his hand. He heard the strike of flint, smelled the wispy smoke of their tinder, and saw the first flickers of the fire they were building—a fire to guard them against the night.

His chuckle was a rumble of contempt, deep within his huge chest. It was a campfire to heat their meager foods and to protect them from whatever might be out there, watching. Humans! His chuckle became a deep, rumbling growl. Like all of the lesser races, the small, frail races, they put their trust in a handful of fire and thought they were safe.

Safe from me? His wide mouth spread in a sneering grin, exposing teeth like sharpened chisels. Contempt burned deep within his eyes. Safe? No human was safe from Krog.

Krog knew how to deal with humans—and with anyone else who ventured into his territory. He found them, tracked them down, and killed them. Sometimes they carried something he could use, sometimes not, but it was always a pleasure to see their torment as he crushed and mangled them, a joy to hear their screams.

There were a dozen or more in the party below him. Four were armed males, the rest a motley, ragged group bound together by lengths of rope tied around their necks. Slaves, Krog knew. The remnants of some human village ransacked by slavers. There were many such groups roaming the countryside in these days—slavers and their prey. Small groups like this, usually, though sometimes the groups came together in large camps, to trade and to export their prizes to distant markets. Those, the big groups, he enjoyed most, but now he was tired of waiting.

He studied them; his cunning eyes counted their shadows in the dusk below. The slaves were grouped just beyond the little fire, but it was their captors he watched most closely, marking exactly where each of the armed ones settled around their fire. Experience had taught him to deal first with the armed ones. He carried the scars of sword and axe cuts, from times when armed humans had managed a slash or two before he finished them. The cuts had been annoying. Better, he had learned, to deal with the weapon-bearers quickly. Then he could finish off the others in any way that amused him.

For a long time now, ever since the beginning of the strangenesses that some called omens, humans and other small races had been wandering into the territory that Krog considered his—the eastern slopes of the Khalkist Mountains. Chaotic times had fallen upon the plains beyond, and the people of those plains were in turmoil. Krog knew little of that, cared less. Every day, humans and others were drifting westward toward the Khalkists, some fleeing, some in pursuit . . . and they all were sport for Krog.

Below him on the slope, the humans' campfire blazed brightly, and the humans gathered around it. He watched, and repressed the urge to rush down at them, to hear their first screams of terror. Let them have a minute or two to stare into their precious fire. Let them night-blind themselves so they would not see him until he was among them. It would make his attack easier, with less likelihood of any of them fleeing into the darkness.

Stare into the light, he thought, licking wide, scarred lips with keen anticipation of the pleasures to come. Stare into the fire, and . . .

He raised his head; his grin faded. He stared into another fire, a fire that sprang from a glowing coal in the overhead sky and grew until it seemed to fill half the sky. Searing light far brighter than firelight, brighter than the light of day, billowed out and out until the entire eastern sky was ablaze with it. Sudden winds howled high above, shrieks and bellows of anguish as though the very world were screaming. The radiance aloft grew and intensified, instant by instant, a blinding blaze of sky in which something huge, something enormous and hideous, coalesced, spinning and shrieking, and plunged downward to meet the eastern horizon in a blinding blast of fury.

Stunned and half blinded, he stood on the slope, barely aware of the sounds all around him—birds taking terrified flight, small creatures scurrying past, the screams and shouts of the terrified humans just down the slope. Panic and fear, everywhere . . . then silence. A silence as complete as the recesses of a cavern seemed to grow from the world itself as the brilliant, distant light dimmed beyond the horizon. A slow, agonizing dimming, like the reluctant ebbing of a hundred sunsets, all at once descended.

Out of the silence came a sound that was not a sound as much as a tingling in the air, a mounting of invisible tensions. Past the eastern horizon, where the immense flare still lingered, lightning danced and black clouds like mountain ranges marched up the sky, one after another. The inaudible sounds grew and grew, becoming a torrent of vibration that strummed the winds and made rocks dance on the slope. In the distance, gouts of brilliance spewed upward, rising above the clouds to shower the eastern world with marching storms of fire.

Shouting and screaming, terrified creatures rushed past him, the largest among them less than half his size and wide-eyed with fear. The humans from the slope below, slavers and enslaved, fled together in panic. They ran within arm's reach of him, and he barely noticed them as they passed. Dazed and dazzled, he stared out across a landscape gone insane, a landscape where distant mountains writhed and shattered and sank from view, where serpentine brilliance danced in a fire-lit sky gone black with climbing smoke, where the horizon heaved upward like a tidal wave, rushing toward him.

Winds like hammers swooped down from aloft and struck him with a force that sent him tumbling backward, arms and legs flailing helplessly as oven-hot gusts rolled him uphill a dozen yards and dropped him into a heaving pit. His club was wrenched from his fingers and flew skyward, carried by raging winds. Struggling, fighting for balance, he got his feet under him and climbed, drawing himself over the edge of the chasm just as it closed with stone jaws behind him.

In a bedlam of howling, furnace winds, shattering stone, and deep, bone-jarring rumbles from beneath the ground, he lay gasping for breath, then raised stricken eyes as the nearer mountains to the west began to explode.

Huge boulders rose into the sky like grains of flung sand, then showered back down onto the slopes, bounding and rolling downward, bringing other debris with them as they came.

He struggled upward, dodging and dancing, flinging himself this way and that as monstrous rock fragments shot past, shaking the ground with their force. A tumbling boulder the size of an elven mansion bore down on him, and he flung himself aside, hugging the ground as it hit, bounced and sailed over, missing him by inches. He raised himself and turned to watch it go, and something hit him from behind—something massive and stone-hard that smashed against his head, bowling him over. Chaos rang in his ears, and he saw the hard, shaking ground rise to meet him . . . then saw nothing more.

Where he fell, shards of stone skidded and bounced, piling up in drifts around him. After a long time, the stone-falls slowed and stopped, and a creeping, gurgling torrent of mud and silt from ravaged slopes above rolled down to bury the lesser debris. He was not aware of being buried. He wasn't aware of anything now. The flowing soil found him, covered him and passed on, and there was nothing there to see.

With the winds came clouds, and with the clouds came rain—torrents of rain washing over a ravaged land, rain and more rain, scouring channels and gullies in the sediment among the tumbled stones.

The rains came and went and came again, and between storms the ravaged land lay in silence.

* * * * *

On a caprock hillside, where scoured stone rose in stacked layers above the climbing slopes, evening light made a patchwork of shadows, hiding indentations in the stone cliffs, camouflaging them from prying eyes. Here on the south face of the cliff, low in its surface, one of those somber shadows might have seemed slightly different from those around it, to the practiced eye—darker and deeper, the opening of a cavern that opened to other caverns beyond.

Screened from view by jutting rock, the spot was just the sort of place the combined clans of Bulp had been seeking for weeks—a place that could be This Place until it was time to move on to Another Place.

And, seeking it, they had found it and moved right in. Furtively, they entered, scouted around, were satisfied, and reported the find to their leader.

With great ceremony, then, His Royalness Gorge III, Highbulp by Choice and Lord Protector of This Place and Who Knew How Many Other Places, made his own brief tour of inspection, strutting here and there, looking at this and that, muttering under his breath and in general behaving like a Highbulp.

Various of his subjects trailed after him, occasionally stumbling over one another.

At a wall of rock, Gorge stopped and raised his candle. "What this?" he demanded.

At his shoulder, his wife and consort, the Lady Drule, peered at the wall and said, "Rock. Cave have rock walls. Wouldn't be cave without walls."

Old Hunch, the Grand Notioner of the Bulp Clan, padded forward, leaned on his mop-handle staff, to ask, "What Highbulp's problem?"

"Want to know what is that." The Lady Drule pointed at the wall.

"That wall," Hunch said. "Rock wall. So what?"

"Highbulp doin' inspec . . . explo . . . lookin' 'round," Gorge proclaimed. He moistened a finger, touched the wall, then tasted his finger. "Rock wall," he decided. "Cave got rock wall this side."

"Other sides, too," Hunch pointed out. "Caves do."

Satisfied, Gorge wandered away from the wall, raised his eyes to look critically at the rock ceiling, and tripped over a bump in the rock floor. He sprawled flat and lost his candle.

"Highbulp clumsy oaf," Drule muttered, helping him to his feet. Someone returned his candle to him, and he looked around, found a foot-high ledge, and sat on it. "Bring Royal Stuff," he ordered.

Several of his subjects scouted around, found the tattered sack that was the Holder of Royal Stuff, and brought it to him. Digging into it, throwing aside various objects—a rabbit skull, a broken spearhead, a battered cup—Gorge drew forth a broken antler nearly as tall as he was. An elk antler, it once had been part of a set, attached to a tanned elk hide. The hide and the other antler were long gone, but he still had this one, and he raised it like a scepter.

"This place okay for This Place," Gorge III decreed, "so this place This Place." The ceremony ended, he tossed aside the elk antler. "Get stew goin'," he ordered. " 'Bout time to eat."

The Lady Drule stepped aside to confer with other ladies of the clan. There were shrugs and shaking heads. She paused in thought, gazing into the murky reaches of the cavern.

"Rats," she said.

Gorge glanced around. "What?"

"Rats. Need meat for stew. Time for hunt rats."

Within moments, small figures scurried all around the cave and into the tunnels leading from it. Their shouts and chatter, the sounds of scuffing, scrambling feet, the thuds of people falling down and the oaths of those who stumbled over them, all receded into the reaches of the cavern.

Gorge looked distinctly irritated. "Where ever'body go?"

"Huntin' rats," the Lady Drule explained.

"Rats," Gorge grumbled. No longer the center of everyone's attention, he felt abandoned and surly. He wanted to sulk, but sulking usually put him to sleep, and he was too hungry to sleep.

It was a characteristic of the race called Aghar, whom most races called gully dwarves: Once a thing was begun, simply keep on doing it. When at rest, they tended to stay at rest. But once in motion, they kept moving. One of the strongest drives of any gully dwarf was simple inertia.

Thus the rat hunt, once begun, went on and on. The cave held plenty of rats, the hunting was good, and the gully dwarves were enjoying the sport . . . and exploring further and further as they hunted.

Stew, however, was in progress. Seeing that her husband was becoming more and more testy, the Lady Drule had rounded up a squadron of other ladies when the first rats were brought in. Now they had a good fire going, and a stew of gathered greens, wild onions, turnips and fresh rat meat was beginning to bubble.

Gorge didn't wait for the rest to come to supper. He dug into one of the clan packs, found a stew bowl that once had been the codpiece on some Tall warrior's armor, and helped himself.

He was only halfway through his second serving when a group of gully dwarves came racing in from the shadows at the rear of the cave and jostled to a stop before him.

"Highbulp come look!" one said, excitedly. "We find . . . ah . . . " He turned to another. "What we find?"

"Other cave," the second one reminded him.

"Right," the first continued. "Highbulp come see other cave. Got good stuff."

"What kind good stuff?" Gorge demanded, stifling a belch.

The first turned to the second. "What kind good stuff?"

"Cave stuff," the second reminded him. "Pretty stuff."

"Cave stuff, Highbulp," the first reported.

"Better be good," Gorge snapped. "Good 'nough for inter . . . int . . . butt in when Highbulp tryin' to eat?"

"Good stuff," several of them assured him.

"What kind stuff? Gold? Clay? Bats? Pyr . . . pyr . . . pretty rocks? What?" Another resounding belch caught him, this one unstifled.

The first among them turned to the second. "What?"

"Pretty rocks," the second reminded. "Highbulp come see!"

"Rats," Gorge muttered. Those around him seemed so excited—there were dozens of them now—that he set down his codpiece bowl, picked up his candle, and went to see what they had found. A parade of small figures carrying candles headed for the rear of the cavern—the guides leading, Gorge following them, and a horde of others following him. Most of them—latecomers on the scene—didn't know where they were going or why, but they followed anyway. Far back in the cavern, a crack in the rock led into an eroded tunnel, which wound away, curving upward.

As he entered the crack, Gorge belched mightily. "Too much turnips in stew," he muttered.

By ones and threes and fives, the gully dwarves entered and disappeared from the sight of those remaining.

The Lady Drule and several other ladies were just coming back from a side chamber, where they had been preparing sleeping quarters. At sight of the last candles disappearing into the tunnel, Drule asked, "Now what goin' on? Where Highbulp?"

Hunch was inspecting the stew. He looked up and shrugged. "Somebody find somethin'. Highbulp go see." He tasted the stew. "Good," he said. He tasted again, then turned away, philosophically. "Life like stew," he said. "Fulla rats an' turnips."

The Lady Drule glanced after him, mildly bewildered, then glanced around the cavern. Only a few of the males were there, some asleep, some more interested in eating than in following the Highbulp around, and two or three who had started on the trek into the tunnel, then lost interest and turned back.

She could see them clearly, she noticed. The cavern suddenly was very well lighted, light flooding in from the entrance and growing brighter by the moment. Near the fire, a sleeping gully dwarf rolled over, sat up and blinked, shading his eyes. "Huh!" he said. "Mornin' already?"

The light grew, its color changing from angry red to orange, to yellow and then to brilliant white, nearly blinding them, even in the shadows of the cavern. Other sleeping souls awoke and gaped about them.

"What happenin'?" the Lady Drule wondered.

Hunch returned with a bowl and filled it with stew. "Gettin' lighter," he said, absently. Abruptly there was a howling at the entrance, and a gust of wind like an oven blast swept into the cave. The stew in Hunch's bowl seemed to come alive. It spewed up and out, showering gravy halfway across the chamber. The bowl followed, wrenched from the Grand Notioner's grip, and Hunch followed that, rolling and shouting, his mop-handle flailing.

Everywhere, then, gully dwarves were scurrying for cover—stumbling, falling, rolling, fleeing from the brilliant, howling entrance. They scurried into crevices, rolled into holes, dodged behind erosion pillars . . . and abruptly there was silence. The bright light still flooded in from the entrance, but now not quite so blinding. The roaring wind died away and the howling diminished to a low, continuing rumble almost below hearing.

Silence . . . then the rumbling increased. The floor of the cavern seemed to dance, vibrating to the sound. Bits of stone and showers of dust fell from the walls, and chunks of rock parted from the ceiling to crash downward. A rattling, bouncing flood of gravel buried the stew pot and the fire, and there was a new sound above the rumbling—the high, keening wail of stone splitting.

The cavern's entrance collapsed with a roar. Tons of broken stone slid across the opening, burying it, sealing it. Within, the rumbling and the rattle of rockfall were a chaos of noise, but now the noise built in darkness, for there was no light to see.

*   *   *   *   *

The tunnel from the back of the cavern called This Place wound deep into the capstone of the hill, bending and turning, always angling upward. His Royalness Gorge III, Highbulp and leader of clans, was somewhat to the rear of his expedition when the rest of them rounded a bend in the rising tunnel and saw the light ahead. Somewhere along the way, Gorge had decided that his feet were sore, and had taken to limping whenever he thought about it.

But when he heard the shouts and exclamations ahead of him—cries of, "Hey! This pretty!" and "Nice stuff, huh?" and "Where that light comin' from?"—he forgot his limp and hurried to see what was going on. Rounding a bend, he found a traffic tie-up in a well-lighted cave, where the light seemed to grow brighter moment by moment. The first arrivals there had stopped in awe; others had piled into them from behind, and several had fallen down. Wading around and through tangles of his subjects, Gorge pushed past them and stopped. The cavern was a wide oval, an erosion chamber where ancient seeps had collected, and at the top of it was a hole that opened to the sky . . . a sky that suddenly was as bright as day.

"What goin' on here?" Gorge demanded. "What light through yonder . . . yon . . . why hole all lit up?"

"Dunno," several of his subjects explained. Then one of them pointed aside. "See, Highbulp? Pretty rocks."

He looked, and his eyes widened. One entire wall of the cavern glistened like brilliant gold, layer upon layer of bright embedment shining in the dark stone. "Wow," the Highbulp breathed . . . and belched. As though echoing him, the whole cavern shuddered and rumbled.

"Way too much turnips," Gorge decided, as those around him looked at him in admiration. He turned his attention again to the wall of pyrites. He moistened a finger, rubbed it against a glittering lode, then licked it. "Real nice," he said. "Good pyr . . . pyr . . . pretty rocks."

Spying an exceptionally bright nodule, he reached for it. The cavern belched again—a deep, rumbling roll of sound—and the node fell loose in his hand. Gorge belched in surprise, and the cavern echoed him. The light in This Place had dimmed slightly, and suddenly became murky with dust. Gravel fell and rattled around them as the whole cave shook in a spasm.

"Hiccups?" someone asked.

"Not me," the Highbulp declared. "What goin' on here?"

As though the mountain had given a stone belch, the cavern vibrated and began to shake. Gully dwarves danced around in confusion, stumbling and falling over one another. The spasm subsided slightly, then came again, this time far more violently. Fallen gully dwarves piled up on the gravel-strewn floor, and the Highbulp was thrown head over heels, to land atop them.

" 'Nough of this!" he shrieked. "Ever'body run like crazy!"

They would have, gladly, but a rumbling like approaching thunder growled all around them. Debris from above pelted down on them, and the cavern's floor heaved and rose, pitching them into the center, where they piled up in a writhing, struggling mass with the Highbulp buried somewhere within.

Then, with a tremendous roar, the hole in the ceiling split wide, the cavern's floor heaved upward, the very world seemed to belch mightily, and the hilltop above erupted in a gout of gravel, pyrite fragments, dust and tumbling gully dwarves.

The Highbulp found himself airborne, and shrieked in terror, then he was falling, and thudded onto hard ground beneath a smoky red sky. Someone landed on top of him, and others all around. For a time he lay dazed, then he raised eyes that went round with wonder. He was on a hilltop, surrounded by other stunned gully dwarves, and all around was confusion. In the distance to the east, the horizon and the sky above it were a cauldron of blazing, writhing flames, where smoke and black clouds marched across a howling sky. And in the opposite direction, to the west, mountains were exploding.

"Wha' happen?" several voices echoed one another.

"Cave all turnippy," someone said. "Burp us out."

For long minutes, the ground beneath them shook and danced, and they hugged its surface in panic. The sky rained dust and cinders on them, and huge winds howled overhead. Then there came a lull, the quaking subsided, and dark raindrops thudded into the dust around them.

One by one, the gully dwarves got to their feet. They crowded around the Highbulp, making it almost impossible for him to get his feet under him.

"Back off," he growled. Those nearest backed away, creating a ripple effect in the crowd that knocked some of those on the outside down again. Gorge stood up, tried to dust himself off, and a large raindrop splattered on his nose. He looked around at his gathered followers, squinting in the darkness that had replaced the brilliant light.

Lightning split the sky overhead, illuminating everything, and Gorge's latest belch turned to a shriek of panic. All around them were Talls—humans—armed men with swords and axes that glistened in the storm light—armed, determined human slavers . . . and there was nowhere for the gully dwarves to run.

* * * * *

The rains came and went and came again, scouring a savaged land that never again would be as it had been before. Gray morning light shone on silent chaos, a land rent and ripped and devastated, a landscape of desolation, where huge boulders lay scattered upon silt-buried slopes, a place of sundered silence in a land torn and rent by cataclysm.

Mountains no longer had the dagger-spire silhouettes of yesterday, but instead presented cratered and tumbled faces to the dawn. Their slopes were strewn with boulders. Jagged shards jutted like teeth from the pitted flows of settling topsoil scoured from ravaged ranges above.

On one such slope a searching falcon circled near the surface, drawn by scurrying rodents among the stones. The bird spiraled downward, gliding just above the stones, then beat its wings and darted away when something moved in a place where nothing should be.

The falcon beat away, and behind it a grotesque, recumbent figure stirred. Half buried in silt, it had seemed only a fragment of thrown rock—until it moved. It stirred, shifted a portion of itself upward, and drying mud sloughed away to reveal a large, rounded head surmounting great, knotted shoulders. It raised its head and opened puzzled eyes, peered this way and that for a moment, then pushed its huge torso upward on massive arms, and the rest of it became visible. Legs the size of tree trunks bent and flexed, and the creature paused on hands and knees to look around again, then shifted to a sitting position.

Big, calloused hands went to its head, and it closed its eyes in momentary pain. A growl like distant thunder escaped it. Its grimace revealed teeth like yellow chisels, in a mouth that was wide and cruel.

The jolt of pain passed, and the creature sighed, opening its eyes again. Something had happened. Something inconceivable that seemed at the edge of memory but was just beyond recall. In a muttering voice as deep as gravel in a well, it faltered with words. "Wha . . . what? What happen? Where?" Wincing at the effort, it tried to remember . . . and could not. Only a word came to memory, one significant word. A name? Yes, a name.

His own name. Krog.

Sore and shaking, he stood. Small, unseen things scurried away among the tumbled stones.

Krog. "I . . . am Krog," he muttered. It was true. He knew that, but nothing more. His name was Krog, but what had happened to him? Where was he? And *why*?

"Who am I?" he whispered. "Krog . . . what is Krog? *Who* is Krog?"

The battered landscape told him nothing. In the distance, where dawning grew, were smoke and haze. In the other direction were high mountains, but they meant nothing to him. Everywhere he looked, he saw a bleak and sundered landscape that was the only landscape he knew because he remembered no others.

It was as though he had just been born, and abruptly he felt a terrible loneliness—a need for . . . something . . . for belonging. There must be someone somewhere, someone to care for him. Someone to teach him, to help him understand. There *had* to be someone.

He turned full circle, big hooded eyes scanning the distance. Nothing moved. Nothing anywhere suggested that there was another living creature other than himself.

"Not right," he muttered, the words a low growl that came from deep within a great chest. "Not just Krog. Not all alone. Has to be . . . somebody else here."

He started walking on unsteady legs. All directions were the same, so he went the way he had been facing, with the mountains to his left and the gray, hazed morning to his right. Ahead was a caprock hill, and he headed toward it. Remembering nothing except his name, knowing nothing except that he had awakened from nowhere and was headed to a place, aware of nothing except his aching head and the driving need not to be alone, Krog went looking for someone.

* * * * *

"Even the mountains are different," one of the men said, pointing with a coiled whip at the distant peaks standing against a high gray sky. "What in the names of all the gods could have done this?"

Those nearest him shrugged and shook their heads. Men of the tribe of Shalimin—reviled by those who knew them as "the raiders," or "marauders," or, simply, "the slavers"— were men who knew the ways of the wild, not the ways of the world. The changes they saw now in that world were abrupt and massive; the night of change had been terrifying. Yet, whatever had done it, now it seemed to be past. And if sawtooth crags now stood where before had been dagger-spire peaks, if what had been meadows now were fields of strewn stone, if entire forests that had stood yesterday now lay fallen and desolate, it was not theirs to worry about.

It was over. The world was still here, and they still walked on it, and it was time to regroup.

"You!" one of them shouted, brandishing a whip. "Back in line and stay there!" Ahead of him, a small, terrified creature scurried back into its place in the ragged line proceeding northward. "Gully dwarves!" He spat. "We won't show much profit from this haul, Daco."

"Better than nothing, though," his companion said. "They can be sold for simple work. They're strong enough to tote and fetch."

"They won't bring a copper a head." Daco sneered. "Slave buyers know about gully dwarves. They're unreliable, they're clumsy, and they can't be taught anything useful."

"Devious, I've heard," someone added. "I wouldn't want one for a slave of my own. Always plotting and scheming. They'd be a danger to have around if they could concentrate on anything for more than a minute or two. You, there! Get on your feet and walk! Nobody said you could stop and sleep!" He turned to the flanker opposite him. "See? That's what I'm talking about. The one with the curly beard there . . . just like that, he was taking time out for a nap."

The motley assemblage made its way northward across a strange and tumbled land, a dozen armed men driving several dozen gully dwarves. The little creatures—barely half the size of their captors—stumbled in an erratic double line, each bound to those in front and behind by a length of cord tied around his neck. The men surrounded them, herded them like cattle.

The slavers had been two separate parties only days before, and each party had been successful. Good slaves for the market. Human slaves—men, women and children. Then the Cataclysm—whatever it was—had occurred. Each party had lost its captives in the ensuing chaos, and now they had nothing to show for their expeditions except these pitiful gully dwarves they had chanced across.

Little enough to show, when they arrived at the main camp. Still, the gully dwarves were better than nothing.

The line topped a ridge, and they looked out on yet another scene of chaos. A forest of tall conifers once had lined the narrow valley. Now, hardly a tree was standing. The valley was a patchwork maze of fallen timbers, scattered this way and that as though some giant thing had trod there and paused to scuff its feet.

The men stared at the scene in wonder, then movement

caught their eyes. "Ah," Daco breathed. "There. Look."

Among the fallen timbers were people, a ragged line of them making their way northward. Even from the ridge top, it was obvious that they were refugees . . . from something. There were at least a dozen of them, maybe more, and among them were women and children.

No more than two or three carried weapons of any sort.

"Well, well." Daco grinned. "It seems our luck has just improved. That lot will bring a fine price at the pens."

*　*　*　*　*

This Place was a mess. Whatever had happened was through happening, but the entire cavern was a litter of fallen stone, gravel dumps, and dust. Holding candles high, the Lady Drule and the others with her poked about, seeing what could be salvaged. There wasn't much: a few iron stew bowls, Hunch's mop-handle staff, about half of the Highbulp's prized elk antler, a few bits of fabric, a reaver's maul, a battered stew pot, a stick used for stirring . . . odds and ends. Most of what the clans had owned was either destroyed or lost.

The Lady Drule shook her head sadly. "Gonna need to forage soon," she said. " 'Bout outta stuff."

She wandered toward the entrance—or where the entrance had been—and looked at a mighty wall of fallen stone. There was no way out. The entrance was sealed.

Behind her, a whining voice said, "So much for that."

She turned to see the Grand Notioner, leaning on his mop handle. "Guess so," she said.

"So what we do now?"

"Dunno." Lady Drule shrugged. "All go find Highbulp, I guess. Let him decide."

"Decide what?" Hunch frowned. "Highbulp dumb as a post. What bright idea he gonna have?"

"Highbulp our glorious leader," Drule pointed out. "He think of somethin'."

"Hmph!"

He followed along, though, with all the rest, when the Lady Drule set out in search of the Highbulp. The last she had seen of him, he and most of the other males had been disappearing into a crack in the back of the cave. The search began there.

Beyond the crack was an erosion seep, a damp, winding tunnel that led away into the hill, curving beyond sight, heading generally upward. Drule started treading along it, and there was a clamor behind her. "What happen?" She turned to look.

"Nothin'," someone said. "Somebody fall down."

"Come on," the Lady Drule urged them. "Keep up."

* * * * *

A smoke-hazed sun had crossed much of the sky, and the hot, searing winds from the east had changed to cool, whispering winds drifting down from the shattered peaks to the west. Time and miles were behind Krog since his awakening, but still he had found no one.

It was as though the world were an empty place, and he the only being on it. Confusion and sheer loneliness drove him on, though his search seemed more and more hopeless.

Then, atop a barren caprock hill, he heard voices. People—somewhere—talking among themselves. With a whimper of sheer glee, Krog searched for the source of the sounds, his eyes alight, his ears twitching. He saw no one, but after a time he heard the voices again and found where they came from. Amidst a pile of rubble was a hole in the ground, and somewhere below were voices, coming nearer. He knelt, peered into the darkness. He could see nothing. He tried to lower himself into the hole, but only his head would go in. The hole was far too small for his shoulders. He backed out, sniffling in frustration, and heard the voices again—various voices, close enough now that he could almost make out the words.

Knowing nothing else to do, Krog lay beside the hole, listening. The sound soothed and comforted him. He was not alone after all. He sniffled again, and tears glistened in his eyes as he closed them.

* * * * *

The old seep wound upward, and upward again, and the gully dwarves followed it, their candles casting weird shadows on the stone walls. It was slow going. Whatever had made the cavern shake and had sealed its entrance, had littered the tunnel with shards and slabs of broken rock. Footing was tricky, requiring more concentration than most of the Lady Drule's followers could maintain in a place with so many distractions—layers of fresh stone to be looked at and tasted, small, furry things to be noted in case there was time later for a rat hunt, and their own distorted shadows bobbing here and there.

As a result, the journey was punctuated with thuds and bumps, trips and falls, and a running commentary up and down the line:

"Look here! Pretty shine."

"What that over there? Dragon?"

"Not dragon, dummy, just bat shadow."

"Oops!" Thud.

"Hey, floor bouncy!"

"Not bouncy. You fall on me. Get off."

"Somethin' shiny there? Nope, just Bipp's eyes."

"Anybody bring stew?"

"Where we goin', anyway?"

"To find Highbulp."

"Find Highbulp? Why?"

"Dunno. Lady Drule say so."

Then, from the head of the line, "Sh!"

The Lady Drule had rounded a bend and saw light ahead. She stopped, and several of her followers bumped into her. "Sh!" she repeated.

Behind her, around the bend, someone complained, "Hunch! Get staff off my foot!" Then, "Hunch? Hunch! Wake up, get staff off my foot!"

There were sounds of a tussle, and the Grand Notioner's voice, "What? What goin' on?"

The Lady Drule turned, frowning. She put a finger to her lips. "Sh!"

This time the message was relayed back down the line, and there was silence. She turned again, peering toward the dim light ahead. The tunnel seemed to widen there, and something glistened. Raising her hand to keep the rest hushed, Drule crept forward. Another cavern was just ahead, its floor strewn with broken rock and glitters of pyrite, and the light came from overhead. She tiptoed into the open, peering around. The light was daylight and came from a hole in the ceiling. There was no sign of the Highbulp and his explorers, but among the glitters lay two or three candles, a forage pouch, and a shoe. The others had been here.

The Lady Drule's ears perked at a sound that was like faraway thunder—or someone snoring. It came from overhead, and her eyes brightened. "Gorge?" she called softly. "Highbulp, where you?"

"Lady Drule find Highbulp?" someone asked.

"Must be close," someone else suggested. "Sure sounds like him snorin'."

Drule looked up at the opening in the ceiling, then handed her candle to the one nearest her. "All wait here," she said. "Maybe they up there. I go see."

Clambering onto a pile of fallen stone, she found handholds on the stone wall and climbed toward the light. The opening above was small—about two feet across—but it was big enough for any gully dwarf to go through.

The Lady Drule climbed, then hoisted herself into the hole. The sound of snoring came again, very close. If that was Gorge snoring, he was outdoing himself. She had never heard even the Highbulp sleep so loudly.

With a final pull, she raised her head above the hole and looked around. She was on a hilltop littered with stone. Fragments and grotesque shapes were all around, and a particularly ugly large boulder blocked her view on one side. She raised herself from the hole, dusted herself off, and started to climb over the boulder, then stopped in confusion. It didn't *feel* like stone. As she bent to look at it more closely, the snore came again, then cut off abruptly. A pair of huge yellow eyes opened directly in front of her. For an instant, Drule froze in panic, then she pivoted and tried to run . . . and had nowhere to go. A pair of enormous hands rose behind her, blocking her escape, and the big head with the yellow eyes came upright and gazed at her. Below the eyes, a huge mouth opened, exposing great, chisellike teeth.

In horror, the Lady Drule gaped at the monster, and it grinned back, then the big mouth moved, and it spoke one word. "Mama?"

* * * * *

In the cavern below, the rest of the ladies—and the few males with them—waited with growing impatience. They could no longer see the Lady Drule, and could no longer hear the snoring. There were voices somewhere above—or a voice and intermittent rumbles of thunder—but they couldn't hear what was being said.

By threes and fives, they started wandering around the cavern, looking at the pyrite deposits, the fallen stone, anything of momentary interest. Several had nearly decided to go back down the tunnel to the lower cavern and put on a pot of stew, when the hole above darkened and Drule's voice came down. "Ever'body come up," she called.

Hunch peered upward. "Lady Drule find others? Find what's-'is-name . . . th' Highbulp?"

"Not here," she called back. "Tracks, though. Maybe we follow an' find."

The first ones to the top glanced at the Lady Drule, started to hoist themselves out of the hole, then spotted the huge, ugly creature crouched nearby—its gaze fixed lovingly on Drule—and retreated in panic, dislodging those below them. Within seconds, there was a tumbling pile of gully dwarves on the cavern floor and nobody climbing.

The Lady Drule appeared at the opening again, looked at them curiously. "What happen? Ever'body fall down?"

"What that you got up there?" someone asked. "Big, ugly thing."

"Oh." She glanced around, then looked down again. "That just Krog. Stop wastin' time! Come up."

Several of them began climbing again. Heads reached the surface and poked out, wide eyes looking past Drule at the creature still squatting nearby.

"That Krog?" someone asked.

"Krog," Drule assured them.

"What Krog?" another demanded.

"Dunno," she shrugged. "Just Krog. That all he remember. All come on now. Got to find Highbulp."

"Why?" several of them wondered. Then one added, "We don' like Krog. Make him go 'way."

Drule stamped her foot impatiently, then turned and walked to Krog. "Go 'way, Krog," she said. "Shoo!"

Obediently, the creature stood and backed away several steps.

"More go 'way than that!" somebody called from the hole.

"Shoo!" Drule repeated, waving her arms at Krog. "Shoo! Shoo!"

Looking very puzzled, the creature retreated farther, then squatted on its haunches again, a smile of contentment on its face.

It was some time before the Lady Drule got all of her people out of the hole. When she did, they crowded around her, staring at the creature she had found. She was so hemmed in that she could hardly move, and began pushing her way out of the crowd.

" 'Nough look at Krog!" she commanded. "Come on. We gotta look for Highbulp!"

A layer of dust had settled on the hilltop, and there were tracks all around. Three distinct sizes of footprints—gully dwarf prints, human prints twice their size, and Krog prints twice the size of the human prints.

She showed the rest of them the tracks, then pointed. "Highbulp an' rest go that way with Talls."

Hunch stared at the tracks, frowning. "Highbulp real dimwit to go with Talls," he declared. "Why do that?"

"Dunno." The Lady Drule shrugged. "We go see."

She set out northward, the rest falling in behind her. Behind them, Krog realized that they were leaving. He stood up.

"Mama?" he rumbled. "Wait for me." He hurried to catch up with the Lady Drule, and gully dwarves scattered this way and that to avoid being stepped on.

Drule looked back at the confusion and shook her head.

"Ever'body come on!" she demanded. "No time for fool around!"

"It not us fool around. It Krog!"

"Make Krog go 'way."

After they had gone a few miles, the Lady Drule gave up on getting rid of Krog. She had tried everything she could think of to make the creature "go 'way," and nothing had worked. Faced with the inevitable, she accepted it and just tried to ignore him. It was difficult. Every time she turned around, the first things she saw were enormous knees. Even worse, he insisted on calling her "mama," and kept trying to hold her hand.

Worse yet, Krog's presence tended to discourage the others from following closely. Sometimes, when the Lady Drule looked back, they were barely in sight. Then, when the smoky sun was setting beyond the mountains to the west, she looked around and couldn't see them at all.

On the verge of exasperation, she climbed a broken stump and peered into the brushy distance. "Now where they go?" she muttered.

"Who?" Krog asked.

"Others," she said. "S'posed to be followin'. Can't see 'em."

"Oh," he rumbled. "Here." Great fingers circled her waist, and he raised her high. "See, mama? There they are."

A half mile back, the others had stopped at the edge of a fallen forest and were scurrying about. They had built a fire.

"Oh," the Lady Drule said. "Time for eat."

"Yeah," Krog agreed, setting her on her feet. "Time for eat. What we eat?"

"Make stew," she explained. "What else?" With a sigh, she started back.

"What else?" Krog rumbled, and followed.

Partway back, on a wind-scoured flat littered with fallen stone, Drule saw furtive movement among some rocks, and her nose twitched. "Rat?" she breathed. She circled half around the rocks, saw movement again, and dived at it, her fingers closing an inch behind the rodent's fleeing tail. She stood and shook her head. "Rats," she said.

Krog watched curiously, repeated, "Rats," and squatted beside a boulder. With a heave, he lifted it, and several rats scurried away. The Lady Drule made a dive for one, missed it. Her hand closed around a stick. A second rodent raced by. Drule swatted it on the head.

She picked it up, looked at it, then looked at the stick in her hand. It was a sturdy hardwood branch an inch thick and about two feet long. "Pretty good bashin' tool," she decided.

"Bashin' tool," Krog rumbled.

By the time they got back to the others, Drule had three rodents for the pot and Krog was busy fashioning a bashing tool of his own. He had found a section of broken tree trunk about five feet long, and was shaping it to his satisfaction by beating it against rocks as they passed. It was a noisy process, but the implement pleased him. It felt right and natural in his hand. He held the forty-pound club in front of him, studied it with satisfied eyes, tossed it in the air, caught it, and studied it again. "Pretty good bashin' tool," he said.

By the time the stew was ready, daylight was gone. "Better stay here for sleep," the Lady Drule told the others. "Go on tomorrow."

"Go where, Mama?" Krog wondered.

"Find others."

"These others?" He indicated the crowd around the fire.

"No," she said. "Other others."

"Fine," the Grand Notioner said, picking out a stew bowl. He dipped it and sat down to eat as others made their way to the pot. There weren't enough iron bowls to go around—much had been lost when the cavern of This Place had collapsed—but they made do with vessels of tree bark, cupped shards of stone, and a leather boot that someone had found and cut down.

Drule had just started eating when she heard a sniffle in the gloom, a very large sniffle. She looked up. "What matter with Krog?"

"Want some, too," the monster explained.

The Lady Drule filled a tree-bark bowl and gave it to Krog. He sniffed it, opened his mouth, and popped it in, bowl and all. He swallowed. "Good," he said. "More?"

Hunch, the Grand Notioner, stared up at the big creature in disbelief. "Gonna need lots more rats an' greens," he said. "Bark, too, if Krog keep eatin' th' bowls."

"Rats?" Krog's eyes lit up. "Krog get rats with bashin' tool."

He stood, picked up his club, and vanished into the darkness. He was gone for a long time, and most of the gully dwarves were asleep when he returned.

Drule saw him approaching and held a finger to her lips. "Sh!" she said.

Quietly, Krog came to the waning fire, found a clear spot and dropped something on the ground, something very big. "Rats too quick for Krog," he whispered. "Can't catch 'em. This do?"

Drule gaped at the thing. She had seen cave bears before, but never a dead one, and never up close. It certainly would make a lot of stew, she decided.

* * * * *

The Highbulp Gorge III was not happy. First to be snatched up by armed Talls and herded cross-country with a rope around his neck, lashed with whips and insulted at every stumble, then to be thrown into a cage with the rest of his followers and dozens of Tall captives as well—Gorge was almost certain that his dignity had been offended, among other things.

"This intoler . . . outra . . . unforgiv . . . this stink!" he grumbled, pacing back and forth in the corner of the roofed pen where the gully dwarves were huddled. "Slave, Talls say. Not slave. I Highbulp!"

"Not slave either," several of his subjects agreed.

A voice growled, "You gully dwarves pipe down or you'll feel the lash."

"Hmph!" Gorge muttered, but lowered his voice. "Maybe dig out? Skitt? Where Skitt?"

"Here," a sleepy voice said. "What Highbulp want?"

"Skitt, you dig hole."

"Tried it," Skitt said in the gloom. "Rock underneath. Need tools, no tools. G'night."

"Might cut through bars," another suggested. "Bars are wood."

"Cut with what?" still another pointed out. "Same thing. Got no tools. If had anything for cut, could—"

"Shut up over there!" a human whispered from the other side of the pen. "You'll get us all in trouble!"

"Hmph!" Gorge said, feeling helpless and hopeless.

Armed guards patrolled around the pen. Nearby, the fires of the slavers' camp burned bright. They had been coming in all day, groups of four to eight at a time, most of them bringing captives, and now there were at least thirty in the camp, and dozens of slaves in the pen.

A guard passed near the wood-barred enclosure, and a human voice inside said, "If only I could get my hands on a sword, I'd . . ."

The guard laughed. "You'd what, slave? Fight? By the time we sell you, we'll have beaten all the fight out of you. Now shut up."

Another guard strolled past on the gully dwarves' side, and the Highbulp and his followers cringed away from the bars. They didn't like the way these Talls talked, at all.

* * * * *

At first dawn, the ladies packed as much bear meat as they could carry, while the Lady Drule went looking for tracks to follow. Krog tagged along, happy as a duckling following its mother.

Drule searched northward, then stopped and scratched her head. There had been tracks before, she was certain, but now there were none. "Where they all go?" she wondered.

Krog squatted beside her, scratching his head in imitation. "Who?" he asked.

"Highbulp an' th' rest," she reminded him. "Ones we been tryin' to find."

He scowled—a frightening and fierce expression, on his face. "Mama want find those ones?"

"Sure," the Lady Drule said. "Don't know where to look, though."

"No problem," Krog said, standing and pointing northward. "They over there."

"Where?"

"There. See smoke? That where other others go."

He seemed certain of it, so Drule said, "Fine. We go there, too. Highbulp prob'ly need 'tendin' to 'bout now."

She called to the rest, and they set off northward—a nine-foot creature guiding, a long line of three- to four-foot creatures tagging after. In the distance, far across a wide, sundered valley littered with the debris of nameless catastrophe, was a ridge. Beyond the ridge, Krog said, were their lost people. It would take all day to get there, Drule guessed, but they had nowhere else to go.

It was midday when Drule and Krog rounded a spire of rock that might once have been a mountaintop, and came face-to-face with a stranger, a human, carrying an axe.

As any good gully dwarf would do, faced with an armed Tall, the Lady Drule shrieked, turned and ran. Behind her, gully dwarves scattered in all directions.

Krog looked after Drule for a second, thoroughly puzzled, then looked again at the bug-eyed man standing there, gawking up at him in terror. Krog shrugged eloquently, then voiced a mighty shriek, flung up his hands just as Drule had done, and pounded away after her. His shriek drowned out the screams of the man, who was now bounding away in the other direction, shouting, "Ogre! Ogre!"

Some distance away, Krog found the Lady Drule hiding behind a clump of grass. Krog did the same, though his clump of grass covered no more than the lower part of his face and maybe one shoulder. He stayed there until Drule rose. Deciding the danger was gone, she went to regather her followers. Krog didn't know why they had been hiding, but whatever suited Mama was all right with him.

* * * * *

It was late evening. Hazy dusk lay in the long shadows of the Khalkists, and the smoke of campfires hung in the air when a gully dwarf named Bipp crept through the brush to the shadowed slave pen and looked inside. He squinted.

"Highbulp?"

Several faces turned toward him. "Hey," someone said. "That Bipp."

"What you doin' out there, Bipp?" another asked.

Bipp put a finger to his lips. "Sh!"

"What?"

"*Sh!*"

"Oh. Okay."

"Where Highbulp?" Bipp whispered.

"Right here, somewhere. Highbulp? Highbulp, wake up. Bipp here." A pause, then, "Highbulp! Wake up! Highbulp sleepy oaf. Wake up, Highbulp! Bipp here."

"Who?"

"Bipp."

"Shut up over there!" a human voice shouted. "Can't you little dimwits ever be quiet?"

At the sound, an armed guard at the far corner of the pen looked around, and Bipp flattened himself in the shadows. "Shut up in there, or you'll wish you had," the guard ordered.

Then Gorge was there, peering through the lashed-post bars. "What Bipp want?"

"Lady Drule send me. She lookin' for you. Why ever'body here?"

"Can't get out," the Highbulp said, peevishly. "Talls got us incarcera . . . in custo . . . got us locked in for sell."

"Oh." Bipp studied the bars, shrugged, and turned away. "Okay," he said. "Have nice evenin'. I go tell Lady Drule."

In a moment he was gone, but behind him a babble of voices echoed, and a guard roared, "You slaves heard what I said!"

A torch flared. A guard with a patch on one eye drew a sword and thrust it viciously between the bars. A human screamed, and the scream became a whimper as the guard withdrew the sword, bloody.

The man put away his sword, grinned at another guard. "That ought to quiet them," he said. "Slaves don't need two ears, anyway."

* * * * *

Atop the ridge, the Lady Drule and the others listened wide-eyed as Bipp made his report. He told them what he had seen and what he had heard, and there was no doubt what it all meant. Most of the males of the Bulp clan were prisoners of heavily armed Talls, and would be sold into slavery.

Drule scratched her head, wondering what to do about that, then gave up and went to find Hunch. "You Grand Notioner," she reminded him. "Time for Grand Notion."

The Grand Notioner was preoccupied, trying to repair the bindings on his feet after a long day's walk. "What about?" he grumbled.

" 'Bout how get Highbulp an' all away from Talls! Pay attention."

"Oh." He thought about it for a while, then shrugged and pointed at the stick in her hand. "Use bashin' tool, I guess."

"For what?" Drule looked at the stick.

"For bash Talls," he explained.

To the Lady Drule, that didn't sound like much of an idea, but when several long minutes of fierce concentration didn't produce a better one, she resigned herself to it. Bashing Talls, in her opinion, was a very good way to get into a lot of trouble, but maybe it was worth a try.

"Anybody wanna bash Talls?" she asked around, hoping for volunteers. There were none. She would just have to do it herself, then.

Nearing the foot of the ridge, Drule suddenly was aware that Krog was right behind her, mimicking her stealthy approach. She turned and raised a hand. "Krog wait," she whispered. "I got somethin' to do."

In a rumbling whisper, the big creature asked, "What Mama do?"

She pointed toward the pen, where a guard was sitting on a rock. "See Tall there? Gotta bash him. Now be quiet."

"Oh," Krog said. "Okay."

With Krog silenced, the Lady Drule crept on down the slope toward the guard. Even sitting on a rock, the man was taller than she was, and his ready sword glinted in the starlight.

Trembling with dread, Drule crept up behind him, raised her rat-bashing stick, and brought it down on the back of the man's head as hard as she could.

"Ow!" the man said. His hand went to his head. "What th'—" He reached for his sword.

The Lady Drule tried to run, but tripped over her own feet and fell.

The raider guard spied her, spat. "Gully dwarf!" He grasped the hilt of his sword . . . then raised his eyes to see the last sight of his life—a massive club descending on his skull.

The Lady Drule got her feet under her, started to run again, then saw the squashed body of the man sprawled across the rock. Krog stood to one side, disinterestedly gazing out over the fire-lit camp.

"Wow!" Drule breathed. Raising her rat-stick, she stared at it in amazement. "Pretty good bash!"

Quietly, then, she crept toward the pen, bright eyes looking for other Talls to bash. Somewhere nearby, a rumbling whisper said, "Ones with weapons first, Mama."

That, she realized, made pretty good sense. She wondered how Krog came to know such sound strategy. At the bottom of the slope, she began to circle the slave pen. The gully dwarves were all crowded into one corner of the wooden cage enclosure, spurned by the humans inside.

As Drule neared that corner, a voice whispered, "There Lady Drule! Hi there, Lady Drule." Another voice whispered, "Highbulp! Wake up! Lady Drule here . . . Highbulp? Highbulp sleepy oaf. Wake up, Highbulp!"

Drule said, "Sh!" and went on. Behind her, a giant shadow moved, but those inside were too busy watching her to notice it.

Just beyond the corner of the stockade, a man stood leaning on a spear staff. He yawned, and a stick smacked him sharply across the buttocks. "Here now!" he started to say, but only part of it was ever said. The club that smashed into his skull put an end to it.

"Wow," the Lady Drule muttered.

Another guard stood at the next corner, and just beyond him burned the coals of a cook-fire. Other men lay in sleep, their weapons at hand. Quietly, Drule approached the guard, raised her stick, and whacked him on the back. The man said, "Ow!" and spun around, raising his spear. "Gully dwarf," he said. "And a female one. Where did you come from?"

"Woop," Drule shouted. She raised her stick and struck again.

The stick whacked across the man's knuckles, and he dropped his spear. His eyes narrowed. "Why, you little snake," he hissed. "You'll pay for that." He drew a long knife from his boot and lunged at the gully dwarf, who dodged aside, tripped, and fell.

The slaver aimed another thrust, then stopped. A chorus of shrieks sounded from inside the pen. Some of the slaves had just noticed Krog stepping into the light of the fires. Crashing, thudding sounds erupted. Thuds, rending snaps, and a high-pitched scream abruptly silenced.

The guard turned, gaped, screamed, "Ogre!"

He started to run, tripped over the Lady Drule, and sprawled facedown.

A stick whacked him on the back of his head, and a voice said, "Take that!" Then, "Don' know what wrong with this bashin' tool. Used to work real good."

As the man got to his knees, Drule decided she had done enough bashing, and ducked away. The area around the nearby campfire was a shambles—sprawled bodies everywhere, dropped weapons lying here and there . . . and blood, lots of blood. Krog had finished there and gone on to the next fire, unleashing havoc. There were screams of fear, screams of agony, the rhythmic thudding of a huge club against flesh and bone.

Like huge death, Krog strode around and through the sleeping-fire, a growling, implacable horror with rending fingers, ripping teeth, and a great club as tireless and relentless as a harvester's scythe. Wide-eyed, terrified slavers came out of their blankets, grabbing up weapons to confront him. Some never even got to their feet before the heavy club flattened them and great feet trod across their bodies. Others tried to regroup and fight, and were splattered with their companions' blood even as their own blood splattered others.

A man with an eye-patch rolled aside, hid for a second in shadows, then sprang to his feet, aiming a heavy sword at the marauder's backside. He swung—and the sword thudded into hard wood, embedded itself, and was torn from his grasp. A huge hand closed around his helmed head and squeezed, and the iron helm collapsed, crushing the skull within. Krog flung him aside and went on, growling his pleasure.

Somewhere, deep in Krog's mind, a glimmer of memory awakened—memory triggered by the violence and the smell of fresh blood. Rampant and towering in the remains of the sleeping camp, Krog raised his club toward the sky, and a growl sounded in his throat—a growl that became a roar that echoed from the hillsides, a roar of challenge and of pleasure, the cry of a rampaging ogre.

Ahead of him were other fires, where men with weapons scrambled in all directions, and his eyes lit with pleasure.

But then, behind him somewhere, a voice called, "Krog! 'Nough foolin' 'round! Got better things to do!"

The glimmer of memory held for a moment, urging him on, then became tenuous and faded. Feeling a disappointment he didn't understand, Krog turned and headed back, pausing only for a casual swat that brained a panicked, fleeing slaver. "All right, Mama!" he thundered, his lower lip jutting in a huge pout. "Comin'!"

The ladies of Lady Drule's retinue, and the few males with them, had followed Drule and Krog as far as the pen. Not finding a hole in the cage, they made one. Using the edges of burnished iron stew tureens, they chipped away enough sapling bars and lashings for the gully dwarves to come tumbling out, and a flood of crouched Talls right behind them. Pushing past and through the gully dwarves as though they were not there, the Talls grabbed up fallen weapons and launched a murderous attack on the stunned and disorganized slavers.

The minute Gorge III, Highbulp of This Place and Those Other Places Too, was free of captivity, he threw back his shoulders, donned his most regal pose and issued the orders of a true leader. "Everybody run like crazy!" he commanded.

* * * * *

It was many hours later, and broad daylight, when the reunited Clan of Bulp paused on the devastated lower slopes of the Khalkist Mountains to regroup. Through night and morning they had fled, each and severally. But now Gorge remembered that he had sore feet and decided it was a good time to stop and reassert his authority. He proclaimed a temporary This Place, and by threes and fives they gathered around him.

There was one small problem. Through it all, nobody had thought to tell Gorge about Krog, so when the Lady Drule and her band showed up, shrieks and screams filled the hazy air and they found a This Place with no one in attendance except old Hunch, sitting on a rock.

Drule looked around in confusion. "Where Highbulp? Where ever'body go?"

"All run an' hide." Hunch shrugged.

"Why?"

"Dunno. Didn' say. Ever'body just holler an' run an' hide."

Impatiently, Drule set her fists on her hips, stamped her foot, and shouted, "Gorge! Where you?"

Here and there, shadows moved. From brushy crevices and piles of stone, faces peered out. The Highbulp's voice said, "Yes, dear?"

"What goin' on?" the Lady Drule demanded. "You playin' game?"

More of the gully dwarves peered from hiding places, all gaping at the towering Krog. "What that you got with you, dear?" the Highbulp called.

Drule looked up at the ogre, then turned toward the voice. "Nothin'! Just Krog! Stop fool 'round!"

Reassurance didn't come easily, but lapse of attention did, and soon the whole tribe was gathered.

Within an hour, they had stew on, and the Lady Drule handed a tureen to Gorge III. He sniffed, tasted, and proclaimed, "This superi . . . excep . . . pretty good stew! What in it?"

"Cave bear an' skinny green plant," she said. "An' mushroom an' tall-grass seed an' leftover bird nest."

He took another sip and nodded. "Good stuff. Best I . . . *cave bear*? Where get cave bear?"

Offhandedly, Drule pointed at the hulking Krog, who was waiting for the crowd around the stew pot to disperse so that he could finish the pot. "Krog get," she said. "Krog not much for hunt rats, but bash bears real good."

"Krog," the Highbulp said, scowling in thought as he studied the amiable monster. He hadn't really thought much about Krog since the first shock of encounter, but when he did, troubling notions tumbled around in his head. He glanced at Drule suspiciously. "Krog call you Mama," he said. "You been up to somethin', dear?"

"Krog lost, needed mama." She shrugged. "Keeps callin' me that."

"Oh." Gorge sipped at his stew, relieved but still troubled. "Dear, wha' happen to Talls at slave camp? Somethin' squash 'em?"

"Mostly Krog," she explained. "He got th' hang of bashin' Talls pretty quick. Had lotta fun."

"Hmph!" Gorge sat in thought for a time, then asked, "How you an' others find us?"

Again she pointed at the huge creature nearby. "Krog find place. Krog pretty handy have around, right?"

"Right." The Highbulp scowled. Tossing aside his empty tureen, he stalked away, sulking.

The Lady Drule stared after him, then beckoned the Grand Notioner. "Hunch, what wrong with Highbulp?"

"Highbulp?" Hunch shrugged. "Highbulp is Highbulp. That his main problem."

"What that mean?"

"Highbulp gotta be Highbulp alla time," he explained, puzzling it out as he went. "Gotta be big cheese, top turkey, main mullet, otherwise, no good be Highbulp."

"So what?"

"So now Krog big hero. Ever'body lookin' up to Krog. Not good for Highbulp. Steal his thunder."

The Lady Drule pondered, trying to understand. "Okay," she said finally. "What do about it, then?"

"Maybe Highbulp make Krog a knight," Hunch said simply, "like Tall kings do. Heroes real nuisance to kings, but if king make hero a knight, alla glory belong to king again."

"Oh," Drule concurred. "Okay." With renewed purpose, she strode to where the Highbulp was sulking and faced him. "Highbulp better knight Krog," she told him.

He frowned a puzzled frown. "What?"

"Knight Krog, then Highbulp be like a king, get glorious."

"Highbulp already glorious," he pointed out, then squinted at her. "Knight Krog good idea, huh?"

"Real good idea."

"Right," he decided. "Jus' what I was thinkin 'bout."

Gorge strode to the middle of the camp and raised his arms. "All pay attention! Highbulp got announ . . . proclam . . . somethin' to say!"

When he had their attention, he pointed at Krog. "Highbulp gonna . . . Ever'body! Stop lookin' at Krog! Look at Highbulp!"

When he had their attention again, he said, "Highbulp deci . . . conclu . . . make up mind to do Krog big honor, for—" he turned to Drule "—for what?"

"For be hero," she whispered. "For valor an' service. For be brave an' . . . an' bashful."

It was a bit complicated for the Highbulp. Turning back to his assembled subjects, he said, "For bein' a good guy, make Krog be *Sir* Krog. Krog!" he ordered. "Go over by big rock an' prost . . . recumb . . . hunker down real low."

With a nod from Drule, the big creature did as he was told. Kneeling before a boulder, he bent low enough that it was almost as tall as himself. Gorge walked around him, trying to remember what he had heard about knighting. He glanced at the huge club in Krog's hand and pointed at it. "What that?"

"Bashin' tool," the Lady Drule said. "Krog made it."

"Good," Gorge said. "Krog, give bashin' tool to Highbulp."

Hunkered low before the boulder, Krog turned his head, saw Mama's nod of approval and extended his club. The Highbulp took it and, when Krog released it, sat down hard with the club across his lap. It weighed almost as much as he did.

"Gonna need volunteers," the Highbulp muttered. He pushed the club away, stood and called, "You, Chuff. An' Bipp. An' Skitt, all come help."

Three sturdy young gully dwarves stepped forward. Gorge climbed to the top of the boulder and beckoned. "Bring bashin' tool up here."

Between them, the three managed to hoist the club and themselves onto the boulder, scattering dust from its top. Beside it, Krog wrinkled his nose, shook his head, and began to fidget.

"Hol' still, Krog," the Lady Drule told him.

With the Highbulp supervising, the three volunteers positioned the club above Krog's left shoulder.

Gorge drew himself up regally. "Krog, 'cause of exce . . . unusu . . . for doin' good stuff, I dub you *Sir Krog*." To the volunteers, he said, "Dub Krog on shoulder now."

Falling dust tickled Krog's nose. He sneezed. A cloud of dust blew up around the boulder, blinding the dubbers. Bipp sneezed and lost his grip on the club, Chuff fell over backward, and Skitt, suddenly lifting the full weight of the thing, lost control of it. With a resounding thud, the club descended on the back of Krog's head.

For a moment there was a stunned silence, then Krog shook himself like an angry bear, raised his head . . . and the Highbulp found himself staring into a huge face that was no longer amiable. A growl like approaching thunder shook the slopes. Krog's once-innocent eyes brightened with a flood of returning memory—brightened and glittered with a killing rage.

"Uh-oh!" the Highbulp gulped. He turned, leapt from the stone, and shouted, "Ever'body run like crazy!"

Gully dwarves scattered in all directions, disappearing into the shattered landscape. Behind them, a mighty roar sent echoes up the mountainsides—the roar of an ogre unleashed.

Krog stood, picked up his club, and brandished it, roaring again. "Krog!" he thundered. "I am Krog! Not Krog Aghar! *Krog ogre*! Krog!"

Seeing movement, he sped after it, his feet pounding. Beyond a shoulder of stone, he skidded to a stop. A female gully dwarf lay there, staring up at him in horror. "Krog?" she said.

Her voice—the remembered voice and the remembered face of the little creature—made him hesitate, and his hesitation angered him. For an instant he felt . . . soft. "Shut up!" he thundered. "I am Krog! Krog ogre!"

She blinked, and a tear glistened in her eye. "Krog . . . not want Mama anymore?"

"I am ogre!" he roared. "You . . . nothing to me!" Furious, he raised his club high, then hesitated as another small figure darted out of a shadowed cleft to face him, a little gully dwarf male with curly whiskers, the one they called Highbulp. The gully dwarf faced him with terror in its eyes and an elk tine in its hand, and again Krog hesitated.

The absurd little thing was challenging him! A snarl tugged at Krog's cheek, but still he hesitated, looking from one to the other of the puny creatures. They meant nothing to him, nothing at all, and yet, there was something about the pair . . .

For a moment Krog stood, his club lifted high to strike, then he shook his head and lowered it. Wrinkling his nose in disgust—mostly at himself—he turned and stalked away.

Behind him, the Highbulp Gorge III lifted the Lady Drule to her feet with trembling hands. They clung together, staring at the monster's receding back.

"'Bye, Krog," Drule whispered.

The Cobbler's Son

ROGER E. MOORE

The Authentic Field Reports of Walnut Arskin
To Astinus of Palanthas,
As Set Down by Me, Walnut,
Foster Son of Jeraim Arskin,
Famed Amanuensis, Scribe of Astinus,
and Licensed Cobbler
(Open All Week Long)
Newshore-Near-Gwynned, North Island, Ergoth

Report Number One
Year 22, New Reckoning
Spring day 12 or maybe 13 (I forget), dawn

Hi, Astinus! It's just after dawn and I'm now your newest field recorder, and I'm making my very first official field report to you on official Palanthas paper with my brand-new steel pen while wearing my once-holy symbol of Gilean and my official gray recorder's robes and my best walking boots. I've even put on clean underwear. I just want you to know, Astinus, that I will be your best field recorder ever, and someday I might even become a great amanuensis like Ark!

It's pretty cold outside for springtime right now, so my handwriting is sorta wiggly, but I can still read it. Can you? I'm a little hungry, as I would have had breakfast by now only I lost it after Ark sent me out of the shoe shop right after he made me his official field recorder, which is an interesting story, and I should write it down in case it's important, and anyway there's not much else to do in this alley at this hour of the morning.

Ark—known to you as your loyal scribe and amanuensis Jeraim Arskin from Newshore, but known to me as Ark and sometimes Dad, and known to everyone else in Newshore as Arkie—woke me up early and told me to get ready for the ceremony. I'd been begging him to let me be a scribe for ages, and Ark said he was going deaf from hearing me beg, but then something happened last night and he said he had something important for me to do today, but I'd have to be out on my own and out of his way. He was awfully nervous, and when he got me up he looked like he hadn't slept much, and he wanted to hurry through everything, and when I asked him what was wrong, he just said, "Don't be a kender right now," which I can't help, since I am one.

Ark first gave me a set of gray scribe's robes that he had hemmed up, which I put on, and then he gave me some official paper from Palanthas, where you live, and this new steel pen and this once-holy symbol that used to belong to a real cleric of Gilean until he disappeared (the cleric, that is) when the gods lowered the boom on Istar twenty-two years ago and left without telling anyone their next address, but I guess you know that part, since you're a historian.

I looked over at the wall mirror then and saw all three feet nine inches of me in the candlelight, with my dark brown hair combed out and bound in a high tassel and my gray robes with the nice silver borders and my writing paper and once-holy symbol and official steel pen. It was strange, because I didn't look like me, and that made me feel funny. I looked like a kender I didn't quite know.

Ark stood behind me, and in the candlelight he looked old, and that made me feel funny, too. He's about average in size for a human and is almost bald and has a hooked nose and a potbelly, and I knew who he was, but just then he didn't look much like the man who had raised me and told me funny stories when I was sick and took me fishing and bailed me out of jail every so often. Maybe it was the hour, but he looked old and tired, like something was bothering him. I worry about him sometimes.

Ark sighed after a moment and said, "Well, let's get started. I've got a lot of work to do today—and so do you, of course." Then he put his hand on my head and used some big words that I didn't know, but you probably do, and when he was done, he said, "Walnut, you are now my official field recorder. Your mission is to go out among the people of Newshore and record all things of importance. I know I can trust you to do a good job. Don't come back until sundown, stay out of jail, take lots of notes, don't upset anyone, and let me get my correspondence done. I'm a little behind, and Astinus will use my skin for book covers if I don't get those reports to him."

(I should say here that I certainly hope you do not intend to skin Ark, Astinus, especially not for book covers. You may skin me instead if you have to, as Ark is late with his correspondence only because I made paper fishing boats out of his last reports. I thought they were just waste paper, like when he writes letters to you when he's mad and tells you to jump off the roof of your library but then never sends them. He says it makes him feel better, and he gives the letters to me to make boats out of them. I grabbed the wrong stack and am sorry.)

Anyway, I am now a field recorder, which Ark tells me is the first step toward becoming a real-live scribe and eventually an amanuensis, which is the most incredible word, isn't it? I've wanted to be a scribe for years, ever since Ark taught me to read and write, and I've learned almost every word there is, except the biggest ones (except for "amanuensis") and I've practiced and practiced at my writing until Ark says that if I write on the walls or furniture one more time, he will put me in jail himself, but I think he was only kidding, except maybe once or twice.

I am determined to make Ark proud of me, and after the ceremony, I said, "Ark, I will be the best field recorder ever, and you are going to be so proud of me that you will bust."

Ark smiled without looking happy and said, "Good, good. Just stay out of jail." Then he hurried me toward the door and gave me a pouch with some hard rolls and cheese and dried bacon and raisins and other stuff in it, which I dropped when I cut through the Wylmeens' garden on the way into town and their big brown mastiff, Mud, chased me out. Stupid dog.

I tried to get my pouch back, but Mud tore it apart and ate it, so I went back to the shoe shop after that to get another bag for breakfast, and when I went in, Ark was sitting at the kitchen table, sound asleep. He had all of his papers out and his pens and his ink bottles, and he had just started what looked like a long report to you about the political and religious situation in Newshore, but he must have been pretty tired, what with staying up so late last night, and I wondered if it was because I had been up late, too, because I was so excited about being made a recorder, and maybe I shouldn't have tried to make tea, because I spilled hot water all over the dirt floor in the kitchen so that it turned to mud. I didn't want to bother Ark, so I went looking for food, and while I was doing that I found his "facts machine," which is why you are getting my reports the moment I write them down.

The facts machine was in a leather satchel by Ark's feet, and I couldn't help but look at it, because Ark usually throws a fit if I get near it. He says gnomes and wizards made it and that all you have to do is put a page of paper in the machine and it sends the page by magic to your library so you can read all the facts right away. What will those gnomes and wizards think of next? Ark said only the most trusted scribes get their own facts machines, and the machines are the most incredible secret, and I must never tell anyone about them, and I never have, not even Widow Muffin, who comes over to see Ark and me now and then and is the sweetest person, so don't worry, because you can trust me.

As I was looking through the satchel I also found the letter you sent to Ark yesterday, telling him he had better send in his assignment to find out how people feel about the Cataclysm (as you call it) and how peeved you were that Ark had not done so before now. I also read the part where you said you understood Ark's concerns about talking to the wrong people and being lynched, but his job required dedication, and you seemed to imply that being lynched wasn't half as bad as what you had in mind if Ark missed his next deadline, which was tonight at sundown.

You said that Ark's assignment was important because you were concerned that the purpose and lessons of the Cataclysm were being lost in a sea of deliberate ignorance and intolerance that could lay the foundation for future disasters (I'm copying from your letter now), and you said you counted on Ark and others like him to keep you informed of the condition of the land and its peoples, because if the peoples couldn't get off on the right foot (or is that feet?), then maybe they never would and one day we'd be sorry.

Well, I was amazed that anyone wouldn't know why Istar had a flaming mountain dropped on it, since Istar was such a poop nation and went around enslaving and torturing and killing people, all the while saying the people were being killed for their own good, until the gods got fed up and turned Istar into the bottom of the Blood Sea of Istar for everyone else's own good. Ark taught me all that, and I always thought everyone knew that but then I never asked, and I was surprised to read that Ark said he was afraid to ask, and I couldn't figure out why not understanding the Cataclysm meant we would be sorry later. Are we going to be tested on it?

Anyway, you had told Ark to send in his report by sundown tonight or else, and I knew Ark couldn't very well do that while he was asleep, so I've decided to do his work for him and surprise him when he wakes up. Isn't that great? I'm going to find out what everyone thinks of the Cataclysm, and I'll write it all down and send it right to you on the facts machine, which I took with me. Ark will be so proud! Sometimes, when he's bailing me out of jail, he says that he should have left me by the side of the road, which is how he became my foster father, as he found me on his way into town when I was a baby just after the time of the Cataclysm. He raised me and showed me how to fix shoes and how to count and read and everything, but we do have our moments when things don't go right, which seems to happen more often lately, now that I'm bigger, but that's how families work sometimes, you know.

Anyway, here I am now, down by the harbor in the alley beside Goodwife Filster's bakery, trying to stay out of the wind and keep warm. Ark said I should write down important things while I'm out today, so I will do that and send them to you, and I think I should write down something about Newshore and its politics and religion, but Newshore doesn't have much of either. I could also talk about how Newshore got its name, as it used to be a farm until Istar got mashed and the sea came up and northern Ergoth turned into an island, and you can still see the sunken foundation stones of an old barn just offshore, in a place Ark shows me when we go fishing, but everybody here knows about that. I could talk about Goodwife Filster's sugar rolls, which I can smell baking now, and they are on my mind a lot because I forgot to get something to eat before I left the shop the second time, but no one would want to read that, either. I should just get started on my assignment.

But, first, I am going to get a sugar roll.

* * * * *

Report Number Two
Same day, about midmorning

Hi, Astinus! I am writing this from the Newshore magistrate's jail in cell number four. It is dark in here, and I cannot see what I am writing or even if my pen is still working. It smells like somebody drank too much ale and it didn't agree with him, so he got rid of it in every way he could and then didn't bother to clean it up. I can hear someone snoring in cell number one, and cell three has someone in it who needs to use a handkerchief.

How I got here is very interesting, so I will put it down in case it is important. I was really hungry and was getting cold in the alley, so I went on into the bakery, which smelled of fresh-baked sugar rolls and breakfast pastries, the whirly kind with the melted cheese stuff on top that Ark says gives him gas but which I like anyway (the pastries with cheese I mean, not the gas, which is awful).

Ark always buys pastries from Goodwife Filster by himself. When I tell him I want to get them, he always says, "That wouldn't be a good idea," and he buys the pastries. Goodwife Filster always frowns at me while I wait for Ark outside her shop. She knows I'll be eating the sugar rolls Ark is buying, which I think makes her mad, but I have no idea why. She's one of the people I want to understand by being a recorder, but so far I haven't figured her out.

When I opened the oak door and went inside where it was toasty warm from the baking ovens and smelled the way I imagine Paradise does, Goodwife Filster saw me and frowned (she never smiles) and said in a nasty voice, "I'm not open yet, kender."

I said, "I thought you always opened about now."

And she said, "Get out of here, before I call the magistrate. Go on!"

About then I knew I wasn't going to get a sugar roll or even a cheese pastry, because Goodwife Filster is funny sometimes about people who aren't human like her, only she's not really funny as in funny ha-ha, she's funny as in funny uh-oh. Ark calls her the Minotaur, on account of she's strong and heavy and has such a terrible temper, but he says it's because she's as ugly as one, too.

I was leaving when I remembered what you had asked Ark to do, so I stopped and said, "I have just one question to ask before I go."

Goodwife Filster's face knotted up in a way that reminded me of the Wylmeens' dog, but she didn't say anything, so I quickly got out my papers and pen and got ready to write down her answer. When she looked like she was going to yell at me, I asked my question, which was, "Do you think the gods did the right thing when they struck down Istar so that the balance of the world was preserved and freedom of thought, will, and action was granted to all once more?" I'm not sure I asked the question exactly as you wanted Ark to, and I borrowed some of your phrases from your letter to get it right, but I figured I was close enough and didn't think it would hurt.

On the other hand, maybe I didn't ask the question properly after all, since Goodwife Filster called me a name that meant that my real parents weren't married, which for all I know they weren't, but that wasn't any business of hers, and then she came at me with a bread knife, so I ran outside and down the street and was cold and hungry again before I knew it.

As I was standing outside her shop with my arms crossed under my robes because it was too cold to write this down yet, a fisherman came up to go into the bakery, and I said, "It's not open yet," because I'd never known Goodwife Filster to lie, even if she once said that all elves carried diseases and kidnapped children, which I don't think they do, or at least not all of them, or at least not the ones I know. Anyway, the fisherman said, "Oh," and left.

Then the Moviken kids came up, and I said, "It's not open yet," so they made faces at the bakery window and left. Then the spinster sisters Anwen and Naevistin Noff came up, and I said, "It's not open yet," and they groaned and left.

Then Goodwife Filster came out, wiping her hands on a towel, and she looked around and frowned at me, and I said, "Are you open yet?"

And she made a snorting noise through her nose and said, "When Istar rises, you damn kender," then went back inside to bake some more.

Then Woose, the dwarf, came by and said, "Morning, Walnut," and I said, "Morning, Woose. The bakery's not open yet."

Woose peered at the bakery door and scratched his beard and said, "That's funny. She's usually open at this hour," and then he left. Woose isn't a human, but he has lots of steel coins from his mining business, and maybe Goodwife Filster forgives him for not being human on account of that.

Five more people came by whose names I've forgotten, and they left, and then Goodwife Filster came out and mumbled to herself and looked around and glared at me and said, "What did you tell those last two people who were here just now?"

And I said, "That you weren't open yet," and she got a look on her face that reminded me of the Wylmeens' dog when it bit me on the finger, and she called me a name that meant I liked my mother more than normal people were meant to, which was silly because I don't even remember my mother, and Goodwife Filster grabbed me by my robes and brought me here to the magistrate to be hanged.

We had to wait until Jarvis, the magistrate, could get out of bed and find his spectacles, and he was as tall and thin as ever, and his black hair was all messed up from sleeping on it. He combed out his hair and big moustache, then looked at me and said, "You again?" and looked sad, probably on account of this being the fifth time this year he would have to throw me in jail for being a public nuisance, which Jarvis says is really just a way to let everyone cool off and forget whatever I had done so they wouldn't tie me to a rock and drop me on a kelp farm, as Jarvis puts it, which sounds interesting but which I don't understand, since that would mean I was underwater.

"What now?" said Jarvis to Goodwife Filster, who then said a lot of things that weren't true, like that I was a plague carrier and a thief and a liar, and she was about to explain what she meant by my being responsible for the fall of Istar when Woose, the dwarf, ran into the magistrate's office and yelled, "Fire! Fire at Goodwife Filster's!"

Then Woose saw Goodwife Filster and yelled, "Gods, woman, your bakery is on fire!" and Goodwife Filster went all white and staggered like someone had hit her, then she ran out, and Woose ran out, and Jarvis ran out, but before Jarvis ran out he locked me in here and said he would be back.

So here I am with my facts machine and nothing to do. I should write down some notes on the economic situation in Newshore after Istar blew up and the crops drowned because of the ocean that used to be two days north of here but now comes up to the place where the Karkhovs once had a giant melon field and is where Ark and I fish for moonfins, but Jarvis is back now, and he's waiting for me to leave my cell after I finish this first.

"What are you writing?" he just now asked me, and now he's looking and . . .

* * * * *

Report Number Three
Same day, about an hour after noon

Hi, Astinus! I'm writing this from the rooftop of the Cats & Kitties, which is really just a tavern with a sign showing a woman's bosom with no dress on and isn't a pet shop at all, which was what I thought all the time I was growing up but Ark wouldn't take me there to find out. It's warmer now, and the sun is out and the sky is clear blue, and I can see lots of bird droppings on the roof from last year now that the snow is gone, and I might be sitting on some but I can't help it. Someone should clean this roof up, but then no one is supposed to be up here and I wouldn't be either except that Magistrate Jarvis said I was safer here than in jail, and he's gone to try to calm down the mob before I show up in town again.

So here I am, writing away on the roof and reading over some letters that Ark left in the satchel with the facts machine, and those letters are very interesting, though I can't imagine why Ark put them in here since I doubt very much he meant to send them to you. I think Widow Muffin wrote these letters to Ark, and she says a lot of things that make me think that maybe they aren't telling me the whole truth whenever Ark asks me to go into town to buy groceries when Widow Muffin comes over, and when I get back they tell me they were just talking. I was quite amazed at some of the things she said, and I don't think I will ever be able to look at either her or Ark again and not think about them playing "warming the weasel," which I should probably explain but am too embarrassed to do, and you wouldn't believe me anyway.

How I got up here on the roof is an interesting story, and I will write it down in case it is important. After I left off last time, Magistrate Jarvis took my satchel away while I was sending my report through the facts machine inside, and he took me out of jail, then gave me my satchel back and said that I could leave now, but I shouldn't try to talk to Goodwife Filster for a few years.

"What happened to her bakery?" I asked, and he said, "Oh, the old windbag left a cloth sitting on an oven when she went outside, and the cloth caught fire, and that spread to the wall and ceiling. The place is pretty well ruined now. She's probably going south to Gwynned to stay with her brother until she gets things sorted out."

I felt bad for her having to leave town, but I also felt bad for myself and everyone else, since she had the only good bakery. Jarvis went on about there being a lot of confusion as they were trying to put out the fire, but when Woose tried to get people organized, no one would listen to him, because he was rich or a dwarf or both, so the whole place burned up and took the tailor's shop with it. Jarvis said a lot of things about certain people that I should probably not put down here, because I think he was just angry, and I doubt he would really know if those people were as much in love with their barn animals as he implied they were.

Magistrate Jarvis stopped and rubbed his face and then looked at me and said, "By the way, where did you get those?" and he pointed at my gray robes, so I said, "Ark made me his official recorder this morning, and these are my official recorder's robes, and this is my official Palanthas paper, and this is my steel scribing pen, and this is my once-holy symbol," and I showed him my silver necklace that has the tiny silver open book with the tiny little scribbles in it that you can't read no matter how close you hold it to your eye, which I did once when I was smaller but poked myself in the eyeball and couldn't see for two days, so I don't do it now.

Magistrate Jarvis snorted and said, "Arkie'd be better off sticking to his shoe business. People don't have a need to read or write all that much. A little bit of knowledge goes a long way."

I was going to ask what he meant by that, but he looked at my satchel and asked about that, too, and I said it was just to hold all my papers.

Jarvis sighed and said, "You'd better be getting on out now. Try not to get yourself killed before nightfall," and I promised, and he let me go.

I was almost out the door when I remembered what you wanted, so I turned around and said, "Can I ask just one question?"

Jarvis was heading back to bed, but he groaned and said, "If it means I can get to sleep afterward, sure, anything."

So I took out my papers and my pen and tried to remember the question, and I asked him, "Do you think the gods did right when they sank Istar to preserve the balance of the world and to protect the freedoms of will, thought, and action among all beings?"

Jarvis stood real still for a while, which made me a bit uneasy, and I slowly began to roll up my papers in case I had to run for it. His face got old and white, and his black moustache looked droopy and dark, but he only said, "Why would you ask me such a damned foolish question as that? By the Abyss and its dragons, no, that wasn't good at all. The gods ruined everything for us. Istar had evil on the run. We had those goblins and minotaurs and other scum in our grip, and we were smashing down the wizards' towers right and left. We could have had a golden age here on our world, the first true age of freedom ever, but the gods broke Istar and turned their backs on us. I was a soldier for Istar before the fall. I was out here in Ergoth hunting down blood-crazed barbarians when the sky lit up to the east and the mountain fell on my homeland. Then the earthquakes and windstorms came, and there was suffering and starvation for all of us who were left, every damn one. That was twenty-two years ago, and I remember every moment of it, every single thing, just like it was yesterday. The gods did us wrong. The good gods turned evil and sold us out. They sold us into a pit of serpents like the lowest goblin whelp."

Jarvis didn't look much like the Jarvis I knew. He looked more like someone else, and I thought maybe I'd better be going before he threw something at me even if he did promise not to. But Jarvis only stared at me some more and then said, "Get out of here," so I left and didn't write anything down at all until now.

I walked around town for a little bit after that, thinking about what Jarvis had said and wishing I could get something to eat, because I hadn't had anything so far, what with being chased and thrown in jail and starting fires by accident. I wasn't getting very far on my assignment, and I didn't feel very good at all. I finally got a drink of water from the town fountain, and that helped a little, so I sat on the fountain rim and bunched myself up because it was still a little cold, and I wondered why you were so worried about Ark finding someone who understood why the gods had destroyed Istar, and how you would feel if no one ever understood but Ark and me, and how you would feel if sometimes even Ark and me don't quite understand, either, since the Cataclysm seems to have made everyone so rude-minded. And I didn't understand how not understanding would cause everyone more problems later. Nothing made any sense then, and it still doesn't now, but I'm getting ahead of myself, because it's boring to be here on the roof-top, even with the nice view.

Anyway, I was sitting by the fountain when a man riding a horse came over. He wore a little bit of armor, so I knew he wasn't from town even if I didn't recognize him anyway, since no one here wears any armor because goblins never come to the coast and the barbarians aren't bothering any-body this year, because they're all sick. The man looked like he was very old but very strong, and he had a moustache bigger and thicker than Jarvis's, but it was full of gray hair. He rode his horse up to the fountain and got off and let his horse drink while he stretched and scratched his backside and began to rub his horse down. It was about the time when he pulled a cloth out of his pocket and began wiping off his armor that I thought he might be a knight, because only a knight would do that. Nobody else cares what his or her armor looks like.

Ark had told me a lot about the Knights of Solamnia when I was younger, and I never knew if he liked them or didn't like them, because the knights did both good things and bad things, but they often did them both at the same time, so I was pretty confused as to which side they were on. I got out my papers and pen so I could ask my question, but I saw the knight pull out a long steel sword with notches and scrapes cut into the blade, so I decided I would wait a little while and ask about the weather first instead. Ark always says I should think first, since I'm not very good at it sometimes, and maybe I would live longer that way, and right then I decided that maybe he knew what he was talking about.

The knight glanced at me a few times but said nothing as he cleaned his armor, every bit of it, then got himself a drink from the fountain. He acted like I wasn't really there. I forgot how hungry I was getting because I had never seen a real knight up close, and this one smelled like old sweat and leather and fur and steel. His eyes were like a gray winter sky, and the more I looked at him the less I wanted to ask my question, but I knew I'd have to do it anyway for Ark and you. I was just clearing my throat and was trying to get the question framed properly, so that I could run if necessary, when I saw Kroogi walk up from the blacksmith's shop to wash his face before lunch like he always does, and I knew I was saved. I would ask Kroogi the question first.

I smiled at Kroogi and sat up straight when he came over, only he wasn't looking at me. He was looking at the knight and the knight was looking back, and neither was looking away, and they didn't look too happy about seeing each other. I waved at Kroogi to get his attention, but he didn't wave back. He slowly stripped off his shirt to wash, and you could see the old tribal tattoos on his chest and arms from when he was a warrior with the Red Thunder People who lived east of here before they all died from fighting or being sick, which was why Kroogi left them. The knight stared at Kroogi's tattoos and Kroogi stared at the knight's armor, and neither of them said a thing.

"Kroogi!" I said, waving my arms. "Kroogi, I have a question. Do you have a moment?" I felt safe asking Kroogi, because he was real quiet and never did anything mean, even if Jarvis said Kroogi once cut two men in half using a hand axe in a battle with Istarian army renegades before the fall of Istar, but that wasn't anything anyone would hold against him, as Istarian army renegades were not very nice and they're mostly dead now anyway.

Kroogi didn't look at me, because he was still staring at the knight, and then Kroogi began flexing his huge arm and chest muscles so you could see the places where spears or swords or arrows had cut him here and there. Finally, he looked away and ber *t down to soak his shirt in the fountain water, ignoring the knight.

Several more people had wandered over to the fountain in the meantime, so I knew I'd have lots of other people to ask if the knight or Kroogi didn't give me an answer. "Kroogi!" I said.

Kroogi glanced at me as he began to wash himself using his shirt, and I knew I could go ahead and ask my question. He never said much, but he always made what he said count.

"I just have one question," I said, and cleared my throat. It would be easier to get a response from the knight after asking Kroogi first. "Kroogi, do you think the gods did right in dropping the flaming mountain on Istar so that—"

"Yes," said Kroogi. He lifted his wet shirt and ran it across his chest, washing away the ash and dust.

"Wait," I said. "I didn't get to finish the question. Do you think the gods did right when—"

"Yes," he said again. "They did right in killing the murdering mongrel dogs of Istar and their Solamnic iron-assed lackeys. The blessed gods, praise their names, did right in crushing out the Kingpriest's filth and purifying the lands that Istar and Solamnia had defiled, washing them with clean fire and water." He dabbed at his forehead. His face never changed expression. It rarely did.

"Oh," I said in surprise. This was easier than I'd thought. "Oh, well, would you—"

"I agree that the gods did right," interrupted the knight. His voice was like low thunder from a distant storm. "They killed the mad murderers of Istar, who would have chained or slain us all, but afterward they allowed evil to roam the lands in the form of ignorant, filthy, barbarian scum who spread plague as they looted and burned their way across the injured lands. The gods did right in destroying Istar, but they didn't finish the job when they let hordes of masterless vermin prey on innocent and law-abiding people. The gods instead left the cleaning up to those with the wisdom to separate the grain from the chaff, and the strength to dispose of the chaff properly."

Well, I thought this was great! Here I had two people who completely agreed that the gods had done right. I was going to ask both of them to detail their answers just a little bit more, when Kroogi's arm snapped out and he flung his wet shirt into the knight's face and knocked him off balance. Then Kroogi screamed at the top of his lungs so loudly that my ears rang, and he leapt at the knight with his big hands going for the knight's throat.

I was so surprised that I just sat there with my papers and pen and satchel and watched the two of them fighting and rolling in the dirt, yelling and cursing each other and using words that Ark would have slapped my face for using, as he'd done once when I said a word I'd heard a fisherman use but which I won't say ever again, or at least not when Ark is around.

More townspeople gathered around, shouting at Kroogi to beat the knight up, but some people came who yelled for the knight to beat up Kroogi because they didn't like the fact that Kroogi was once a barbarian, even if he was a nice guy mostly and made toys at Yuletime for some families when he had the chance.

Then someone pushed someone else, and then the whole crowd was going at it and everyone was kicking and punching and shoving and flailing away, and grown men had blood coming from their noses and mouths, and their hair was pulled out, and some had clubs and hoes, and someone else screamed like he was dying, and about then I felt someone grab me around the waist and drag me off, and it was Jarvis.

"Damn you!" he shouted at me as he dragged me off. "What in the Abyss did you do now?"

So I told him, and he put me up here on the roof of the Cats & Kitties, where he said I couldn't cause any more trouble while he tried to restore order in town. It's nice and warm up here, and I have a great view of the town and sea and farms, but I can still hear people yelling, and some lady is wailing over and over, and I wish I had asked Jarvis for something to eat, because now I am really hungry. I think Jarvis is coming back up the ladder now, so I'd better close this up. Oops! I see that it isn't Jarvis, it's Goodwife Fils—

* * * * *

Report Number Four
Same day (Cotterpin says the 13th), late afternoon

Hi, Astinus. I'm a few miles outside of town now, sitting under a tree, where no one except Cotterpin can find me, I hope. This is probably my last official report to you, because there doesn't seem to be much point in continuing to try to find someone who understands why the gods got so tired of Istar, when everyone gets so upset about the whole issue and thinks either that Istar was wonderful or that Istar was bad but wasn't as bad as some other places around here that should have gotten hit with their own fiery mountains first.

My stomach hurts but I'm not hungry, and I feel just awful, like I'm going to have a good cry in a minute after I finish writing this all down, even if Ark says boys shouldn't cry, but I'm a kender and not a human so maybe it's okay if I feel bad for just a little while.

Everyone hates me, and I hate me, and I hate being a recorder, and I hate sitting out here on a rock in the wilderness because I have no one to talk to except for Cotterpin, the tinker gnome, but he's already gone to sleep in his steam-powered lawn chair under the oak tree here. Ark is going to be very disappointed that I got thrown in jail and made part of the town burn up and started a riot and everything. I'll write down how I got here, but I don't care if it's interesting or important anymore.

After Magistrate Jarvis caught Goodwife Filster on the tavern roof and wrestled with her and they both almost fell off and he took her butcher's cleaver away and made her get down the ladder again and leave me alone, he said it would be best if I left town for a while.

"How long is 'for a while'?" I asked, and he said, "Until Goodie Filster leaves town, that's how long. Maybe it would be even better if you were gone for good. Permanently. Forever."

We climbed down from the roof of the Cats & Kitties, and he took me by the arm and ran me back to his office. I could hear people fighting in town all the way there, and I wondered how they could keep it up for so long and wouldn't they be tired of it all by now, but obviously they weren't yet.

Jarvis kept me inside his office long enough to give me a blanket, a bag of bread rolls with no sugar, some cheese, and a skin he said was full of water but which was really only half full of ale, which I hate and have already poured out. Then he said, "Just get out of here. It's for your own good as well as everyone else's. You can't stay here any longer until Goodie Filster's out of here."

And I said, "Where can I go?" And he said, "Gods, you idiot, anywhere! Just get out of this town. She'll kill you if she sees you here!" And I said, "But what about Ark? Can't I go see Ark?" Then Jarvis called me a name that means my head looks like my backside and told me to leave, so I left.

I walked and walked until I was past the Dormens' farm, which was as far as I'd ever gone away from town in my whole life, and then I went around a hill I always used to look at when I was small but had never visited, and I looked back one last time at the town and felt like part of my insides had fallen out and been left behind, and I missed Ark terribly but didn't know if I could ever go back, because things were in such a mess.

There was smoke drifting over the town near the waterfront, but I couldn't see if it was from Goodwife Filster's bakery or someone else's place that was burning up. I turned around and walked on down the road, scuffing my feet in the dust and kicking rocks and holding my blanket and wishing I was dead.

I thought of you, Astinus, and Ark, and I was ashamed because I had promised to do my best to find out if anyone understood the Cataclysm, but I had done it all wrong and now I would never get to be a real scribe, much less an amanuensis. Even worse, I was afraid that because I couldn't find out the answer to the question, then something would go wrong someday and no one would know what to do about it and it would be all my fault.

But even this was not as bad as missing Ark, because Ark is my father, even if he isn't my real father, because he took care of me when no one else would, and I knew he would be upset with me, and I missed him so much that I just couldn't feel anything at all. I was empty inside and knew I would be empty forever. I wasn't even hungry anymore.

I walked a long time, but I didn't walk very fast. Part of me wanted to keep on walking forever, but I got so numb and tired that I found a rock under an oak tree by the road and dropped my blanket and satchel and just sat down and didn't move at all. I must have sat there a long time before I noticed that a donkey cart had stopped in front of me and the driver had come over and was asking me something. The driver was shorter than I am and had wrinkled leathery skin and a snow-white beard and eyes like the deep sky. He wore a red and brown outfit covered with belts and pockets and tools. It was Cotterpin, the tinker gnome.

Cotterpin has been visiting all the villages in a huge circle around the coast of northern Ergoth for years, and everyone knows him. When I was small, he let me play with some of the toys he had in his cart, and he was always careful to take most of them back from me so other kids could play with them in other towns, but he always left some toys behind. I think now that he did it on purpose, but I used to think he was just forgetful.

"Obviously a newly generated social outcast," he was saying to me as I sat under the oak tree. "Sociological tragedy of the first magnitude. Disgraceful phenomenon."

I just looked at him, then looked at the dirt at my feet as I had been doing for however long I'd been there. I thought for a moment that I should ask him the question you wanted Ark to ask, but I didn't want to ask anyone that question ever again. I knew if I asked him, he would hate me like everyone else hated me, and I just couldn't stand that.

Cotterpin went back to his cart and heaved something out of the back, then began to set up something beside my rock that looked like a box with a metal plate on it and a switch on one end, with red gnomish lettering all over it that I couldn't read. He fiddled with the box for a bit, then went back to the cart and got a clay mug from it and filled it with liquid from a tap on the side of his cart, then set it on the box and flipped the switch. I knew I should run or hide or shield my face when he did that, as everyone knows that gnome-built things can make craters as big as the one Istar now rests in, but I didn't feel like running, and I thought maybe it would be best if I blew up with the box.

But the box didn't blow up; it just got warm after a while and the tea in the mug got warm, too. I was trying to figure that one out while Cotterpin went back to the cart and brought back a steam-powered folding chair that also failed to blow up and which he set up next to me under the tree so he could relax in it and enjoy the same warm setting sun that I was not enjoying.

"A pleasant respite it is to renew our long acquaintance, Walnut Arskin," he said in his same old deep but nasal voice, "though I suffer some concern about the circumstances. Perhaps you would care to elaborate on your condition."

I thought about it and finally said, "No."

"Mmm." Cotterpin took a sip of his tea, then held the mug in his short, thick fingers and swirled the contents. "I am not unaccustomed to seeing wayfarers as youthful as yourself fall victim to any number of unfortunate mishaps in the undisciplined confines of the wilderness. Being moderately fond of our visits together in the recent past, I was hoping to hear some motive or rationale for your presence here before you, too, encounter any of the aforementioned mishaps. Are you perhaps running away from home?"

"No," I said, and then I said, "Yes," and then I said, "No. Maybe. I don't know."

"Mmm." Cotterpin took another sip of his tea and looked off at the sun, which was just above the hill that hides Newshore from view. He didn't say anything more for a long time, and before I knew it I had told him everything, even the part about the question that you wanted Ark to answer (but I didn't tell him about the facts machine).

"Mmm," he said when I was done. "I see." Cotterpin was quiet for a while, and we looked at the open fields around us and watched deer graze and a hawk hunt for rabbits. The wind was getting a little cooler, but it was still okay to be out.

"It seems like an eon ago that I dwelled in Istar," said Cotterpin at last, watching the hawk with a peaceful face. "Yet even now I remember it far better than I would like. In the twilight years of that sea-buried land, I labored as a menial slave, the chattel of a priest. I had arrived there but scant decades before as a fully accredited diplomat from my homeland—the extinct geothermal vent called Mount Nevermind by the knights. Unfettered I was at first, able to commune with priest and commoner alike in that proud city, until the Istarians manifested great annoyance with my fellow diplomats and me over the failure of one of our gifts of technology. We had directed the construction of a new mode of urban transport, a steam-powered cart that traveled over fixed rails, but on its trial run it caused considerable damage to some important buildings in the capital. I was put on trial and sentenced to enforced servitude for the remainder of my life, as were my fellow diplomats, whom I never saw again.

"My overseer, whose glacial visage I shall bear with me to my grave, brought me along on an inspection tour of a distant military encampment just before catastrophe overtook Istar. In the anarchy and discord that followed, I was able to effect my escape and leave my overseer and his retainers to their own fate, which could not have been pleasant given the multitude of ills that plagued the region at that time. I journeyed westward on foot, feasting on the meager bounty of nature like an untamed beast, until I found a bare remnant of civilization in old Solamnia. There, among bitter-eyed men who cursed the gods and slew one another over trifles, I labored until I had saved enough steel to cross the new sea to Hylo, on this island's eastern shore. I then purchased a cart and a donkey—dear old Axle, whom you see now—and took up my most recent and probably final vocation as a tinker. As such, I am now content with my lot and desire nothing more."

"Did you ever want to go home to Mount Nevermind?" I asked. I had forgotten all about my problems and was trying to imagine what it would be like to walk across the whole continent, from Istar to northern Ergoth. I couldn't imagine it. I was also thinking about Ark and wishing that I could go home myself.

"Mmm," Cotterpin mumbled. "The thought has made its disquieting presence known to me on occasion, but I take thorough comfort in the realization that Mount Nevermind will continue to exist regardless of my actual physical location. I have determined that my best course is to find my own footway in the world and meanwhile examine the long-range consequences of the catastrophe that the gods visited upon Istar. I have been content with my work since then and have not regretted a moment of it. My original life quest was to have something to do with mass transit, but given the results of my development of the prototypical urban travel system in Istar, for which I was enslaved, I decided that another form of life-quest expression was called for. I also fear that I've been much contaminated socially by my contact with humans, and I am concerned that my brethren at Mount Nevermind might find my speech and mannerisms peculiar and would perhaps ask me to volunteer for psychiatric research, which at this time I am minded to avoid. No, I'd rather not voyage to fair Mount Nevermind again. I am an itinerant vagabond, happy at last, and wish to remain so to the end of my vagabond days."

We sat there for a while longer, and Cotterpin sighed. "Would that I could render some comfort to you, Walnut," he said, "but I wonder if perhaps your father, Jeraim, might give you more comfort than I, and if perhaps a visit with him might not reassure him that you have not fallen victim to tragedy. You have taken up a dreadful and thankless assignment. It might be time to recuperate from your excursion and renew your personal energies."

Cotterpin yawned and set aside his mug. "Tea always has a soporific effect on my psychomotor system," he said, his words slurring a bit. "The local angle of solar radiation is also inducing drowsiness, and if you would be so generous as to excuse my lapse, I would like to take a brief moment to relax my . . . to relax my eyelids." He closed his eyes, and, only two heartbeats later, he began to snore.

I looked at the countryside for a while more, then took out my paper and pen and wrote all of this down. The sun is about to sink behind the hill, and I can hear crickets chirping and birds singing, and I can still see a deer across the field, near some trees.

I stopped after I wrote the last paragraph above and thought for a while like Ark told me to do. I don't feel as upset as I did when I started to write down this report. I've just put my blanket over Cotterpin and left my bag of food with him after I ate some of it, and I've made sure that Axle has enough grass where she is standing, off to the side of the road. I am taking my papers and pen and facts machine, and I am going back to see Ark. I might have something to write to you about later, but if not, then it won't matter.

*   *   *   *   *

Report Number Five
Same day, after midnight, I think

Hi, Astinus! It's really late, I know, but I had to get one last report to you about how everything went. Ark doesn't know that I'm up or that I found out where he hid the facts machine after I gave it back to him and he ordered me never to touch it again or else I'd go to jail for a year, so don't tell him, please. He and Widow Muffin are asleep right now, and I don't think they could wake up for anything, and I'd rather not wake them up anyway. It's been a busy evening.

I went back into town right at sundown and went home to the shop, though part way there I slowed down a lot and was worried about what Ark would do when he found that I had his facts machine and had burned down the town and all, even if the last part was an accident. I felt bad, too, because I had failed to find out everything I think you wanted and Ark would be angry and disappointed in me, and I was also rather mortified that Ark might find out that I read Widow Muffin's letters, but I didn't read them all, just the first twelve.

The town was quiet again, though I could smell some smoke, and I saw candles burning in the window at the back of the shop where I usually go in. As I got closer, I saw that the back door was open, and I could hear voices inside the shop. The light inside was flickering, and at first I thought it was the stove. As I got even closer, I could tell that one of the voices was Ark's and one was Widow Muffin's, and I almost stopped, but I kept going anyway, even if my face was red.

It was when I got even closer still, almost up to the doorway, that I could hear a third voice in the shop, and that voice was Goodwife Filster's.

I stopped right then, holding the satchel and not moving a muscle. Goodwife Filster was saying something in a loud voice, growling like the Wylmeens' mastiff when he catches scent of me walking through the garden that he thinks is his territory. After a moment, I edged up to the door on one side, so no one could see me, and I listened to them talk, though Ark had once told me to never spy on anyone, and I never have, except just then and maybe two other times.

"You have to be reasonable about this," Ark was saying. His voice was a little too high and tight. "If you could just listen to me for a minute and think about—"

"Shut your dung-eating trap," shouted Goodwife Filster. "You brought that wicked little monster into this good town, and look at me now! My bakery's burned down, and I've got nothing left to my name except the clothes on my back. My whole life has been a sewage pit ever since blessed Istar died, and it's all because of vermin like that kender and maggot-brained asses like yourself who feed and clothe them! You're to blame for this even more than he is. You brought him among us, and you blinded everyone to his evil nature. You let him work his evil on us, and now he's had his way, and good people like myself are destroyed! I'm ruined!" And then she called Ark some names that I'm not going to write down here, because they were awful and I don't think I could spell them correctly anyway. I might ask Ark about them tomorrow.

When Goodwife Filster stopped for breath, I heard Widow Muffin say, "Goodie Filster, please, listen to us. You need to go back to the inn and rest for a while. If you do anything to hurt us, you'll feel terrible about it. You've had some terrible things happen to—"

"Shut up!"

The wall I was leaning against vibrated when Goodwife

Filster yelled, and among other things she called Widow Muffin a prostitute, only she didn't use that word.

"You can't talk to me!" Goodwife Filster finished. "You have no right to say anything to me! You deserve the same fate that the kender should have had years ago! He should have died out there, eaten by rats and wolves. It's your fault, Arskin, for dragging that demon child in among good folk."

"He's not a demon," Ark said, his voice shaky. "You're just upset, now. He's a kender, and they're just like you and me, even if they cause a little more—"

"The Abyss take you!" screamed Goodwife Filster. "The evil gods delivered him into your hands to destroy us!"

"Goodie, he was just a little baby, and his mother was dead. She'd been wounded by goblins or bandits, and she'd carried him all the way through the wilderness to get him to safety. I couldn't leave him there after I buried her. If you had been me, you would have done the same. You know it!" Ark sounded like he was trying to reason with a swamp viper he'd almost stepped on.

I was shocked to hear about my mother, because Ark had never said a word to me about her, and for a moment I couldn't think of anything else until Goodwife Filster laughed.

"I would have known what to do to the little bastard," she said, and my insides went cold when she said it. "I would have spared us all this torment. But because of you and that kender, I lost everything I ever owned. It's only right that you should suffer as I have, just exactly as I have."

I slowly moved around the door frame. No one was by the door, but I could look into the wall mirror nearby and see part of Goodwife Filster's back and one of her arms. She was holding a torch in one hand and had a meat-cutting knife stuck in her belt. That was bad enough, but, being so close to the door, I could also smell something like lamp oil, only it couldn't have been—or so I thought—because Ark doesn't own any oil lamps, because he says the local oil burns too fast and smells awful, like burned fish, which is what it comes from (we call them greasegills).

Of course, my next thought was that Goodwife Filster

had brought her own lamp oil, and that she meant what she said about Ark suffering exactly as she had, and suddenly all I could think about was my growing up in the shoe shop and how it was the only home I had ever known and how Ark and I, and later Widow Muffin, had always had so much fun here. I realized I had no idea how much lamp oil Goodwife Filster had brought in with her, but it smelled like enough to burn up my memories and the shoe shop and maybe some people with it.

I stopped listening then so I'd have a chance to think. Think first, Ark always tells me, even if it's just for a moment. At first I thought I should run for help, but I didn't know if Goodwife Filster would behave herself long enough for me to find Magistrate Jarvis and get back without anyone being hurt. I carefully put down the satchel with the facts machine and looked down at the steps and thought and thought. Goodwife Filster was saying something about beasts and dragons and fires from the Abyss, and she wasn't making a lot of sense, though in a way she was, even if it was a very awful sort of logic.

About then I remembered a trick I had once played on Ark when I was small, something I had sworn never to do again after I'd tried the trick, and Ark had broken two of his fingers, for which I'd been spanked and felt bad over for weeks. I was looking at the bottom of the door frame, where part of the frame had fallen off but left some nails sticking out, just enough to tie a string across the bottom of the door above ankle height.

I felt in my robe pockets for some string, but I didn't have any. Then I remembered my once-holy symbol of Gilean, and I carefully slid its chain off my neck and knelt down by the door as quietly as I could. It took a few seconds for me to wrap the chain around the nails on either side of the doorway. It was dark, and I didn't think Goodwife Filster would see the chain until it was too late. Then I grabbed the satchel.

I thought about calling for Goodwife Filster to come outside, but I thought she might say no and burn down our home. That left only one solution, and from the sound of things inside, I was going to have to do it now.

"Don't set the house on fire," Ark was begging. "I don't want any of us to get hurt. Please take the torch outside."

"I have no fear of you," cried Goodwife Filster. "I am the arm of righteousness. I am the avenger of fallen Istar."

"Goodie, that's crazy talk!" said Widow Muffin, and right then I knew she had said the wrong thing. I leaped up the two back steps, stepped over the chain at the bottom of the doorway, and stomped into the shop as loudly as I could.

"You—!" Goodwife Filster was starting to shout a bad word, but she stopped when I came in and turned around. When I saw her, I wondered if I had made a very bad mistake, because Goodwife Filster had a hatchet in the hand that didn't have the torch. Her eyes were shining like black stones at the bottom of a cold creek. Ark and Widow Muffin were bunched up in a corner, and Ark was holding a footstool with the widow back behind him. The place stank of burned fish. Everyone froze as I came in. The only thing I could hear was the crackling of the torch flames.

It was time to do something, so I waved my arms and the satchel and shouted the first thing that came into my head. "Hey!" I yelled at Goodwife Filster. "Got any sugar buns?"

I didn't know what to expect, but I certainly didn't expect that Goodwife Filster could move so fast for someone built so dumpy. She didn't say a thing, at least not that I remember, but she came at me like a wild horse, and I knew I was going to be a very sorry kender if I didn't move. I ran for the back door, and my plan to trip Goodwife Filster and hit her over the head with the satchel would have been perfect, except that I forgot about the chain at the bottom of the door in trying to get away from her and that axe and torch she had, and the chain snagged my foot, and I fell out the back door and down the steps into the dirt.

I got up right away, and it was a good thing I did, too, because Goodwife Filster hit the chain right after I did and fell down the steps, too, but she fell right next to me, and the torch singed my hair before it stuck in the dirt and went out. I had no time to do anything with the facts-machine satchel except hold it. I had to run, so I did.

I took off for the low place in the stone wall between

Ark's place and the Salberins' property, and it was hard to see where I always came up and hoisted myself over the wall, but I could hear Goodwife Filster behind me, her thick feet thumping on the ground, and suddenly I had the idea of vaulting over the wall on my hands, so I did exactly that—the first time I ever did it—and I sailed over the wall on one hand, holding the satchel in the other, just as something struck the top of the wall by my hand and threw up sparks as it went by. It looked like her hatchet, but I didn't want to find out for sure, so I hit the ground on the other side and almost lost my balance and the satchel, too, but I managed to keep running. I thought I could hear Ark shouting my name way back behind me, but it didn't make much difference to me right then.

As I tore across the Salberins' flower beds and headed for the rail fence between their place and the Wylmeens' property, I heard someone scrambling over the wall behind me, screaming something like "evil spawn" over and over. For a moment, I wondered if Goodwife Filster had always been strange in that way, and if she was really crazy or was just so angry she couldn't think straight anymore, and maybe having her bakery burn down was just the last straw. She had always been mean but never really awful or strange like she was now.

I reached the rail fence, slowing down just enough to climb over it with one hand because it was too high to vault over. I couldn't seem to get a grip on the wood for a moment, but I heard her shout, "Evil spawn!" right behind me, and in moments I was over the fence and on my back in the Wylmeens' tomato bed. I scraped my leg on a tomato post in falling over the fence and the satchel banged my nose, but none of it hurt very much and I had a lot more to think about right then than a scratch. I also thought that I didn't have the faintest idea of where I was going to go, but I just wanted to get Goodwife Filster and her torch away from Ark and Widow Muffin and our shoe shop. That was all that mattered.

I got up and started running across the tomato bed and into the cucumber vines, but it was dark and my foot caught in a bunch of vines and I fell flat on my face and knocked all the wind out of my lungs. I still had the satchel, so I started to get up and run again, but I fell down right away because my ankle felt like someone had stuck it with a red-hot iron. I heard someone scramble over the fence and land on the ground a dozen feet behind me, so I got up again but couldn't run on my bad leg or even hop on my good leg, and I fell again and said the very same bad word I'd heard the fisherman use, the very same word Ark had told me never to say again, and I said it real loud.

And that's when I heard Mud coming.

The Wylmeens call their dog Mud because he has the same color coat as the mud in the road after a heavy rain. He comes up almost to my shoulders and has eyes that glow white when he sees something he wants to kill, and the Wylmeens haven't been very good about teaching Mud not to kill everything that comes into his yard. He killed a wolverine one year in an hour-long battle, and the Wylmeens stuck the carcass on a post by the road, where it stayed until Mud figured out how to get it down and tore it into little pieces. I sometimes slip through the Wylmeens' garden because I figured out how to get to the other side before he could get off the back porch and catch me, and I have to confess that it was a little exciting to tease him like that, even though I knew I shouldn't if I wanted to live a long time.

Unfortunately, I had never expected to fall down in the Wylmeens' garden, though I had long ago figured out from the number of close calls that I'd had with Mud that falling down meant I would probably not get a second chance to get out of the garden in one piece. I heard Mud coming off the back porch, and I looked up over the vines in front of my face to see him hurtling across the garden right at me, moving like a wild black shadow with white moons for eyes. I couldn't see much of him but I saw enough, so I wrapped my arms over my head and curled up and hoped the Wylmeens would be able to call him off me before I looked like that wolverine.

Mud was on me in a rush. Then he was over and past me, and I heard a shriek that could have awakened a graveyard full of dead people. Mud was snarling and fighting, and someone was screaming, and I decided it was time to get out of there no matter what had happened to my ankle. I started to crawl away on my hands and knees as fast as I could, but as I was trying to leave I heard Goodwife Filster screaming *"Help me!"* at the top of her lungs, and I did what I had never thought I would do. I crawled back to save her.

Humans think that because I'm a kender I am not supposed to be afraid of anything, and I guess it's true, but I must admit that my stomach turned over when I saw how big Mud was and what he was doing to Goodwife Filster on the ground. Mud wasn't paying any attention to me, so I crawled over and got up on my knees and banged him twice on his dog butt with the satchel. It was like hitting a tree stump for all the good it did, and the satchel handle broke right then anyway, and the facts machine fell out in the dirt and cucumber vines. Goodwife Filster was screaming, and Mud was about to tear her arm off, so I picked up the facts machine and threw it at Mud, and I hit him.

I have to admit that I didn't expect the facts machine to light up like it did and shoot out little lightning bolts and make Mud flip up into the air and spin around for a moment before he crashed back into the cucumbers and wiggled around in really bizarre ways. I found the facts machine, and it didn't seem to be broken, so I put it back in the satchel and crawled over to see what I could do for Goodwife Filster, who was groaning and holding her arms in front of her face.

About then Ark came over the fence and all twenty of the Wylmeens came out of their house and ran over to help, too, which was a good thing, as I had never seen someone with so many cuts and bites before and I wasn't sure where to start in trying to fix them all.

They carried Goodwife Filster into the Wylmeens' house and washed her off and wrapped up her arms and face and legs and everything else in white bandages until she almost looked like one of her own sugar buns. It seemed to me that she was going to live, though she wasn't going to be chasing people around with sharp objects and torches very much in the foreseeable future. They also wrapped up my ankle, which wasn't broken, only sprained, and made me sit off to the side out of sight while they made Goodwife Filster more comfortable. I admit that I was a little jealous of the attention she got because, after all, she was the one who had been chasing me with a knife and axe and torch and had wanted to burn down Ark's shoe shop, but I decided not to point that out. It was when I was watching everyone get Goodwife Filster fixed up that I had a funny thought, and I hopped over to ask her a question.

They had finished wrapping up her head and everyone was gathering around her to talk when I came over. No one paid any attention to me, so I went right up and stood beside the cot where she lay, and I put down the satchel, which Ark had forgotten to take back from me right then but did later. Goodwife Filster looked terrible, but she was breathing and that was good, I guess.

"Goodwife Filster?" I whispered, and when she didn't do anything, I asked again, "Goodwife Filster?"

She groaned then and half-turned so she could look at me through all the rags that were tied over her head. Her eyes opened, but they looked like they were dead.

"You were pretty mad at me for asking about Istar, weren't you?" I asked.

Goodwife Filster just stared at me and didn't make any noise, but I assumed her answer was yes. No one else said anything. They all just looked at me, so I kept going.

"I was supposed to ask that question for Astinus of Palanthas, to help out Ark," I said. "I was just thinking about it all, and I think I know the reason Astinus wanted to find out what people thought of the Cataclysm. It goes like this: Nobody liked Istar very much, except maybe for you and a few other people. But, then, from what I've heard, nobody really liked anybody at all very much back then, and things don't seem to have gotten much better now, because everyone down deep still hates everyone else. Asking people about Istar brings out all the worst in them and opens up all the old wounds, though I'm saying that as a metaphor and not because you have so many wounds right now, really. I think Astinus knew that would happen, and he wanted to find out just how bad things really were now, and maybe he wasn't so much interested in Istar after all. Astinus is really worried that someday something bad will happen that will need all of us to pull together and work together and maybe fight together to set things right again, and if we don't learn that being different is really okay, then we aren't going to make it in the long run and we'll be just like the Karkhovs' melons and be swept away by the ocean or whatever it is that Astinus is afraid will come at us. What do you think?"

Goodwife Filster kept staring at me while her lips moved. I had to lean close to hear her. "Astinus and you?" she asked. "You were both doing this?"

I nodded. "Yup. See, Ark made me a field recorder, and I decided to—"

I'm afraid I didn't get much further with my explanation, because at that point Goodwife Filster sat up on the cot and yelled out that both you and I should get together and do something that was remarkably disgusting and which I'll bet is physically impossible, but which I have to admit sounded pretty funny to me later on, though you might not think so. Then she tried to get off the cot and come after me, but the Wylmeens got to her first.

After things calmed down a bit, Ark and Widow Muffin carried me back to the shop. On the way, we picked up Woose, the dwarf, and Cotterpin, the tinker, and Magistrate Jarvis and Kroogi and several other people who were friends of at least one of us, and when we got back to the shop, Ark closed the back door and everyone cleaned me up and fed me while Ark and the widow told the story of how I had saved them. They put fresh dirt over all the lamp oil Goodwife Filster had spilled in the shop and swept it out, but it still smelled almost as bad as the gas Ark gets from eating cheese pastries, which I guess he won't eat anymore. In the process, I heard that the Wylmeens' dog, Mud, was still alive but he wasn't the same old Mud and was actually pretty quiet now and wasn't chasing or biting anyone this evening and maybe won't do it again, or so I hope.

Eventually everyone went home and Ark took his facts machine and satchel away from me, and the machine was a little dirty but not broken, and Ark never once asked me if I'd seen the widow's letters, and I never once brought it up. I never even asked why the widow happened to drop by the shop while I was gone or where her shoes had gone. (When I got the satchel and facts machine back just a few minutes ago to send this to you, I noticed that Ark had taken the letters out of the satchel and had hidden them somewhere else, but I won't try to find out where they are, as I don't think I could stand the shock. Widow Muffin stayed on with us tonight, but I didn't mind. She and Ark seem the happier for it.)

This will be my last report to you, Astinus. I told Ark that being a recorder was very exciting, but it was maybe a little too exciting, and I would rather be a cobbler for now and later an amanuensis, though to tell the truth I have given some thought to being a cave explorer or a sea pirate (I didn't tell him that part, though).

I also asked Ark if tomorrow he would show me where my mother is buried so I could say hi to her and maybe visit her once in a while. Ark said yes and also said he was sorry he had never told me about her before and said it had hurt him to even think about it. All he could remember about her was that she was pretty. I thought about it and finally figured that I could forgive him, because I don't know what I would have done had it been me finding a baby Ark, and it was all past anyway.

I have been thinking about the question I tried to answer for you and how much trouble that one question caused, and for a while I was feeling bad about myself for asking it, but now I don't so much. I feel sorry for Goodwife Filster, even if she is so crazy and angry that she lost control of herself, but there are a lot of people like her around who have bad attitudes and don't want to make life better for anyone else. If you are afraid that people haven't learned anything about working together as a lesson of the Cataclysm, then it seems to me you have a lot to worry about. But Ark and I (and maybe the widow, too, though I haven't asked) have it figured out most of the time, so there's still hope.

It was fun working for you, Astinus. Maybe I will get to see you again someday when I sail my own pirate ship. Be looking for me!

The Voyage
of the Sunchaser

Paul B. Thompson
and Tonya R. Carter

***

A DENSE RED HAZE SURROUNDED THE SUN IN A HOT, silent sky. The sea was calm, though swirls and eddies showed on its surface. The violent upheavals in the air and water had lasted through the long night; now they were done. Across this desolate scene drifted the merchant ship *Sunchaser*, listing hard to port, its tangled yards and spars trailing in the oily water.

The ship's master, Dunvane of Palanthas, slipped the loops of rope from around his wrists. In the worst part of the storm, he had lashed himself to the ship's wheel. His wrists were raw and bloody from the hemp's chafing. Dunvane took the wheel now and turned it left and right, but the steering ropes were slack and the ship did not respond.

He drew in a deep breath and coughed. Feathers of smoke clung to the *Sunchaser*; the shredded sails were still burning. Dunvane had never seen anything like the blazing hot tempest that had swept down upon them. The wind was like fire itself, and it consumed more than the ship's sails. Those sailors who'd had the ill fortune to be standing on the windward side of the ship had ignited like candles. Half of Dunvane's crew of fourteen died in that instant. He and the others who'd been on deck had burns on their faces and hands and arms.

Then came the waves. Breakers as high and solid as cliffs fell on them. Only Dunvane's seamanship had saved the *Sunchaser*, as he turned stern first to the crushing waves.

***

The ship rode out the extraordinary storm, but with all the spinning and turning, the captain had no idea where they'd come to be.

What crewmen remained were scattered on deck, laid out by exhaustion. Dunvane staggered to the waist of the ship, shaking the sailors awake. Four men, he found, were beyond waking. Within a short time, the only three survivors of the *Sunchaser*'s crew were on their feet.

"Set the lads to clearing away those fallen shrouds," Dunvane said.

First Mate Norry croaked the order, then asked his captain, "As we're short-handed, sir, will we be puttin' back for Palanthas?"

Dunvane squinted into the billowing clouds. "Nay. We've come more than halfway. It's better to make for Gardenath, on the Istar coast." He shook his head and tugged thoughtfully at his dark brown beard. "I haven't a clue where we are, Norry."

"Surely the Solamnic coast lies south," offered the mate, pointing over the starboard rail.

Dunvane was not sure of anything, and said so.

"Well," Norry said, "at least the cargo is safe."

Dunvane looked at the reason for their voyage. Lashed to the deck hard by the mainmast was an enormous bowl, carved out of serpentine stone by master artisans in Palanthas. Dunvane and his crew were being well paid to ferry this stone bowl from Palanthas to Istar. The sight eased Dunvane's fear.

"I'll speak with the Revered Son," the captain said. "He'll know what's going on. In the meantime, keep the men busy. Don't give 'em time to think too much."

"Aye, aye, sir."

Dunvane circled the serpentine bowl, watching the iridescent colors flare and die on its surface as he moved around it. Although made of stone, the bowl was remarkably light, in part because of the skillful fluting of the underside. It was seven feet in diameter and two feet deep in the center, yet four Palanthian stevedores had loaded it without strain. Once the captain was satisfied that its lashings were intact, he went aft to the sterncastle.

A gust of wind disturbed the eerie calm. Something borne on the wind pattered on the deck and stung his face. He stared at it—fine, black dirt. Here was a fresh wonder—a shower of dirt this far out at sea! The wind swirled and stole the dark dust from his sight.

Dunvane hurried aft and knocked loudly on the stern cabin door. "May I enter?" he called.

"Yes, come."

Dunvane pulled off his knitted wool cap and raised the latch. The cabin inside was hot and dark. The sole candle had gone out. Dunvane's eyes adjusted to the lack of light, and he saw a pale face emerge from the shadows near the cabin berth.

"Are you well, Revered Son?"

"I am well, Captain." The passenger stood and stepped into the well of faint light from the open door. A tall, ascetic-looking man, not yet thirty years of age, his fair skin and blond-white hair shone in the gloom. Despite the violence of the night, he appeared remarkably composed. His white priestly robes were neatly draped around his narrow shoulders, and his hair was smoothed back from his forehead. Composure came easily to Revered Son Imkhian of Istar. He wore it as part of the costume of his office.

Seating himself at the table in the center of the cabin, Imkhian asked in a calm, deep voice, "What has happened?"

Dunvane opened the side shutters and let diffuse red light fill the cabin. "A storm like no other I ever encountered in my life, Revered Son. I shot the stars just before eight bells, and everything was as calm as a farmer's pond. The sky was fair. Then the lookout called, 'Fire! Fire!' 'Whereaway?' says I. 'In the air,' says the lookout."

"Fire in the sky? Most strange," Imkhian said coolly. "Then what?"

"A great globe of fire fell into the sea, and a burning hot wind struck us." Dunvane went on to enumerate his losses—sailors, sails, rigging. "But your special cargo is safe, Revered Son, safe and undamaged."

The priest nodded. "That is well. The Kingpriest himself is expecting the serpentine bowl before the great Festival of Purification."

"If I may ask—what is it for?"

Imkhian folded his hands. "It will be placed in the great temple in the center of the city, and there an eternal flame will be kindled. That is why it must be made of serpentine; any other stone would eventually crack under the continuous heat."

Cries outside interrupted the priest. "Heave away!" yelled a voice, and there was a loud crash. The ship slowly righted itself.

"The men have cut away the broken foremast that was making us list," Dunvane explained. "The hull is undamaged."

"How will we proceed without sails?"

"There is spare cloth on board. We'll patch together a small sail, Revered Son. We are being drawn by a current. Our progress will be slow, but we can proceed."

Imkhian frowned, his pale blue eyes narrowing. "Time is short, Captain. The voyage was only supposed to last a week."

The captain shifted nervously, his head still bent in a posture of deference. "No one could have foreseen the tempest last night, but I don't think it will delay us more than a day. But . . . Revered Son, what could that globe of fire have been?"

The priest looked thoughtful. "Forces of evil are rampant, Captain, and the work of our great Kingpriest is often threatened. Since the Proclamation of Manifest Virtue, evil sorcerers have plotted to stop this great cleansing work. Perhaps some wizard sought to prevent the serpentine bowl from reaching Istar." Imkhian drew himself up taller, his eyes glinting proudly. "But the will of the Kingpriest is not easily thwarted."

"May his blessings continue upon us," Dunvane murmured with feeling.

Imkhian frowned and studied the sea captain intently, as if searching for some sign of insincerity. Dunvane shifted uneasily.

"Ahoy! Shipwreck, ahoy!" came a cry from on deck.

Bowing, Dunvane hastily quit the cabin, jamming his hat back on his head. The mate and the other two members of his crew stood at the starboard rail, peering into the murk. The first mate put his hands around his mouth and crowed again, "Shipwreck, ahoy!"

Then the captain saw it. Lying very low in the water, some thousand yards off, was a dark, floating object. It resembled a fair-sized vessel, lying on its beam ends.

"Is the helm answering?" asked Dunvane.

"Aye, Captain, but without sheets, we're flowing with the current," Norry replied.

"That will do. Bring her about, four points to starboard."

Sluggishly, the *Sunchaser* turned its bluff bow toward the distant wreck. The smoky dust hanging in the air parted silently as the *Sunchaser* glided along.

"Two points more," called Dunvane. He climbed the rigging and clung to the shrouds, studying the wreck as they came steadily closer. From his loftier perch, he saw that the sea ahead was flecked with flotsam of every kind: tree branches, boards, straw, bottles, the carcasses of drowned animals. Norry steered the ship until the bow was dead-on to the half-sunken vessel.

The water was muddy, a turbid brown mixture. It was impossible to see the usual changes in sea color that warn of shallows. Dunvane stared hard at the water, praying they wouldn't run aground.

"Keep us off that wreck," ordered the captain. "I don't want to foul her."

A sailor went forward with a hefty boat hook in hand. At the last moment, Norry spun the wheel, and the *Sunchaser* sheered left of the wreck.

A figure rose up on top of the hulk and waved both arms.

"Bring him aboard!" shouted Dunvane, and the sailor with the boat hook held it out to the castaway. The mud-coated figure threw both arms around the pole. The sailor levered him up and around.

Dunvane's attention was drawn from the rescue by a scraping sound below him. He looked down to where the side of the *Sunchaser* was brushing against the wreck. Tufts of hay, tied with string, broke loose and floated away from the sunken ship. Bundled straw . . . thatch from a roof . . .

"I'll be damned!" Dunvane exclaimed. "That's no ship!

241

It's a house!"

The rescued castaway collapsed on deck. Dunvane slid down a line and dropped onto the deck beside the stranger—a woman.

"Thank you!" she gasped, brown eyes gleaming out from under a thick mask of mud. She kissed Dunvane's hand fervently. "Bless you, sir! I saw your ship and thought it was a vision—!" Her voice choked off.

Embarrassed, the captain pulled away and stood up. He ordered a sailor to push them off from the wreck, and soon the unusual current was once more pulling them along. Norry fetched a bucket of clean water and a rag. The woman wiped her face, then raised the heavy bucket to her lips, drinking deeply. The water cut rivulets in the mud plastered on her throat.

"Who are you?" asked Dunvane. "Where do you come from?"

"My name is Jermina. I am from Gardenath."

Dunvane stared. "*Where?*"

The woman repeated her answer.

"How in all Chaos did you get out here, in the middle of the ocean?" he demanded.

Jermina looked forlornly at the receding bulk of the wreck. "This was Gardenath," she said. "Right where you stand."

"You're lying!" said Norry.

She shook her head, dazed, in shock. "That house was Herril's Inn. It stood on the highest hill in Gardenath. The wall of water fell upon us, covering the land in a single night. Nothing remains. . . ."

"Bah!" Norry snorted, but the others weren't so sure.

"Can it be true, Captain?" one of the sailors asked.

"I cannot count it so. There was an upheaval, we know that, but I cannot believe that a town of ten thousand souls has sunk beneath the sea."

"So it happened," said Jermina softly.

The sailors frowned, exchanging glances. It was obvious they were beginning to believe her.

"I will ask the Revered Son," said Dunvane firmly. "He will know the truth!"

242

He took hold of the woman and headed for the priest's cabin. Dunvane knocked until the door opened and Imkhian appeared. The captain brought Jermina forward. She told her story.

The priest's composure remained untouched, and he spared no more than a glance at the muddy, bedraggled woman. "It is a lie, Captain," he said flatly. "Such things do not happen. The Kingpriest does not permit them to happen."

Jermina blinked at him. "Why would I lie? I tell you, the town of Gardenath lies under the water around you!"

Imkhian's impassive gaze remained on the captain. "Resume your course, Master Dunvane. I am on an important mission, given me by the Kingpriest himself. The serpentine bowl must arrive in Istar for the ceremony. Don't waste any more precious time worrying about this ridiculous tale."

"We'll set to work on the sail at once, Revered Son," said Dunvane, relieved, as Imkhian slammed shut the cabin door.

"Captain!" shouted Norry.

The *Sunchaser* shuddered and heeled slowly to port. Dunvane and his men ran to the rail. The strange current that had been carrying them along was changing direction, and the ship's rudder, tied straight ahead, was fighting the pull.

"Look!" Norry pointed.

"By all the holy gods," breathed Dunvane.

Off the port side was a scene from a nightmare. A vast shoal of floating debris covered the water. Clinging to the mass of logs, shake roofs, and uprooted trees were bedraggled, muddy, sunburned people. All stared hopefully at the oncoming *Sunchaser*.

The first cries from parched throats reached their ears. "Help . . . help us . . . water, water . . . help . . ."

The captain recovered from his shock. "Norry. Take the wheel. Steer wide of them." Dunvane ran to Imkhian's door once again. "Revered Son! Come out, please! You must see this!"

Imkhian emerged. The captain pointed at the scene ahead.

A flicker of surprise marred the smooth surface of the priest's composure. His eyes moved left and right, taking in the dreadful panorama.

The flotsam shoal was only a ship's length away. Norry wrestled with the wheel, but, without sails, the *Sunchaser* could not resist the current. The ship's blunt bow was pointed at the thickest concentration of rafts. The people were making ready to climb on board.

"Do not stop," Imkhian said swiftly.

"But, Revered Son, a seaman's duty is to aid—"

"We cannot help them," answered the priest. "There is neither food nor water enough on this ship to save twenty, much less such a multitude. We can do nothing for them. You must fulfill your mission, Captain. The serpentine bowl must be delivered."

"Help us . . . mercy, please . . . save my baby . . ." came the cries.

The cutwater struck the first line of rafts with a sickening crunch. Dunvane saw Norry's hands trembling violently on the wheel. In a cold, anguished fury, the captain shoved the mate away and took the wheel himself. The *Sunchaser* rode over everything in its path. The screams and groans of the dying people were horrible to hear. Dunvane knew he'd be haunted by the memory for the rest of his days.

Jermina, left to herself, cast about wildly for some succor to give to the people in the water. She found a coil of rope and threw its free end over the side. The castaways clung to it, trying to climb the rope onto the ship.

Dunvane saw her as she steered to starboard in an attempt to miss a raft laden with people. "The Revered Son is right," he said through clenched teeth. "We've not enough food or water to share. Cut the line, Norry."

Jermina screamed. Norry pulled out his sheath knife, casting a look of agony at his captain. Dunvane could not speak the order again, but he nodded once. Norry cut the rope with one stroke, just as a pair of raw, blistered hands reached for the rail.

Dunvane would never forget that dreadful voyage. When at last they were clear of the floating refugees, he tied off the wheel and slumped against the sterncastle behind him.

"Captain."

Dunvane opened his eyes. Norry stood before him. "We're with you, sir," the mate said. "Me and the men, we don't want to die, but we're scared. What's happened, Captain? Who were all those people?"

"Pirates," said Imkhian, looming in the doorway to his cabin. "Thieves."

"Your pardon, Holy One, but those were ordinary towns-folk, not even sailors, by the look of their pale skin," Dunvane replied.

"Could they be? Could the woman be telling the truth?" Norry asked slowly. "Were those the people of Gardenath?"

"You're speaking blasphemy," warned the priest.

Still sobbing, Jermina cried, "Since when is the truth a blasphemy?"

"Enough," Dunvane barked. The sullen sky was darkening to purple as the sun began to set. "If there is a coast to find, it's got to be south. Norry, you and the men work on rigging a trysail on the foremast. Once it's done, maybe we can steer ourselves out of this current."

The sailors dispersed to their tasks. The woman, Jermina, went forward to sleep in the shadows on the foredeck. Imkhian began to speak of faith and trust in the gods, and faith in the goodness and power of the Kingpriest. After a few minutes, the priest realized no one was heeding him. Scowling, he withdrew in offended dignity back to his cabin.

*　*　*　*　*

A wind sprang up before midnight. The breeze scoured the smoke and clouds away, and stars glittered overhead. Dunvane called for his quadrant. He shot the stars and called out their positions to Norry, who scratched figures on a wax tablet.

"Something's not right about these figures, Captain," Norry muttered. He chewed the blunt end of his wooden stylus. "We're nowhere near where we should be."

Dunvane sent below for a chart of the Istar coast. By lantern light, he compared the figures he'd just taken to the ones given on the parchment scroll. His jaw dropped in astonishment. He shot the stars again, with the same result. The heavens did not lie. He stabbed his knife into the map at their position. "We're a hundred miles from the Istar coast," said Dunvane. "A hundred miles *inland* of the coastline!"

"The woman's right," said Norry grimly. "The land's gone under the sea. What do we do now, sir?"

Dunvane snatched up lantern, knife, and chart. "The Revered Son must see this." He burst into the priest's cabin without knocking. Imkhian stirred sleepily in his berth.

"What's the meaning of this disturbance?" he asked sternly.

"I have important news, Holy One," Dunvane replied.

"We have reached Istar?" Imkhian sat up. "The Kingpriest will be very pleased! We're a day early—"

"We're in Istar all right, Revered Son, but Istar is not here."

"Did you wake me to ply me with riddles?"

Dunvane spread the map on the table and set the lamp on it. "By the stars of heaven, which I shot not five minutes ago, I got this as our position." He pointed to the hole in the chart made by his knife point. Imkhian bent over to study the map.

"You've simply made an error—"

"I shot our position twice, Holy One," the captain interrupted. "The woman was right. What we took for a tempest was some kind of great upheaval. There's no way of knowing how far the destruction spreads."

Imkhian straightened. He ran his fingers through his mussed hair and tugged his wrinkled robe into a semblance of order. "I am certain the city of Istar is safe, Captain. The Kingpriest's power is proof against any catastrophe or evil magic."

Imkhian's voice was strong, positive, calm. But this time, the captain's fears were not stilled. The two men stared at each other for a long minute.

"I hope you're right, Revered Son," said Dunvane at last. He rolled up his chart. "I'd best take the wheel. We're in unknown waters now, and a captain's place is at the helm."

He turned to go, but Imkhian caught his arm. "Leave the lantern," he said. "I wish to pray."

Dunvane pulled the cabin door shut quietly. Norry came up behind him.

"The trysail's been rigged, sir," he reported, "and we've spotted lightning. Looks to be a terrible storm, dead ahead."

What else could happen? Dunvane sighed and followed his mate to the wheel. A red glow lit up the horizon, too early and too easterly to be the dawn. "What is that?" asked the captain, staring.

"Dunno, sir. Could be a ship on fire."

Dunvane squinted through the tangle of rigging, masts, and the billowing trysail. "If so, it's a big one," he muttered.

"Aye."

Lightning flickered around the scarlet glow. An uncommonly warm wind blew over them; patches of mist rose from the cooling sea. They could hear the sound of thunder. The previously calm sea was roughened by rising swells. The *Sunchaser* wallowed in the waves. The motion roused Jermina, who came aft to see what was going on.

"What's that light?" she asked, clutching at the binnacle for support.

Before anyone could reply, Imkhian, white robe flapping in the increasingly hot wind, appeared like a pale ghost at the captain's elbow.

"Let the gods steer your ship, Captain," he commanded. "We are in their hands now."

"Every sailor is in the hands of the gods," Dunvane said, "but my hands stay on this wheel, Holy One."

A thunderclap was punctuated by a stinging hail of dust. The wind crackled the frail trysail. The ship glided along with the speeding current. The dust storm passed quickly, replaced by a steady blast of furnace-hot air. The sailors and Jermina coughed and covered their faces. Dunvane blinked through the grit lodged in his eyes and stared at the rapidly brightening red glow. It soon filled the sky from port to starboard. From its midst rose a column of smoke, reaching from the sea surface up to the sky, where it spread into a flat-topped cloud.

"The whole world's on fire!" Norry gasped.

"The water's starting to seethe like a soup kettle," cried the lookout.

Dunvane stared over the bow. Steam rose from the sea. The water was the color of blood. "I'm putting about," Dunvane said and tried to put the helm over to starboard.

Imkhian's long white fingers gripped the wheel. "Go forward, Captain. In my prayers I was given to know that we must seek out the fire, not hide from it. Fire purifies all it touches. The gods will protect us."

The priest's voice was calm, his gaze fixed upon the crimson glow before them.

Dunvane shook his head. "We must turn away, Revered Son. The ship would go up like a torch."

The priest made his way past the sailors and stood by the rail. His gaze roved around the spectacle before them, the unknown red light, the pillar of smoke, the steaming, blood-red water. He turned abruptly, his eyes blazing. "Keep going!"

Lightning flickered overhead as the hot, glowing column of smoke closed out the last bit of night. The red glow lit them like a bloody sunrise. Dunvane spun the wheel left and right, but the *Sunchaser* could not break out of the rushing stream that propelled it.

"It doesn't look as if we've got much choice," Dunvane said bitterly. Norry and the other two crewmen began to fidget and cast anxious looks at the churning sea.

Something boomed against the hull. A sailor bent over the side and sang out, "Timbers! There's timbers in the water! Heading straight for us!"

Unable to steer, Dunvane could do nothing. Massive building timbers rammed into the *Sunchaser*. Dunvane held grimly to the wheel. The ship rolled and pitched and they were still being drawn toward the great shaft of smoke, fire and lightning.

"Have no fear!" called Imkhian above the thunder and booming waves. "We are being tested! We must not be afraid! Istar lies beyond the wall of fire; we must penetrate the wall!" The priest knelt by the great serpentine bowl, clinging to its smooth surface.

Norry staggered across the canted deck. "Captain! What can we do?"

A bolt of lightning struck the mainmast. The foot-thick oak mast splintered down its length, and the heavy crossyard crashed to the deck, knocking Dunvane back from the wheel. He hit the sterncastle and slid down, stunned. The useless wheel spun freely.

The *Sunchaser* heeled sharply to port. Dunvane shook the mist from his brain and stood, grasping Norry's arm for support.

The rudder had been carried away. The fallen crossyard had torn the puny trysail like a cobweb. *Sunchaser* wallowed dead in the water. The racing current caught its blunt stern and swung the ship in a half circle. Scalding-hot spray, whipped up from the churning water, burst over the rail. Dunvane, his men, and Jermina sought vainly for cover.

Imkhian stood alone on the foredeck, clutching the capstan and staring into the hellish tempest. His hair was slicked down by the hot sea spray. His lips moved, though no one could hear his words. He gazed up at the heavens, as though praying.

Norry prodded Dunvane. The captain shielded his face from the droplets as his gaze followed the first mate's pointing arm.

Great piles of wreckage whirled on the sea's surface—fragments of gilded roofs and plastered walls, furniture, corpses, uprooted trees. The wreckage spun about in the blood-tinged water, then vanished into a gigantic whirlpool in the ocean. Dunvane knew then they were doomed. Smoke rose from the funnel, and lightning flashed in the skies above. "This is the force that has drawn us on since yesterday morning," Dunvane said.

One sailor shrieked a warning. A gigantic bronze statue was coming up fast on the starboard beam.

Dunvane grabbed the person nearest him—it happened to be Jermina—and held on. The hurtling statue smashed into the ship.

The *Sunchaser* heeled halfway over, burying its port rail in the blood-red sea. A sailor somersaulted over the rail into the water and was swept away by the current. The ship shuddered like a wounded beast, its timbers groaning as it slowly righted itself partway. It was impaled on the wreckage, and sinking by the bow.

The colossal statue—seared by fire, melted and misshapen—lay across the foredeck. "Where's the Revered Son?" Dunvane demanded. He ran forward and found Imkhian crumpled against the capstan. Blood was running from a gash on his forehead.

"Revered Son! Are you all right?"

The priest blinked and looked up at the face of the statue. "Kingpriest!" he cried hoarsely. "You stood upon the arch of Paladine's Gate!" He covered his face with his hands and uttered a long, tearing wail. "What has the world come to, that the most righteous nation on Krynn can be dealt such a blow? The Great Temple—the Kingpriest—the Revered Sons and Daughters—all thrown down! Istar is destroyed! Istar is destroyed!"

Imkhian bolted to the starboard rail. He stared straight into the whirling maelstrom and threw a leg over the rail.

"Stop, Imkhian!" Dunvane yelled.

The sound of his own name made the priest pause. He looked over his shoulder at the captain. His face was twisted with fury. "The gods have abandoned us! The world is at an end." Turning back to face the boiling sea, he raised his other leg over the rail.

"You don't have to die!" Dunvane shouted.

Imkhian's reply was a snarl. "Fools! You are already dead!" He let go and fell from the ship.

Dunvane and Norry ran to the rail. To his horror, Dunvane saw Imkhian break the surface of the bubbling ocean, hands reaching up to the ruined image of the Kingpriest. Without a sound, he sank below the surface.

Hatch covers all over the ship burst off as the flooding seawater filled the hold. Norry pulled Dunvane away from the rail. The *Sunchaser* was going down.

"Go aft!" Dunvane yelled. There was a small dinghy lashed to the transom stern. It was the only escape craft they had. Norry and the other sailor worked their way up the port side. Jermina and the captain crawled up the starboard. Blood-red saltwater lapped at Dunvane's heels.

"Don't let the dinghy fall!" Dunvane ordered. "It'll break." The sinking ship had lifted the stern so high he didn't dare release the lifeboat's moorings for fear of it plunging into the water and breaking apart. Norry and the sailor tried to free the dinghy, planning to drag it amidships and launch it there. They were so intent on cutting the knots that they didn't see the mizzen yard teeter above them.

"Look out!" the captain shouted.

Norry looked up in time to see the yard falling. He threw himself back. The railing he landed against gave way and, with a shocked outcry, he plunged overboard. The sailor, crouched by the dinghy, had no time to escape. The heavy yard crushed him and the dinghy in one devastating blow.

The ship's bow slipped under the waves. The bronze statue broke loose and was sucked away into the maelstrom by the racing current.

Water advanced slowly up the deck. Jermina clutched the captain's arm. "There must be something we can do," she pleaded.

"No one can live in that current," Dunvane said grimly. "The priest was right. The gods have abandoned us. We are as good as dead."

"No!" Jermina cried. "I don't believe it. The gods help those who help themselves."

Seawater bubbled around the serpentine bowl. It remained lashed to the deck, though the mainmast yard had fallen across it. Steam billowed up as the hot water touched the cool stone.

"Will that float?" Jermina asked, pointing to the sacramental bowl.

"Float? Maybe. It's light for its size, but why—?"

"Come on!" She seized his arm and dragged him along.

They had to wade in ankle-deep blood-red water to reach the bowl. Dunvane was almost numb with shock. "Hopeless," he muttered, but he let Jermina carry him along.

They managed to climb into the gigantic serpentine bowl. Jermina snatched the captain's knife from his belt and tried to hack through the lashings. They were too thick, and she made little progress. At last, Dunvane took the knife from her and set to work. Jermina reached out and snagged a boat hook floating nearby.

When the last line parted, the bowl was free of the ship. Jermina pushed them away with the boat hook. The bowl slid off the canted deck and into the water. The rushing current caught them.

They huddled in the bottom of the sacramental bowl, clinging to each other. The stone's fireproof properties protected them from the heat of the water, but the low sides let gouts of hot spray wash over them. The maelstrom spun them in tighter and tighter spirals toward the huge column of smoke and flame in its heart. Other wreckage crashed into them. The roaring of the rushing water filled their ears. They coughed and gasped in the fiery, choking air.

The serpentine bowl struck hard against something—the statue of the Kingpriest. Dunvane, certain this was the end, shut his eyes. The heat overcame them. They both lost consciousness.

* * * * *

Jermina awoke, sat up slowly. She looked around, dazed. Behind them, the column of fire that marked the grave of the city of Istar burned and flashed. The serpentine bowl she and Dunvane were in, along with other wreckage and rubbish, had been propelled out of the maelstrom. They floated quietly in a backwater.

"Dunvane!" she said, shaking him. He sat up, staring in wonder.

A cool drop hit his face. Another followed, then another, and soon rain was pattering on the ocean. The shower strengthened. Dunvane lifted his head and let the water wash over him. The sound of hysterical laughter grated on his nerves. Jermina was laughing and sobbing at the same time.

"What's funny?" he asked.

"The Revered Son was wrong," she said. "We're alive."

The High Priest of Halcyon

Douglas Niles

FROM THE CONTINUING RESEARCH OF FORYTH TEEL, Chief Scribe Assisting Astinus, Eternal Lorekeeper of Krynn.

Most Esteemed Historian:

It is with reverence approaching awe that I again pursue the lost histories of Krynn. It seems to me that now, more than ever before, the search for truth must be pursued with unrelenting courage and diligence. By all reckonings during this bleak era, the gods have abandoned us. Godly powers have been unknown for generations. The scars of the Cataclysm ravage the land. Thus, it falls to us—the historians— to follow the flickers of light that will lead us to a brighter future!

Those flickers, as Your Excellency well knows, have grown faint. During the bleak century since the gods rained their ruin upon Istar, the tragedy of the Dwarfgate War hangs over the south. The violent Newsea, tortured since its very creation by typhoon and cyclone, divides the peoples of central Ansalon, fragmenting the countryside into tiny partitions of its former greatness.

And everywhere, the people seek their gods. They call to Paladine, plead for Gilean or Reorx to answer their prayers. Yet the gods of good and neutrality and evil do not reply. These sad worshipers find not even the hint of the once-manifest presence of immortal beings. That, my lord, must certainly be deemed the most dire of the many effects attributable to the Cataclysm, for without gods, the people see no hope in the future.

On a brighter note, I am pleased to report that my health has been restored. As I have indicated previously, Your Grace's generosity in providing me with comfortable convalescence cannot be overthanked. With remarkable good luck—I dare not say the grace of the gods—I have regained full use of my limbs and the disfigurement left by the frostbite is only faintly visible.

In sum, my recovery is complete. Now, too, I have heard news that again compels me to walk the pathways of history! The information comes to me by a most reliable source (more about him in a moment).

I have received word of one who claims to have touched a higher power—and whose claims can be supported by creditable witnesses. A messenger arrived here, after many days of riding, from a land to the east. He tells me of a priest who has performed actual miracles. Having heard of we scribes who quest for the truth, the priest sends me testimonials by this messenger and extends an invitation to witness proof that the gods have not abandoned Krynn.

I understand that, if your calculations are correct (as they must undoubtedly be, Your Eminence!) and the gods have not left man, but man has left the gods, then there will be evidence of godhood found somewhere in the world. In a place distant or near, anywhere from the war-ravaged depths of Thorbardin to the crimson flowage of the Bloodsea, there exists proof of godly powers, whether they be curative or corruptive, beneficial or deadly.

The priest goes by the name of Erasmoth Luker. He dwells near a small town on the shore of the Newsea—a place called, oddly (symbolically?), Halcyon. Claiming that he can wield the powers of the gods, Erasmoth has established himself in a temple on a hilltop and preaches to all who will listen.

The source of my information—the one who dispatched the messenger to me—is a man known to you, Excellency. He is Underscribe Tyrol Deet, a historian of unusual acuity and perception. (Do you remember him—the young fellow who wanted to be a soldier until he lost his eye in a hunting accident? Now he wears a black patch over the socket and swears that the focus of his other eye has improved tenfold!) He says he has not witnessed the miracles wrought by Erasmoth—those traditionally have been reserved for the initiates, and, naturally, no historian could become such an initiate and still maintain the objective viewpoint required for our craft. Nevertheless, young Tyrol is convinced that there is truth to the tale and has persuaded the priest to allow your representative to witness and record the proof.

That one, needless to say, is me. The cleric has invited me, in my capacity as official scribe, to join his flock at the temple, there to witness the miracles of godhood and provide proof of their existence to you, Most Gracious Master Lorekeeper!

A ship awaits me at the wharf below. The captain has promised to carry me to Halcyon, though he warns that the waters will be rough. We embark with the morning tide, shortly past the dawn.

My lamp flickers as the oil runs low, and I realize that most of the night has passed. I will close for now. A rider departs for Palanthas in the morning, and he will carry this parchment with all the speed he can muster. I hope, Excellency, that it reaches your hands in good order. My next communication shall be sent by more unpredictable means, for it will originate from the vale of Halcyon itself.

Until such time, I remain your devoted servant:

Foryth Teel,
Senior Scribe to Astinus Lorekeeper

* * * * *

Most Merciful Master,

I pen this missive from my room in the quaint shoreline town of Halcyon. The sun shines through my windows. The wetness of the recent rain steams on the cobbled street. Indeed, this is the first glimpse of sunshine I have seen since weeks before my departure. Perhaps the gods *do*, in fact, favor this corner of Ansalon with their presence.

The voyage itself was a nightmare, from embarkation until I stepped onto the docks of Halcyon. Mountainous seas tossed the galley about like a matchstick. My poor body suffered countless bruises from the beating inflicted on it by collision with random parts of the vessel.

The voyage melded into a blur of seasickness; drenching, ice-cold rains; and even a night attack by some monstrous sea-beast. I could not get a look at the scaly horror in the darkness, but, whatever it was, it took two crewmen with it before it was driven off!

But, then, Halcyon hove into view, and the clouds lifted from my spirits as they did from the skies above. Green hills rise beyond whitewashed huts, huddled in a wide valley that breaks into a sheltered bay. Two broad arms of encircling ridge protect the waters, which seem too shallow for a vessel of any great draft but accommodated our galley with no difficulty.

I had expected Tyrol Deet to meet me at the dock, and I looked for his unforgettable eye-patch, but I was disappointed. He was not here. Seizing my small baggage, I hastened down the plank and was relieved to plant my feet once again upon a motionless surface.

I asked several people, but none of them knew the young scribe. I could think of no way to find him. As he gave me no address, I have reserved a room at the Halcyon Inn, the largest and grandest establishment of its kind within the town. I assume that Deet will look for me here.

This is the first night of my stay. I am hopeful that on the morrow the scribe will find me and we can commence our quest for the truth. In the meantime, I rejoice in the discovery of this tiny port—a place where the overcast breaks, at least momentarily, to allow Krynn to catch a little glimpse of the sun.

My next missive to Your Excellency will follow as shortly as circumstances allow. I remain your ever-devoted servant,

Foryth Teel

* * * * *

Most Esteemed Historian:

I resume my communication two days since my previous letter, which I trust has reached you in good order. Much has happened since that missive, which I will attempt to summarize for Your Grace as best I can.

The first news I received was not a positive harbinger. The morning following my arrival, I was greeted at my inn by a tall, slender man dressed in brown robes, who located me in the common room as I broke my fast. The gaze of his eyes, of clear and light blue, fastened on me from across the chamber, and I felt at once the presence of an unusual individual. As he approached, his narrow lips parted in a smile—though still I sensed those eyes appraising me, as if evaluating my fitness.

I must confess, Excellency, that I squirmed somewhat under that penetrating gaze, but nevertheless rose to my feet and took his hand as he reached my table.

"I am Erasmoth Luker," he said in a deep and powerful voice. "You are the scribe—the historian?"

"Indeed," I replied, not surprised to find that this was the priest of whom I had been informed. Something in the force of his gaze, in the depth of his voice, told me I faced an extraordinary person. "I am Foryth Teel, but I was supposed to be met by my colleague, Tyrol Deet."

"Alas," answered the priest. "I am sad to bring you unhappy tidings. The young scribe was taken by fever shortly after he wrote you. He was a strong lad, and held on for several days, but, in the end, to no avail."

"He's dead?" I asked, astonished. The news struck me with unexpected force. Deet was not a close friend of mine—we barely knew each other—but it was as if a promising lead had drawn me this far, only to vanish before my eyes.

"I see the news has affected you grievously," observed the priest, his tone sympathetic. "Would you want to see where he is buried? We have given him the full honors of the church, though, of course, he was not an initiate."

"Yes . . . yes, I should like that," I replied.

The priest led me through the streets of Halcyon—which then, alas, were dark beneath the same gray overcast that so thoroughly blankets Ansalon these days. We passed from the town and climbed a smooth dirt track that progressed into the surrounding hills.

Erasmoth has an elegance about him—a grace, if you will—that made me feel immediately at ease. His hair is dark and long, combed back to his neck, and shows traces of silver at the ears. His skin is smooth, but there is a maturity in his bearing that causes me to guess his age at perhaps fifty. Nevertheless, he moves easily—with far more energy than I can manage!

Soon the priest turned onto a side trail, and we quickly passed between a pair of looming pillars into a small, sheltered grotto—a small niche protected by the much larger hills. A clear pool of water, surrounded by drooping willows, formed the centerpiece of the vale. Among the broad tree trunks I noticed several headstones. It was the most peaceful and pastoral setting for a cemetery this well-traveled scribe has ever seen.

"I hope you approve of the arrangements," said Erasmoth when, at length, we had passed among the graves to reach a flowered mound with an admirable granite marker, clearly bearing the name of Tyrol Deet, and marking his station as a scribe of Your Greatness.

(Indeed, though his actual rank was a mere assistant scribe, I saw that insufficient space remained upon the stone for a correction; therefore, I let the matter lie.)

"Very nice," I said. "You have honored him well."

"No more than you honor us by your presence," Erasmoth informed me.

"The honor is to my master's name—Astinus, Lorekeeper of Krynn," I reminded him.

"Quite. The written affirmation of a historian such as yourself will validate the truth of my faith. The gods have not abandoned Krynn! They merely require the proper forms of approach from those who would worship them."

"In reference to these gods," I responded, grateful for the

opportunity to broach the subject of my quest, "young Deet was quite vague in his letter. How do you intend to prove their presence?"

"I'm glad you asked!" he declared, positively beaming. His enthusiasm, I must admit, was quite contagious.

Before he spoke further, he took my arm and led me back along the forested path, toward the rocky notch leading into this grotto. He explained as we climbed steadily upward.

"There are powers in the world that derive from sorcery," he said, "and others—reputedly vanished since the Cataclysm—that can be traced only to the gods and their faithful priests and priestesses. These powers, these clerical abilities, have been long since lost, abilities that no sorcerer can wield. Surely an astute historian like yourself is familiar with examples of those who have tried and failed."

"True," I allowed. "Such things as the healing of wounds and sickness, the communing with gods, auguries of the future, powers over trees and water and air, come only from the gods and are granted only to their most faithful servants—not to mention darker powers," I added as an afterthought. "From gods of evil."

He brushed that aside. "Surely you see, then," he noted, "that any who can wield these powers must have gained knowledge of the true gods—and more than that, he must be the recipient of their favor!"

We came through the rock-bordered notch, and I saw several people waiting for us.

Where they had come from was a mystery, for there were no dwellings—not even a simple homestead or farm—within sight. The group included a dozen or so people dressed in plain, dark brown robes, each person's face concealed by a blank plaster mask. A tall woman, unmasked and wearing a lovely red dress, stood at the center of the gathering.

"My higher-ranking initiates," explained the priest, as we continued to advance. "They have come to meet us here, as I instructed them earlier."

Erasmoth gestured to the woman. "The high priestess Kassandry," he said. She stepped forward to meet me.

The woman was, even to my old and weary eyes, a person of exquisite beauty. Tall and lithe, her gown of shimmering red silk flowing around her; she moved like ripples of water across the surface of a pool. Her skin was pale, almost as if it had been powdered white, and her hair of deep black contrasted sharply with both her complexion and gown. She had high cheekbones and deep brown eyes flecked with green. Her long neck bore a collar that appeared to be a single bar of gold.

"These are my acolytes, the faithful initiates of my temple." Erasmoth gestured to the dozen or so masked figures who remained in their watchful semicircle around us. They regarded me impassively, their eyes invisible behind the dark holes in their white masks. "They will be our escort, as we take you to the entrance to our temple."

"Why are they masked?" I inquired.

"They have all witnessed the glory of my god," Erasmoth explained, "but they do not know the full extent of that glory, or its attendant power. Their masks are a sign of their endeavors to learn. Only when they have achieved mastery will they again bare their faces to the world."

"You will give me proof of that power today?" I asked, striving to contain my excitement.

"Patience," the priest said, softly. "First you must be prepared for the miracle."

Erasmoth took my arm and escorted me in the forefront. The priestess Kassandry raised her hands and uttered a sharp cry. The acolytes fell into rank behind us. The group led me higher into the hills of Halcyon.

We made an odd procession—the priest and myself marching in the vanguard, followed by the crimson-gowned priestess immediately behind and the silent file of masked apprentices, making our slow and deliberate way in a winding column up the twisting trail.

This lofty solitude seemed an appropriate place for the worship of gods. Blankets of mist shrouded the valleys, draping the gray-green domes of the hilltops like fine linen. Above, soft crests of heather and grass rose in pleasant majesty, without the craggy menace of higher mountains such as the Khalkists.

We came upon a small valley, where stood a cluster of neat, thatch-roofed houses, whitewashed and surrounded by bright flower gardens. A crystal pool of water, formed by the damming of a narrow stream, looked cool and inviting after the exertion of the march.

"There!" proclaimed the priest, seizing my arm and gesturing with a finger toward the upper distance.

My eyes swept across the vast shoulder of the nearest hill, following the rising ground until I saw a tall white arch. A long white wall expanded out from either side of the arch. Several tall spires dotted the length of the barrier.

"What is it?" I asked.

"My temple—the holy place of the gods!" he proclaimed. "Tonight you will stay here in the valley, the outer sanctum of my temple. We shall endeavor to familiarize you with certain keystones of our faith. Tomorrow, or the next day, you will accompany the worshipers onto the mountain—there to witness the miracles wrought by me, in the name of the gods of Krynn!"

I studied the temple above with some trepidation. Your Excellency may recall, from my previous adventures, the vertigo that tends to grip me at the prospect of heights. The road that ascends to this temple is a sheer and winding track that would challenge a mountain goat—yet it was my goal!

The great temple arch was flanked by a pair of slender towers, an inherent part of the structure's design. The long, white wall stretching along the mountainside must enclose a compound of some sort.

Erasmoth led me on and, in a few moments, we had reached the houses in the valley. The high priestess went into one to arrange for my lodgings. I stood waiting on the shore of the pool.

"We call it the Mirror of Souls," Erasmoth said. "It is a splendid focus for meditation and introspection." Indeed, the water's dark surface lay as still as glass, and it seemed that one could imagine it as a repository for the fathomless depths of knowledge.

I stood entranced for some minutes, unaware of time's passage. At some point Erasmoth left, to arrange our dinner, as I recall him saying, but my gaze remained rapt on that magnificent reflecting pool.

"This scroll and package arrived in Halcyon for you. They were delivered to your assistant before he succumbed to the fever. Erasmoth directed me to save them for you."

Kassandry's voice brought me out of my meditation. She smiled, which was quite charming, and handed me a glass globe and a small scroll.

"Thank you," I said, surprised.

(Of course, Your Excellency is familiar with the package—the Jar of Sending, with which I shortly will try to convey this missive. At the time I did not know what it was, but I have since read your enclosed instructions.)

"We are pleased that you have come," said Kassandry, her tone surprisingly gentle. She no longer seemed the commanding high priestess. Instead, she was like any young maiden, eager to make her honored guest feel welcome, and fearful that he will not find matters to his liking.

"I'm grateful for the invitation and the hospitality."

She shook her head, as if I had missed the point. "No! The story must be told. The world must learn of our discoveries."

"It could be very important," I agreed, taken aback by her passion.

"Everything will have meaning then. If only you can convince the historian that the gods have not abandoned us!"

To my surprise, then, she leaned toward me, took my gray head in her hands, and kissed me full upon the lips!

I must admit, Your Grace, that it has been many years since I have received the attentions of a young woman—not to mention one of such stunning beauty.

"Er . . . delightful," I stammered, somewhat slow to respond, "but I really . . . my task is to observe . . ." In retrospect, I find that my words were a trifle confused.

Her gaze burned into mine with a secret smile—a smile that kindled spiritual fires I had thought long extinguished. Fortunately (unfortunately?) Erasmoth called us to dinner just then.

We dined on rib of lamb, accompanied by spiced potatoes. Our meal was a most pleasurable experience, prepared and served by Erasmoth alone. Only the high priestess, the priest, and myself were seated at the well-laden table; the acolytes presumably shared some plainer fare elsewhere.

During the dinner, Erasmoth proved himself a gracious and charming host. He is well-educated, though he lacks the polish of formal schooling. By his accent, I place his home in Ergoth somewhere, though I gather from his remarks that he has been in nearly every part of Ansalon. He probably is the most well-traveled person I have met— outside of our own ranks, in any event.

His dinner was excellent—the meat delicately cooked, tender and succulent; the bread crusty and hot from the oven. His amusing remarks on the antics of his apprentices were delightful. I left his company—and that of the priestess—with true regret.

Now my bed has been prepared, and the weariness of the day's march propels me there. Nevertheless, my pulse quickens at the thought of the morrow, and the promised miracle. May we find proof that gods can work their powers upon Krynn!

I tremble with anticipation of the joyful news that might be contained in my next communication. Until then, Your Grace, I am your obedient slave:

Foryth Teel,
Senior Scribe of Astinus

* * * * *

O Learned One:

A day has passed, and success! The priest has just pronounced me ready to bear witness at the inner sanctum of his temple! The activities of today have included exercises in meditative discipline and discussions with Erasmoth of the role of spiritual faith, which I quite enjoyed. We had a lively debate on the moral state of the Kingpriest prior to the Cataclysm and what effect, if any, that had on it. We debated the implications of the Newsea on trade in Ansalon.

I also spent time with Kassandry, and, though it was not

so intellectual, it was no less stimulating, if Your Excellency understands my meaning. There was an air of desire—almost hunger—in her attitude toward me that, I confess, tempted me in ways I had thought long forgotten. I assure Your Grace that my impartiality remains intact, though her beauty and charm has put considerable strain on my sense of duty and discipline. Indeed, were I a younger man . . .

In any event, Excellency, the priest Erasmoth has agreed that tomorrow I will be given the opportunity to witness an actual demonstration of clerical powers!

He does not reveal the exact nature of the miracle he plans—nor even the nature of his god—but he has assured me that I will find it convincing. I am prepared for anything, hoping that soon I can relay a communication of truly historical import.

As to the strange globe you provided, Excellency, it seems to me that it functioned flawlessly. I inserted the letter into the jar as you instructed and screwed the top tightly in place, then I held it over the flame of a bright candle for a few seconds and—poof—the parchment vanished in a bright flash of light. I trust that it arrived safely in Your Great Library. Such a device has obvious advantages, Lord, in that it avoids the use of unreliable post. And, too, it allows me to report from locations where I must otherwise remain discreet. I will employ it in all future correspondence.

But that was last night. My day in this pastoral vale has passed swiftly, and once again it is after sunset that I relate my experiences to you now.

Those times I was not in the company of the priest or priestess I spent in contemplation beside the Mirror of Souls—a remarkably invigorating pastime.

Once again we dined sumptuously, just the three of us. Indeed, the valley has been empty most of the day, though toward sunset I witnessed a file of the brown-robed acolytes winding their way up the trail toward the gleaming arch of the temple gate. They go, Erasmoth informs me, to prepare for tomorrow's ceremony.

Kassandry was a delightful dining companion. She has not kissed me again, and I confess to a certain disappointment there—though, of course, her restraint does make my position of impartiality easier to maintain.

Until my next missive, Excellency, I remain loyal to the service of our cause! Your devoted servant of history:

Foryth Teel

* * * * *

Your Grace,

I inscribe this from the dizzying ledge that serves as portal to the temple, halfway up a mountain that is much steeper than it appeared from the valley. I steal a moment to inscribe some quick observations, prior to entering the stone-walled temple compound. I will endeavor to complete this later and send it to you by means of the magical device you provided to me.

Erasmoth himself led the procession to the gates of his temple. We stand beneath the alabaster arch, which looms high above, and wait for the priest to perform his incantations and gestures, all of which are rendered in a tongue indecipherable to myself. His apprentices, masked and silent, remain immobile while he performs his rites, with Kassandry at his side. Today the high priestess has been surprisingly aloof, and I wonder at the change in her attitude. She does not seem unfriendly, merely preoccupied.

I will spare you the details of the perilous ascent to the temple. Suffice to say that I survived by dint of concentration on the objective, with oft-repeated reminders to myself about the significance of the historian's role and the importance of diligence and integrity in research. I made it this far . . . and when we pass within the temple walls, at least the threat of a fatal fall will be removed!

The temple, which has been dedicated to the worship of Erasmoth's gods, looms above me. The walls are solid, smooth, and much higher than they appeared from below. Each is topped with an array of spikes resembling the bristling spears of a rank of soldiers. The towers that flank the gate are tall, and I sense the presence of watchful eyes observing me and my escort. When I asked him about this, however, Erasmoth assured me that the place is empty.

The gates themselves are impressive doors made of pure silver. Even to my untrained eye, the aura of power protecting them is visible; a hazy and ominous film sparkles from the metal, bidding the unwary or uninitiated to remain at bay.

"We may now enter," Erasmoth announced.

The great gates swung soundlessly open, revealing a courtyard of dazzling white stone, with a beautiful fountain splashing just beyond the gate. The wondrous sight infused me with joy of discovery. We shall enter at once.

I hasten to close, Your Grace, with the hope that you will hear from me soon with the proof that our poor people have so long been seeking!

* * * * *

I resume:

I begin with the presumption that the enchanted globe performs its task and carries this information to you. Without that, all my labors shall have been spent in vain.

I return to the moment when the portals of silver spread wide, and I followed my host beneath the tall archway. The high priestess Kassandry walked at my side, her step light, eyes shining. She did not speak, and her attitude toward me remained distant.

The courtyard was filled with flowers, blazing with color. Walkways of white gravel meandered through the garden, as if to acknowledge that any course plotted straight through these wonders meant too hasty a passage. There are no buildings within, though the face of the mountaintop has been scored with several apertures.

We approached the inner doors of the temple, set in the mountain itself. These gleamed with a pure surface of burnished gold and, like the outer gates, seemed to forbid intrusion. Erasmoth approached them and barked a sharp word of command—required, apparently, to loosen the hold of magic and cause the doors to swing wide.

A dark tunnel led into the mountain. I hesitated for a moment, surprised by the sudden darkness, but Erasmoth entered and gestured to me with the imperious order, "Come."

Wondering at my sudden unease, I passed the gilded portal. Darkness washed over me. The gates closed with a resounding clang.

The heat was intense. I realized that the corridor must lead directly into the heart of the mountain itself! Great columns of basalt lined the walls to either side, with dusty alcoves lost in the shadows between them. Torches sputtered infrequently, cast inadequate light. It seemed a lifeless place, undisturbed for a long time, and I wondered how it could be the center of worship for the priest's faith.

"Why did you build the temple to your god—here—in this dark place?" I asked.

"I didn't build it. I discovered it." Erasmoth's voice rang with triumph. "It was placed here for me! I was a simple stone mason before I discovered my true calling. I was exploring, seeking materials for my trade, when I came across what was then only ruins. Now they are the magnificent gardens you have seen outside. I followed it to its heart . . . and learned of the glories of the gods!" Light flamed in his eyes, and his tone vibrated with intensity.

Sudden movement in the shadowy corridor seized my attention. Ghostlike shapes advanced all around me, and I gasped in terror.

Then a torch flared, and the forms were revealed as Erasmoth's acolytes, in their robes and flat masks. I heaved a sigh of relief and began to follow the priest and priestess down the long corridor, accompanied by the silent apprentices.

"How much farther do we have to go?" I asked the priestess. I found the darkness and the heat oppressive.

"Be patient, Historian!" said Kassandry softly. "We must display no unworthiness before we participate in the glories of the gods!"

"The role of the historian is not to participate—merely to observe and to report," I corrected mildly.

She regarded me strangely, her eyes flashing. Her once-pallid cheeks grew quite flushed, and her lips parted. She licked them, invitingly, I thought, but said nothing further.

I grew more uncomfortable. "Why did the gods choose you?" I asked the priest.

But Erasmoth did not seem to hear. "Await me here while I complete the preparations," he said abruptly, stopping and pointing to one side of the trail.

I noticed, for the first time, that what I took for an alcove between the arches of the tunnel wall was, in actuality, the entrance to a doorway. The priest chanted a word and waved his hand. This portal swung silently open to reveal a chamber of surprisingly comfortable appointments. A snap of his fingers brought a clear yellow flame to the wick of a glass lamp.

"I will return for you when all is ready," he announced, refusing my entreaties to watch his preparations.

I entered the room. The door closed behind Erasmoth. I was alone. The priestess Kassandry had already gone on ahead, striding toward the heart of the mountain.

Now I sit writing at a table of darkened wood, its surface polished and smooth. Lush carpets of fur and wool line the floor; soft chairs offer me comfort. The oil lantern burns without smoke, its light steady and bright.

But, now, Excellency, I bid farewell. I hear footsteps approaching down the hall, and hasten to complete the enchantment that will send this missive over magical pathways to your desk.

I pray that my next missive will contain the proof we both desire! Your ever-devoted servant:

Foryth Teel

*   *   *   *   *

Most Learned Master:

You probably are wondering at the delay. It has taken me time to regain my composure, so dramatic and terrible have been the experiences of the last few hours. Indeed, the palpitations of my heart bring tremors to my hand— I beg Your Excellency's pardon for my awkward script.

Immediately after I sent my last report, Erasmoth entered my chamber. He was a man transformed. The flush of rapture tinged his cheeks, and a supernatural glow burned in his eyes. His appearance alone was almost enough to convince me that some divine force was at work here.

The priest gestured to me, and I fell into step behind him. I noticed as I emerged from the room that two ranks of acolytes stood, waiting silently, their expressions concealed behind those featureless masks.

We followed the black-walled, torch-lit passage for a distance I estimated as more than a mile. Finally, the narrow passage led us into a much larger chamber. The yellow glow of torches was lost in the vastness of the space. For a moment, I thought all was blackness, but as my eyes adjusted, I realized that a sullen crimson glow emanated from all around me—pools of molten rock, bubbling and flaming.

"My temple!" proclaimed Erasmoth.

The first thing that struck me was the size of this cavelike expanse. Judging from the distant echoes of our footsteps and the dim glow of the pits of lava and deep wells of burning coals, I could guess that we stood in a vast room.

The floor was smooth beneath my feet—as if hundreds of hours of labor had been expended to polish the natural rock to an unnatural perfection.

My next observation, as we stepped away from the tunnel that had led us here, was an unpleasant—almost nauseating—odor. I was reminded of the thick, close air of a charnel house. I gagged convulsively. For a moment, Excellency, I was quite overcome, and would have fallen, if not for the supportive grip of the priest upon my arm. Remembering the dignity of my station, I recovered my composure. Politely declining Erasmoth's assistance, I once again walked forward under my own power.

I could see by the irregular shape that the shrine was a natural cavern, not an eccentric excavation. Nevertheless, it showed signs of centuries of use—such as the smoothness of the floor. Great, fluted columns, obviously wrought by hand, extended from floor to ceiling around the periphery.

I became aware of someone approaching out of the darkness. It was the priestess Kassandry. Her arrival sent a wave of relief through my body. I had become uneasy, due to the heavy stench and the unusual surroundings, no doubt.

A holy fire glowed within her, shining as a flaming light in her eyes. Her lips were moist; her tongue flicked back and forth across them. She wore no mask, and I feel certain she had not painted her skin in any way, yet the excessive pallor of her complexion was as white as if she had coated herself with chalk.

Her eyes passed over me, and I saw none of the warmth, the friendship, or affection that she had displayed in the vale beyond this temple. In fact, the priestess appeared to take little note of me. She drew near Erasmoth and seemed to meld her body to his. Her voice was a throaty whisper.

"All is readied," she told the priest.

My heart pounded with excitement. The ceremony, which would provide the most valuable find of my career, was, I believed, about to start.

"What do you do now?" I inquired, prepared to make mental notes.

"First, my acolytes take their proper stations." The priest gestured to his dark-robed, masked assistants, who had gathered in an arc around us. I noted that there were more than two dozen of them in all.

Erasmoth gestured imperiously to one of his masked apprentices, who shambled forward, stopping before Erasmoth. The acolyte waited for another command.

"Remove your mask!"

The acolyte did so. Forgive me once again, Excellency. The memory of what I saw causes a weakness in the very fiber of my being—a sensation like a stream of icy water infusing my limbs and paralyzing my heart.

The face was recognizable, barely, as having once been human, but now! Horrible! One cheek had rotted away, displaying a patchwork of grisly muscle and dank, decaying gum. Yellow teeth jutted like tusks from the slack-jawed mouth. The nose was a useless lump of cartilage and gore. Withered eyes rolled sightlessly in sockets.

The creature before me was unquestionably one of the walking dead—a zombie. It stood, pathetic and unknowing, awaiting the command of its master.

"Bear witness!" cried Erasmoth. "See the miracle of the gods!"

Kassandry watched him with rapture gleaming in her eyes. Her slender hands clasped before her, she paid no heed to myself, nor to the ghastly acolyte.

"You killed your own apprentice?" I gasped.

Your Excellency can imagine my shock.

"All of them!" he cried. "They know bliss now! Joy! An eternal freedom from want and desire!"

The other masked acolytes gathered close, removed their masks to reveal a gallery of horror. Each face was marred by decay, with peeling flaps of flesh and loosely hanging skin. Hair sprouted from the scalps of many; the pates of others gleamed as pure white bone.

"Who were they?" I cried. "Where did you find them?"

"They came to me!" Shrill triumph rang in the priest's voice. His words were addressed to the heavens, and it seemed that I overheard him as a mere eavesdropper.

"You tricked them, then killed them," I challenged him.

"They understood!" Erasmoth's voice hissed. "They offered their souls to the god! The god claimed them, and then gave them to me as slaves."

I noticed suddenly one of the zombies wore a black eyepatch covering one of its dead orbs. It all seemed some hideous joke, but I recognized, by that sign only, for his face was ravaged by decay, Tyrol Deet!

"This is your miracle?" I gasped, appalled. "The secret of undeath!"

"Approach the altar!" commanded Erasmoth. He reached to push me, but I avoided his shoving hand.

Kassandry took my arm, surprising me with the gentleness of her touch. I looked at her face, now so close to mine, and saw nothing but the rapture of one who believes she has found a greater truth. She paid no attention to me, save for the slight pressure of her grip upon my arm. Her bright eyes remained focused on the far side of the cave.

As if on command, fires surged upward from several of the great basins in the cavern, and for the first time I received a more accurate picture of this dreadful temple. It was monstrous, Excellency. Five pits belched columns of hissing flame into the air. The central flame was highest and flared as a bright red. Fires of blue and green surged to its left; a small fire of purest white flickered to the right.

The fifth flame I did not see immediately, and then I noticed it only as a shifting shade before the backdrop of several red pools of lava. Upon closer inspection, I saw that this was a fire of black! It absorbed the light around it, rather than casting illumination of its own, and thus was visible only by the outline of its greater darkness. Five fires, of black, white, red, green, and blue—the holy altar of this deity worshiped by Erasmoth Luker.

"Witness the power of my god," announced Erasmoth. The arrogance of his tone was now palpable. Clearly, he regarded me as little more than a tablet for the purpose of recording his mighty deeds.

Excellency, at this point in the course of events, I am afraid that my mind ceased to function with its usual acuity for detail and observation. Instead, I recall only a series of impressions—each, it seemed, more garish and terrifying than the one preceding.

I recall those five columns of flame. We were quite close to them, now, and I could feel the heat radiate from every direction. The spouts of fire sputtered and hissed and crackled, yet I could see no fuel of any sort. The pits were smooth bowls of black stone, deeper than a man's height, but rounded into the shape of a great cauldron.

The red flame—the centermost and tallest of the pillars—stood in front of the others. The black flame was farther removed from the group.

A circular depression, with four or five concentric rings of steps, allowed easy descent into the circle. Within the circle rested a block of stone, square and solid.

"Behold the altar of godhood!" Erasmoth cried. "Behold and tremble!"

A deeper pit opened in the floor before the altar. It was from this ghastly hole that the unspeakable odor flowed, as if all the foulness and perversion across the face of Krynn had been gathered into one place. The priest led me around this pit to stand before the altar.

Next in my recollection come images of my two

companions—the woman, so slender and wanton in her god-inspired desire, and the man, his face distorted by shadow and by the intensity of his passion, as he focused upon the approaching ceremony. Kassandry, who had ignored me during the approach to this central altar, now turned her luminous eyes to my face.

She dropped her robe to the floor. She was naked, except for a belt of leather and steel gauntlets on her wrists. Two slender stilettos hung from the belt. Seizing one in each hand, she raised them toward the roof of the cavern.

Erasmoth, too, lifted his hands. Together the priest and priestess wailed a chant, repeating the beastlike sounds over and over, their voices rising to a pitch of ecstasy. I had no doubt but that the culmination of this ceremony would be the plunging of those razor-edged blades into my breast.

I confess, Excellency, that the thought of my duties, of the sacred trust of the historian, vanished from my mind. Fear consumed me. All I could think of was escape. The wailing of the clerics rose to a hysterical crescendo. Only a few feet away from me I saw steps that would lead me out of this unholy circle. Beyond—a desperate sprint away—the tunnel would take me to the surface. So convoluted was my own reasoning that I completely forgot about the gates of gold and silver that must eventually block my exit.

I sprang away from the priest and priestess, made a dash for the stairs. The two made no reaction; their chant continued without interruption. I reached the bottom step and leapt upward, passing in two bounds out of that hateful arena. Still Erasmoth and Kassandry chanted.

My breath came in ragged gasps. My heart pounded. I turned to look for the tunnel by which we had entered this accursed cavern.

But where was it? My surroundings looked different, as if this was not the place I had passed mere minutes before. Dark shadows stood in places where I remembered glowing patches of light. The five columns of flame still burned, however, and they gave me my bearings. I started in the direction I believed would offer escape. My feet skimmed across the smooth floor, and still the two clerics stood, locked in the grip of their unholy ritual.

I sensed the movement of the darkness against the fiery background. My heart chilled at the sound of approaching footsteps. Hands reached for me. The cloying scent of death was all around me. An arm, like a sodden piece of old meat, struck my chest, knocking me backward.

I collapsed into another animated corpse, and retched as I felt my hand sink into the rotted satchel of its belly. The zombies were all around me, reaching with horrible hands.

With a cry of horror, I broke free, lunging in the only direction that would take me away from the ghastly figures—back toward the pit and the Altar of Erasmoth.

"Come to us now, Historian!" cried the priest, ceasing his chant. Kassandry licked her gleaming lips. She held the two daggers high, crossing the blades over her head.

The ranks of the undead pressed forward, and in the surging light of the fires I could see scores of them. They emerged from the shadows around the periphery of the great cavern, shambling slowly out of the darkness to gather in an attentive circle around their master and mistress.

The close-packed ranks of the zombies pressed in on me, forcing me onto the top step leading into the circular altar pit, toward the doom that awaited me below. In desperation, I looked for some avenue of escape through the steadily closing circle. There were none!

"Make haste, Historian!" The priest's tone contained an element of irritation.

I could delay no longer. The zombies had driven me to the bottom step of the circle, and thence into the pit itself.

Kassandry's gaze locked on to mine. It was the priestess, in the end, who compelled me to step slowly across the floor of the circle, until I stood before her. Behind her was the black pit, which exuded that terrible odor.

"Now!" cried Erasmoth, raising his hands, his fists clenched in triumph. "In the name of the gods!"

Kassandry raised the knives, still staring at my face. I was transfixed, unable to break that hypnotizing gaze. I waited for the stabbing of that keen steel into my flesh.

Kassandry struck, slicing each blade through the neck, severing the two arteries that carry blood to the brain. But, as I live to write this, Excellency, it was not my flesh. Nay, and I swear by the sanctity of my Historian's Oath, Your Grace, she slashed her own neck as she stood before me! The priestess took her own life!

Blood spurted from the two wounds, drenching me. Kassandry remained standing, that same expression of rapture etched into her features. Then she started to topple forward and I—out of instinct—reached to catch her.

But Erasmoth knocked me out of the way. Kassandry's blood sprayed, slicking the smooth floor.

"I must make haste!" shouted the priest.

With surprising strength, he lifted her into his arms, turned toward the dark pit in the center of the circle, and threw the still-bleeding corpse into that blackened hole.

The five pillars of fire surged upward, their light illuminating the great cavern, washing across the senseless, unknowing faces of the zombies and the smiling visage of the triumphant priest.

O wise Astinus, here, it seemed, my historian's instincts took over, rescued me as I teetered at the brink of madness. Shock welled within me and my legs grew weak, too feeble to support me. I remained senseless of the blood—Kassandry's blood—that stained my robe, or even of the fact that, for the time being, I had been spared.

I watched the proceedings with a sort of detachment—no longer was I a participant, as indeed I never should have been in the first place. I stared into that black pit. The zombies around us were still, and even Erasmoth's breathing had become slow and labored.

Then, from out of that obscene darkness, a hand reached forth—a slender, female hand, wet with blood. Another hand appeared, followed by a pair of arms. Then the face, now deathly pale, was visible—and then the mortal flesh that once had been the priestess called Kassandry.

The creature that emerged from the pit was dead, as insensate as the rank of rotting corpses that stood around us. The female zombie, her nearly naked flesh smeared with the gruesome refuse of the dark pit, climbed laboriously from the hole in the floor. The thing's—I cannot think of it, anymore, as female, or even human—movements were jerky and uncoordinated, as if it must learn to walk anew.

But the aspect that shocked me the most was the vacant stare of those once-bright eyes. Kassandry's gaze had been so intense, so vital, that it had fascinated me even as it made me quiver with uncertainty. Now the dull, deadened eyes of a corpse roamed sightlessly in that awful, pallid face.

"Before we proceed further," Erasmoth declared to me, "I want to show you something."

Numbly, still anticipating my imminent death, I nonetheless followed him. I believe I was in shock and would have jumped into the pit itself, then, if he had ordered it. My captor led me to the pillar of black flame.

"The black fire, as you can feel, radiates no heat," he said, as we approached the shadowy column.

Indeed, the flickering fire actually seemed to absorb warmth from the air. I felt as if I faced the open night, with my back to the comfort of a house or inn. A limitless well of cold seemed to emanate from the fire, sucking all that was living and warm into its black and soulless depths.

"A curious phenomenon, don't you agree?" he said. "Now, study the white one."

We moved to this pale phantasm. This column of fire was translucent and pearly as smoke, but possessed a definition of form and purpose that belied a vaporous nature. The chill of the blaze was like a forceful attack, like a blast of subfreezing wind across a field of ice. I recoiled, to the amusement of the priest.

"She saps your life, does this fire," Erasmoth said, "but gives you the eternal life of my goddess in return!"

"Life?" I cried, quite losing the impartiality of a historian, for which Your Eminence will no doubt chastise me severely. "How dare you call this evil abomination life!"

"Ah—but it is truly the greatest life!" responded the priest. "For it is life without end!"

"A life without awareness!" I retorted. "No life at all!"

"I did not expect you to understand," he announced, his tone filled with supreme arrogance, "but I have shown you the proof of a miracle. You, Historian, must take this message to the world."

"You have shown me proof of the presence of an evil god," I continued, still choosing my words with caution.

278

"And that, in itself, is a remarkable discovery in this era when all gods were thought to have abandoned Krynn! But will you not tell me the name of this god?"

"Goddess," he corrected. "You already know her."

I looked again, realizing that I gazed at the five pillars of fire, the five colors . . . of evil dragonhood! "She is the Nameless One," I said quietly, "driven from the world more than two thousand years ago! She whose dark power once brought Krynn almost to the point of subjugation."

"The Queen of Darkness!" he shouted in ecstasy. "Mistress of the evil dragons, the five-headed wyrm!"

"Takhisis!" All of the horrors I had witnessed paled when compared with the menace raised by this dark priest. "Do you mean to tell me that she returns to the world?"

"Not yet, Historian, not yet, but her presence can be felt, by myself and others. She grows in power, and she is patient. She is not defeated. Never make that mistake, Historian. She will not be vanquished!"

Abruptly, he raised his voice, pointed. "Go, now! Take your notes and report to your master what you have learned! Let the great Astinus know and tremble! Let everyone know! The Queen of Darkness will return, and glory is the destiny of those who worship her name!"

His triumph ringing in my ears, I departed—precipitously, if the truth be told (as, of course, it must). The zombies parted, let me pass. The gold gates, and the silver as well, stood open for me. I ran through the sun-dappled courtyard, raced all the way down the winding trail to Halcyon. And even here, I do not feel safe.

Not because I fear the priest. If Erasmoth had wanted me, he could have taken me at his altar. My fear is deeper. It touches on the very survival of our world.

For I swear, Master Astinus—it is all true! The Queen of Darkness lives, and she longs to project her power into the world! She has found a cleric in Erasmoth. Will she find (or has she found) others?

What, then, can be the fate of the world?

Foryth Teel,
In the cause of Astinus and the Great Histories of Krynn.

True Knight

Margaret Weis and Tracy Hickman

Part I

Nikol and Brother Michael left the Lost Citadel and traveled the forest, now bereft of its enchantment, with the dazed and bewildered expressions of those who have undergone some awful, wondrous experience and who do not, on reflection, believe in it.

They had evidence the events had occurred—the blood of Nikol's twin brother and the blood of the evil wizard who had been responsible for Nicholas's death stained Nikol's hands. The holy medallion of Mishakal, which once had glowed with the blue light of the goddess's favor, hung dark around Brother Michael's neck. All the true clerics had departed, gathered by the gods to serve on other planes. The dark clerics, worshipers of the Queen of the Abyss, had not succeeded in their scheme to fill the void left by the departure of the other gods' faithful. The words of the strange mage, who called himself Raistlin, echoed in their hearts.

In thirteen days' time, the gods in their wrath at the folly of men will hurl a fiery mountain down upon Ansalon. The land will be sundered, seas will rise, and mountains topple. Countless numbers will die. Countless more, who will live in the dark and terrible days to follow, will come to wish they had died.

Michael and Nikol reached the edge of the forest, came to the clearing where Akar had received his prize—the dying knight, Nicholas—from the goblins who had captured him. The knight's blood still stained the crushed grass. Both paused, without a word spoken. Neither had said a word to each other, following their departure from the Lost Citadel.

Thirteen days. Thirteen days until the destruction of the world.

"Where do you want to go, my lady?" Michael asked.

Nikol glanced around the clearing, slowly darkening with the coming of night. The dazzled bewilderment was fading, a numbness and lethargy that was not so much a weariness of body as it was a weariness of spirit that made her feet seem too heavy to lift, her heart too heavy to bear.

She had only one thought. "Home," she said.

Michael looked grave, opened his mouth, probably to protest. Nikol knew what he was going to say, stopped the words on his lips with a glance. Her manor castle, which had been in her family for generations and had housed the three of them in far happier days, had probably been attacked and sacked and looted by goblins. She would return to find the castle charred and gutted, a ghastly skeleton. She didn't care. The castle was her home.

"It's where I want to die," she said to Michael.

She started walking.

* * * * *

Brother Michael was astonished to discover the castle had been left in relatively good repair, perhaps because the goblins had decided to make it their base while they despoiled the countryside. Noting from a distance that the castle was still standing and was not a burned-out hulk, Michael was more than half convinced that the goblins were still around. A day's watching persuaded him that the goblins had moved on, perhaps in search of richer pickings. The castle was empty.

Inside, he and Nikol found a horrible mess; both gagged from the stench, fled back outside to fresher air. Filth and remnants of dread feasting choked the halls. The heavy oaken furniture had been axed, used for firewood. Curtains had been torn down. The ceremonial armor was gone, probably being worn now by some goblin king. Yule decorations and the tapestries had been desecrated, burned. Vermin roamed the halls now extremely loathe to leave.

The villagers and manor tenants all had fled and had not come back, either out of fear of the goblins or because they had nothing to which to come back. Not a house remained standing. Stock had been slaughtered, granaries raided and burned, wells poisoned. At least most had escaped with their lives, if little else.

Michael gazed at the destruction and said firmly, "My lady, Sir Thomas's manor is a fortnight's journey. Let me take you there. We can travel by night. . . ."

Nikol didn't hear him, walked away from him in midspeech. Stripping off her armor, she stacked it neatly in a corner of a blackened wall. Beneath the armor she wore the cast-off clothes of her brother that she had worn when the two of them practiced their sword work together. Binding a strip of torn linen, found hanging from a tree limb, around her nose and mouth, she entered the castle and began the thankless task of cleaning.

She was vaguely aware, after a time, that Michael was at her side, attempting, when he could, to take the more onerous tasks upon himself. She straightened from her work, brushed a lock of her ragged-cut hair from her face, and stared at him. "You don't have to stay here. I can manage. Sir Thomas would be glad to have you."

Michael regarded her with an air of exasperation and concern. "Nikol, don't you understand by now? I could no more leave you than I could fly off into the sky. I want to stay. I love you."

He might have been speaking the Elvish tongue, for all she understood him. His words made no sense to her. She was too numb, couldn't feel them.

"I'm so tired," she said. "I can't sleep. It's all hopeless, isn't it? But, at least we'll have a place to die."

He reached for her, tried to take her in his arms. His face was anxious, his expression worried.

"There is always hope. . . ."

Nikol turned away from him, forgot about him, began again to work.

* * * * *

They made preparations in order to survive the coming Day of Destruction. That is, Michael made preparations. Nikol, once the castle was clean, sat, talking and laughing, in the room where she and her brother used to sit during the long evening hours. She sat, doing nothing, staring at the empty chair across from hers. She was biddable, tractable. If Michael found some slight task for her to do, she did it without comment, without complaint, but then she would return to her chair. She ate and drank only if Michael put the food into her hand.

He was gentle with her at first. Patiently, he tried to coax her back to the life she was fast leaving. When this failed, his fear for her grew. He argued, shouted at her. At one point, he even shook her. Nikol paid no attention to him. When it seemed she thought of him at all, he was a stranger to her. At length, he grew too busy to take time to do more than see to it that she ate something.

Michael was forced to spend his days roaming the countryside, foraging for whatever the goblins had left behind, which wasn't much. He found a stream that had not been fouled and, though he had never been taught the art of fishing, managed to catch enough to serve their needs. He knew nothing about setting traps, nor could he bring himself to snare small animals. He had not eaten animal flesh since he had come to serve the goddess of healing. He was knowledgeable about berries and herbs, wild vegetables and fruits, and these kept them alive. Although the strange, hot wind that blew incessantly day and night was rapidly drying up the land, he set in a store of food that could feed them for a long time, if they ate sparingly.

And he firmly put aside the chilling thought that, unless something happened to shake Nikol out of her dark melancholia, he would have only himself to worry about.

He prayed to Mishakal to help Nikol, to heal the wound that had not touched the flesh but had torn apart the woman's soul. He prayed to Paladine as well, asking the god of the Solamnic Knights to look with favor upon the daughter who had fought evil as valiantly as any son.

And it was, or so it seemed at first, Paladine who answered.

They had no visitors; the countryside around them was deserted. Michael watched for travelers closely, for he desperately wanted to send a message to Sir Thomas, to warn him of the coming destruction and to ask for whatever aid the knight could give them. No one came. The thirteen days dwindled to nine, and Michael had given up looking for help. At twilight, the stillness was broken by the sound of hooves, clattering on the paved courtyard.

"Hail the castle!" shouted a strong, deep voice, speaking Solamnic.

The sound roused Nikol from her dread lethargy. She glanced up with unusual interest. "A guest," she said.

Michael went hurriedly to look out the window. "A knight," he reported. "A Knight of the Rose, by his armor."

"We must make him welcome," said Nikol.

The Measure dictated the treatment of a guest, who was said to be a "jewel upon the pillow of hospitality." The honor of the knighthood bound Nikol to offer shelter, food, whatever comfort her home could provide to the stranger.

She stirred, rose from her chair. Glancing down at her shabby men's clothes, she seemed perplexed.

"I'm not dressed to receive visitors. My father was very strict about that. We always put on our finest clothes to honor the guest. My father wore his ceremonial sword. . . ."

Looking around, as if she thought a dress might materialize from out of the air, she caught sight of her brother's sword, standing in its place upon the weapons' rack. She buckled the sword about her waist, and went to make the guest welcome—her first voluntary actions in days.

Michael followed her, silently thanking this knight, whoever he was, whatever his reason for being here. The man obviously had traveled far; his black horse was coated with dust and sweat.

Nikol entered the courtyard. If the strange knight was shocked at her shabby appearance, he politely gave no indication. In this day and age, perhaps he was used to the sight of impoverished members of the knighthood. He drew his sword, held it to his helm, blade upward, in gesture of salute and peace.

"My lord," he said. "I regret that I have no squire to ride forward and give notice of my coming. Forgive my intrusion at this unseemly time of night."

"Welcome to Whitsund Manor, Sir Knight. I am not lord of the manor, but its lady. I am Nikol, daughter to Sir David Whitsund. Dismount your noble steed and give yourself rest and ease this night. I regret I have no groom to lead your horse to stable, but that task I will take upon myself and count it an honor."

The knight, who traveled in full armor, the breastplate decorated with the rose that marked his high standing in the knighthood, removed his helm. Shocked, Michael moved a step nearer Nikol.

"Forgive me, my lady," the knight was saying. "I can only plead dusk's shadows as an excuse for having mistaken noble lady for noble lord."

Nikol accepted the compliment with a smile and a nod, turned her attention to the man's fine horse.

Michael could not take his eyes from the knight's face. The strong and darkly handsome visage was gaunt and haggard. He looked exhausted to the point of falling. But it was the knight's eyes that arrested Michael, caused the words of thanksgiving that had been on the cleric's lips to die. The black eyes burned with a strange and terrible fire that seemed to be consuming his flesh. So fey was the knight that Michael feared they were dealing with a madman. Nikol had not noticed. Her attention was for the fine horse, which was accepting her overtures at friendship with gracious forbearance.

"My lady," Michael began, licking dry lips, not certain how to proceed. "I think perhaps . . ."

"Now it is I who ask forgiveness," Nikol said, glancing up. "I present our family chaplain, Brother Michael."

The knight bowed.

"I am honored to meet you, Brother Michael. My name is Lord Soth, of Dargaard Keep. Lady Nikol, I thank you for your kind offer of hospitality, but it is an offer that I regretfully must refuse. Urgent need carries me back on the road this night. I will not even dismount, by your leave. I only stopped to ask for water for myself and my horse."

The knight's words were cool and courteous, but they were tinged with the crackling of the flames that burned in the eyes. Nikol gazed up at him in admiration. Perhaps night's shadows blinded her as well.

"Gladly, Lord Soth. I will fetch the water myself."

The daughter of a knight, Nikol recognized the knight's need for haste and did not waste time in further niceties. She left immediately to find water. Michael went to find a bucket and some straw for the horse. He returned to find the knight drinking slowly and sparingly from the iron dipper. Michael placed the bucket down before the horse, who drank more deeply than its master.

"I would not have disturbed you at all, my lady," said the knight, "but would have stopped at stream or pond. I could find no pure water in these parts, however. Goblins attacked you, I take it." He glanced about the ruined castle with the air of an experienced warrior.

"Yes," said Nikol softly. She stroked the horse's neck. "They fell upon us about a fortnight ago. My brother died, defending the castle and our people."

"He was not the only one who defended it, seemingly," said Lord Soth, the burning eyes fixing upon the sword Nikol wore easily and confidently at her side.

Nikol flushed. "It is my home," she said simply.

"Your home. And a blessed one, despite all," said the knight. The flames in the black eyes blazed higher. The countenance grew grim, scarred by bitterness and regret. He stirred restlessly in the saddle, as if in pain.

"I must be on my way." He handed the dipper back to Nikol.

"I would not hinder you on whatever urgent business takes you out into the night," said Nikol, "but I repeat again, you are welcome in my home, Lord Soth."

"I thank you, Lady Nikol, but I may not rest until my task is complete. I ride to Istar and I must be there in four days' time."

"Istar!" cried Michael, shaken. "But you should not go there! In four days time—" He paused, uncertain of what he was going to say, not sure how he knew what he knew or how he would explain it.

The knight's burning eyes seared Michael. "You know, then, Brother. You know what terrible fate hangs over this world. Then I leave you with this hope: With the help of the gods, I will prevent it, though it cost me my life."

The knight bowed again to Nikol. Replacing his helm, he turned his horse's head out into the night and soon was lost to their sight.

"Though it cost him his life," said Nikol softly, gazing after him with shining eyes. "He is a true hero. He rides forth to save the world, though it cost him his life. And what do I do? What have I done?"

She turned, stared at the castle, perhaps truly seeing it for the first time since they had returned.

"The Measure. The Oath. 'My honor is my life.' I came near forgetting that, came near failing the memory of my father, my brother. This knight has reminded me of my duty. Perhaps Paladine sent him for that very reason. I will always honor his name: Lord Soth of Dargaard Keep."

Michael would have added his own fervent blessing on the knight, who had brought Nikol back to life, but a shadow drifted across the cleric's heart, like smoke from a distant fire. The effect was chilling. He could not speak.

Part II

Nikol's melancholia vanished, borne away by the Knight of the Rose. She began to believe, once again, in a future, to find hope in it, and threw herself into preparing for it with her usual energy. It was a future of promise she believed in, a future unscarred by the terrible calamity foreordained by the gods.

Michael, whose fears were growing, not receding, sought to gently temper this newfound hope.

"I have had dark dreams of late, Nikol. I see the Kingpriest confronting the gods. He does not approach them in humility, remembering that he is man and mortal. He makes demands of them. He has come to think of himself as equal to the gods. I feel their wrath. This strange wind . . ."

Nikol interrupted him, placed her hand upon his with a patronizing air, "Brother, be at peace. A Knight of Solamnia rides to Istar to stop this. *He* goes with Paladine's blessing."

He knew she did not mean to hurt him by adding that unconscious emphasis on the word. Perhaps she wasn't even equating the two of them—the knight who rode with Paladine's blessing, the cleric who had given up the favor of his goddess by choosing to stay in this world—but the pain burned. He said nothing, however.

She might think he was jealous of the knight, but Michael wasn't, not really. Nikol was not in love with Lord Soth. She saw in him what she had been raised to see—the epitome of honor, godliness, nobility. The Oath and the Measure placed the knights above the faults and foibles of other, lesser men.

Michael left the castle for a few hours, until his hurt subsided. Catching fish, wading up to his shins in the stream, helped him rationalize, understand. Her faith was touching, childlike. Who was he to destroy it?

"Perhaps, if more had believed as she does, we would not be facing this dreadful fate," he said to the strange wind and the cloudless, lead-colored sky.

The night before the Cataclysm, Michael woke from dreams of fire and blood to find himself prostrate upon the floor, shivering and sweating. The gods' anger crackled in the air, rumbled in the empty sky. A timid knock at his door roused him.

"Are you all right, Brother?" called Nikol.

Michael flung open the door, startled her. She stared at him, backed up a step. He knew he must look wild, disheveled—thin from lack of food, bleary-eyed from sleepless nights. He caught hold of her.

"We must go somewhere, somewhere safe."

"It's a storm, that's all," said Nikol, uneasy, nervous. "Michael, you're hurting me."

He did not loosen his hold. "It is coming. The Day of Wrath."

"Lord Soth—" she began.

"He couldn't stop it, Nikol!" Michael had to shout to be heard over the low rumble of thunder that shook the manor walls. "I don't know why or how or what happened, but he failed! Men do fail, you know! Even Knights of Solamnia. They're human, damn it, like the rest of us."

"I have faith in him!" Nikol cried angrily.

"He is a man. We must have faith in the gods." Saying this, reminding himself of it, Michael was calm. "This house, these walls are strong. Blessed, the knight said. Yes, here, inside these walls, we will be safe."

"No! It cannot be! He *will* stop it."

She broke free of his grasp, ran inside the small family chapel. Michael followed her, to try to reason with her. Looking around, he realized at once that this room—built in the castle's interior, without windows—was the safest place. Nikol was kneeling before the altar.

"Paladine! Be with Lord Soth! Accept his sacrifice, as you once accepted Huma's!"

The strange wind, hot and dry, blew harder and harder, shrieked about the castle walls with inhuman voices. Lightning slashed, split trees. Thunder shook the ground, like the footsteps of an angry giant.

All that morning the storm raged, growing more and more intense. The sun vanished. Day became darker than night. Violent winds blew, lifted huge trees from the ground, hurled them about like newly planted saplings. Those trees that held fast against the wind fell victim to the savage lightning. Michael, daring to leave the chapel, ventured back into his room, stared out the window.

Fires lit the darkness, trees consumed by flames. Grass fires scorched the land. Nikol, shivering, came to stand by his side. "The gods have forsaken us," she whispered.

"No," said Michael, taking her in his arms. "It is we who have forsaken them."

They returned to the chapel. The wind blew harder. The voices in it were horrible, conjuring up visions of dragons, screaming over their kill. It buffeted the castle walls, trying to beat them down. The earth began to shudder, as if the very ground was appalled at the horrors it was witnessing. The first quakes hit. The castle rocked and shivered. The two crouched before the altar, unable to move, unable to speak or even pray. Beyond the chapel, they could hear crashes, shattering cracks.

Michael knew they were doomed. The walls must collapse, the ceiling cave in. He held fast to Nikol's hands and began to describe, in a feverish voice, the beautiful bridge of starlight he'd seen before, the wondrous worlds where they soon would find peace and freedom from this terror.

Then it was over.

The tremors ceased. The storm abated, clouds blown away as if by a mournful sigh. All was quiet. They were not dead.

"We're safe, beloved!" Michael cried, not thinking of what he was saying. He clasped Nikol in his arms.

She was stiff, rigid in his grasp. Then, suddenly, she threw her arms around him, held him fast. They sank to the floor, before the altar of Paladine. Huddled in each other's grasp, they were grateful for the comfort of being together.

" 'The land will be sundered, seas will rise, and mountains topple. Countless numbers will die. Countless more, who will live in the dark and terrible days to follow, will come to wish they had died.' That's what he said, the black-robed wizard. Why? Why did this happen, Michael?" Nikol cried brokenly. "Certainly, some deserved the gods' wrath—that horrible, fat cleric who came here before Nicholas died—but this terror has surely destroyed the innocent as well as the guilty. How can the gods, if they are good, do this?"

"I don't know," Michael said helplessly. "I wish I had the answer, but I don't."

"At least I'm not alone," Nikol continued softly. "You're here. I'm glad you're here, Michael. It's selfish of me, I know, but if you had left with the goddess, I think I would be dead by now."

He didn't answer. He couldn't. The words wouldn't come past the ache of love and longing.

"Hold me closer," she said, burrowing into his arms.

He did as she commanded, pressed her head against his breast, bent, and kissed the shining hair. To his amazement, Nikol returned his kiss. Her lips met his hungrily.

"Nikol," he said, when he could breathe, "I've no right to ask this. You're the daughter of a knight. Your family is noble. My father was a shopkeeper in Xak Tsaroth, my mother a nomad, who roamed the plains. I have nothing to give. . . ."

"I will marry you, Michael," she said.

"Nikol, think about what I said—"

"Michael," she whispered, laying her hand upon his lips. "You think about it. Does any of that matter now?"

Perhaps Paladine heard their vows of marriage, spoken silently in their hearts. Perhaps the god turned aside his wrath one moment to bless their union, for the manor walls continued to stand strong and sheltering above them.

When the morning came, a heavy sadness, mingled with their joy, oppressed them both. Nikol stood before the altar of Paladine, which now had a crack in it, traced the crack with her finger. "We will find out why, won't we, Michael," she said firmly. "We will find out why this happened. We will search until we discover the answer. Then you and I will make it right."

In a world of the faithless, you are the only one who is faithful. And, because of that, you will be reviled, ridiculed, persecuted. But I see one who loves you, who will risk all to defend you.

The words of the black-robed wizard, Raistlin.

"Yes," Michael answered, as he would have answered yes to anything she asked of him at that moment. "We will search for the answer."

Part III

A cold and bitter winter closed in on them soon after the Cataclysm. Their small supply of food dwindled rapidly. The stream in which Michael fished vanished during the quakes, swallowed by the ground. A killing frost shriveled any plants that had survived the fires.

Then, one day, a small band of humans, traveling up from the south, had offered to trade game for shelter. The manor, they said, looking at it in awe, was one of the few buildings in these parts still standing. Michael agreed, was forced to eat animal flesh to stay alive. He hoped, all things considered, the goddess would forgive him.

But, once they were rested and had buried their dead, the refugees left, looking for new hunting grounds. Michael had figured, only this morning, that they had dried meat and berries to last them another few days. South, at least, there apparently was game to be had in the forests, the plains. Besides, Michael had a sudden urgent longing for his home.

"Xak Tsaroth," said Michael.

"What about it?" Nikol asked him.

"The Temple of Mishakal is there. And so are the holy disks. Why didn't I think of those sooner?" He began to pace the room excitedly.

"What disks? What are you talking about?"

"The Disks of Mishakal. All the wisdom of the gods are written on these disks. Don't you see, beloved? It's on those disks that we will find the answers!"

"If there *are* answers," Nikol said, frowning. "We buried a child yesterday. A little child! What had that babe to do with Kingpriests or clerics? Why should the gods punish the innocent?"

"If we find the disks, we'll find the answers," he said.

"In Xak Tsaroth!" Nikol scoffed. "Don't you remember what those refugees told us about Xak Tsaroth?"

"I remember." Michael turned, started to walk away. Having been born and reared in Xak Tsaroth, he had listened in disbelief to the tales of its destruction, told by the refugees. He had to see for himself.

Nikol ran after him, laid a remorseful hand on his arm. "I'm sorry, dearest, truly I am. I wasn't thinking. I forgot that was your home once. We'll travel there. We'll leave tomorrow. We have nothing to keep us here. We would have had to leave soon anyway."

As they were leaving, Nikol pulled shut the castle's heavy oaken door, made to lock it. Then, abruptly, she changed her mind. "No," she said, shoving it wide open. "This home is blessed, as the knight said. Let it shelter those who come. I have the feeling I will never see it again anyway."

"Don't speak words of ill omen," Michael warned her.

"It's not an ill omen," Nikol said quietly, looking up at him with a sad smile. "Our path lies far from here, I think."

She placed her hand upon the cold stone wall in final farewell, then the two gathered their meager belongings and started down the road, heading south.

* * * * *

If they had known how long the journey would take them, or how hard and dangerous it would be, they would have never left the castle's walls. They had been forewarned of terrible destruction farther south, but they were unprepared for the tremendous changes that had occurred, not the least of which was a sea where no sea had been before.

Reaching Caergoth, they were amazed to discover that the ground had sunk. Seawater, rushing in from the Sirrion Sea, now hid the scars of sundered lands. The two were forced to halt and work to pay their passage on a crude raft, run by a group of villainous-looking Ergothians, who had been separated by the sea from their homeland to the west.

The Ergothians ambushed them outside of Caergoth, demanded they hand over food and valuables. Nikol, disguised as a knight, refused. A fight ensued that left no one seriously injured, but gained Nikol the men's respect. They eyed Michael's blue robes with sneering suspicion but accepted Nikol's explanation that "her brother" had made a vow to their dying mother to remain faithful to his goddess.

As it turned out, the Ergothians were basically honest folk, made savage in their ways by the hardships they had been forced to endure. Nikol, maintaining her disguise as a knight, aided them in wiping out a band of goblins that had been raiding their hovels. Michael showed them plants and herbs they could use to supplement what had been a steady diet of fish. In return, the Ergothians ferried them across what they were calling "Newsea" and promised that they would have a return voyage, should they care to come back. Which they soon would, they promised, once they saw what had become of Xak Tsaroth.

On the opposite shore, Michael and Nikol soon lost their

way, wandered in the mountains for weeks. No map was trustworthy. The land had altered and shifted beyond recognition. Roads that once led somewhere now wound up nowhere—or worse. Survival itself was a struggle. Game was scarce. Farmland was either scorched by drought or flooded by newly created rivers. Famine and disease drove people to flee wrecked homes and villages and seek a better life that, rumor had it, was always over the next mountain. Even good men and women became desperate as they listened to their children cry from hunger. Rumor had it that several elven cities in nearby Qualinost had been attacked by humans.

This must have been true, for when Michael and Nikol accidentally came too near the borders of that land, a flight of elven arrows warned them to turn aside.

Nikol wore her sword openly; the bleak and chill sun shone on the blade. Her armor and breastplate and her knightly air of confidence daunted many. Most robbers were nothing more than ruffians, who wanted food in their bellies, not a sharp blade. But, on occasion, she and Michael met with those who were well armed and were not afraid of a "beardless knight."

Nikol and Michael fought when they were cornered, ran when they were outnumbered. The cleric had taken to carrying a stout staff, which he learned to swing with clumsy effect, if not skill. He fought for Nikol's sake, more than his own. Plunged into despair over the chaos he saw in the world, he would, if he had been alone, gone the way of so many others before him.

Nikol credited him with keeping her alive during the dark days before the Cataclysm. Now it was she who returned the favor. Her love alone bore him along. Michael even ceased to ask Mishakal's forgiveness when he bashed a head. Eventually, after many months of weary travel, they reached their destination.

* * * * *

"The Great City of Xak Tsaroth, whose beauty surrounds you . . ." Michael whispered the inscription on the fallen obelisk, traced it with his hand on the broken stone. His voice died before he could finish reading. He lowered his head, ashamed to be seen weeping.

Nikol patted his shoulder. Her hand was roughened, its skin tough and calloused, cracked and bleeding from the cold, scarred from battle. But its touch was gentle.

"I don't know why I'm crying," Michael said harshly, wiping his hands over his cheeks before his tears froze on his skin. "We've seen so many horrible sights—brutal death, terrible suffering. This"—he gestured at the fallen obelisk—"this is nothing but a hunk of stone. Yet, I remember . . ."

His head sank into hands, hurting sobs wrenched him. He thought he'd prepared himself. He'd thought he was strong enough to return, but the devastation was too much, too appalling.

From this point, long ago, one could have seen the city of Xak Tsaroth, heard its life in the throbbing, pulsing cries of its vendors and hawkers, the shrill laughter of its children, the rush and bustle of its streets. The silence was the most horrible part of his homecoming. The silence and the emptiness. They told him Xak Tsaroth was gone, sunk into the ground on which it had been built. He had not believed them. He had hoped. Bitterly, he cursed his hope.

Nikol pressed his arm in silent sympathy, then drew away. His grief was private; she did not feel that even she had a right to share in it. Hand on her sword hilt, she kept watch, staring out over the ruins that surrounded the obelisk, peering intently into the shadows beyond.

Gradually, Michael's sobs lessened. Nikol heard him draw a shivering breath.

"Do you want to keep going?" she asked, purposefully cool and calm.

"Yes. We've come this far." He sighed. "It's one thing to see strange cities lying in ruins, another to see one's home."

Nikol climbed on the obelisk, used it as a bridge to cross the swamp water. Michael, after a moment's hesitation, followed after her. His feet trod over the inscription: *The gods reward us in the grace of our home.* Grace. The land was barren, almost a desert, its trees charred stumps, its flowering plants and bushes nothing but soft ash. There was no sign of any living being, not even animal tracks.

Michael looked out over the ruins of the city's outskirts. "I can't believe it," he said softly to himself. "Why did I come? What did I expect to find here?"

"Your family," said Nikol quietly.

He looked at her in silence a moment, then slowly nodded. "Yes, you're right. How well you know me."

"Perhaps we will find them," she said, forcing a smile. "People might live around here still."

Nikol tried to sound cheerful, for Michael's sake. She did not believe herself, however, and she knew she hadn't fooled Michael. The quiet was oppressive, perhaps because it was not true quiet. A thin undercurrent of sound disturbed the surface. She could tell herself it was the wind, sighing through the broken branches of dead trees, but its sorrow pierced her heart.

Michael shook his head. "No, if they survived, which I doubt, they must have fled into the plains. My mother's people came from there. She would have gone back to find them."

Nikol paused, uncertain of her way. "You know, I could almost think that Xak Tsaroth *is* haunted, that its dead do lament."

Michael shook his head. "If any of the dead walk these broken streets, it is those who are unable or unwilling to pass beyond, to find the mercy of the gods."

What mercy? Nikol almost asked bitterly, but she bit her tongue, kept silent. Their relationship over these past hard months had deepened. Love was no longer the splendid, perfect bridal garment. The fabric was worn, now, but it fit better, was far more comfortable. Neither could imagine a night spent outside the refuge of the other's arms. But there were several rents and tears in the shining fabric.

The terrible things they'd seen had left their mark upon them both. When these cuts were mended, they would serve to make the marriage stronger, but now the arguments were growing bitter, had inflicted wounds that were still tender and sore to the touch.

"It's midafternoon," she said abruptly. "We don't have

much time if we're going to make use of the daylight to aid our search. Which way do we go?"

He heard the chill in her voice, knew what she was thinking as well as if she'd said it.

"Straight ahead. We will come to a large well and, beyond that, the Temple of Mishakal."

"If it's still standing. . . ."

"It must be," said Michael firmly. "There we will find the answers to your questions and to mine."

The remnants of what once had been a broad street took them to an open, paved courtyard. To the east stood four tall, free-standing columns that supported nothing; the building lay in ruins around them. A circular stone wall, rising four feet above the ground, had once been a well. Nikol stopped, peered down, and shrugged. She could see nothing but darkness. Michael ran his hand over the low wall.

"We used to come out of temple classes and sit on this wall and talk of our plans—how we would go forth and, with the help of the gods, change the world for the better."

"Obviously, the gods weren't listening." Nikol gazed around. "Is that the temple?" She pointed.

Now it was Michael who bit his lips on the words that would have precipitated yet another quarrel.

"Yes," he said instead. "That is the temple."

"I see *it* escaped the destruction unscathed," Nikol stated, her tone bitter.

Michael walked toward the building that was so familiar—its beautiful white stone shining pure and cold— and, at the same time, so alien. Perhaps that was because he missed the sight of the other buildings, now lying in rubble; missed the crowds of people strolling about the courtyard, meeting at the well to exchange the latest news. He ascended the stairs, approached the large, ornate double doors that led into the temple. Made of gold, the doors gleamed coldly in the winter sun. Michael pushed on them.

They did not open.

He pushed again, harder. The doors remained shut fast. Stepping backward, he stared at them in perplexity.

"What's wrong?" Nikol called from her place, guarding

the foot of the stairs.

"The doors won't open," Michael answered.

"They're barred, then. Keep a look out, will you?" Nikol climbed the stairs, studied the doors. "But they should be easy to pry apart—"

"They're not barred. They couldn't be. They had no locks on them. The temple was always open. . . ."

"This is ridiculous. There *must* be a way inside."

Nikol shoved at the doors, leaned her shoulder against them. The temple doors did not move.

Nikol stared at them, frustrated, angry. "We have to get inside! Is there another way?"

"This was the only entrance."

"I *will* enter, then!" She drew her sword, was about to thrust it between the doors.

Michael laid his hand upon her arm. "No, Nikol. I forbid it."

"You *forbid* it!" Nikol rounded on him in fury. "I'm the daughter of a Knight of Solamnia! You dare to give me orders, you who are nothing but a—"

"Cleric," finished Michael. "And now not even that." He touched the holy medallion around his neck, the symbol of the goddess. He looked at the temple sadly. "She will not open her doors to me."

"Now is not the time," came a voice.

Nikol drew her sword. "Who's there?" she demanded.

"Put your weapon away, Knight's Daughter," said the voice meekly. "I mean you no harm."

A middle-aged woman clad in threadbare clothing sat at the foot of the stairs. She sat very still; the dark shadow of a broken column had hidden her from view. Perhaps that was why neither Michael nor Nikol had noticed her until now. Nikol sheathed her sword but kept her hand on the hilt. The Cataclysm had not destroyed magic-users, or so rumor had it. This seemingly harmless woman might be a wizardess in disguise.

They both descended the stairs, walking slowly, warily. Nearing her, Nikol saw the woman's face more clearly. The sorrow etched on the aged and wrinkled skin was heartbreaking. Nikol's hand slipped from her sword's hilt. Tears came to her eyes, though she had not cried in all the long months of weary journeying.

"Who are you, Mistress?" Michael asked gently, kneeling beside the woman, who had not moved from where she sat. "What is your name?"

"I have no name," said the woman quietly. "I am a mother, that is all."

Her clothes were thin. She had no cloak and was shivering in the chill twilight. Michael took his own cloak from his shoulders, wrapped it around the woman.

"You cannot stay here, Mistress," he said. "Night is coming."

"Oh, but I must stay here." She did not seem to notice the cloak. "Otherwise, how will my children know where to find me?"

Nikol knelt. Her voice, which had been so strident when she was arguing with Michael, was now soft and low and filled with compassion. "Where are your children? We'll take you to them."

"There," said the woman, and she nodded toward the destroyed city.

Nikol caught her breath, looked at Michael. "She's gone mad!" she mouthed.

"How long have you been waiting here, Mistress?" he asked.

"Since that day," she answered, and they had no need to ask which day she meant. "I have never left them. They left me, you know. They were supposed to meet me here, but they didn't come. I'll keep waiting. Someday, they will return."

Nikol brushed her hand across her eyes. Michael gazed at the woman. He was at a loss to know what to do. He couldn't leave this poor, mad creature here. She would surely die. But it was obvious that she would not go without a struggle, and the shock of that might well kill her. Perhaps, if he could draw her thoughts away from her tragedy . . .

"Mistress, I am a cleric of Mishakal. I have returned to the temple in search of the disks that were kept here. You said that now is not the time to enter. When will the golden doors open?"

"When the evil comes out of the well. When the blue crystal staff shines. When dark wings spread over the land. Then my children will come. Then the doors will open." The woman spoke in a dreamy voice.

"When will that be?"

"Long . . . long." The woman blinked dazedly. The mists of madness parted, and she seemed to return to reality. "You seek the disks? They are not in there."

"Where, then?" Michael asked eagerly.

"Some say . . . Palanthas," the woman murmured. "Astinus. The great library. Go to Palanthas. There you will find the answer you seek."

"Palanthas!" Michael sat back on his heels, appalled. The thought of more months of traveling, of venturing back out into the savage land, came close to driving him to the pathetic state of this pitiable woman.

But Nikol's eyes shone. "Palanthas! The High Clerist's Tower, strong bastion of the Solamnic Knights. Yes, *that* is where we will find answers. Come, Michael," she said, rising briskly to her feet. "We can get in an hour's journeying before sunset."

Michael stood reluctantly. "Are you sure you won't come with us, Mistress?"

"This is my place," she said to him, fingering the cloak. "How will they know where to find me otherwise? Thank you for this wrap, though. I will be warm now, as I wait."

He started to go, felt a strong tugging at his heart. Turning, he stared at her. Suddenly, she seemed very familiar. Perhaps he'd known her—a friend, a neighbor.

"How can I leave you?"

She smiled, a strange, sad smile. "Go with my blessing, child. Someday, you, too, will return. And when you do, I will be waiting."

Part IV

The great seaport city of Palanthas, built by dwarves, fabled as far back as the Age of Might, was, according to swift-flying rumor, one of the few cities to come through the Cataclysm almost unscathed. Michael and Nikol, to their astonishment and disquiet, found themselves two drops in a steadily flowing stream of refugees, flowing toward what was purportedly a rich, safe harbor.

Located in western Solamnia, on the Bay of Branchala, the Cityhome, as it was known among its inhabitants, was governed by a noble lord under the auspices of the Knights of Solamnia, whose stronghold—the Tower of the High Clerist—guarded the mountain pass that kept goods and wealth flowing from Palanthas to the lands beyond.

But, though the city's walls and pavement, its tall towers and graceful minarets, may have survived the Cataclysm without damage, the disaster opened cracks within its population. These cracks had always been there, but the rifts had been covered by wealth, reverence for the gods, respect for (and fear of) the knights.

Now, almost a year after the Cataclysm, wealth had ceased to enter Palanthas. Few ships sailed the sea. Beggars, not gold, came pouring through the gates. The city's economy collapsed beneath the weight. Here, as in other places throughout Ansalon, the people looked for someone other than themselves to blame.

Michael and Nikol, along with numerous other fellow travelers, arrived at the city of Palanthas in midmorning. They'd heard rumors in abundance, some good, but many more dark—tales of beating, looting, murder. Mostly, they'd discounted them, but rumor had not prepared them for the sight that met their eyes.

"May the gods have mercy," said Michael, staring in pity and horror.

Throngs of people—ragged, wretched—crouched on the road outside the walls. At the sight of new arrivals, they surged forward, begging for anything that might, for a moment, relieve their misery and suffering.

Michael, sick at heart, would have given them all he owned, but Nikol, her face pale, her lips pressed tight, steered him with a firm hand through the grasping, wailing mob that surrounded the city gates.

The gates stood open wide, people pouring in, shoving their way out. The guards kept traffic moving, but did little else. One of them, however, eyed Nikol, and the weapon she wore, with interest.

"Hey, you. Mercenary. The Revered Son's looking for swords," said the guard. "You can earn yourself a meal, a place to sleep." He jerked a thumb. "Head for Old City."

"Revered Son?" Michael repeated, in disbelief.

"Thank you," said Nikol, catching hold of her husband and dragging him away. Outside the walls, they could hear the disappointed cries of the beggars.

Inside the walls, things were not much better. People lay sleeping in doorways or on the bare, cold pavement. Evil-looking men drifted near, saw Nikol's sword and Michael's stout staff, and drifted away. Two slatternly women caught hold of them and tried to drag them into a tumble-down hovel. The city stank of filth and death and disease.

They were loathe to stop and ask anyone directions. Nikol's father had visited Palanthas often, however, and had described the layout of the city, which was like a gigantic wheel. The great and ancient library stood in the city's center, known as Old City, along with the palace, the homes of the knights, and other important structures. They made their way through the wall that separated Old City from the New. Here the streets were not as crowded, almost empty. The air was cleaner, easier to breathe.

Michael and Nikol hurried forward, certain that the library must be a haven of peace in this wretched city. They had barely passed through the Old City wall when they discovered why the streets had been deserted. All the people—and there must have been hundreds—were gathered here.

"Where's the library?" Michael asked, peering over the heads of the crowd.

"There," said Nikol, pointing to the building the mob surrounded.

"What's going on here?" Michael asked a woman standing near him.

"Hush!" she said, glaring at him. "The Revered Son is speaking."

"Over here!" Nikol drew Michael into a grove of trees

that bordered one of the broad avenues of Old City. From this vantage point, both could see and hear the speaker, who stood upon the very steps of the Great Library of Palanthas.

"Do you know what is behind those walls, good citizens? I'll tell you! Lies!" A man pointed an accusing finger at the large, elegant, columned building behind him. "Lies about the Kingpriest!"

The crowd gathered around him muttered angrily.

"Yes, I've seen them, read them with my own eyes!" The man tapped those eyes, remarkable only for the fact that they were squinted and sly-looking. "The great Astinus"—the voice was poisoned with sarcasm—"writes that the Kingpriest called down the wrath of the gods by making demands of them! And who had a better right? What man has lived who was as good as that man? I'll tell you the real reason the gods hurled the fiery mountain upon Istar!"

He paused, waited until the crowd hushed.

"Jealousy!" he breathed in a stage whisper that carried clearly through the chill air. "They were jealous! Jealous of a man more godly than the gods themselves! They were jealous and afraid that he might challenge them. And so he might have! And he would have won!"

The crowd roared its approval, with an undercurrent of anger frightening to hear.

"But, though he is gone," continued the man, clasping his hands in pious grief, "some of us have vowed to carry on, to keep his memory alive. Yes," he cried, raising his fist to heaven. "We defy you, gods! We are not afraid! Drop a fiery mountain on us if you dare!"

Michael stirred restlessly, opened his mouth.

"Are you mad?" Nikol whispered. "You'll get us killed!" Taking hold of his medallion, she tucked it down the front of his blue robes, hiding it from sight.

Michael sighed, kept silent.

No one else in the crowd saw them. All eyes were on the speaker.

"Lord Palanthas sides with us," the man cried. "He would agree to pass our laws, for he knows they are right and just, but he is prevented from doing so by that old man in there!"

Again he pointed at the columned building behind him.

"Then *we'll* pass the laws and enforce them ourselves!" shouted a voice from the crowd, who, by the quickness of his response, obviously had been waiting for a cue. "Read us your laws, Revered Son. Let us hear them."

"Yes, read us the laws!" The crowd picked up the shout, turned it into a chant.

"I will, good citizens," said the squint-eyed speaker. He drew forth a scroll from the bosom of robes that were rich and snowy white—a marked contrast to the worn and shabby clothing of those who hung upon his every word.

"First: no elf, dwarf, kender, gnome, or anyone with so much as a drop of blood of any of these races is to be allowed in the city. Any now residing here will be expelled. Any caught here in the future will be put to death."

The people looked at each other, muttered their approval.

"Second: any wizard or wizardess, witch or warlock, apprentice mage, sorcerer or sorceress"—the man ran out of breath, paused to catch it—"caught within these city walls will be put to death."

This met with nods and shrugs and even some incredulous laughter, as though such an occurrence was almost beyond the realm of possibility. Palanthas had divested itself of such evil long ago, though at a heavy cost.

"Third: all Knights of Solamnia—"

Boos and hisses and angry shouts interrupted the speaker. He smiled in satisfaction and raised his voice to be heard above the uproar.

"All Knights of Solamnia or any member of a knight's family found henceforth within the city limits shall be expelled!"

A loud cheer.

"All lands and goods and properties of said Knights of Solamnia shall be confiscated and turned over to the people!"

An even louder cheer.

Now it was Nikol who flushed in anger and seemed about to speak.

"Are *you* mad?" Michael whispered, wrapping her cloak

more closely about the telltale breastplate, twitching the folds over the sword in its antique silver sheath, decorated with kingfisher and crown.

The two drew back to stand in the shadows of a large, spreading oak.

"Fourth: the library will be razed to the ground! All the books and scrolls and the lies that they contain will be burned!"

The speaker snapped his own scroll shut. Leaning toward the crowd, he made a sweeping gesture with his arm, as if he would scoop them up and send them in a surging tide toward destruction. The mob shouted its agreement and made a tentative movement toward the steps of the ancient library.

No one came out from the library. No defender appeared in the doorway. The building itself, the weight of years, its age and veneration and dignity, spoke a silent, eloquent defense and daunted the crowd.

Those in the front ranks seemed unwilling to proceed, fell back to let those behind come forth if they wanted. Those behind, finding themselves about to become those in front, had second thoughts, with the result that the mob began to mill about aimlessly at the foot of the library stairs. Some shouted threats; others threw rotten eggs and vegetables at the venerable structure. No one wanted to go any nearer.

The speaker gazed at them with a grim face, realized that the time was not propitious. He stepped down from his platform and was immediately surrounded by people, who cried out for his blessing or reached out to touch him reverently or held up their children for him to kiss.

"In the name of the Kingpriest," he said humbly, moving from one to another. "In the name of the Kingpriest."

"What is this mockery?" Michael gasped, appalled, no longer able to keep quiet. "I can't believe this! Haven't they learned? This is worse, far worse—"

"Hush!" Nikol hissed and dragged him even farther back into the shadows.

The speaker moved through the crowd, handling the people skillfully, giving them what they wanted, yet subtly ridding himself of them. A small retinue, led by the man who had asked the speaker to read the laws, formed a circle around the Revered Son and managed to extricate him from the press. He and his henchmen emerged near where Michael and Nikol stood, hidden by the trees.

Some of the mob continued to surge sluggishly about the library steps, but most grew bored and wandered off to the taverns or whatever other amusements could cheer their dreary existence.

"You had them eating out of your hand, Revered Son. Why didn't you urge them on?"

"Because now is not the time," the Revered Son answered complacently. "Let them go to their friends and neighbors and tell what they have heard this day. We'll have a hundred times more people than this at our next rally and a hundred times a hundred more after that. In the meantime, we'll whip up their fear and their hatred.

"Remember that half-elf baker we talked to yesterday, the stubborn one, who refused to leave the city? See to it that his loaves make a few people sick. Use this." The Revered Son handed over a small glass vial. "Let me know who's taken ill. I'll be around to 'heal' them."

One of the henchmen, taking the vial, looked at it dubiously. The Revered Son regarded him with some impatience. "The effects wear off naturally after a while, but these ignorant peasants don't know that. They'll think I've performed a miracle."

The man pocketed the vial. "What about the library?"

"We'll hold another rally in front of it day after tomorrow, after we've had time to stir up trouble. If you could get me one of those books, the one with the lies about the Kingpriest—"

The man nodded, shrugged. "Nothing to it. That fool old man, Astinus, lets anyone read 'em."

"Excellent. I'll read it aloud to the crowd. That should seal the library's fate and the old man's. He's been the main one opposing my takeover of the city's government. Once he's out of the way, I'll have no trouble with that namby-pamby Lord Palanthas.

"Now, tonight," continued the Revered Son, "I want you and the others in the taverns, spreading stories about that knight, the one that was god-cursed—"

"Soth."

"Yes, Lord Soth."

Nikol sucked in her breath softly. Michael caught hold of her hand, squeezed it, counseling silence.

"I'm not certain we should rely on that story to drive the mob to attack the knights, Revered Son. There's more than one tale about him going around."

"What's the other?" the speaker asked sharply.

"That he was forewarned about the Cataclysm. He was riding to Istar, planning to try to *stop* the Kingpriest—"

"Nonsense!" The Revered Son snorted. "Here's the story you tell them. Soth was furious because the Kingpriest was about to make public the knight's dalliances with that elven trollop of his. Make that clear. Oh, and throw in that bit about him murdering his first wife. That always goes over—"

"Shush, someone's wanting a blessing."

A young woman, carrying a baby, was hovering timidly on the outskirts of the group. The Revered Son glanced about, saw the woman, and smiled at her benignly.

"Come closer. What may I do for you, Daughter?"

"Pardon me for disturbing you, Revered Son," the woman said, with a blush, "but I heard you speak at the temple yesterday, and I'm confused."

"I'll do my best to help you understand, Daughter," said the Revered Son humbly. "What do you find confusing?"

"I have always prayed to Paladine, but you say we're not to pray to him or any of the other gods. We're to pray to the Kingpriest?"

"Yes, Daughter. When the wicked Queen of Evil attacked the world, the other gods fled in terror. The Kingpriest alone had the courage to stand and fight her, just as did Huma, long ago. The Kingpriest fights her today, on the heavenly plane. He needs your prayers, Daughter, to aid him in his struggles."

"And that's why we must drive out the kender and the elves—"

"And all those whose disbelief come to the aid of the Powers of Darkness."

"I understand now. Thank you, Revered Son." The young woman curtseyed.

The Revered Son laid his hand upon her head, and upon her child's. "In the name of the Kingpriest," he said solemnly.

The young woman left. The Revered Son watched after her, a pleased smile upon his lips. He cast a glance at his cohorts, who grinned and nodded. Their heads bent together in continued plotting, the Revered Son and his minions walked off in the opposite direction.

Neither Nikol nor Michael could speak for long moments. The shock of what they'd heard and seen took their breath, made them dizzy and sick, as if they'd been physically assaulted.

"Oh, Michael," murmured Nikol, "this can't be happening! I don't believe it. Lord Soth was so valiant, so brave. No knight would do such terrible things—"

"Lies!" said Michael. His face was pale. He literally shook with anger and outrage. "That false cleric has twisted the truth—"

"But what is the truth, Michael?" Nikol cried. "We don't know!"

"Hush, we're attracting attention," he cautioned, noting that several men were casting suspicious glances in their direction. "The truth about that friend of ours," Michael continued loudly. "We'll find out, I'm certain, now that we're here in this fair city. A city obviously blessed."

Several men, burly and unwashed and smelling strongly of dwarf spirits, lurched over to stare at them.

"Strangers, are you?" one said, scowling.

"From Whitsund, Sire," said Michael, bowing.

"At least you're human. Refugees? Thinkin' of movin' in?" He glowered at them. " 'Cause if you are, you got another think comin'. We got beggars enough as it is." Those with him muttered their assent. "Why don't you two just head on back to wherever it is you came from?"

Nikol shifted restlessly; her armor jingled, her sword clanked. The man turned, looked at her with drunken interest.

"That steel I hear?" The man took a step nearer Nikol.

Reaching out a filthy hand, he caught hold of her by the chin, wrenched her face to the light. "You look as if you've noble blood in you, boy. Don't he, fellas? Not some noble's son, by any chance? With a fat purse?"

"Let go of me," said Nikol through clenched teeth. "Or you're a dead man."

"Please," said Michael, trying to come between them, "we don't want any trouble—"

But he only made matters worse. His staff caught on Nikol's cloak, dragged the fabric aside. The shining breastplate she wore glittered in the sun.

"A knight hisself!" The man howled in glee. "Look, fellas. Look what I've caught! I'm gonna have a little fun.' " He drew a long dagger from his belt. "Let's see if your blood does run yellow—"

Nikol thrust her sword into the man, yanked it out before he or his drunken companions knew what had happened. The man stared at her in blank astonishment, then groaned and toppled to the ground. A pool of blood spread beneath him. The sight sobered up his friends, who growled in anger. Some drew knives; one wielded a blackthorn cudgel. Michael whirled his staff. Nikol set her back to his, her sword, red with blood, swinging in a slow arc.

The men made a half-hearted show of attacking. Michael's staff lashed out, caught one on the side of one man's head, sent him into the dust. Nikol gave another a slash on his cheek that he would carry to his grave. The men, eyeing the knight and the cleric, decided they'd had enough. They broke and ran.

"Cowards!" jeered Nikol, cleaning her sword with the tail of the dead man's shirt. "Thieves and knaves."

"Yes, but they'll be back," said Michael grimly. "And they'll bring help. We can't stay in the city. We'll have to leave." He cast a longing, disappointed glance at the great library.

"We'll return," said Nikol confidently. "I have an idea. Hurry up. One of those thugs is talking to that so-called Revered Son."

Sure enough, the Revered Son was turning, staring hard in their direction. The man was pointing at them excitedly.

The two ran, blended in with the rest of the flotsam and dregs of humanity that had washed ashore in Palanthas. Reaching the gates, they were walking out just as one of the Revered Son's henchmen came pounding up, breathless, to deliver a message to the guard.

Michael and Nikol ducked behind a wagon that had become mired in the crowd.

"Knight of Solamnia!" the man shouted. "A huge fellow with a sword six feet long! He's got a friend, some fellow wearing the blue robes of the false goddess."

"Yeah, sure, we'll watch for them," said the guard, and the henchman dashed off, to spread the alarm at other gates. "Get that wagon moving! What's the matter with you?"

Nikol drew her cloak close around her, pressed her sword against her thigh. Michael made certain his holy medallion was well hidden. The guard didn't even bother to spare them a glance. Once outside the gate, they fended off the beggars, traveled some distance up the road, finally stopping in a grove of stunted trees.

"What's your plan?" Michael asked.

"We'll travel to the High Clerist's Tower," Nikol replied. "The knights must be told about what is going on in Palanthas, how this false cleric is plotting to take control. They'll soon put a stop to it, then we can go into the library and find the Disks of Mishakal. We'll use them to prove to people that this Revered Son is a crook and a charlatan."

Michael looked doubtful. "But surely the knights must know—"

"No, they don't. They can't or they would have stopped him before now," Nikol argued. Serene, confident, she looked up into the mountains that loomed over Palanthas, to the road that led to the knights' stronghold. "And we'll find out the truth about Lord Soth, too," she added softly, her cheeks flushing. "I don't believe what they said, not a word of it. I want to know the truth."

Michael sighed, shook his head.

"What?" Nikol demanded sharply. "What's the matter?"

"I was thinking that perhaps there are some truths we are better off not knowing," he replied.

Part V

A chill wind, which blew from the plane of dark and evil magic, tore aside the cloak of the knight who stood upon that plane, allowed the icy blast to penetrate to the center of his empty being. He drew the cloak closer around him—a human gesture made from force of habit, for this ephemeral fabric, spun of memory, would never be sufficient to protect him from death's eternal cold. The knight had not been dead long, and he clung to the small and comforting habits of blessed life—once taken for granted, now, with their loss, bitterly regretted.

Other than drawing his cloak closer around the body that no longer was there, he did not move. He had urgent business. He was spying on the city of Palanthas. And though he was quite near it, none of the living saw him or were aware of his presence. The shadows of his dark magic shrouded him, hid him from view. The sight of him would have terrorized these weak vessels of warm flesh, rendered them useless to him. He needed the living, needed them alive, and, knowing his own cursed power, he wasn't certain how to approach them.

He watched them, hated them, envied them.

Palanthas. Once he'd owned that city. Once he'd been a power there. He could be a power still, a power for death and destruction. But that wasn't what he wanted, not now, not yet. A city saved from the terror of the Cataclysm. There had to be a reason, something blessed within it, something he could use.

The Revered Son? The knight had assumed so, at first. A dark joy had filled what once had been his heart when he'd heard that a Revered Son had arrived from the east, claiming to be a survivor of shattered Istar, come to take over the spiritual well-being of the populace. Was it possible? Had he discovered a true cleric left in the land? But, after long days and longer nights (for what was time to him?) spent listening to the Revered Son, the knight came to the conclusion he'd been decei ed.

In life, he'd known men and women like this charlatan, made use of them for his own ends. He recognized the man's tricks and deceits. He toyed with the idea of destroying this Revered Son, found it amusing, for the knight hated the living with a hatred born of jealousy. And he would be doing these fool Palanthians a favor, ridding them of one who would end up tyrant, despot.

But what would he gain out of it, except the fleeting pleasure of watching warm flesh grow as cold as his own?

"Nothing," he said to himself. "If they are stupid enough to fall for that man's lies, let them. It serves them right."

Yet something within Palanthas called to him, and so he stayed, watching, waiting with the patience of one who has eternity, the impatience of one who longs for rest.

He was there, invisible to living eyes, when two people—a beardless youth armed with a sword, and a man in shabby blue robes—emerged from the city gates with haste enough to draw the knight's attention, piqued his interest by taking themselves away from the sight of the guards.

The knight gazed at the man in blue with interest that increased when he saw, with the clear sight of those who walk another plane of existence, the symbol of Mishakal hidden beneath the man's robes. And the beardless youth; there seemed something familiar about him. The dark knight drew closer.

"We'll travel to the High Clerist's Tower," the youth was saying to his friend. "The knights must be told about what is going on in Palanthas, how this false cleric is plotting to take control. They'll soon put a stop to it, then we can go into the library and find the Disks of Mishakal. We'll use them to prove to people that this Revered Son is a crook and a charlatan."

High Clerist's Tower! The knight gave a bitter, silent laugh.

The youth's friend appeared to share the listener's doubts. "But surely the knights must know—"

"No, they don't," the youth returned. "They can't or they would have stopped him before now. And we'll find out the truth about Lord Soth, too. I don't believe what they said, not a word of it. I want to know the truth."

The knight heard his name, heard it spoken in admiration. A thrill passed through him, a thrill that was achingly human and alive. Soth was so astounded, so lost in wonder and puzzlement, trying to think of where he'd known this young man, that he didn't hear whatever reply the friend made in response.

The two started on their way up the winding road to the High Clerist's Tower. Summoning his steed, a creature of flame and evil magic as dark as his own, Lord Soth accompanied them—an unseen companion.

*　*　*　*　*

The Tower of the High Clerist had been built by the founder of the knights, Vinas Solamnus. Located high in the Vingaard Mountains, it guarded Westgate Pass, the only pass through the mountains.

The road to the High Clerist's Tower was long and steep, but, because it was so well traveled, the knights and the citizens of Palanthas had always worked together to keep it in good repair. The road had become legendary, in fact. A quick route to anything was termed "as smooth as the road to Palanthas."

But that had changed, as had so much else, since the Cataclysm.

Expecting a swift and easy journey, Michael and Nikol were dismayed and disheartened to discover the once smooth road now in ruins; at points, almost impassable. Huge boulders blocked the way in some places. Wide chasms, where the rock had split apart, prevented passage in others. Mountain wall on one side of them, sheer drop on the other, Michael and Nikol were forced to climb over these barriers or—heart in mouth—make a perilous leap from one side of a cut to another.

After only a few miles journeying, both were exhausted. They reached a relatively level place, a clearing of fir trees that once might have been a resting area for travelers. A mountain stream ran clear and cold, bounding down the cliff's side to disappear into the woodlands far beneath them. A circle of blackened rocks indicated that people had built campfires on this spot.

The two stopped, by unspoken consent, to rest. Although the way had been hard, both were far wearier than they should have been. A pall had come over them shortly after starting out and lay heavily on them, drained them of energy. They had the feeling they were being watched, followed. Nikol kept her hand on her sword; Michael stopped continually, looked behind. They saw nothing, heard nothing, but the feeling did not leave them.

"At least," said Nikol, "we have a clear view of the road from here." She stared long and hard down the mountain, down the way they'd come. Nothing stirred along the broken path.

"It's our imagination," said Michael. "We're jumpy, after what happened in Palanthas, that's all."

They sat down on the ground that was smooth with a covering of dead pine needles and ate sparingly of their meager supplies.

The sky was gray, laden with heavy clouds that hung so low, wisps seemed to cling to the tall firs. Both were oppressed, spirits subdued by a feeling of dread and awe. When they finally spoke, they did so in low voices, reluctant to shatter the stillness.

"It seems strange," said Michael, "that the knights do not clean up this road. The Cataclysm was almost a year ago, time enough to build bridges, remove these boulders, fill in the cracks. Do you know," he continued, talking for the sake of talking, not realizing what he was saying, "it looks to me as if they've left the road in disrepair on purpose. I think they're afraid of being attacked—"

"Nonsense!" said Nikol, bristling. "What do the knights have to fear? That drunken scum in Palanthas? They're nothing more than paid henchmen for that false cleric. The citizens of Palanthas respect the knights, and well they should. The knights have defended Palanthas for generations. You'll see. When the knights come riding down in force, those cowards will take one look and beg for mercy."

"Then why haven't they ridden forth before now?"

"They don't know the danger," she snapped. "No one's brought them word."

Rubbing her shoulders beneath her heavy cloak, Nikol abruptly changed the subject. "How hard the wind blows up here, and how bitter it is. The cold goes through flesh and bone, strikes at the heart."

"So it does," said Michael, growing more and more uneasy. "A strange chill, not of winter. I've never known the like."

"I suppose it's just the high altitude." Nikol tried to shrug it off. Rising to her feet, she paced the clearing, peering nervously into the woods. "Nothing out there."

Coming back, she nudged Michael gently with the toe of her boot. "You didn't hear a word I said. You're smiling. Tell me. I'd be glad of something to smile about," she added with a shiver.

"What?" Michael jumped, glanced up, startled. "Oh, it's nothing, really. Funny, what memories come to you for no good reason. For a moment, I was a child, back in Xak Tsaroth. An uncle of mine, one of the nomads, came into town one day. I don't suppose you ever saw the Plainsmen. They dress all in leather and bright-colored feathers and beads. I loved it when they came to visit our family, bringing their trade goods. This uncle told the most wonderful stories. I'll never forget them, tales of the dark gods, who were never supposed to be mentioned then, in the time of the Kingpriest. Stories of ghosts and ghouls, the undead who roam the land in torment. I was terrified for days after."

"What happened?" asked Nikol, sitting beside him, crowding near for warmth and comfort. "Why do you sigh?"

"I told my teacher one of the stories. He was a young man, a new cleric sent from Istar. He was furious. He called the Plainsman a wicked liar, a dangerous blasphemer, a corrupting influence on impressionable youth. He told me my uncle's tales were ridiculous fabrications or, worse, downright heresy. There were no such things as ghosts and ghouls. All such evil had been eradicated by the almighty good of the Kingpriest. I can still feel the knock on the head the priest gave me—in the name of Mishakal, of course."

"What made you think of all this?"

"Those ghost stories." Michael tried to laugh, but it ended in a nervous cough. "When one of the undead comes near, my uncle says you feel a terrible chill that seems to come from the grave. It freezes your heart—"

"Stop it, Michael!" Nikol bounded to her feet. "You'll end up scaring us both silly. There's snow in the air. We should go on, whether we're rested or not. That way, we'll reach the tower before nightfall. Hand me the waterskin. I'll fill it, then we can be on our way."

Silently, Michael handed over the waterskin. Nikol walked over, filled the skin at the bubbling brook. Michael pulled the symbol of Mishakal out from beneath his robes, held it in his hand, stared at it. He could have sworn it glowed faintly, a shimmer of blue that lit the gray gloom surrounding them, deepening around them, deepening to black. . . .

And in the black, eyes of flame.

The eyes were in front of Nikol, staring at her from across the stream. She had risen to her feet, the waterskin in her hand, water dripping from it.

"This is how I know you," came a deep and terrible voice.

Michael tried to call to her, but his own voice was a strangled scream. He tried to move, to run to her side, but his legs were useless, as if they'd been cut off at the knees. Nikol did not retreat, did not flee. She stood unmoving, staring with set, pale face at the apparition emerging from the shadows.

He was—or once had been—a Knight of Solamnia. He was mounted on a steed that, like himself, seemed to spring from a terrible dream. A strange and eerie light, perhaps that cast by the black moon, Nuitari, shone on armor that bore the symbol of the rose, but the armor did not gleam. It was charred, scorched, as if the man had passed through a ravaging fire. He wore a helm, its visor lowered. No face was visible within, however. Only a terrible darkness lighted by the hideous flame of those burning eyes.

He came to a halt near Nikol, reached down a gloved hand, as if for the waterskin. In that motion, Michael knew him.

"You gave me water," said the knight, and his voice

seemed to come from below the ground, from the grave. "You eased my burning thirst. I wish you could do so again."

The knight's voice was sad, burdened with a sorrow that brought tears to Michael's eyes, though they froze there.

The knight's words jolted Nikol, drove her to action. She drew her sword from its sheath.

"I do not know what dark and evil place you spring from, but you desecrate the armor of a knight—"

Michael shook free of his fear, ran forward, caught hold of her arm. "Put your weapon away. He means us no harm." Pray Mishakal that was true! "Look at him, Nikol," Michael added, barely able to draw breath enough to speak. "Don't you recognize him?"

"Lord Soth!" Nikol whispered. She lowered her sword. "What dread fate is this? What have you become?"

Soth regarded her long moments without speaking. The chill that flowed from him came near to freezing their blood, the terror freezing their minds. And yet Michael guessed that the knight's evil powers were being held in check, even as he held the reins of his restive steed.

"I hear pity in your voice," said the knight. "Your pity and compassion touch some part of me—the part that will not die, the part that burns and throbs in endless pain! For I am one of the undead—doomed to bitter agony, eternal torment, no rest, no sleep. . . ."

His fist clenched in anger. The horse shied, screamed suddenly. Its hooves clattered on the frozen ground.

Nikol fell back a step, raised her sword.

"The rumors we heard about you, then, are true," she said, trying to control her shaking voice. "You failed us, the knights, the gods. You are cursed—"

"Unjustly!" Soth's voice hissed. "Cursed unjustly! I was tricked! Deceived! My wife was warned of the calamity. I rode forth, prepared to give my life to save the world, but the gods had no intention of being merciful. They wanted humankind punished. The gods prevented my coming to Istar and, in an attempt to cleanse their hands of the blood of innocents, they laid this curse on me! And now they have abandoned the world they destroyed."

Michael, frightened and sick at heart, clasped his hand

around the symbol of Mishakal. The death knight was swift to notice.

"You do not believe me, Cleric?"

The flame eyes seared Michael's skin; the dreadful cold chilled his heart. "No, my lord," said Michael, wondering where he found the courage. "No, I do not believe you. The gods would not be so unjust."

"Oh, wouldn't they?" Nikol retorted bitterly. "I've kept silent, Michael, for I did not want to hurt you or add to your burden, but what if you're wrong? What if you've been deceived? What if the gods *have* abandoned us, left us alone at the mercy of scoundrels like those in Palanthas?"

Michael looked at her sadly. "You saw Nicholas. You saw him blessed, at peace. You heard the promise of the goddess, that someday we would find such peace. How can you doubt?"

"But where is the goddess now, Michael?" Nikol demanded. "Where is she when you pray to her? She does not answer."

Michael looked again at the medallion in the palm of his hand. It was dark and cold to the touch, colder than the chill of the death knight. But Michael had seen it glow blue—or had he? Was it wishful thinking? Was his faith nothing but wishful thinking?

Nikol's hand closed over his. "There, you see, Michael? You don't believe. . . ."

"The Disks of Mishakal," he said desperately. "If we could only find those, I could prove to you—" Prove to myself, he said silently, and in that moment admitted for the first time that he, too, was beginning to lose his faith.

"Disks of Mishakal? What are these?" Lord Soth asked.

Michael was reluctant to answer.

"They are holy tablets of the gods," the cleric said finally. "I . . . hoped to find the answers on them."

"Where are these disks?"

"Why do you want to know?" Michael asked, greatly daring.

The shadows deepened around him. He felt Soth's anger, the anger of pride and arrogance at being questioned, his will thwarted. The knight controlled his anger, however, though Michael sensed it took great effort.

"These holy disks could be my salvation," Soth stated.

"But how? If you don't believe—"

"Let the gods prove themselves to me!" said the knight proudly. "Let them do so by lifting this curse and granting me freedom from my eternal torment!"

This is all wrong, Michael thought, confused and unhappy. Yet, in his words, I hear an echo of my own.

"The disks are in the great library," said Nikol, seeing that Michael would not reply. "We would have gone to look for them, but the library is in peril from the mobs. We travel to the High Clerist's Tower to warn the knights, that they may ride to Palanthas, quell this uprising, and restore peace and justice."

To their horror and astonishment, Lord Soth began to laugh—terrible laughter that seemed to come from places of unfathomable darkness. "You have traveled far and seen many dreadful sights," said the knight, "but you have yet to see the worst. I wish you luck!"

Turning the head of his wraithlike steed, he vanished into the shadows.

"My lord! What do you mean?" cried Nikol.

"He's gone," said Michael.

The darkness lifted from his heart; the icy chill of death retreated; the warmth of life flowed through his body.

"Let's leave this place swiftly," he said.

"Yes, I agree," Nikol murmured.

She went to lift the waterskin, hesitated, loathe to touch it, fearful, perhaps, of the death's knight return. Then, resolute, face pale, lips set, she picked it up. "He has been cruelly wronged," she said, flashing Michael a glance, daring him to disagree.

He said nothing. The silence became a wall between them, separated them the rest of the way up the mountain.

Part VI

The Tower of the High Clerist was an imposing structure, its central tower rising some one thousand feet into the air.

Tall battlements, connected by a curtain wall, surrounded it. Michael had never seen any building this strong, this impregnable. He could now well believe the claim made by Nikol that the "tower had never fallen to an enemy while knights defended it with honor."

Both stopped, stared at it, overcome with awe.

"I have never been here," said Nikol. The lingering horror of the meeting with the undead knight had faded; her lingering anger at Michael was all but forgotten. She gazed on the legendary stronghold with shining eyes. "My father described it to Nicholas and me often. I think I could walk it blindfolded. There is the High Lookout, there the Nest of the Kingfisher—the knight's symbol. We planned to come here, Nicholas and I. He said a man was never truly a knight until he had knelt to pray in the chapel of the High Clerist's Tower—"

She lowered her head, blinked back her tears.

"You will kneel there for him," said Michael.

"Why?" she demanded, regarding him coldly. "Who will be there to listen?"

She walked up the broad, wide road that led to one of several entrances into the fortress. Michael followed after, troubled, uneasy. The tower was strangely quiet. No guards walked the battlements, as he might have expected. No lights shone from the windows, though the sun had long since sunk behind the mountains, bringing premature night to the tower and its environs.

Nikol, too, appeared to find this silence, this lack of activity odd, for she slowed her walk. Tilting back her head to try to see through the gloom, she started to hail the tower. Her call was cut off.

Cloaked and hooded figures surged out of the night. Skilled hands laid hold of Michael, swiftly relieved him of his staff, pinned his arms behind his back. He struggled in his captors' grasp, not so much to free himself, since he knew that was impossible, but to try to keep sight of Nikol. She had disappeared behind a wall of bodies. He heard the ring of steel against steel.

"You are a prisoner of the Knights of Solamnia. Yield yourself," said a harsh voice, speaking in the crude trade tongue.

"You lie!" Nikol cried, answering in Solamnic. "Since when do true knights move in the shadows and ambush people in the darkness?"

"We move in the dark because these are days of darkness." Another man approached, emerging from the gate leading into the High Clerist's Tower. More men followed after him.

Torchlight flared, half blinding Michael. Its light shone on polished armor, steel helms, and, beneath the helms, the long, flowing moustaches that were the knights' hallmark. One man, the one who'd answered Nikol, wore on his shoulder a ribbon. Once bright, it was now somewhat frayed and discolored. Michael had lived among knights long enough to recognize by this insignia a lord knight, one who commands in time of war.

"What have we here?"

"Spies, I believe, my lord," answered one of Michael's captors.

"Bring the torches closer. Let me take a look."

Michael's guard escorted him to the front. The knights were efficient, but not rough, according him a measure of respect even as they let him know who was in charge.

Nikol looked somewhat daunted at the sight of the lord knight, but she flushed angrily at the charge.

"We are not spies!" she said through clenched teeth. Remaining on guard, she used the flat of her blade to strike out at any who came near her.

The knights outnumbered her, could have taken her, but that would have meant unnecessary bloodshed. They glanced at the lord knight for orders.

He walked over to her, held the light to shine upon her. "Why, it is but a beardless youth, yet one who wields a sword with a man's skill, it seems," he added, looking at a companion who was wiping blood from a cut cheek. Frowning, he studied the sword in Nikol's hand. The lord knight's face hardened. "How did you come by such a weapon and this armor that belongs to a Knight of the Crown? Stolen from the body of a gallant knight, no doubt. If you thought to sell it to us for your own gain, you have made a mistake that will prove costly. You will end up paying—with your life!"

"I did not steal it! I carry it by—" Nikol paused. She had started to say she carried it by right, but the thought occurred to her that she did not have the right to bear the arms of a true knight. Flushing, she amended her words. "My father is Sir David of Whitsund, now deceased. My twin brother, Nicholas, who is also dead, was a Knight of the Crown. This sword is his, as is the armor. I took them from his body—"

"And she put them on and cut her hair and bravely defended the castle and those of us within it," struck in Michael.

"And who are you?" The lord knight glowered at Michael.

"Perhaps that false cleric from Palanthas, my lord," said a knight. "See, he wears the holy symbol of Mishakal."

The lord knight barely spared Michael a glance, turned to stare at Nikol.

"*She*?" the lord knight repeated. He stepped forward, scrutinized Nikol's features, then fell back, his gaze traveling swiftly over her body. "By Paladine, the false cleric speaks the truth. This is a *woman*!"

"Michael is not a false cleric," Nikol began angrily.

"We will deal with him later," said the lord knight. "You have yourself to explain first."

Biting her lip, her face stained crimson, Nikol looked irresolute. Michael guessed at the struggle within her breast. She had lived the Oath and the Measure, fought evil, defended the innocent. She had come to think of herself as a knight. Yet, by the Measure, she knew she was in the wrong. Kneeling on one knee before the lord knight, she presented her sword hilt-first, over her arm, as was correct for a knight, when yielding to one superior in rank or to a victor in a tournament.

"I have broken the law. Forgive me, my lord."

Nikol was pale and grave, but she held her head proudly. She did not kneel from shame, but out of respect.

The lord knight's face remained stern and cold. Reaching out, he took hold of the sword she offered him and tried to remove it from her grasp. She let it go reluctantly. Not since her brother's death had anyone other than herself handled his blade.

"You did indeed break the Measure, Daughter, which prohibits the hand of a woman from wielding the blade of a true knight. We will take into consideration the fact that you came to us of your own free will, to surrender yourself—"

"Surrender? No, I have not, my lord!" Nikol stated. Rising to her feet, she shifted her gaze, which had been fixed wistfully on the sword, to the lord knight's granite face. "I have come to warn you. That false cleric, of whom you speak, is rousing the citizens to violence against the great library! Tomorrow they threaten to burn it, and all the knowledge it holds, to the ground."

Nikol looked from one to the other, expecting shock, action, expressions of outrage. No one moved, no one said a word. The knights didn't even seem surprised. Their faces grew more grim and rigid, and dark lines deepened.

"Am I correct in understanding that you did not come here to ask forgiveness for your crime, Daughter?" the lord knight said.

Nikol stared at him.

"You . . . What . . . *My* crime? Didn't you hear what I just said, my lord? The great library is in danger! Not only that, but the city of Palanthas itself could fall into the hands of this evil man and his henchmen!"

"What happens in Palanthas is none of our concern, Daughter," said the lord knight.

"None of your concern? How can you say that?"

"Many of these men came from Palanthas, as did I myself. The people drove us out. They attacked our homes, threatened our families. My own lady died at the hands of the mob."

"Yet," said Michael quietly, "by the Measure, Sir Knight, you are bound in Paladine's name to protect the innocent—"

"Innocent!" The lord knight's eyes flashed. "If the city of Palanthas burns to the ground, it will be no more than the rabble deserve! Paladine, in his righteous wrath, has turned his face from them. Let the Dark Queen take them and be damned!"

"The wrath of the gods has fallen upon all of us," said Michael. "How can any of us say we didn't deserve it?"

"Blasphemy!" thundered the lord knight, and he struck Michael across the face.

He staggered beneath the blow. Putting his hand to his cut lip, he saw his fingers stained with blood.

The lord knight turned to Nikol. "The blasphemer will not be allowed within our walls. You, Daughter, since you are the child of a knight, may stay here in the fortress, safe from harm. You will remove your armor, turn it over to us, then you will spend night and day on your knees in the chapel, begging forgiveness of the father and the brother whose memories you disgrace."

Nikol went livid, as if she'd been run through by her own sword, then hot blood flooded her cheeks.

"I'm not the one who has disgraced the knighthood. You! You're the disgrace!" Her gaze flashed around at the knights. "You hide away from the world, whining to Paladine about the injustice of it all. He doesn't answer you, does he? You've lost your powers and you're scared!"

Moving swiftly, she reached out, grabbed hold of her sword, wrested it from the lord knight before he knew what was happening. Lifting her weapon, she fell back, on guard.

"Seize her!" the lord knight ordered.

The knights drew their swords, began to close in.

"Hold," came a deep voice.

A blast of bitterly cold wind blew out the torches, chilled flesh and blood. Swords fell from numb hands, clattered to the ground with a hollow sound that was like a death knell. The knights' faces went stark white beneath their helms. Their eyes widened in horror at the sight of the terrible apparition riding down upon them.

"The Knight of the Black Rose!" cried one, in panic.

"Paladine forfend!" shouted the lord knight, raising his hand in a warding gesture.

Lord Soth laughed, a sound like the grinding of rocks in a mountain slide. He reined in his nightmare steed, regarded the knights cowering before him with scorn.

"This woman is far more worthy than any of you to

---

wield the sword and wear the armor of a knight. She stood up to me. She faced me, unafraid. What will you do, noble knights all? Will you fight me?"

The knights hesitated, cast terrified, questioning glances at their leader. The lord's face was yellow, like old bone.

"They are all in league with the Queen of Darkness!" he shouted. "Retreat, for the sake of your souls!"

The knights picked up their swords. Massing around their leader, they fell back until they had reached the massive wooden doors, which opened wide to let them in. Once inside, the doors slammed and the portcullis rang down.

The High Clerist's Tower stood dark and silent, as if it were empty.

Part VII

Nikol and Michael spent the night in a cave they found in the mountains. Huddled together for warmth, they slept only fitfully. Again they had the feeling they were being watched. Both were up with the dawn, made haste to return to Palanthas, though what they would do when they arrived was open to question.

"If we can only find the holy disks, then all will be put right," Michael said more than once.

"We can warn Astinus about the library's danger," said Nikol. "And we can take the Disks of Mishakal to safety."

"Take them to Lord Soth, don't you mean?" Michael asked her quietly.

"He saved us at the tower. We are in his debt. If I can end his torment, I will. *He* is a true knight," she added, casting a sad and wistful look back up into the mountains. "I know it in my heart."

Michael said nothing. Soth had saved them, but for their sake or his own? Had he been cursed unjustly or had his dread fate been forged by his own evil passions? Michael could only repeat what had become a litany: the blessed disks would make everything clear, everything right again.

Neither wayfarer was overly concerned at the thought of reentering the city. Having seen the confusion at the main gate, they doubted if the guards would even remember they were supposed to be searching for a beardless knight and blue-robed cleric. They timed their arrival for midday, when the traffic should be at its peak.

But, when they reached Palanthas, they found the road before the city empty, its gates standing wide open.

Alarmed at the sudden and inexplicable change, they ducked into the same grove of stunted trees, waited, and watched.

"Something's definitely wrong," said Nikol, eyeing the city walls. "I haven't seen one guard go past on his rounds. Come on." She buckled on her sword, wrapped her cloak around her. "We're going inside."

No beggars accosted them. No guard hailed them. No one challenged them or demanded to know their business within the city. The walls were deserted, the streets empty. The only living being they saw was a mongrel dog, trotting past with a dead hen in its mouth, having taking advantage of the situation to raid an unguarded chicken coop.

They hurried through the merchandising district of New City, the streets of which should have been filled with people at this time of day. Stalls were closed. Shop windows were barred and shuttered.

"It looks like a city preparing for a holiday," said Michael.

"Or a war," Nikol said grimly. She walked with her hand on the hilt of her sword. "Look. Look at that."

One of the shops was not closed. It had been destroyed, its windows smashed. The shop's goods—gaily colored silks from the elven lands of Qualinesti—lay strewn about the streets. Ugly epitaphs had been scrawled across the walls, written in blood. Lying in front of the shop was the body of an elven woman. Her throat had been cut. A dead child lay beside her.

"May the gods forgive them," murmured Michael.

"I trust your disks can explain this," Nikol said bitterly.

They continued on, passing other sites of senseless destruction, other wanton acts of violence. Palanthas itself may have escaped the ravages of the Cataclysm, but the souls of its people had been cracked and shattered.

It was at the Old City wall that they first heard the sound

of the mob, the sound of a thousand people gone mad, a thousand people finding anonymity in their numbers, driven to commit crimes one alone would have been ashamed to consider. The noise was frightful, inhuman. It prickled the hair on Michael's neck, sent a shiver down his spine.

Smoke boiled up from beyond the walls of Old City. Under its cover, Michael and Nikol slipped through the gates without attracting anyone's attention. Reaching the other side, they came to a halt, stared in disbelief. Nothing, not the sight of the destruction, not the tumult that raged around them, prepared them for what they saw.

Several large and beautiful houses had been set ablaze and were burning furiously. Large crowds danced drunkenly in front of the fires, cheering and waving bottles and other, more gruesome, trophies. But the largest concentration of the mob was farther on, gathered around the great library.

Here the crowd was more or less hushed, heads craning to see and hear. A voice rose, exhorting them to further acts of terror. Nikol climbed a drainpipe that ran up the side of a house, and stood on the roof to gain a better view.

"The Revered Son is on the library stairs," she reported on her return. "His men are there with him. They're armed with clubs and axes and carrying torches. He's—" Her words were drowned out by a roar that set the windows rattling.

"We must get inside the library!" Michael was forced to shout to be heard over the clamor. He was starting to feel panicked. The idea that the holy disks might fall victim to this unholy chaos appalled him.

"I have an idea!" Nikol shouted in return, then motioned him to follow her. They slipped past on the fringes of the crowd, ducked down an alleyway, ran its length. Reaching the end, they stopped, peered out cautiously. They stood directly opposite one of the library's semidetached wings. The mob, intent upon hearing the speaker, blocked the front, but not the sides, of the building.

"We can climb in through the windows," said Nikol.

They headed for the ornamental grove of trees, the same grove that had provided them shelter the last time they were here. Keeping to the shadows, they trampled on dead, unkempt flower beds and shoved through hedges, once clipped, now left to grow wild. A narrow strip of open lawn stood between them and the library. Breaking free of their cover, they ran across the well-kept grass, came to a window on the ground level. They flattened themselves against the building, trying to keep out of sight of the mob.

"The window's probably guarded," said Michael.

Nikol risked peeping over the ledge. "I don't see anyone, not even the Book Readers," she added, using a common slang term that referred to the Order of Aesthetics, followers of the god Gilean who devoted their lives to the gathering and preserving of knowledge.

Nevertheless, she drew her sword from its sheath. "Quickly!" whispered Nikol.

A blow from Michael's staff broke the window, knocked down fragments of glass. Nikol clambered through, kept her sword raised. She stared about intently. Seeing no one, she reached back to help Michael.

He climbed inside, came to a halt. He had heard all his life about the great library, but he'd never seen it, and this was beyond anything he could have imagined. A vast room held row after row of bookshelves, each shelf filled with neatly arranged, lovingly dusted, leather-bound volumes. His heart yearned, suddenly, for the wisdom stored within these walls, ached to think that all this irreplaceable knowledge was in such dire danger.

"Michael!" Nikol called a warning.

A robed monk, wielding a sword, had crept out from the shadows of one of the bookcases, stood blocking their path.

"Hold . . . hold right th-there," stammered the Aesthetic. "Don't . . . don't m-m-move."

The monk was thinner than the heavy, antique, two-handed broadsword he was trying his best to hold. His face was chalk-colored, sweat ran down his bald head, and he shook so that his teeth clicked together. But, though obviously frightened out of his wits, he was grimly standing his ground. Nikol had been about to laugh. She remembered the brutal mob, their hands already stained with blood, and her laughter changed to a sigh.

"Here," she said, stepping forward, accosting the terrified monk, who stared at her, wide-eyed. "You're holding that sword all wrong." Wrenching the poor man's hands loose from the weapon, she repositioned them. "This hand here, and this hand here. There. Now you have a chance of hurting someone besides yourself."

"Th-thank you," murmured the monk, gazing at the weapon and Nikol in perplexity. Suddenly, he brought the sword, point-first, to her throat. "Now . . . I s-s-suggest you . . . you leave."

"For the love of Paladine! We're on *your* side," said Nikol in exasperation, shoving the wavering blade away from her. Outside they could hear the mob raise its voice in response to the Revered Son's harangues.

"We want to help you," Michael said, coming forward. "We don't have much time. We're looking for the disks—"

"What is going on in here, Malachai?" questioned a stern voice. "I heard glass breaking."

A robed man who seemed old, but whose face was unlined, smooth, and devoid of expression, entered the library room. Calm and unruffled, he walked down the aisle between the bookcases.

"They . . . broke in, M-master," the monk gasped.

The man's stern gaze shifted to the couple. "You are responsible for this?" he said, indicating the broken window.

"Well, yes, Master," answered Michael, astonished to feel his skin burning in shame. "Only because we couldn't get in the front."

"We don't mean any harm," said Nikol. "You must believe us. We'd like to help, in fact, Master—"

"Astinus," said the man coolly. "I am Astinus. Did I hear you say you were searching for the Disks of Mishakal?" His gaze went to Michael's breast.

The cleric had been careful to hide the medallion beneath his robes, but this man's ageless eyes seemed able to penetrate the cloth.

"The *true* clerics have all departed Krynn," observed Astinus, frowning.

"I was given the chance," said Michael, defensively. "I chose to stay. I could not leave—"

"Yes, yes. It is all recorded. You've come for the disks. This—"

A howl rose from the mob outside. Shouts of anger and rage surged up against the library walls like the pounding of a monstrous sea. The monk, hearing that terrible sound, seemed likely to faint. He was sucking in breath in great gulps. His eyes were white-rimmed and huge.

"Sit down, Malachai. Put your head between your knees," advised Astinus. "And for the gods' sake drop that sword before you slice off your toe. When you feel better, fetch a broom and sweep up this glass. Someone could get cut. Now, if you two will come with me—"

Nikol stared at the man. "You daft old fool! Listen to that! They're out for blood! *Your* blood! You should be preparing for your defense! Look, we can barricade these windows. We'll overturn these bookcases, then shove them up against—"

"Overturn the bookcases!" Astinus thundered, his placid calm finally disturbed. "Are you mad, young woman? These hold thousands of volumes, catalogued according to date and place. Do you realize how long it would take us to put every volume back in its proper position? Not to mention the damage you might do to some of the older texts. The binding is fragile. And the method of making paper was not as advanced—"

"They're about to burn you to ground, old man!" Nikol shouted back. "You're not going to have anything *left* to catalogue!"

Astinus pointedly ignored Nikol, shifted his gaze to Michael. "You, Cleric of Mishakal, are, I take it, not here to overturn bookcases?"

"No, Master," said Michael hurriedly.

"Very well. You may come with me." Astinus turned, started to leave.

"Pardon, Master," Michael said meekly, "if my wife could accompany us . . ."

"Will she behave herself?" Astinus demanded, regarding Nikol dubiously.

"She will," said Michael. "Put your sword away, dear."

"You're all mad!" muttered Nikol, staring from one to the

other.

Michael lifted his eyebrows. "Humor the old man," he said silently.

Nikol sighed, slid her sword in its sheath. The monk, Malachai, was sitting on the floor, his hand still clasped over the hilt of the sword.

Astinus led them out of the room, into the main portion of the library. He walked at a leisurely, unhurried pace, pointing out this section and that as they passed. Outside they could hear the mob gathering its courage. Smoke, drifting in through the broken window, hung ominously in the still air.

Michael moved as if in a dream. Nothing seemed real. Inside the library, all was as quiet, calm, and unperturbed as Astinus himself. Occasionally, they caught sight of some monk running down a hallway, a scared look on his face, some precious volume clutched in his arms. At the sight of the master, however, the monk would skid to a halt. Eyes lowered before Astinus's frown, the monk would proceed at a decorous walk.

They passed from what Astinus said were the public reading rooms, through a small hallway, up two flights of stairs, into the private section of the library. Here, at high desks, perched on tall stools, some of the Aesthetics sat at their work, pens scratching, a ghastly counterpoint to the roaring outside. But a few had left their work, were clustered in a frightened knot at one of the windows, staring down at the mob below.

"What is the meaning of this?" Astinus barked.

Caught, the monks cast swift, apologetic glances at the master and hastened back to their seats. Pens scratched diligently. Work resumed.

Astinus walked among them, eyes darting this way and that. Pausing beside one pale-faced older man, the master of the library stared down at the manuscript, pointed.

"That is a blot, Johann."

"Yes, Master. I'm sorry, Master."

"What is the meaning of that blot, Johann?"

"I—I'm afraid, Master. Afraid we're all going to die!"

"If we do, I trust it will be neatly. Start the page over."

"Yes, Master."

The Aesthetic removed the offending sheet, slid a clean one in its place. He bent to his task, but, Michael noticed, the monk's fear had eased. He was actually smiling. If Astinus could be concerned over blots at a time like this, surely there was no danger—that's what he was telling himself.

Michael would have liked to believe that as well, but more and more he was becoming convinced that the master of the library was either drunk or insane or perhaps both.

They left the main library, entered what Astinus termed the living area. He guided them through long hallways, past the small, comfortless cells where the monks resided.

"My study," said Astinus, ushering them into a small, book-lined room that contained a desk, a chair, a rug, a lamp, and nothing else. "I rarely permit visitors, but today I will make an exception, since you seem unduly disturbed by the noise in the streets. You"—he indicated Michael—"may sit in the chair. You"—he glowered at Nikol—"stand by the door and touch nothing. Do you understand? Touch nothing! I will be back shortly."

"Where are you going?" Nikol demanded.

He stared at her, face frozen.

"Master," she added in a more respectful tone.

"You asked for the Disks of Mishakal," said Astinus, and left.

"At last!" Michael said, sitting in the chair, glad to rest. "Soon we'll have the disks and the answers—"

"If we live long enough to read them," Nikol stated angrily. She left her place by the door, began pacing the small room, waving her hands. "That old man is a fool! He'll let himself and these poor, wretched monks be butchered, his precious library torn down around his ears. When we get the disks, Michael, we'll take them and leave. And if that old man tries to stop us, I'll—"

"Nikol," said Michael, awed. "Look . . . look at this."

"What?" She stopped her pacing, startled by the odd tone of his voice. "What is it?"

"A book," said Michael, "left open, here, on the desk."

"Michael, this is no time to be reading!"

"Nikol," he said softly, "it's about Lord Soth."

"What does it say?" she cried, leaning over him. "Tell me!"

Michael read the text silently to himself.

"Well?" Nikol demanded, impatient.

He looked up at her. "He's a murderer, Nikol, and worse. It's all here. How he fell in love with a young elven maid, a virgin priestess. He carried her off to Dargaard Keep, then murdered his first wife, to have her out of his way."

"Lies!" Nikol cried, white-lipped. "I don't believe it! No true knight would break his vows like that! No true knight would do such a monstrous thing!"

"Yet, one did," came a deep voice.

Lord Soth stood in the room.

Part VIII

Michael, trembling, rose to his feet. Nikol turned to face the knight. Her hand went to her sword, but fell, nerveless, at her side. The accursed knight's chill pervaded the small room. His flame-eyes were fixed, not on the two who stood before him, but upon the book.

"That tells my story?" Soth asked, gesturing with his gloved hand to the book on the table.

"Yes," Michael answered faintly. Nikol fell back, to stand by his side.

"Turn the book toward me, that I may read it," Soth ordered.

Hands shaking, Michael did as ordered, shifting the heavy, enormous volume around for the death knight to view. An awful darkness filled the room, doused the lamplight, grew deeper and darker as time passed. The only light was the burning of the flame-eyes, which did not read, so much as devour, each page. Michael and Nikol drew near each other, clasped each other tightly by the hand.

"You did these terrible deeds?" Nikol asked, her voice as small and unhappy as a child's, whose dream has been shattered. "You murdered . . ."

The blazing eyes lifted; their gaze pierced her heart.

"For love. I did it for love."

"Not love," Michael said, the warmth of Nikol's touch giving him strength. "Lust, dark desire, but not love. She—the elven maid—she hated you for it, when she found out, didn't she?"

"She loved me!" Soth's fist clenched in anger. He glanced down at the page. His hand slowly relaxed. "She hated what I had done. She prayed for me. And her prayer was answered. I was to be given the power of stopping the Cataclysm. I was on my way to do so, when I stopped at your castle, Lady."

The deep voice was sad, filled with regret, a bitter sorrow that wrung the heart. The darkness deepened until they could see nothing except the flaming eyes, the reflection of their fire in the charred and blackened armor. The noise of the mob faded away, became nothing more than the keening of the wind.

"And I turned aside, as it says here." Soth gestured at the flame-lighted page. "But it was Paladine who tempted me to do so. Elven priestesses, enamored of the Kingpriest, told me that the woman I loved was unfaithful. The child she had borne was not mine. Wounded pride, soul-searing jealousy, overwhelmed me, drove me to abandon my quest. I rode back, accused my love, falsely accused her. . . . The Cataclysm struck. My castle fell. She died in the fire . . . and so did I.

"But not to stay dead!" Soth's mailed fist clenched again. His anger flared. "I awoke to endless torment, eternal pain! Free me, Cleric. You can. You must. You are a true cleric."

He stretched out his ghostly hand to the medallion. "The goddess has blessed you."

"Yet she does not bless you," said Michael, the words falling from fear-numbed lips. "You lied to us, my lord. The gods did not curse you unjustly, as you would have had us believe. All the evil passions that led you to disgrace and downfall are still alive within you."

"You dare speak so to me? You dare defy me? Wretched mortal! I could slay you with a word!" Soth's finger hovered near Michael's heart. One touch of that death-chilled hand, and the heart would burst.

"You could," Michael answered, "but you won't. You

won't kill me for speaking the truth. I hear your regret, my lord. I hear your sorrow. Better feelings within you war with the dark passions. If you were wholly given over to evil, my lord, you would not care. You would not suffer."

"Bitter comfort you offer me, Cleric." Soth sneered.

"It could be your redemption," Michael said softly.

Soth stood long moments in silence. Slowly, his hand lowered. It went to the book, lying on the table. The fingers followed the words, as though the death knight were reading them again. Michael clasped the medallion in one hand, Nikol's hand in the other. Neither spoke. Not that it would have mattered. The death knight seemed unaware of their presence. When he spoke, it was not to them.

"No!" he cried suddenly, lifting his head, his voice to the heavens. "You tempted me, then treated me unjustly when I fell! I will *not* ask your forgiveness. It is you who should ask mine!"

Flames sprang up, engulfing the page, the book, seemed likely to set fire to the room. Michael fell back with a cry, shielding Nikol with his body, his hand raised to ward off the searing heat.

"*What* is the meaning of this?"

Astinus's voice fell over them like cool water, doused the flames in an instant. Michael lowered his hand, blinked, staring through an afterimage of fiery red that momentarily blinded him.

Lord Soth was gone; in his place stood the library's master.

"I cannot let you two out of my sight a moment, it seems," stated Astinus coldly.

"But, Master. Didn't you see him?" Michael gasped, pointed. "Lord—"

Nikol dug her nails into his arm. "Tell this old fool nothing!" she whispered urgently. "Forgive us, Master," she said aloud. "Have you brought the Disks of Mishakal?"

"No," said Astinus. "They are not here. They have never been here. They will never be here."

"But . . ." Michael glared at the man. "You said you went to get them . . ."

"I said you wanted them. I did not say I would get them,"

Astinus replied with calm. "I went to open the doors."

"The great doors! The doors to the library!" Nikol gasped. "You . . . opened them! You're mad! Now there's nothing to stop the mob from entering!"

"At least," said Astinus, "they will not harm the woodwork."

The rising clamor of the mob was much louder than before. They were chanting, "Burn the books, burn the books, burn the books!"

Michael looked at the book on the desk. It was whole, unharmed. The fire had not touched it. He stared at Astinus and thought he saw the tiniest hint of a smile flicker on the stern lips.

"You two can escape out the back," said the master.

"We should," said Nikol, regarding him with scorn. Shoving past Michael, she drew her sword, started for the door. "We should leave you to the mob, old man, but there are others here besides you and, by the Oath and the Measure, I'm bound to protect the innocent, the defenseless."

"You are not bound. You are not a knight, young woman," said Astinus testily.

Nikol, however, had already gone. They could hear her booted footsteps racing down the hall. And they could hear, as well, the rising tumult of thousands. Michael took hold of his staff, set out after Nikol. As he passed Astinus, who continued to regard him with that faint smile, Michael paused.

" 'This woman is far more worthy than any of you to wield the sword and wear the armor of a knight,' " he quoted, pointing back at the book that stood upon the desk. "Soth said that. You can read it here."

He bowed to Astinus and left to join Nikol in death.

* * * * *

The mob had been astonished to see the master open the great doors that led into the Library of Palanthas. For a moment, the sight of Astinus, standing framed in the doorway, even curbed the loquacity of the Revered Son, who certainly had never expected such a thing. His jaw went slack.

He stared foolishly at the master, who not only opened the doors, but bowed silently to the people before leaving.

Then Nikol appeared. Alone, she advanced to stand before the great doors.

"Astinus asked me to tell you," she called, spreading her hands in a gesture of welcome, "that the library is always open to the public. The wisdom of the ages is yours. If you enter, do so with respect. Lay down your weapons."

The cruelest, most murderous villain in the crowd could not help but applaud such courage. And most of the people were not murderers or villains, but ordinary citizens, tired of fighting poverty and disease and misfortune, seeking to place the blame for their problems on someone else. They looked ashamed of what they'd done, what they'd been about to do. More than a few began to slink away.

The Revered Son realized he was losing them.

"Yes, it's open to the public!" he shouted. "Go inside! Read about the gods who brought this misery upon you! Read about the elves, the favored of the gods, who are living well while you starve! Read about the knights!" He pointed at Nikol. "Even now, they feed off your misery!"

The people stopped, exchanged glances, looked uncertain. The Revered Son sent a swift glance at the leader of his henchmen, who nodded. A stone hurtled from the crowd, struck Nikol on her shoulder. Hitting her breastplate, the stone knocked her back a step but did no harm.

"Cowards!" Nikol cried, drawing her sword. "Come and fight me face-to-face."

But that is not the way of a mob. A second stone followed the first. This one hit its mark, struck her on the forehead. Nikol reeled, dazed from blow, and fell upon one knee. Blood streamed down her face. At the sight, the crowd howled in glee, excited. The henchmen, shouting, urged them on. Nikol staggered to her feet, faced them alone, glittering steel in her hand.

* * * * *

Michael saw her fall. He started toward the door, to her. A hand clapped over his shoulder.

The touch chilled him to the very marrow of his bones, drove him to his knees. Looking up into fiery eyes, Michael stifled a gasp of pain, knowing that the touch, if the knight had wanted, could have killed him.

"The book will remain here forever—for all to read?" Lord Soth asked.

"Yes, my lord," Michael answered.

Soth nodded slowly. It had not been a question, so much as a reaffirmation. "I cannot be saved, but perhaps my story can save someone else."

The flame-eyes seemed to burn clear for a moment in what might have been a smile. "Ironic, isn't it, Cleric? Two false knights defending the truth." He let go his hold, turned, and walked out the library doors.

* * * * *

The mob surged forward. Men came at Nikol with clubs raised. She struck out at the leader, had the pleasure of seeing him fall back with a cry, clapping his hand over a broken, bleeding arm. For a moment, the rest held back, daunted, fearful of the gleaming steel. Then someone threw another rock. It struck Nikol on her hand, knocked the sword from her grasp.

The mob gave an exultant shout, rushed at her. She tried to reach her weapon, beating those nearest her back with fists and feet, kicking and gouging, knowing all the time she must fall.

She heard Michael shout her name, turned her head, tried to find him, then she was hit from behind. Pain exploded in her brain. She stumbled to her knees, weak, unable to rise.

A shadow fell over her. Someone was standing at her back. Someone was helping her to her feet. Someone had retrieved her sword, was handing it to her. Wiping away blood, she peered through mists of pain and failing consciousness.

A Knight of Solamnia stood beside her. His armor shone silver in the sunlight. His crest fluttered bravely in the wind. His sword gleamed, argent flame, in his strong hand. With respect and reverence, he lifted his sword to her in the knight's salute, then he turned and faced the mob.

Nikol put her back against his, did the same. At least now she would not die alone, without making one last, glorious stand for the honor of the knights. True knights . . .

Nikol blinked, stared in dazed astonishment, unable to comprehend what was happening. She and the knight were outnumbered a thousand to one, yet the mob was not attacking. Faces that had been contorted in bloodlust were now twisted in horror. Curses and threats shrilled to terrified shrieks. Men who had been racing up the library stairs were tumbling over themselves and each other in a panicked race back down.

The Revered Son was among the first to flee, running for his life, driven by such stark terror that it seemed likely he would stop running only when he reached the Newsea.

Nikol's sword was suddenly too heavy for her to hold. It slid from her grasp. She was tired, so tired. She sank to the stone steps, wanting only to sleep. Strong arms took hold of her, gathered her close.

"Nikol!" a voice cried. "Beloved!"

She opened her eyes, saw only Michael's face, illuminated by a soft blue light.

"Is the library . . . safe?" she asked.

Michael nodded, unable to speak for his grief and fear for her.

Nikol smiled. "Cowards," she murmured. "They dared not stand and face a true knight."

"No," said Michael, through his tears, "they dared not."

Blue light surrounded her, soothed her. She slept.

Part IX

"Are you certain you are well enough to travel, my lady?" The young Aesthetic, Malachai, gazed at Nikol anxiously. "You were grievously hurt."

"Yes, I'm fine," said Nikol, with a hint of irritation.

"My dear . . ." Michael reprimanded gently.

Nikol glanced at him, glanced at the young monk, who

was looking downcast. She sighed. She detested being "fussed over."

"I'm sorry I snapped at you. You've all been very kind to me. I thank you for everything you've done," said Nikol.

"We would have done more, much more, but you seemed to be in good hands," Malachai said, with a smile for Michael. "I'll never forget that terrible day," he added, with a shudder. "Looking down from the window, seeing you standing beside that evil knight, so brave, so courageous—"

"What evil knight?" Nikol asked.

The Aesthetic flushed crimson, clapped his hand over his mouth. Casting a guilty look at Michael, Malachai made a brief, bobbing bow and scuttled from the tiny room.

"What was he talking about?" Nikol demanded. "There was no evil knight there. He was a Knight of the Rose. I saw him clearly."

"Astinus wants to see us, before we go," Michael said, turning from her. "Everything's packed. The Aesthetics have really been very kind. They've given us food, warm clothing, blankets—"

"Michael." Nikol came to stand in front of him, forcing him to face her. "What did that Book Reader mean?"

Michael took hold of her, held her tightly, thinking of how he'd almost lost her. "Lord Soth was the one who fought at your side, Beloved."

She stared at him. "No! That's not possible. I saw a knight, a true knight!"

"I think you saw the part of him that still struggles toward the light. Unfortunately, I think it is part of him that few will ever see again." Michael added, with a sigh, "Now, come. We must bid farewell to Astinus."

*   *   *   *   *

The Aesthetics led them to the master's study. The ageless man with his expressionless face was hard at work, writing in a thick book. He did not glance up at their entry, but continued working. They stood for long moments in silence, then Nikol, growing bored and restless, walked over to look out the window.

Astinus lifted his head. "Young woman, you are standing in my light!"

Nikol jumped, flushed. "I beg your pardon—"

"Why are you here?" he asked.

"You sent for us, Master," Michael reminded him.

"Humpf." Carefully Astinus replaced his pen back in the inkwell. Folding his hands, he regarded the two impatiently.

"Well, go ahead. Ask your question. I'll have no peace until you do."

Michael stared. "How did you know I meant to ask—"

"Is that your question?"

"No, Master, it isn't, but—"

"Then out with it! Entire volumes of history are passing while you stand there yammering, wasting my time."

"Very well, Master. My question is this: Why were we directed here to search for the Disks of Mishakal when they are not here?"

"I beg your pardon," said Astinus. "I thought you came here searching for the answer."

"I came here searching for the disks that hold the answer," said Michael patiently. "I didn't find them."

"But did you find the answer?"

"I—" Michael stopped, taken aback. "Perhaps. . . . Well, yes, in a way."

"And that is?"

"Those people out there are searching for the answer. Lord Soth was searching for his answer. The knights in the tower are searching for theirs. They were all looking, like we were, in the wrong place. The answer is here . . . in our hearts."

Astinus nodded, lifted his pen, delicately shook off a drop of ink. "And you discovered that without overturning my bookshelves. Gilean be praised."

"There is one more thing," said Nikol. She laid a bundle that clanked and rattled down on the floor in front of Astinus's desk. "Would one of your people see that this is returned to the knights in the High Clerist's Tower?"

"Your armor," said Astinus, still holding the pen poised above the inkwell. "Or should I say, your brother's armor.

What's the matter? Ashamed of being thought a knight?"

"I am not!" Nikol retorted. "I would wear this armor with more pride than ever, but in the lands where we're planning to travel, the people don't use metal armor. They've never seen anything like it, in fact, and may be frightened."

"You are going to join up with the Plainsmen," Astinus said. He put his pen to paper, began to write. "Some of the few who still believe in the true gods. But, eventually, even their faith will weaken and diminish and die. Still, your mother will be glad to see you, Cleric."

Nikol stared. "His mother! How did you know—We never told anyone—"

Astinus made an impatient gesture. "If that is all the business you have with me, Malachai will see you out."

Michael and Nikol exchanged glances. "He's not even going to say thank you," Nikol whispered.

"For what?" Astinus growled.

Nikol only smiled, shook her head. Malachai waited for them at the door. The two turned to leave.

"Cleric," said Astinus, without pausing in his work.

"Yes, Master?"

"Keep searching."

"Yes, Master," said Michael, taking hold of Nikol's hand. "We will."

AFTERWORD

Michael, cleric of Mishakal, and Nikol, daughter of a knight, left the city of Palanthas, never to return. They traveled south into the plains of Abanasinia. Here they joined a tribe of the nomadic Plainsmen.

A child of a child of a child of a child of Michael and Nikol would come to be called Wanderer—a man whose ancestors, so it was said, never lost faith in the true gods.

And Wanderer would have a grandson named Riverwind.

Meetings Sextet
The Adventures Continue

The Oath and the Measure
Michael Williams

Sturm leaves his friends Raistlin and Caramon to seek a place with the Knights of Solamnia. In searching for the truth about his father, he discovers an old enemy and a new friend, both of whom hide their true intent.

Steel and Stone
Ellen Porath

On his way back from Qualinesti, Tanis encounters the beautiful Kitiara and rescues her. As the two travel together rapport grows, creating a special bond that is later threatened by misunderstanding and conflict.

The Companions
Tina Daniell

Caramon, Sturm, and Tasslehoff are transported by a magical windstorm to the eastern Bloodsea, and Raistlin convinces Flint and Tanis to journey with him to rescue them. Once in Mithas, however, the companions must battle the Nightmaster of the minotaurs, who plans to conquer Krynn.